CORRUPTING VIOLET

AYDEN PERRY

COPYRIGHT
CORRUPTING VIOLET
AYDEN PERRY
COPYRIGHT © 2023 BY AYDEN PERRY
THIS BOOK IS A WORK OF FICTION. ANY REFERENCES TO REAL EVENTS, REAL PEOPLE, AND REAL PLACES ARE USED FICTITIOUSLY. NAMES, CHARACTERS, PLACES, AND INCIDENTS, ARE A PRODUCT OF THE AUTHOR'S IMAGINATION. ANY RESEMBLANCE TO REAL LIFE IS PURELY COINCIDENTAL. ALL RIGHTS RESERVED. THIS BOOK IS INTENDED FOR THE READER OF THIS E-BOOK ONLY. NO PORTION OF THIS BOOK MAY BE REPRODUCED OR TRANSFERRED IN ANY FORM OR BY ANY MEANS, GRAPHIC, ELECTRONIC, OR MECHANICAL, INCLUDING PHOTOCOPYING, RECORDING, TAPING, OR BY ANY OTHER STORAGE RETRIEVAL SYSTEM, WITHOUT WRITTEN PERMISSION FROM THE AUTHORS. ALL SONGS, SONG TITLES, AND LYRICS CONTAINED IN THIS BOOK ARE THE PROPERTY OF THE RESPECTIVE SONGWRITERS AND COPYRIGHT HOLDERS.
COVER DESIGN: AYDEN PERRY
EDITOR: ANNA FROM CORBEAUX EDITORIAL SERVICES

PLAYLIST

THANK LUCIFER - VANT
I WANT OUT - LOWBORN
CHOKE - ROYAL & THE SERPENT
TEARS DON'T FALL - BULLET FOR MY VALENTINE
MANIC - WAGE WAR
STUCK IN MY WAYS - KID BOOKIE, COREY TAYLOR
I SPIT ON YOUR GRAVE - BAND
DEAL WITH IT (FEAT. KELIS) - ASHNIKKO, KELIS
KISS ME AGAIN - HENRY
MAKE ME FEEL - ELVIS DREW
THE BIRD AND THE WORM - THE USED
APPETITE - NATHAN JAMES
KRYPTONITE - 3 DOORS DOWN
DIRTBAG - KID BOOKIE, WHEATUS
OH, PRETTY WOMAN - ROY ORBINSON
I GUESS - SAINT LEVANT, PLAYYARD
ANOTHER LIFE - MOTIONLESS IN WHITE
IDTC - BLACKBEAR
SMELLS LIKE TEEN SPIRIT - WITCHZ
FORMALDEHYDE FOOTSTEPS - BERTIEBANZ
I'M FINE - WITCHZ
HYSTERIA - DEF LEPPARD
HEART OF GLASS - MILEY CYRUS
SMOOTH (FEAT. ROB THOMAS) - SANTANA

THIS IS YOUR WARNING

RUN..!

Subjects pertaining to: breathe play, CNC, electrocution, attempted murder, murder, blood, gore, death, strong adult language, underage drinking and drugs, alcohol, drugs, child abuse, emotional abuse, ageism, anxiety, sexual assault, physical and emotional abuse, bullying, attempted kidnapping, hospitalizsation, emesis, cheating, cults, misogyny, sexism, car accident, self-harm, acrophobia, somnophilia, torture, and violence.

Tropes: sixteen-year age gap, enemies to lovers, step-mom

The activities depicted in this book are not meant to be realistic depictions of BDSM or safe kink play. This is strictly a work of fiction.

PLAYLIST

THANK LUCIFER - VANT
I WANT OUT - LOWBORN
CHOKE - ROYAL & THE SERPENT
TEARS DON'T FALL - BULLET FOR MY VALENTINE
MANIC - WAGE WAR
STUCK IN MY WAYS - KID BOOKIE, COREY TAYLOR
I SPIT ON YOUR GRAVE - ZAND
DEAL WITH IT (FEAT. KELIS) - ASHNIKKO, KELIS
KISS ME AGAIN - HENRY
MAKE ME FEEL - ELVIS DREW
THE BIRD AND THE WORM - THE USED
APPETITE - NATHAN JAMES
KRYPTONITE - 3 DOORS DOWN
DIRTBAG - KID BOOKIE, WHEATUS
OH, PRETTY WOMAN - ROY ORBINSON
I GUESS - SAINT LEVANT, PLAYYARD
ANOTHER LIFE - MOTIONLESS IN WHITE
IDFC - BLACKBEAR
SMELLS LIKE TEEN SPIRIT - WITCHZ
FORMALDEHYDE FOOTSTEPS - BERTIEBANZ
I'M FINE - WITCHZ
HYSTERIA - DEF LEPPARD
HEART OF GLASS - MILEY CYRUS
SMOOTH (FEAT. ROB THOMAS) - SANTANA

THIS IS YOUR WARNING

RUN..!

Subjects pertaining to breathe play, CNC, electrocution, attempted murder, murder, blood, gore, death, strong adult language, underage drinking and drugs, alcohol, drugs, child abuse, emotional abuse, ageism, anxiety, sexual assault, physical and emotional abuse, bullying, attempted kidnapping, hospitalizsation, emesis, cheating, cults, misogyny, sexism, car accident, self-harm, acrophobia, somnophilia, torture, and violence.

Tropes: Sixteen-year age gap, enemies to lovers, step-mom

The activities depicted in this book are not meant to be realistic depictions of BDSM or safe kink play. This is strictly a work of fiction.

DEDICATION

There's a big difference between those who **WANT** you and those who will **KILL** for you.

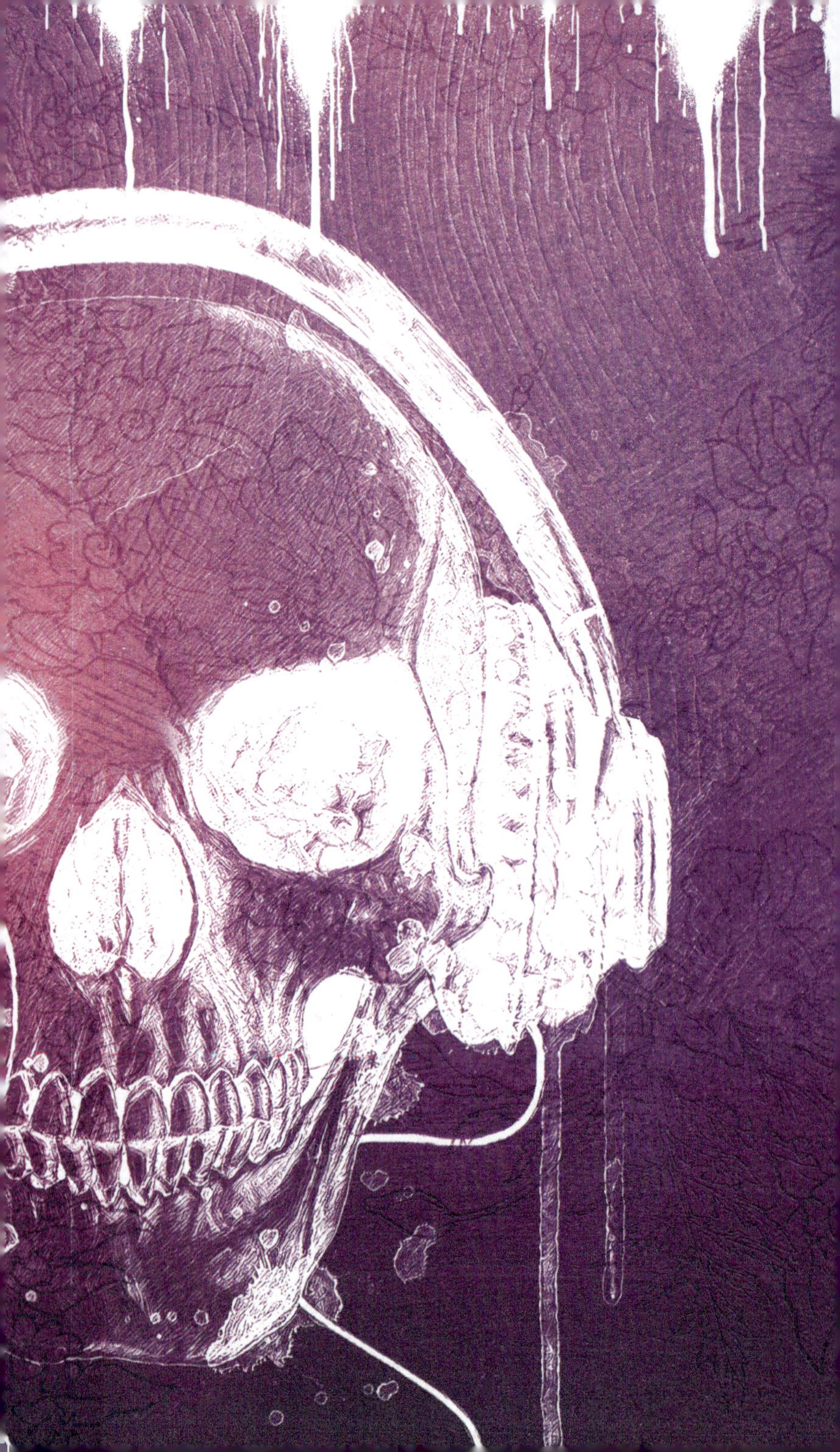

PROLOGUE

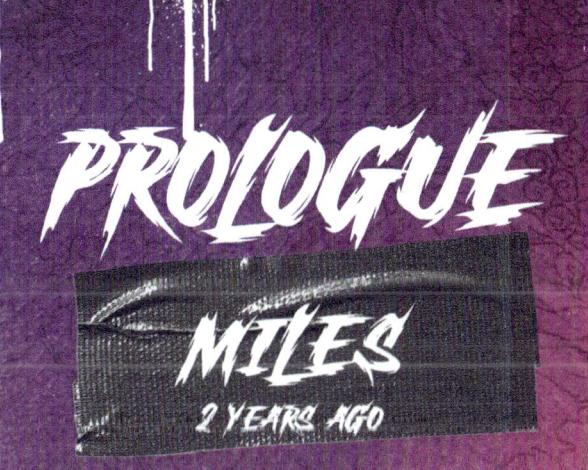

MILES
2 YEARS AGO

"Stuck In My Ways" by Kid Bookie blares from my surround sound speakers, drowning out Christina's breathy moans. Her ass is arched up as I thrust into her. She falls forward, screaming out my name. Her noises egg me on. The pressure of my orgasm builds in my lower spine. I hook my arm around her waist, pulling her back up onto her hands and knees.

"*Fuck, yes,*" I groan as her pussy clenches around my cock.

I've only had sex one other time, at school in the girls' bathroom, and it wasn't from this angle. Her virgin blood coats my lower abs, easing the friction so I glide more easily. I sink into her, bottoming out. She's warm and wet for me. Dipping my hand between us, I gather the blood on my fingertips, relishing in the velvet texture. She asked for this, and I was happy to oblige for my own purposes. My bedroom door is wide open, ready for the show to begin.

I grab on to her hips to hold her in place before I thrust up into her sweet cunt. Her legs tremble around me, and my balls tighten. It doesn't last as long as I thought it would. I can't hold out, but it does the trick. Sweat beads down my face, and I rake my clean hand through my damp hair.

When I look up, my stepmom's face is ghost white in the doorway, and her mouth is agape in horror. "Oh, my god. *Oh, my god*," my stepmom screams. "Wade! Come get your son. I've had enough of this."

Christina scrambles off my bed, grabbing her discarded clothes off my floor. Her blonde hair is knotted and wavy from all the foreplay we've been doing this weekend. She turns to me, eyes the size of saucers. "You told me they would be out till Monday," she hisses.

"Yeah, I lied," I smart off, waving at my stepmom with the blood of a virgin coating my fingers and giving them a wiggle.

My stepmom continues to stand in the doorway with her face twisted in disgust. *Good, now maybe she will fucking leave.* My lips stretch into a grin, hoping this will be the moment that breaks her. I don't even bother getting dressed. My dick swings between my legs as I try to push her over the edge. I have no shame. I'm proud of the goods I have. I stand there exposed until she stomps away on the marble floor with her heels clacking loudly.

If Christina weren't here, I would fist bump the air, but she is pissed I didn't let her in on my plan. Her brows furrow as she yanks her clothes on, letting out a huff of annoyance. She'll get over it, and things will go back to normal on Monday. Especially when she corners me in the bathroom at school, begging to suck my soul out of my dick.

She storms out of my room, her footsteps echoing

down the stairs. In the back of my mind, I feel like I should regret taking her virginity this way. It festers in my brain, but I quickly shut that shit down. This needed to happen in order to get what I want.

The front door slams closed, announcing her departure, and my dad and stepmom waste no time. They argue back and forth about my behavior, which they can never agree on. Why the fuck should they? She's not even my mom, just a gold-digging bitch my dad decided to marry.

After finding my boxer briefs on the floor, I pull them on, and I change the stereo to the next song. Even with the music at full volume, I can still hear their shouts. The last thing I want to hear are her opinions of me and what I should be doing with my life. I pull out my headphones and connect to the Bluetooth, then blast my eardrums with "Dirtbag" by Kid Bookie until their voices are nonexistent.

The chorus seems fitting for what my stepmom thinks of me. I sit on my bedroom couch, laying my head back, and close my eyes. The guitar chords play through their riffs. *Bang!* The song ends at the same time my doorknob hits the wall. My dad looms in the doorway, his face turning red. My abs tighten, ready for what's to come next.

"You little piece of shit," Dad roars, his fists clenching at his sides.

He stalks to where I'm sitting on the couch. I lean forward, resting my elbows on my knees. I'm not scared of him, and my calm demeanor sets him off. "What's the matter, Dad? Can't handle what you dish out?" He grips my throat and pushes back until I see the speckles of popcorn on the ceiling.

"You always have to fuck it up," he hisses, spittle landing on my face. I wipe it off one-handed, running my palm over my face and ending it with a smile. Another show of how he doesn't affect me. His eyes darken and lips pull back in a vicious snarl. He grips my throat tighter, and I don't move or react. I want him to explode.

Fucking. Kill me.

Within a blink, a sharp pain explodes over my eye, my cheek, and finally my nose as his fists land on every inch of my face. If only the school didn't care so much about my dad's donations, they would have called child protective services a long time ago, but instead, they make excuses for him. I'm a shit, a punk, a fuckup. A good-for-nothing teenage rebel. They label me everything under the sun, so why not live up to their expectations? All of them are living for the shit show that is my life. I can't let them down, can I? What else would they whisper and gossip about in the halls of our elite private school.

Dad lets go of me. His demeanor switches to one of calculated calm. "Clean this shit up," he barks.

Black spots dance over my vision. I blink a few times and smile up at him. My eye and lip are already tightening from the swelling.

"Is she gone?" I ask, because if I can't live happily, neither can he.

"You know the answer to that already," he states before exiting my room, leaving the door wide open.

And just like that, we are back to our regular program. I lie there on my overturned couch, staring at the ceiling. The music in my headphones is gone, leaving the silence to rake over my already sensitive nerves. I catch a black blur in the corner of my eye. My phone is on the floor in my periphery, and I grab it, scrolling through my playlist until I see the one. The song that understands me as if the lyrics were written with me in mind. I hit play and lie there, drowning in the words and melody. The tightness in my chest eases.

"I Want Out" by LOWBORN is all I hear as I close my eyes and rest.

AYDEN PERRY 11

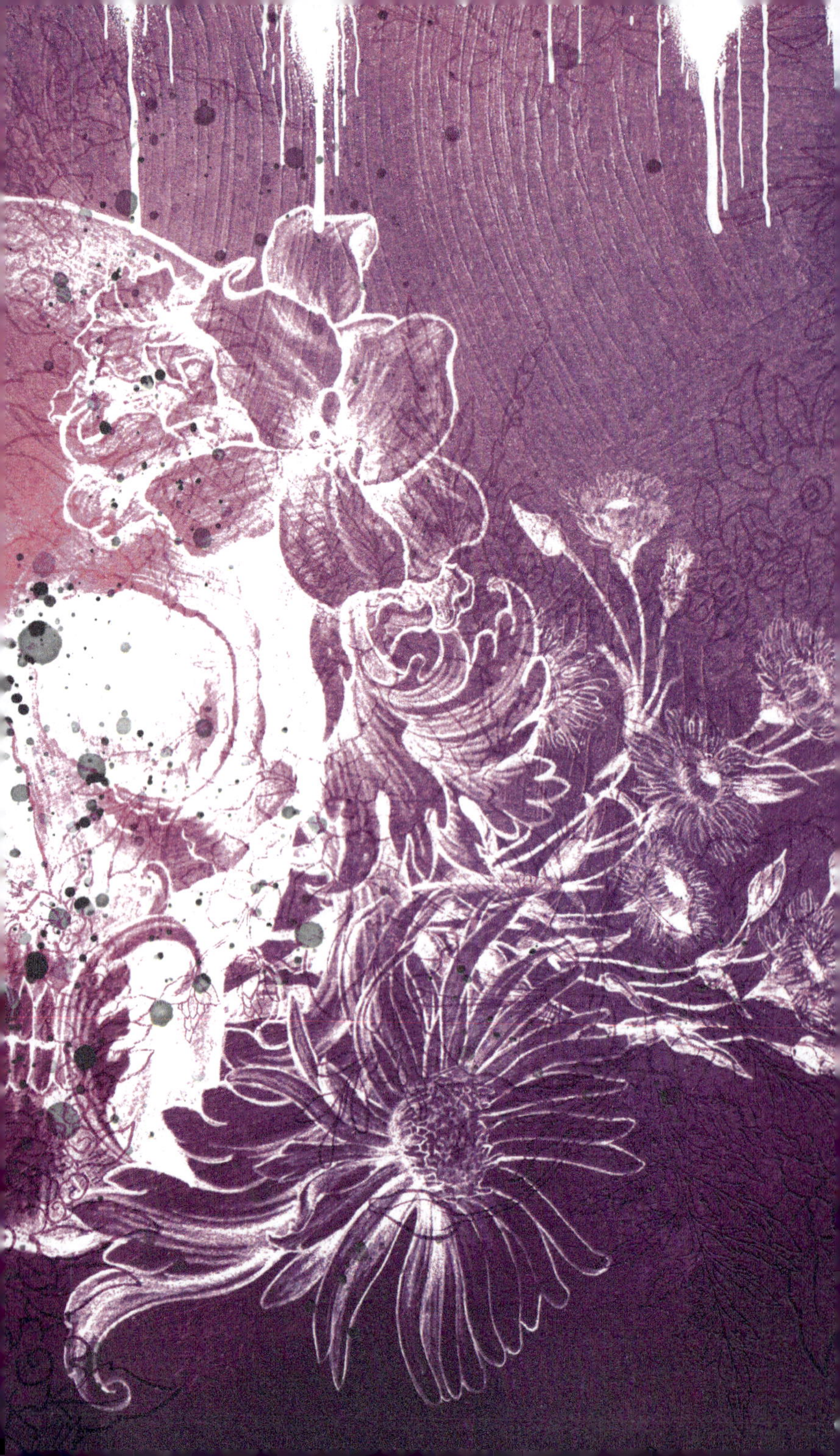

CHAPTER 1

VIOLET
PRESENT DAY

"Hey, Mark. Dani and I are heading out for lunch, if that's okay with you," I shout toward our boss's office.

We are sitting at our desks on the main floor. Dani cuts her eyes to me, biting her lip. We are both eagerly awaiting his response. We've had a shit day so far with all the calls we've had, but we made plans to go to the grand opening of Poppy Valley. What makes this event even better is the mayor of Seattle will be an honored guest.

There's a long pause before Mark hollers, "Yes, fine, but you've got to get me something too."

Dani and I both look over at each other, grinning. I want to jump up and down with excitement, but I contain myself, jogging over to Mark's office door instead. He's leaning over a stack of papers that is the equivalent of a month's worth of work. A small pang of guilt resonates in my chest. I kinda feel bad for leaving him in this mess, but my empty stomach rumbles, reminding me that coffee isn't on the food pyramid.

Rapping on the partly open door, I gain his attention and ask, "Anything in particular?"

"Eh." He shrugs, dropping his pen on the desk. "Just get me a turkey sub."

I pull my lip between my teeth and furrow my brows before responding. "This really isn't one of *those* places. You know?" I wave my hand in the air trying to come up with the words. "It's more like one of those fine dining restaurants with small servings topped with garnishes."

His brows bunch, and his mouth opens and closes like he's hesitating to ask where we're going. Finally giving up, he says, "Just get me whatever sounds good then."

Dani squeals in excitement, jiggling her keys behind me. The signal that I need to hurry my ass up. I wave to Mark, thanking him again before running over to my desk with Dani on my heels.

After grabbing my purse, I turn toward Dani. "Are you ready for this?"

"More ready than that time I went on a date with that hot NFL player. I just hope this doesn't end with you showing me how you can pick up food with your toes and eat with them."

I'm doubled over with laughter before we can make it to the door. "Please, I'm dying," I say between deep inhales of air. "Then. He tried. To take you home. And suck on *your* toes." Each word comes out breathier.

"Right? Like not to kink-shame, but let me wash my feet first. I should have known with the dinner that man's hygiene was subpar," Dani says, grabbing the handle to the front door.

I straighten, wiping the tears from my eyes. I hope I didn't just ruin my makeup. In all seriousness, I ask,

"Do you think *he* will be there?"

"The NFL player?" she asks, scrunching up her face in disgust. "Gah, I hope not."

I only lightly chuckle this time. "No, no. The mayor."

She opens one of the double doors and says, "Well since it's his grand opening, I sure hope so."

We fast walk to her Prius, excitement vibrating off us, but for very different reasons. I slide into the passenger seat, slipping on my sunglasses. She turns up the radio playing the latest pop song by Taylor Swift, and we whip out of the parking lot. Why do all Prius owners drive like they are in a racecar? My heart rate accelerates when she takes out a curb on our way out. I grab on to the *oh shit* handle, and she laughingly apologizes, poking fun as if death isn't a real possibility with her.

The office buildings move by in a blur outside my window. Angry drivers honk, and pedestrians power walk on missions to grab food for lunch. It doesn't take us long to get to First Avenue where the new restaurant is set up. It's been in the media and posted up on flyers with its opening day printed in big bold letters. This is an event that no one wants to miss. Even the investors are going to be there. My palms sweat in anticipation, and I wipe my hands on my thighs.

Dani is more excited than I am, driving with her lead foot and her hand permanently attached to the horn. She whips in and out of the heavy lunchtime traffic. There's no way I can drive like her. I'm still hesitant to use my horn because of how rude drivers are here. They will throw their middle fingers or fists up at you and call you every name under the sun. When her tires screech into an empty parking space, she gets dirty looks from a few bystanders, which she doesn't even notice.

"Do you think we'll be able to get in?" she asks

with her hands clenched together in front of her chest.

"I sure hope so," I fib. I won't tell her I called to make reservations as soon as the date was announced. "Because if we don't bring something back for Mark, we will be eating tuna sandwiches for a month."

Dani's shoulders shiver in disgust. It's not that we don't like tuna sandwiches. We do. It's that when we eat the same thing every day for a month we become completely repulsed by it.

We exit the car and join the large group of people waiting to enter.

A potbellied man calls out over the crowd, "Gather around everyone. Our well-loved mayor, who is always busy and locked in his glass house, has come to grace us with his presence."

Oh, someone is sick of the mayor's PR stunts.

The crowd cheers, but the man waves his hands down. "Save the cheers for the mayor cutting the ribbon."

As if we aren't already in a group clustered together closer than rice in a sushi roll. Three men in various colored suits walk up to the entrance. They must be the investors.

The mayor follows them with a scowl, holding a golden pair of scissors ready to cut the ribbon. His dark hair fades to gray on the sides in a way that makes him look sharp. He's pristine, and his tailored suit hugs his trim waist. He poses perfectly for the cameras, looking very prestigious in his political position. While he is attractive, I'm more interested in what he could do for me. I lick my lips at the thought. If only . . .

Dani's fingers pushed my chin back into place. "You're drooling, girl."

"Oops." I giggle at her.

While Dani is excited about the new restaurant opening, I'm more thrilled for this man. He never steps foot outside of his glass house in the woods unless he's surrounded by security for his political outings.

"Hello, wonderful citizens. We are gathered here today to commemorate our new restaurant's grand opening." His fist covers his mouth before he clears his throat. "And I see we have a great turnout. Even better than the last mayor's." The crowd laughs as if he told a joke. I chuckle to blend in as I look around. *What's so funny?*

"Okay. Okay." He raises his hands to calm down the laughter and capture everyone's attention. "We have these men to thank for their generous investments." Without introducing them, he opens the scissors, smiles for the cameras, and cuts the ribbon. "Let's eat," he finishes. The fabric pieces fall to the ground, and everyone goes wild before charging through the doorway.

"Well, that was a lackluster speech if I've ever heard one," Dani jokes.

"Yeah, maybe he knew if he took any longer someone would have bitten his leg or something."

That gets a hearty chuckle from Dani, and we join the crowd piled up at the door. The entrance is a white awning covered in hanging vines, and the black marble floors gleam, outlining my reflection. I wonder how long this place will stay shiny and brand new as we fall in line with the other patrons checking in at the hostess stand.

Wade is standing off to the side with the men who came up to the ribbon cutting with him, and his gaze is on me, unfaltering. My body heats under his stare, and I cast my eyes downward demurely, pushing a strand of hair behind my ear. I avoid his gaze until we get to the hostess stand. When I look up, he is still staring at me as he smiles at the press.

"Name?" the hostess asks.

"Miss Cosgrove," I say, stealing glances at Wade.

The hostess repeats, "Miss Cosgrove?"

"Yes?"

"You can follow me."

Dani looks at me furrowing her brows, and I shrug. She doesn't need to know that I called ahead of time and made reservations for us.

We follow the waitress into a closed-off back room of the restaurant. I'm guessing it would be an area for an intimate couple to sit together or a private dinner with a group of friends.

While Dani and I take our seats, the waitress announces, "The rest of your party will be here shortly."

When she leaves, Dani asks in a low whisper, "Our party?"

"I have no idea." Because I really *don't* know. I didn't plan on company eating with us when I made the reservations.

My thumbnail is between my teeth before I realize it. A nervous habit of mine that I can't seem to break. Laminated menus are placed before us with names of dishes to choose from, some I've never heard of. I groan. Mark isn't going to enjoy any of this, but we have to bring him back something. Maybe the tomo is something he might like. It's a bowl of angel hair noodles in a cream sauce with baby octopus. If he doesn't like octopuses, he can easily remove them.

We ponder over the menu, and I'm picking Dani's brain on what caviar tastes like when the hostess comes back with a group of men in suits. I'm taken aback, because it's the men who were leading the ribbon-cutting ceremony. The last one to enter is Wade Lynwood, the mayor and wealthiest bachelor in Seattle. The one I have my eye on. If I could bag him, then all my problems would disappear.

They take their seats, leaving the chair next to

mine empty. My hands start to shake, and I hold them together under the table, so no one else will notice how nervous I am.

"Hello." He nods toward Dani and me in greeting. "The two of you wouldn't mind if our party joined yours for lunch, would you?" he asks with a smile, grabbing the empty seat next to mine. He was the last one to walk in, probably since he was held up taking pictures with the press.

The sandalwood cologne he's wearing swarms me like a hive of bees. It makes the spit in my mouth dry as I plaster a polite smile on my face. "No, go right ahead."

"So, Mrs.—" He fumbles for my name.

"*Miss* Cosgrove," I quickly finish, making sure he knows I'm single. Definitely *Not* married. Anymore that is.

"Well, it is very nice to meet you, Miss Cosgrove." He clears his throat before unwrapping the cloth place setting and setting the napkin in his lap. *Very proper.*

"You can call me, Violet, Mr. Mayor." My hand rests over my chest, and my heart races under my palm. *Trust comes hard for me, but trusting the wrong people is what I do best.*

"Wade. You can call me Wade." He gives a half grin.

I point a finger at him and say the first thing that comes to mind. "Like Bruce Wade."

That earns a lighthearted chuckle out of him. "That would be Bruce Wayne. If only I could look as good as Batman."

"Oh, you definitely do," Dani interjects, peering over my shoulder.

I swat her away. Could she really be doing this to me right now? Wade pays her no mind and continues,

AYDEN PERRY 19

"How long have you lived in Seattle?"

"I moved here about six months ago." His eyes roam my body, causing my cheeks to heat. So, he's checking me out. That's why he asked us to sit with them.

"How are you liking it so far?" he asks.

I give in and grant him a flirty smile. Without stopping there, I also give a show of pushing my blonde hair back. "I think I'd like it much better if I had a guide, sir." I lower my voice as I say *sir*, wanting to see his reaction. "I've also heard a lot about how amazing the mayor is here, so I had to come see for myself." I stifle a grin of satisfaction as his pupils dilate. A man who loves attention also enjoys when they sway your decisions.

"I bet they were all good things." A cocky expression takes over his face, and it's hard not to notice how attractive he is. Not my type, but I would be blind not to notice.

"Oh, yes of course. Nothing but the best." I pick up the napkin and do the same as Mayor Wade Lynwood. I'm not sure why since we haven't even ordered yet. I just need something to take my mind off the nerves. "And I'm actually really enjoying it here."

"Good to hear," he says, turning to the rest of the group. Done with our back-and-forth banter for now, he announces, "I've ordered something special for all of us that's not on the menu."

The whole group is nodding and smiling. He's straightforward, not asking if his choice is okay with everyone at the table. Anything the mayor says or does, goes. My guess is everyone is only trying to appease him, to get on his good side, and I most definitely want to be on that side.

He turns to me and whispers, "I hope that's okay with you."

My heart beats faster in my chest. *Can he hear*

that? Pulling myself together, I respond, "Oh, of course. I'm sure whatever you've chosen for us will be lovely." Not that I would have stated otherwise. I don't want to come off as a whiny bitch. I give him a wave of my hand to show all is well, but really, I'm more shocked he considered asking me.

Waiters come from a side door with plates of food and an uncorked bottle of wine. Seafood and sweet fruits assault my senses and have my mouth watering. I'm not sure I've ever smelled anything so divine except for that time I went to this restaurant on the beach in California. They place dishes and wine glasses in front of everyone while one waiter holds a silver bottle of wine in front of Wade. He gives the waiter a curt nod, and the waiter pours a glass for Wade to taste. He swirls the contents of the glass around and smells it before taking a small sip.

He smacks his lips, holding up the glass. "L.W. Blanc de Blancs, best chardonnay in all of Seattle."

Everyone waits for their glasses to be filled and for the go ahead from Wade. Dani and I glance at each other. We did not prepare for a lunch with the mayor himself. Fine dining always goes over an hour, but lunch with *the mayor* is sure to go even longer. I'm sure Mark will understand once we tell him.

When one of the waiters walks past, I hold up my hand, halting him.

"Yes?" he asks.

"Is there a way I can order this plate?" I point to the dish on the menu.

"Will that be included on the tab?" He looks at me skeptically as if I've done something wrong.

"No, no. Sorry. This is to-go for our boss," I say, holding up a hand and shaking it in the air as if to tell him I've got it covered. "It will be on our tab." I motion between Dani and me.

"They will be included on our tab," Wade interjects, jumping into our conversation.

The waiter bows his head. "Very well, sir."

He leaves us, and I'm left speechless. "Um, thank you, Mr. Mayor."

"Call me Wade," he says, supplying a genuine smile. "No need for the formalities, Violet." My heart leaps into my throat, making it hard to swallow. *He's growing more comfortable with me.* "Let's eat." He addresses the table and silverware begins clinking on the ceramic plates.

I take a few bites of the shrimp and mangos coated in a sweet sauce that melts in my mouth before taking a sip of the wine. It complements the seafood wonderfully and causes a soft moan to escape my lips. The only one to notice my minor slip of real satisfaction is Wade, who stares at my lips. My palms sweat, and I wipe them on my slacks. I'm embarrassed by my lack of composure, but the food is just too good. I'm thankful when he turns back to his colleagues, not drawing more attention toward the situation.

The minced mango pieces and grilled shrimp are all mixed together on a bed of rice. I push my food around on my plate as I strain to listen in on their conversation. The only problem is they are giving names and mentioning places I've never heard of like *Santa Rose*, *Miller*, *Davis*, and *McIntire*. The last thing they mention is California's governor, for which Wade gives them a look, and that subject is shut down quicker than Russian roulette. By the end of the meal, I've separated every ingredient into small piles on my plate.

"Violet. Are you okay?" my friend asks me, nudging my arm.

I blink at her a few times trying to figure out why she would think I wasn't okay. It's probably due to the piles of food on my plate, but we are going to sweep that under the rug. The other men at the table start to push back their chairs, announcing the end of the meal. I focus back on the man I came here for, who is talking to one of the other men.

"Yeah, I'm fine." I make sure to address Dani before getting up from my seat.

She looks at me strangely, and I flash her a reassuring smile, not wanting to draw anyone's attention. That doesn't seem to reassure her, but I get up and push my chair in to usher her out before the men realize we are leaving. Just when I think we are going to make it out, someone grabs my arm.

"It was nice to have you ladies join us for the opening lunch." His grip tightens, and his professional smile morphs into a wolfish one, hungry, as if the meal wasn't enough to satisfy him. My gut turns, but I don't react.

"Yes, thank you so much for having us," Dani cuts in. I'm so thankful for her save, because my mouth is still dry, and I'm unable to speak.

She turns to me with a bright smile. Obviously gaining attention from the mayor has put her on some kind of high horse.

"You're a hard man to catch, Mr. Lynwood," I say, making a jab at him always being surrounded by security out in public.

I've been trying to spy on him and get his schedule. I know the route that he drives daily, but as far as seeing him out in public, that hasn't worked.

He chuckles. "Hope you weren't trying to find me to voice a concern about Seattle. We all can't be as amazing as sunny California."

"Nope. I've just heard great things about you and wanted to see the man in action."

That made his chest puff out. He, like any man in a position of power, loves to have his ego stroked. His mouth opens to say something, but one of the men calls for him.

"Excuse me, ladies. Seems I have some more business to attend to," the mayor says before holding a finger up toward the men behind him.

"Don't let us keep you. We actually have to get back to work ourselves."

"I hope to see you again soon, Violet." Wade grabs my hand and plants a kiss on it before turning his back on us.

Dani looks at me sheepishly over her shoulder as we walk out of the restaurant. "Oh, someone has the hots for you, girl."

"Hush it. He does not." I wave Dani off. Even though he did seem forward at times, I still don't think I've won him over just yet.

We walk through the lunch parties of others, who I'd assume are workaholics enjoying a rare lunch outing. I catalog the hostess stand where a man in an untailored business suit is trying to assert his unwelcomed dominance, and then we walk through the glittering shiny doors of the restaurant. The Poppy Valley in classy black block letters on a white background over the door is etched into my brain. This might be the moment that changes the course of everything. I open the passenger door and slide into the seat.

"Man, the sun is shining brightly today," I say as I reach down for my bag, knowing it won't be there. "My purse!" I holler.

"What?" Dani looks over her lap, hands in her hair like I just told her clothes caught fire and she was shirtless in public. I jump out of the car, and I hear Dani screaming my name.

24 CORRUPTING VIOLET

I wave a finger at her and quickly walk inside. My heart is racing, and a lump forms in my throat. I'm making a show, groaning as I walk past the hostess stand. She tries to halt me, but I weave past her with an apology written all over my face.

The door to the back room is just within sight, and I don't see my purse on the ground by the chair I was sitting in. My feet move faster. My breathing labored. I break the threshold of the doorway. My head is on a swivel, looking for my purse. When my face is met with a hard brick wall, and a soft breath of air puffs through my hair, I lose my balance and stagger on my heels.

A rough hand catches me by my forearm, righting me. "Violet," his gruff voice says, sending a shiver down my spine.

"Yes?" I ask, slowly tilting my head back and trailing his broad chest. A flash of my yellow purse catches the corner of my eye. It's looped around his wrist, and he is holding a to-go box in his hand. *Shit,* I did actually forget about Mark's lunch.

"Forget something?" he asks, and I finally meet his looming stare. His eyes are dark and smoldering, making me feel small. I give him a nod and reach for my bag. He pulls it out of my grasp, leaving me standing there awkwardly. "I have something to ask you."

My heart rate spikes higher, creating a heavy thud in my head. I gulp past the sensation of sand on my tongue. "Shoot."

"Come with me to a dinner auction tomorrow," he asks with a smug grin, as if me saying yes is inevitable

"And if I say no?" I ask.

He shrugs and wraps his arm around my waist, pulling me flush against him. My palms rest against his chest, and he whispers in my ear, "Then, I'll have to try another way to get you alone."

"I'm guessing *no* isn't something you hear very often," I say, breathier than intended.

He shakes his head and says, "No is never an option."

His stare is piercing into me as if he is digging up every skeleton I've ever buried. I lick my lips under his hot gaze. I want to say no just to watch what happens to his smug expression. But my racing pulse, and my need to get to know him controls what I say. "Then, I guess I'll see you there."

The grip he has around my waist eases, and I feel like I can finally breathe again, even if just a fraction better. He hands me the white box and my purse. My shoulders relax as relief floods me.

Reluctantly, I ask, "Should I get your number?" I hate that I have to pry this information from him, but how am I supposed to know where this place is or what time I'm supposed to be there?

He moves past me to leave the room. Before he completely exits the room, he says over his shoulder, "Not needed."

Then he's gone, and I'm left standing here with the smell of pasta and seafood.

Lunch took longer than the time we were allotted, which is to be expected with dining out in Seattle, but luckily, I was able to grab Mark's lunch. We did have a deal, and I held up my end of the bargain.

I'm relieved when I see Mark eating his fancy pasta and octopus dish with extreme enthusiasm, licking all the sauce off his fork. "Damn, they know what they are doing at that new place."

Dani nods her head eagerly. "Not only was the food fantastic, but we got to eat with the *mayor.*" His eyes grow large in amazement. "Yeah, and he is just as mouthwatering in person as he is in the tabloids." Her head is propped in her hand, and she's looking off longingly. She snaps out of her reminiscing and addresses me with an arched brow. "Isn't that right, Violet?" She grins proudly, probably thinking of the moment she had to close my mouth at the sight of him.

"Oh, hush." I wave her off to get her to stop talking about it.

"Can I help you?" I hear Mark ask from behind me.

I turn in my seat to see who he might be talking to, and there's a tall, awkward teenager with a face full of acne standing at the entrance of the work space holding a box.

He clears his throat, and his voice comes out as a mixture of squeaky and raspy as his voice is going through the change of puberty. "I have a package here for a," he says, glancing at the card, "Miss Cosgrove?"

I raise my hand. "That's me."

He scurries to place the box on my desk while I reach into my purse for a tip. I hand him a five-dollar bill, and his face lights up. "Thank you, ma'am."

"No problem." I remember the times I used to work small jobs during the summers to be able to hang out with my friends. That was before I had to switch families and got used to living with rich people.

I turn toward the box he set on my desk, and Dani is already hanging over my shoulder to see what it is. "Open it. Open it."

"Okay, calm down, ghost rider," I tell her.

I grab the card on the box and open it.

Violet
You have been invited to The Governor's Annual Auction Ball.
Please be at the Santa Rose Hall at eight p.m. sharp.
Dress formally.
-The Mayor

The note in my hand, with its elegant font and thick card stock, becomes heavy in my grasp. *Trusting my heart though is something I'll keep under lock and key.*

Dani squeals beside me. "You have a date with the mayor," she squeals. "I'm so jealous."

"Ah, it's nothing," I tell her, dropping the note on my desk.

"Well, are you going to open it?" she asks me eagerly.

My fingers trace along the outer rim of the box and lift it open. I'm met with the shine of black sequins, and Dani takes in a sharp inhale. "This is beautiful."

I run my hand along the intricate patterns woven into the material before grabbing it by the top of the dress and pulling it out. It unfurls and reaches the floor. It has an asymmetrical neckline with a built-in choker and a bust to go braless. "It's breathtaking." I have to suppress the smug smile that itches to crawl its way onto my face.

"I'll say it again. I'm freakin' jealous of you," Dani says as she touches the dress. "You have to tell me everything. Especially what he's like in bed." She wiggles her brows at me with a large grin that takes over her face.

"*Dani*," I groan, faking annoyance. *This is exactly what I wanted, right?*

"Don't play coy with me. I know you're just as

excited."

I fold up the dress, close the box, and push it to the far corner of my desk. "You're right."

She beams on her way to her desk. That's the one thing she loves most, being told she is right about something.

The rest of the day passes in a drag. When the clock hits Margaritaville time, I close everything down and grab my belongings. "It's Five O'Clock Somewhere" plays in my mind, and a margarita doesn't sound half bad right now. Dani waits for me by the exit, bag in hand.

"I seriously can't wait for your date with the mayor tomorrow." She's excited, and I'm nervous. Maybe it should have been her that he set his eyes on instead of me. *You deserve this, Violet*, the small voice whispers in my head.

"I wish I had your excitement." I fidget with my keys as we make our way to our cars.

She stops in her tracks and turns to me. "You should take full advantage of this, and don't be nervous. I want to live vicariously through you. I need all the details on whether he is as good in real life as he is in my dreams."

I hang on to the door handle, and before opening it to get in, I tell her, "You know if that ever happens, you will be the first person I tell."

"You better." Her eyes are hard, but the smile on her face tells me she's only partially joking.

The nerves are eating me alive, but I have to put up a confident front. I repeat the mantra in my head. *You deserve this, Violet*. I place the box on my passenger seat and drive home.

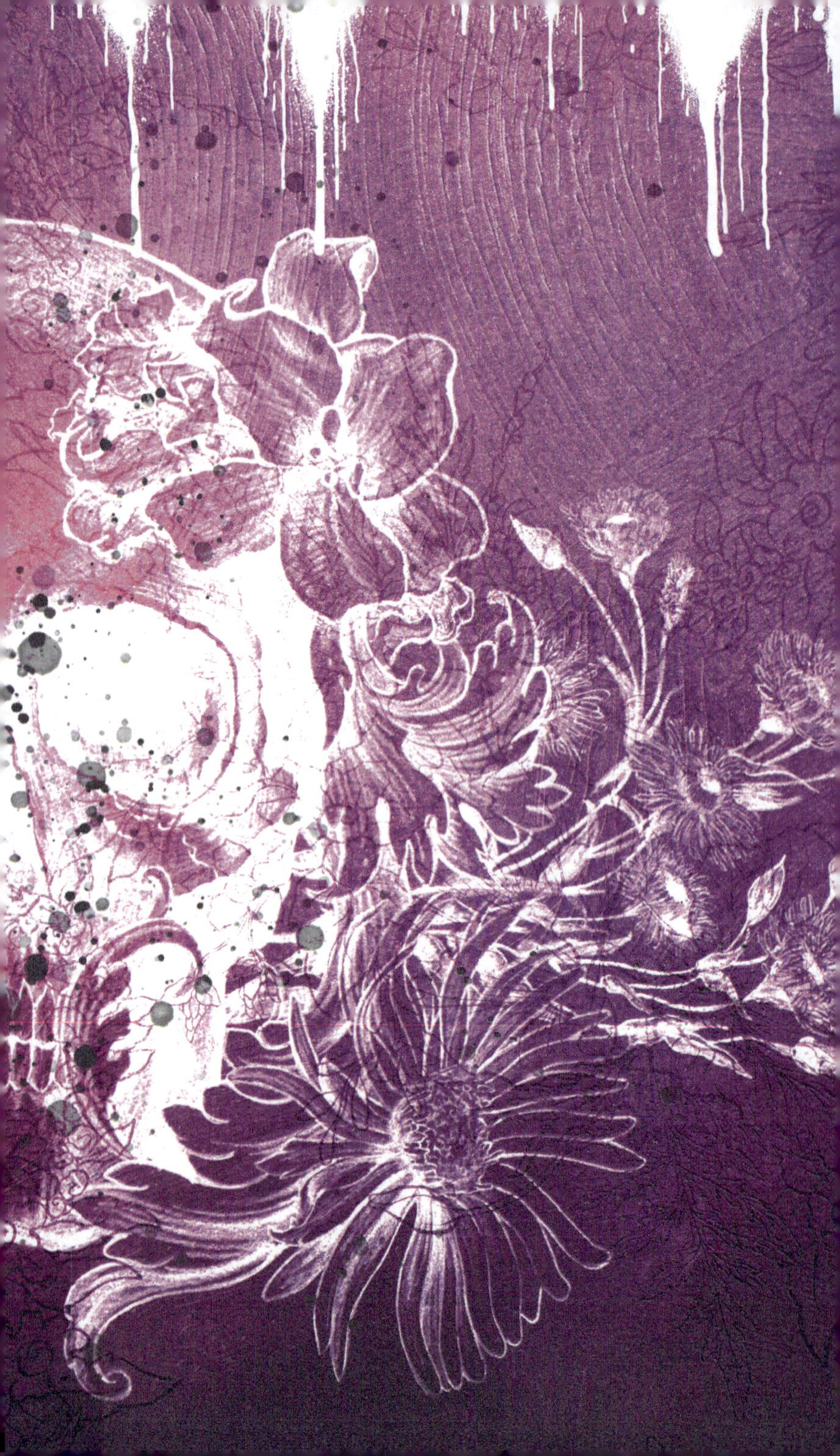

CHAPTER 2
VIOLET

"Are you ready for tonight?" Dani asks.

"A little nervous, but I think I'll be okay," I tell her, putting away the foster paperwork I recently filled out.

"You've got this." She grabs my shoulder, giving me an encouraging squeeze.

After I grace her with a soft smile, she moves back to her desk to finish a case she's working on. We continue through our workday as normal. Answering phones and setting up visitations and check-ins. I lose myself to the steady pace, thinking of the expectations for tonight. I need Wade to fall for me. Be the one he wants to keep for more than one night of intimacy.

"Hey, we just got a call for an urgent case," Mark calls out. He leans out of his open doorway and looks between Dani and me. "I need someone to stay and take this."

His gaze is filled with sorrow, and a cold chill washes over me. "It's another missing mother, isn't it?" I ask, already knowing the answer to my question.

Lips turned down in a deep frown, he says, "It is, sadly. I need someone to take in the child for tonight and call around for relatives. If there are none, then we need a list of open foster homes. Who's going to take it?"

"I will," Dani speaks up.

"Dani, you shouldn't have to do this alone," I say. I want to seem sincere, but I can't miss my plans for tonight.

"No, no. You have a date tonight. I'll stay here and finish out this case," she urges.

"Thank you." I grab her hands in mine and squeeze them. "I owe you one."

She beams at me. "You're damn straight you will."

Mark slaps the doorframe twice. "All right, looks like that's settled."

He goes back to his office while Dani and I part ways to go to our desks. The rest of the day goes by pretty uneventfully. I'm staring at the time, watching the minutes tick down to five o'clock. It's moving like sand in an hourglass. Each piece of sand falling through the skinny sliver of glass, waiting to hit the bottom with all the others. As soon as the little hand reaches the twelve, I let out a breath and pack my things.

"Are you sure, I can't stay to help?" I ask Dani, checking in with her. I don't want to run out of here and leave her hanging, or seem inconsiderate.

"No, the only things I need from you are all the details from your date tonight." She gets up from her desk and starts pushing me out of the door. "Now, go."

"Okay." I chuckle.

Without another moment of hesitation, or show

of one, I walk into the afternoon's muggy heat. Tilting my head back, I look up at the high clouds that streak the sky. It feels like it's going to rain today. I can usually tell by the weight of the air. My mother always told me I was an odd child when it came to the rain. One of my favorite things to do is stand in the middle of a downpour.

When I turn my car on, the air-conditioning and the last thing I played on the radio comes through, blasting in my face. *Shit, guess I really needed a pep in my step this morning.* I immediately turn it off before I have to make an appointment for a new pair of eardrums. The drive to my apartment on the far side of town doesn't take me long. I have two hours to get ready before I have to leave.

The couple out on the sidewalk are arguing, and I groan at the fact that I have to deal with them. My nosey-ass neighbors are always fighting. As soon as I make it to the staircase that leads up to the second floor, I think I'm in the clear, until I hear someone call my name.

"Violet," Venny, my neighbor, shouts. I pick up my pace, wanting to ignore him. A hand wraps around my forearm, spinning me to face him. "I'm talking to you, stuck-up princess."

I pull my arm out of his grip. "What do you want, Venny?"

"You didn't pay your rent." He runs his wormlike tongue over his rotting teeth.

"And I told you, I'll have it to you by Friday." I cross my arms over my chest. Not only is Venny my neighbor, he's also my landlord in this piece-of-shit complex. "Can I go now?"

He adjusts himself in his pants, and I maintain a straight face. "Yeah, yeah. You better have it for me." His hand grips a stray lock of hair that fell in my face, bringing his rancid scent closer to me. "Or I'll have to take my payment some other way."

I push his hand away, causing him to release my hair. "I'll have the money for you."

Not staying to hear anything else he has to say, I walk the rest of the way upstairs to my apartment. One thing is for sure, I can't wait to get out of this dump. I close the door behind me, locking the three different locks that line the frame. The pristine white box sits on my bed. I can't help thinking of how badly I need this to work.

I wash and fix my hair before rubbing on some dollar store makeup. No one ever notices anyway. I left the dress for last, and I pull it out of its box. It glimmers in the yellow light. This dress will get me killed if I wear it out of here. Especially if my landlord sees me in it. He will accuse me of holding out on him. I sadly pack the gorgeous gown into my backpack and throw in the one pair of heels I took when I left my ex-husband. Seems fitting for the occasion.

Sneaking out of my apartment, I hear Venny yelling at his TV. Good, no way I'll run into him again.

"Can you help me?" someone whispers from the shadows when I make it out to my car. The girl who was arguing with Venny before moves out of the darkness and into the glow of the streetlights. She's sporting a shiner that she didn't have there before when I went to my apartment. "I need some money, please," she begs. Her glassy eyes look at me, pleading.

"What's your name?" I ask her.

She inches closer. Her shoulders are hunched as if she is hurting somewhere else. "Merigold."

Her name, a flower just like mine, sends an icy chill down my back. "Merigold, if I can give you anything, it's advice." I look up at Venny's apartment and see his silhouette through the blinds as he gets up to scream at the television. "Find a rich man, and"—she nods, letting me know she's listening—"never give away your heart. Pull it out of your chest and stomp that traitorous bitch into the fucking dirt."

Her eyes are wide when I turn away from her, but she doesn't say anything in return. I hope she takes my advice and lives by it till the fucking end. Life is cold, but you have to learn to be colder.

I drive to the address given with the card stock in my hand. The event is being held in downtown Seattle. I should use the valet, but I don't want the prying eyes of the other attendees, or the valet, to see my clunky car filled with water bottles and wrappers in my passenger seat. I park my car in the closest parking lot and call a cab. A cab seems more acceptable than my old beater. It gets me where I need to go. That's all that matters.

The yellow taxi pulls up in the parking lot, driving slowly, looking for the rusted silver Ford Taurus. I've already slipped on my dress and heels in the car when I get out to flag the driver down. The lights white out my vision until I move out of their direct path, leaving spots to dance along my vision. My palms sweat thinking of the last time I took one of these damn things. I wasn't in a good place. One I refuse to ever go back to.

"Ma'am, you the one who called?" the man asks.

"Yeah, that's me." I'm still holding my hand over my eyes as if the light is still beaming down on me.

"Well." His brow is arched, and he looks confused. I'd be too in his situation. A woman in a formal gown standing in the middle of a packed parking lot calling for a cab. *Yeah, at least he's not one I have to impress.* "Get in."

"One second," I tell him, walking around the front of his cab to the passenger side mirror. I pull out my tube of cherry-red lipstick. One that's rich and smooth as butter as it glides over my cupid's bow. I smack my lips together, checking out my reflection, and slide into the back seat.

The driver huffs out a breath as if this night is already the longest night he's had all week. "Where to?"

"The Convention Center down the street," I say, waiting for his reaction, but instead I get nothing out of him. He clicks on the meter and begins driving. "No need to drive around the block to run up the meter. I'll give you a tip."

That's all he needs to get me to the event in five minutes. There's a valet line and a drop-off line for guests. The cab driver drops me off, and I'm left standing in front of the Convention Center.

A group of women in their various ball gowns whisper, and I overhear them say, "What is she even doing here?" And another comments, "She came in a yellow cab. *Gross*. I wonder whose plus-one she is." The comments cause my exterior to harden and my smile, which is only a thin line, to grow wider. I continue past them to the door with my shoulders pushed back and my head held high. The muscular bodyguard holds a clipboard in front of the double doors. He must be security. It's a private event, so I wouldn't expect anything less.

"Miss Cosgrove," I say to the attendant at the door.

He looks me up and down before checking his list. When he finds my name, he lets the stack of papers fall back to his clipboard before opening the door for me. "Enjoy, ma'am."

Oh, I plan on it.

The large chandelier, the focal point of the room, shines over the round tables covered in white linen beneath it. Everyone looks elegant in their gowns, and the men in their tuxedos look like penguins waddling around. All except for Wade. He commands the attention of the room, surrounded by people all laughing and clapping hands on his back.

"Champagne?" a waiter with a tray of glasses asks me.

I grab a flute off the tray. The chilled glass is a nice contrast to my heated fingers. I wish I could pour the whole glass over my chest, but instead I resort to gulping its contents down in one gulp. The sweet raspberry fizz cools me and calms me at the same time. After swapping out the empty glass for a full one, I make my way over to Wade Lynwood. The man of the hour who will give me more than an hour of his time, if I have my way.

He glances up and our eyes lock. His small smile broadens, lighting a fire in the pit of my stomach. The crowd that surrounds him disperses when he leaves them.

"Violet," he says, towering over me so that I have to look up at him.

"Wade," I whisper, holding my glass of champagne close to my chest.

"I'm glad I didn't have to resort to extreme measures to see you again." He runs his hand over my exposed shoulder and down to my elbow. The motion causes a shiver to run through me.

"Maybe, I shouldn't have come, so that I could see the extremes you would go to see me." I grab one of the lapels of his tux, running my fingers over the soft fabric before looking up into his eyes.

Again, that wolfish grin comes to play on his lips. With his hand still gripping my elbow, he pulls me close to him. The sweat from my glass touches the exposed skin of my chest. It's the only thing holding distance between us.

Wade leans down. His lips brush the shell of my

ear. "Maybe you should have," he whispers.

"It's time for the auction," an announcer calls, breaking the spell Wade was casting on me. "Everyone take your seats."

Wade gently pulls me by the elbow, looping my arm in his before guiding me to our seats. He's one who loves to show off pretty toys that no one else can have. I know I look amazing in this dress because all eyes are drawn to me. With every table we pass, heads turn in my direction, and their eyes consume every inch of me.

Wade stops us at a table close to the front that is slightly off to the side of the stage. We have a great view of the event without being the center of attention. The man who sits front and center leans back in his chair, at ease with his surroundings. The woman beside him—who I'd assume is his wife—sits prim and proper under his arm like a porcelain doll. Her smile is painted on, and her skin is as white as paper. I think if I were to shatter a glass right next to her, she wouldn't even flinch.

"What are you looking so intently at?" Wade whispers in my ear, finding where my eyes are held steadfast.

"Who is that?" I ask, wondering who the man is who demands to be in everyone's line of sight and commanding the attention of the room.

"That's the governor of California and his wife," he says. "She doesn't even hold a candle to your beauty."

I lean away from him sheepishly, covering my face. My fawning embarrassment causes him to smirk. He doesn't act as old as he seems. Or maybe he is just that smooth with women.

"Now that everyone has found their seats. We would like to draw your attention to the founder of this event," the speaker announces. "Andrew Bryson, the governor of California. We thank you for your continued support, which helps generate large donations to help children in need and create temporary homes for orphaned children."

A charity event for orphaned children? Why didn't I know about this?

A round of applause from the attendees serenades the hall until the announcer continues. "We will have each person come forward and then we'll begin the bidding, but before that we will have a few volunteers from the crowd join us."

The man looks around, and Wade grabs my hand from the table. "You should volunteer. You would be perfect."

An unease settles low in my gut. I push the feeling away and plaster on a smile, remembering my rules. *Don't seem easy, or they will lose interest.* I give him a soft chuckle and grip his forearm. "What's the auction for?"

He smiles broadly at me. "For a date. The people in the audience will bid to have a night with you."

It's the first time that I notice one of his front teeth is darker than the rest. I can't help but wonder about the story behind that. "No, I don't think I'd make a good choice for the bidding war," I say, trying to get out of this.

"You are beautiful. Not a single man has been able to keep his eyes off of you," he admits, but I can't risk another man bidding higher than him.

"That's very flattering of you, Wade, but I don't think I'm the right fit for this," I say, shaking my head.

"Of course you are," he urges, pushing me to volunteer myself. "I can't think of another woman here who is more beautiful and cares about children as much as you do."

"I—" I begin to reject him again, but I'm interrupted by the announcer.

"Ahh, this lovely woman." He extends his free hand to a fair-haired woman in a royal-blue dress. "What's your name?" he asks, speaking into the mic, then extending it to the woman for everyone else to hear.

"Mariah McIntire." She speaks softly into the mic. Her fingers tug at the end of her long hair, looping it around and around. If she's nervous, why did she volunteer herself in the first place?

I look around the room for an empty seat and notice one of the men from the luncheon yesterday. He's grinning from ear to ear like the Cheshire cat, and the seat beside him is empty. There are a few more volunteers who come up alongside her that also give their names into the mic. Donna Miller, Emily Davis, and a few more all join Mariah McIntire. All the last names I remember overhearing from the men who had joined us for lunch. *Did they set this up?*

"Wade?" He's grimacing and blatantly upset with me. "I'm going to go to the restroom. Freshen up a bit."

He gives me a curt nod without saying a word. I get up from my seat and head toward the back of the room. The door to the bathroom is labeled with a gold placard, and I let myself in. The attendant in the corner holds a towel over their arm, paying me no mind. I pull out my lipstick from my purse and look in the mirror as I reapply what the champagne glass removed.

A group of women come in, loudly chattering. "And he came in with this woman I saw come in a cab." *That's me.* They quiet down when they see me, and I glare at them through the mirror. *Oh, great.* They are talking about me. I'm the girl who took the yellow cab in. The things they would have said if I pulled up in my beater car would've probably been ten times worse. They scurry to the other side of the sink, snatching glances my way. So, I'm not good enough to be here with *the mayor.*

I close the tube of my lipstick with a loud click and walk away, swaying my hips. *I'll show them. I know how to get what I want.*

When I make it back to my seat, the bidding for the women on stage has already begun. Wade raises his numbered card, and the announcer points calling out a price. He acts as if I'm not even here. *The fuck.* He raises his card again, and I quickly push his hand down.

"What are you doing?" he hisses.

"You don't need to gamble with me around," I say with seduction dripping from my words.

He scoffs. *Too easy, Violet.* I continue, attempting to gain his attention and prevent him from bidding on the women in the auction. Leaning in close to him, moaning with nearly every bite of food. None of my tricks gain his hungry gaze that I so desire and need. My last trick is to drop my fork under the table before running my hand up his slacks. All are too forward, and his only response is to move my palm off his lap.

"What's your problem," I finally snap under my breath.

"I don't have one," he says, coolly.

"Yeah, okay."

Pushing my chair from the table before the event is even over, I stand and march out. My mind is reeling, searching for a way to right this. I need to get close to him. *Next step, walk away.* Men love the chase, the drama. I haven't met a rich man who hasn't come running for it. The only thing I've ever encountered is, when they grow bored, they tend to find a new plaything. That has been my experience anyway.

The night air breezes, moving my baby hairs across my forehead. Cars pass and lights glitter, illuminating the night. Pulling my phone from my purse, I dial a cab. The line rings, and the operator for the company answers. I give them my address and where to pick me up.

"Can we talk?" Wade's gruff voice sounds from behind me.

Without turning to see him, I say, "Maybe." I shrug and peek at him over my shoulder. "Can you?"

"May I?" he asks, stepping up beside me.

This works every time. Make a scene, and they feel the need to console or resolve the issue when they have no idea what they've done wrong. "You may."

"I was upset, because—"

"The first step is always admitting," I say, interrupting his pause.

That causes him to chuckle before continuing. "I wanted to bid on you."

"I told you. You didn't have to bid on me." I cross my arms over my chest, trying to appear smaller.

"I know. I just wanted to show you off," he admits, shoving his hands in his pockets. "Can I give you a ride home?"

A horn honks, interrupting our conversation. *Next, make him work for it.* "That's my cab. Maybe another time?"

"You're not getting in that." Wade grabs my hand, halting me in place.

"Yes, I am," I say, giving the grip he has on me a little tug. "It's my ride home."

His facial features harden into determination before he lets go of my hand and reaches into his pocket, pulling out his clip of cash. He pulls out two twenties and hands them to the cab driver. Without saying a word to the cabby, he addresses me, "No, my driver will take you." Then he raises his hand at the valet.

"Wait, don't drive away," I yell to the cab driver who still has his window open.

But Wade looks at him and commands, "Drive." He doesn't even spare me another glance before he is pulling away from the curb. My shoulders slump. *What the fuck am I going to do now?* "Let me do this for you. There's champagne in the car. You'll be able to relax. Let me make it up to you for this disastrous date. Plus, cabs are filled with germs." He grimaces at the thought.

I know what he means. Activities and fluids end up on those seats, but we pretend those things don't actually happen. That it's only something the movies made up to scare us away or heighten a fantasy, whichever is preferred at the time. Plus, he's trying to make it up to me for his behavior tonight, which is what I wanted.

Hook, line, and sinker. Rich men fall for the damsel every time.

His black town car pulls up to the curb, and I let out a huff. "Fine."

That makes him smile. He thinks he's won, but has he?

He opens the door for me, and I slide in. "I'll see you again."

Placing a finger on my chin as if I'm thinking, I say, "Maybe." Playing hard to get is a game of tug-of-war. Who will be the one to tug the hardest and win?

"There's no maybe." He shuts the door, and the driver pulls aways from the curb.

Good, I'm counting on it.

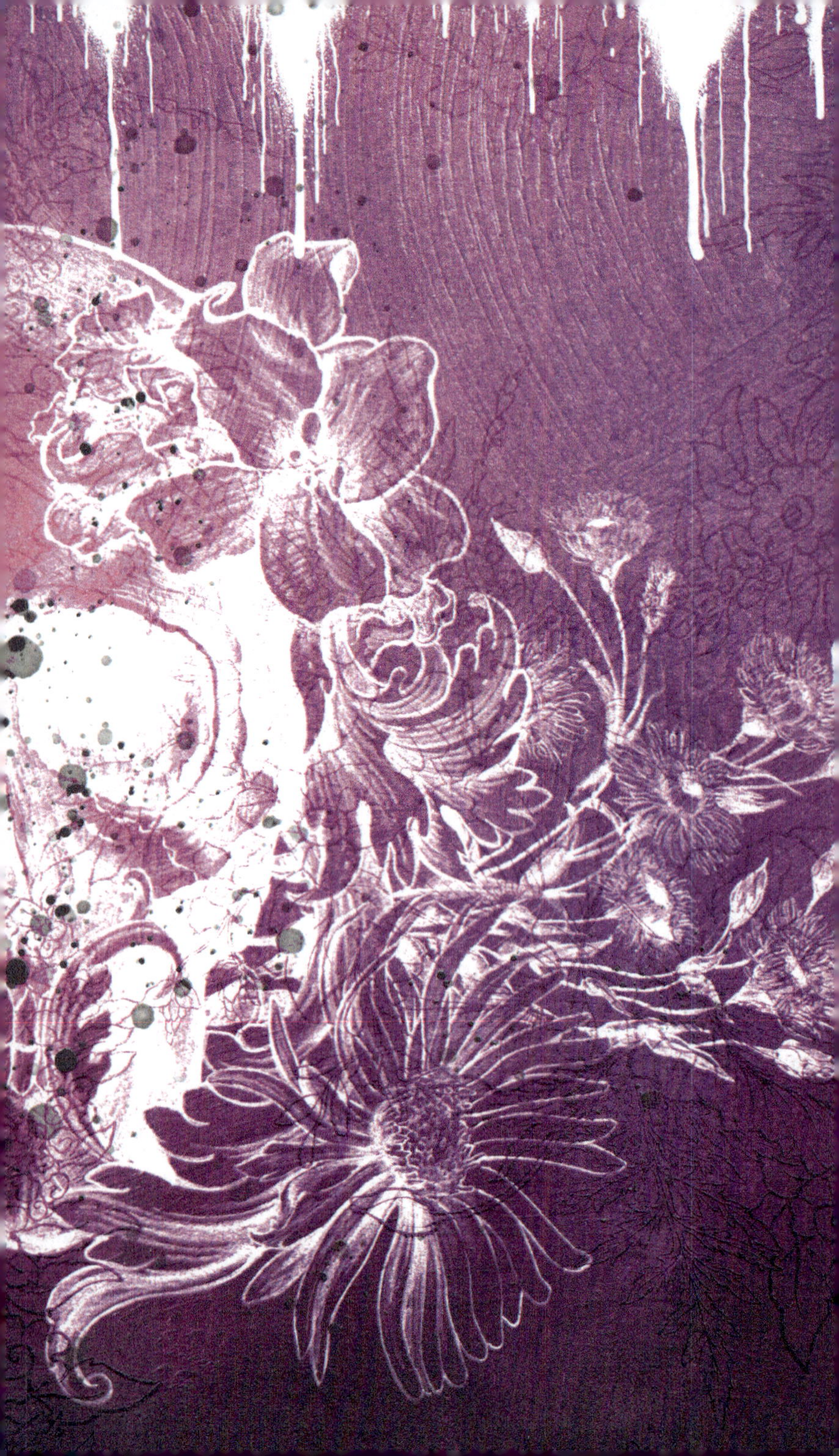

CHAPTER 3
VIOLET

Wade's driver drops me off at my apartment complex. I'm thankful he didn't say anything or ask any questions when I told him where to drop me off at. It's late and dark, but everyone knows this area. It's called the heroine den for a reason.

When I walk up the stairs to the second floor, Merigold is nowhere in sight, and Venny's lights from his TV still flash from behind his blinds. He probably passed out on the couch. My thoughts continue to stray toward Merigold. I hope she found a place to sleep tonight that wasn't in Venny's clutches. Glancing over my shoulder, I look for anyone who may be looking. I don't want them to see me in this gown. What Venny doesn't know won't hurt him. The coast is clear when I unlock my door, and I slink inside before locking all three locks.

My car is in the lot down the street from the convention center. "*Fuuuckkk*," I groan. I'll have to figure that shit out in the morning, but first I need sleep.

I unzip the expensive dress, removing the buttery fabric from my body. Maybe I could sell it for my rent this week. It's not like Wade will ask where it went later. After hanging it up, I place it in the back of my closet behind the few pairs of slacks and dress shirts I have for work. It's the only dress in my possession. Then I wash my face, set my alarm, and go straight to bed.

"Oh, Pretty Woman" plays on my phone, letting me know it's time to get up. The irony of the song isn't lost on me. I actually find it comical and slightly fitting. Stretching my arms over my head, I groan in satisfaction.

I've almost got him where I want him. Only one last move to make.

After dressing for work, I call a cab to take me to where I left my car last night. I should have them on speed dial at this point as much as I've been calling them lately. Once I have all my things together, I unlatch and unlock the door. Taking a deep breath, I peek through the crack and peer around the doorframe. The morning is quiet, and the sun is just beginning to light the sky. Venny, or any one of his minions who could run and grab him, is nowhere in sight. I ease out of my apartment and quickly lock it back up. Still no sounds come from Venny's apartment, which is good. I tiptoe past his door and creep down the stairs to make sure he doesn't wake up, not taking any chances. Once I've made it to the parking lot, I stay among the shadows. I should have waited in my apartment for the cab driver, but I didn't want them to honk and risk pulling more attention to myself as I leave.

"Violet, looking good this morning," Honey calls.

My soul jumps out of me and dives back in when I notice it isn't one of Venny's usual buyers, or Venny himself for that matter.

"Gah, you scared the shit out of me." I place my hand over my chest.

Honey throws her cigarette before striding over toward me. "I see." She chuckles.

"What are you doing out here this early?" I ask.

Honey isn't like the usual crowd around here. She's a badass stripper who works hard as crap for her kids, and I fucking respect the hell out of her.

"I have to go to court this morning for child support," she admits, running her hand over her shaved head. "I was kinda hoping you'd give me a ride, but seeing as your car isn't here . . ."

"Yeah. That's a long story," I tell her, folding my arms over my chest.

"Wanna talk about it?" she asks. Honey reminds me a lot of my sister who I would be closer with, if I hadn't fucked that up.

"Nah, not really."

She just shrugs, letting it drop.

My cab pulls up in front of us. Just in time too, since Venny hasn't come out yet to harass me.

"Come on. You can ride with me," I tell her.

"You sure?" Her brow raises in question.

"Shut the fuck up and come on."

She just smiles before sliding in behind me.

After dropping Honey off at the courthouse, I drive to work. The first thing I see when I walk into the office is a vase full of fresh-cut violets sitting on my desk.

Dani doesn't waste a minute before she is on me. "Oooooo, the date with the mayor went well, I see."

I set my belongings down on my desk and grab the card from the flowers. "Yeah. It went pretty good," I tell her absentmindedly as I look over what the card says.

Two words are written in bold font. *No maybes.*

My stomach flips, and I have to push the excitement down. I've almost got him.

"No maybes?" Dani asks. "What kind of note is that?"

"It's nothing," I say, slipping the card back onto its holder before pushing the vase toward the corner of my desk.

"Oh, it's definitely something. What happened? You have to tell me everything," Dani demands with a shit-eating grin, and I honestly don't have the mental capacity for this.

"It was an auction. We got into an argument because I didn't want to volunteer, and he gave me a ride home," I admit, trying to get this conversation with her over with so that I can get this workday over with.

Her brows pinch together in confusion. "You didn't let him bid on you? I'd have let him bid on my ass," she says before shaking her booty at me.

"Stop." I laugh, slapping her on the arm.

"At least he got you flowers though. That was sweet of him."

"Yeah."

Dani gives up on trying to pull information out of me and begins walking back to her desk. The pep in her step now gone.

I only slightly feel bad that I took all the fun of

gossiping about the mayor out of this for her. My mental spoons are bent and twisted. "Hey, Dani."

She turns toward me, looking over her shoulder. "Yeah?"

"Do you know anything about the charity for orphaned children from the governor of California?" I ask her.

"No? Why?" she asks, hesitantly.

"Just wondering."

Strange, I feel like we would have known something about that.

The rest of our workday passes by in silence. Dani's head is down, and she's pushing papers, much the same as me, with a few phone calls thrown in there. Once the end of our shift comes, I exhale audibly.

"Yeah, I feel that," Dani says from across the room. "I'm so ready to go home. I think I need to sleep as soon as I hit the door."

I slap my palm against my forehead. "I'm so sorry, Dani, I totally forgot you worked late last night." It completely slipped my mind, and I regret brushing her off earlier.

"No, it's fine, really," she says, waving her hand in the air before shoving her laptop into her messenger bag.

"Are you sure?" I ask her, not wanting her to think I'm a complete shit of a person.

"Yeah." Her head is down, and I want to believe it's just because she is tired, but I know I fucked up.

We collect our belongings, saying bye to Mark before we head out. The walk together to our cars is silent and heavy. Once I'm standing outside my door, gripping the handle, an apology weighs on my tongue.

"I'm sorry for crushing your excitement earlier," I tell her over the hood of my car.

She shrugs it off and a smirk plays on her lips. "Yeah. I kind of expected him to be different. It's okay. I hate that it wasn't a better night for you."

"Maybe next time."

She laughs at that. "Is that what the *No maybes* was for?"

I give her a nod.

"Well, good. Make him work for it, girl. See you tomorrow."

That makes me smile. I can always count on Dani to turn things around. We both get into our vehicles. Dani drives off first, and I wait for her to leave. Mark is in his office still working on last-minute paperwork. I have a few minutes before he comes out. My heart rate spikes as I quickly look around. Grabbing my pocketknife, I pop the hood and race to find the radiator line. Wires and tubes surround the motor. I've researched this, but I don't necessarily know what I'm doing. I exhale as I hover my knife on the tube next to the radiator. *Here goes nothing.* The blade cuts through the thick rubber, green fluid falls down, splattering on everything around it, and I cross my fingers.

Starting up the car, the tachometer quickly lifts before settling back down. My temperature gauge starts to rise faster than before. *Perfect, now let's pray this works.* My palms sweat as I recall the vision of Wade's intimidating stare last night. If this goes as planned, my car will sputter to a stop on his normal route home. Hopefully, a damsel in distress is his kryptonite and makes him pull over. If not, this is going to be a bitch of a tow bill.

I cut through downtown Seattle, continuously watching the gauges. A car pulls out in front of me, and I slam on my breaks. *What the fuck, dude.* I lay on the horn, staring at my temperature meter creeping up with this delay. *Fuck, fuck, fuck.* What did I read online? Massaging my temples, I will myself to remember. *Heat good, cold bad.* I would have thought it would have been the opposite, but nope. Cranking on the heater, I watch the gauges intently. A horn honks behind me, causing my heart to beat erratically.

Just breathe. It's going to work out.

The traffic begins to move again, and the temperature gauge bobs at the middle line. Just a little bit farther. My car needs to make it. Turning the wheel sharply, I cut through a side street, barely missing a homeless man. I give him a wave in apology. *Sorry, man this was not a part of the plan. Oh, shit.* I turn back onto another two-lane street. This is it. This is the street. My unexpected detour took me closer to my desired destination than expected. The gasket isn't ready yet. Once I get to a good clearing on the side of the road, I put the car in neutral, blast the AC, and rev the engine, sending silent wishes for this plan to work. The thermostat gauge gets increasingly closer toward the red letter *H*. Small amounts of white smoke flutter from the hood, and with a loud pop, it quickly changes to a billowing cloud. With a large exhale, I put the car in park and turn it off.

Fuck, that was stressful. Glancing at the clock, I notice he should be about to drive this route to get home. Time to get to work. I pop the hood and walk toward the front of the car where the clouds of heat and smoke continue to pour out. I pull off my button-up shirt and wrap it around my waist, leaving just my cami showing. My breasts are perked up high enough for my black lace bra to peek over the top. *Girls are ready and in position.* I lean over the hood and check my watch, only five more minutes. *I'm right on time.* Perfect plans make for perfect executions.

The traffic whips by my car, and I stick my ass out at an angle, so that I'm in view of those driving by. My hope is to garner the attention from the individual I have my sights set on. As I'm waiting, small drops of sweat slowly trail down my spine from the ride here and the overwhelming steam. I hope he drives by soon because this heat is killing me. My stomach sinks when I look back at my watch. It's been *ten minutes*, and Wade is nowhere in sight.

"Fuck!" I bellow as I slam my hood, making the car rock. This isn't working.

I pull out my phone and scroll to AAA, annoyed that I'm having to resort to plan B. A loud screech reverberates off the center divider, causing me to jerk back and look up. *Is it him?* I watch as a sleek black Lexus quickly pulls over ahead of me. My heart thuds against my rib cage as I grip my phone in anticipation. *Please, Please let this be who I hope it is.*

The car door swings open, and a suited pants leg exits. One of the guys from the luncheon steps out. My hand holding my phone drops to my side in disappointment, but I force a smile onto my face anyway.

"Hey, can you help me?" I ask, knowing I still need a ride home.

His head is down as he walks up to me, and he doesn't say a word. I narrow my eyes on him.

"Umm, hello. Can you help me?"

I take a few steps back as a wave of fear rolls over me. Without looking up, he darts forward, snatching my arm before I can make a run for it. His fingers dig into my bicep, and my pulse hammers in my ears. Another car pulls up at the same time, blocking the traffic from seeing me thrash against this man holding me. Panic rises in my throat, and I jerk my arm back until I hear a gruff voice that stops me in my tracks.

"Richard," Wade commands, and my muscles go weak as my eyes fall on him. His brows are furrowed, and his fists are clenched at his sides.

"I was only helping her out, sir."

Wade turns to me and asks, "Is that right Violet?"

"No, I mean, yes . . . I'm not sure. My car broke down and—" I stammer and stumble over my words.

"Here." Wade motions toward his car. "Let me give you a ride, and I'll send someone out to get your car."

I swallow hard, trying to get rid of the cotton ball blocking my vocal cords. "Umm, thank you. I don't know what I would have done if you didn't stop." He opens the passenger door for me to get in. The cold leather caresses my skin, and I sink in. My breathing slows, and the cool air-conditioning is refreshing on my overheated face. *I almost didn't think he would show. Thankfully,* Fifty Shades of Grey *is a great playbook on rich men falling for the damsels.*

Wade gets into the driver seat, adjusting his suit jacket before he turns toward me. "I'm sorry about Richard. He's not as well-mannered as he should be, which will be taken care of immediately."

"It's okay," I whisper as he puts his car in drive, easing away from my car and merging into traffic.

"It's not, and I will reprimand him. Don't you worry, Violet," he promises.

I actually can't believe he is being so nice, or that he is acquaintances with someone who would act like that toward women. *What was Richard planning on doing?* My mind races around the worst-case scenarios.

"Where do you live, Violet?" Wade asks, pulling me out of my head.

"Oh, umm over on East Denny Way at the St. Florence Apartments," I say with some conviction.

AYDEN PERRY 53

Wade turns slightly toward me with a cocked brow. "Violet, you shouldn't be living over there."

"I mean, it's fine. I just keep my head down and my keys between my knuckles. You know, it's really not that bad if you just keep to yourself." I spread my hands out in front of me, because to be honest I can handle myself. He just doesn't need to know that.

"But a beautiful woman like you shouldn't be there. The crime rate is very high in that area, and there are convicted felons who live over there," he tries to inform me, as if I don't already know. He doesn't know that I can take care of myself because he only sees what I show him.

"I know but it's really the only place I can afford with my pay. You don't get paid much as a social worker, you know," I admit, biting my lip for show. Not everyone who lives there is a bad person. He's stereotyping, but I expect that.

We ride in near silence except for Wade tapping on the steering wheel. He looks deep in thought with his lips pressed tightly together and a deep crease between his brows. It seems like time passes us by in a flash before he pulls up to my apartment complex.

I reach for the door handle, and Wade lays his hand on my wrist, stopping me in my tracks.

"Violet, you shouldn't live here," he protests again.

He looks serious and also very concerned for my well-being. My heart leaps into my throat once more, waiting for what he will say next. Part of me worries he will judge me for where I live, but that's part of the plan, right? Why do I care what he *really* thinks about me?

It's as if a lifetime passes between us before I pull my hand away from his. "I'll be okay, Wade," I whisper before exiting the car.

He doesn't say another word. He doesn't even try to follow me.

I begin walking toward my apartment, counting the steps in my head. Once I make it toward the top, I turn to see him still sitting in his vehicle. He hasn't moved an inch.

"New boy toy, Violet?" Venny asks. I quickly spin around to see him leaning against his doorframe. "Maybe you should ask him for your rent?"

A roaring flame boils inside of me, and I set my jaw in a hard line as I pass him to get to my apartment. "Fuck off, Venny," I snap. He can't mess this up for me.

He grabs me, pushing me against the brick wall. The textured edges cut into my exposed shoulders. "What did you just say to me?" he hisses, and his sour breath fans over my face.

I wrinkle my nose at the smell and open my mouth to snap back at him when he is snatched away from me. Wade is glaring down at him. His frame is massive as it towers over Venny.

"You touch her again—" I can't hear the last of what he says because it comes out as a whisper only for Venny's ear, turning him as white as a sheet.

What the fuck?

Wade lets go, and Venny wastes no time as he scurries into his apartment and slams the door closed. Whatever Wade said must've done the trick. "What did you tell him?"

"You don't want to know," Wade answers. His voice is gruff, making my insides melt. His arms cage me in against the wall where Venny just assaulted me, but at least Wade smells so much nicer. "Stay with me. You don't deserve to be here."

There's that word, *deserve*. How does anyone know what I do and don't deserve?

A bubbling laughter builds in my chest, and I'm not quick enough to push it down. "I'm sorry. What? Is this your way of asking me to live with you?"

His brows furrow as the seriousness of the situation settles over me. "I'm not only asking you to live with me, Violet."

I resist the smile that threatens to tug on my lips. I bite the inside of my cheek to pull myself together. *Play the part, Violet. You've almost got him*, I reprimand myself while looking up at him with doe eyes.

"How do you feel about a marriage of convenience?"

"Umm, I'm not sure what you mean, Wade," I whisper, leaving my neck bare for him to claim as if I'm helpless to his allure.

"A marriage where you don't have to live here, Violet. I can take care of you." He traces a finger over my throat before replacing it with his large palm. His grip is loose. Only a show of possessiveness, leaving me in a vulnerable position to have my oxygen stolen from me at any moment.

"Would I have to be your sex slave or something," I joke, but his face remains grave. "I'm sorry. That wasn't funny."

"No." His tone is stern and pressing. "All I would need is you on my arm."

"Really?" I cross my arms over my chest even though his hand remains wrapped about my throat. "That's all?" I'm not convinced that's all he wants. Men always want more from me.

"I have an election coming up," he says as his thumb brushes against my pulse, "and the voters relate better to a family unit."

"A family unit?" Now, I'm really confused. *Family? Unit?*

56 CORRUPTING VIOLET

"Yes, my son needs role model parents." *Son.* It's as if a bucket of ice water were dumped over my head. My face must give away my horror at the idea of being a mother at the young age of thirty-five. Yeah, not so young, but I never wanted *kids*. Why have I never seen pictures of him in the media with his kid? "He's not going to be your concern. It's just for the image."

That seems like Wade's MO, always a golden boy in the eyes of the public. The tightness that started to build in my chest eases, and I let out a huff of air. "Okay."

"Okay?" he asks, skeptically as he searches my eyes for any hint of doubt.

"Yeah, I think I can do that, but what about his mother?" That's the part that confuses me. If he's so worried about looking like a family unit, then where is the baby's mom?

"She left as soon as he was born," he admits.

"Oh," I whisper, feeling terrible for bringing it up.

"But I can't think of anyone more perfect." He removes his hand from around my neck, and it's cold with the loss of him. Then he brushes my hair out of my face, tucking a loose strand behind my ear. "I will have my men come over tonight to gather your belongings," he informs me.

"Wait, what?" I'm genuinely shocked at how fast he is moving with this. I thought I would have more time to come to terms with this.

"Yes," he firmly states. "After residents see me here, you are at a greater risk of the media swarming you and wanting to know our status. They'll see how much I already care for you, and it will be used against me."

"That makes sense," I admit quietly. *Don't seem easy. Too eager, and he will change his mind.*

"So, Violet. Do you agree to the terms?" Wade looks at me with a glint in his eyes that I can't seem to place. This is what I wanted, but why do I feel like I'm entering the lion's den at the same time. I take too long to answer, so he throws in another perk to the deal. "We can even sleep in separate rooms, and if more transpires . . ." He trails off as he struggles to come up with other ways to convince me.

    I swallow hard and answer, "Yes, but . . ."

    "But?" His brow raises.

    The thing about men in power is they feed off the weak.

AYDEN PERRY 59

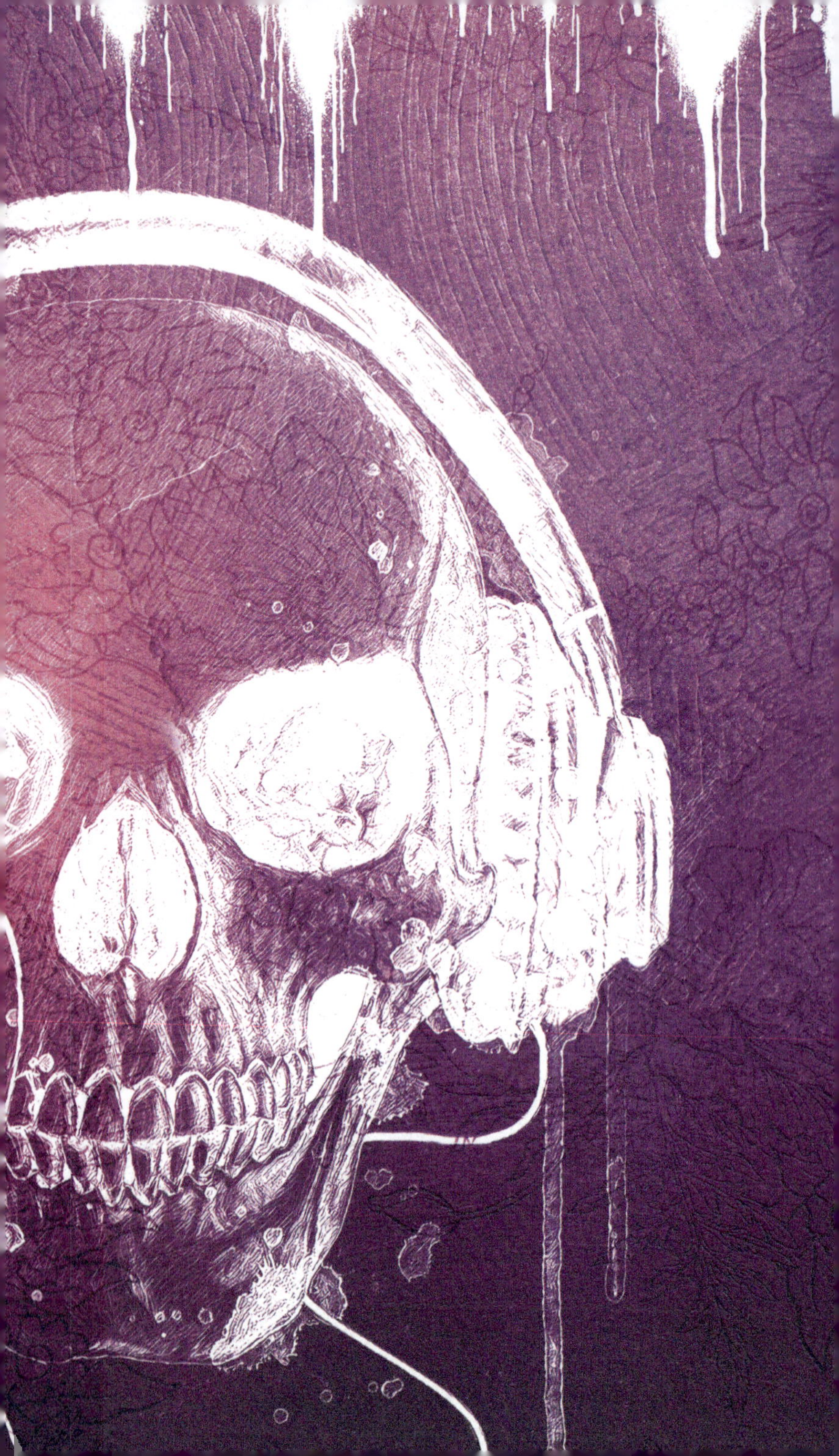

CHAPTER 4

MILES

After coming in from school, I immediately head up to my room, throwing my book bag onto my bed before heading to my desk and starting on my latest project, building a robot. I turn on my surround sound, losing myself to the bass that fills the space as I start to tinker.

This is the only moment of peace I get before Father dearest gets home, and I have to go back to being the son that he always wanted. No music, no gadgets, no reading. The only things that make me, *me*. If it isn't a social hour or hanging out with Christina, it's as if I'm a failure.

He's obsessed with the image of a happy family. I can play nice until he breaks our unspoken rule. Every time he brings in a new stepmom, our agreement breaks. He can keep trying, but I'm not his puppet to manipulate as he pleases, so he keeps me out of the limelight. Good for me, but bad for him, because it makes him have to work that much harder during elections.

"Miles, dinner is ready," our cook, Shannon, announces from the stairs.

I can barely hear her over my music. I turn it off and put my things away. One thing I do know is that if Shannon is here, then *he* is soon to follow. She only comes in a few times a week when he is expected to be here. Since my father's schedule is hectic with trying to keep up his reputation and image of an outstanding citizen in the community, he's rarely here. It'll only get more erratic once elections start. The need for a new stepmommy weighs heavy on him. I wish that keeping up my good behavior would be enough, but I know the truth. He needs a trophy wife on his arm right now more than ever, needs to look like we're the perfect happy family, so it's only a matter of time. Little do they know, it's far from the truth.

The moment I come into the dining room the table is already set. My stomach sinks when I notice Dad is already sitting at the head of the table, glaring at his smartphone.

"Miles," he greets as I take my place in the chair next to him. The smell of lemon-roasted chicken makes my mouth water, but my stomach only churns in his presence, spoiling my appetite. "Miles," he growls, setting his phone down on the table.

"What?" We are roommates in this house, only he is the owner of it and my life. *So, what does that make me?*

"You greet me when I speak to you," he commands.

The innate feeling of defiance is always lingering under the surface. I can only push his buttons so far before I get another black eye and one more excuse about running into a wall.

"Yes, sir," I grumble without looking at him.

We sit in silence for a while, only remaining in each other's company to fulfill the need to feed ourselves. When I'm almost done and think I will make it out of this meal, he speaks.

"How is Christina?"

I groan, internally. *Fuck, me.* This is *not* something I want to talk about with him. He loves Christina, because she fits the image he strives for. Her parents are lawyers, she goes to the same private school as me, and her bank account would triple ours. Everything that he could use for his own gain. While I'm still friends with her, I struggle to drive home the point that we are *not* together.

"I don't know," I say with a shrug. "She has her own life."

"You need to find yourself a woman to settle down with."

I throw my fork down with a loud ring from the porcelain plate. *Here we go again.*

"It's your responsibility to carry on the family legacy," he reminds me as if I don't already know and he hasn't already harped on about this for years. He doesn't allow me the reprieve of forgetting, even for one minute, that he wants me to take over his position one day.

"That's never gonna happen," I whisper under my breath.

He slams his palm flat against the table. "What did you say?" he asks in a low and venomous tone.

"I said"—I grind my teeth together, attempting to hold down the lava boiling inside me—"I don't want your shitty job, or that culty shit you do with your friends," I smart off, the liquid fire dripping from my tongue. Holding it in wasn't an option, it seems

He stands, causing the chair's legs to grate along the marble floor, and points a finger at me. "That's enough from you."

I can't stay here. The need to lash out is eating at me, and the perfect image that I've struggled to maintain is crumpling like a piece of paper. I need to get out of here. I stand up from the table with my plate as I aim for the kitchen, but before I can leave the room, my plate is knocked out of my hands. The white porcelain smashes, echoing off the marble floors as it shatters to pieces.

Dad shoves his finger in my face, causing me to take an involuntary step back. "Don't, you dare, walk away from me." His teeth are bared and spit flies from his mouth. "Or I'll make you participate next Friday." He threatens to get my hands dirty. The only real threat he has in his arsenal. I *fucking* hate him.

I push my shoulders back, hardening my expression as I come toe-to-toe with him. "Yes, sir," I say, but I'd rather bite my tongue off and spit blood in his face than bow down to him.

The need to fight continues to claw at my insides. I hope he doesn't notice my legs shake slightly, the control slowly faltering. He removes his finger from my face and wipes the spit from his chin.

"Good. I'm glad we are clear. Now, clean this shit up. You better act like you have manners when your new stepmom gets here," he commands before heading to his office.

As I stand here, shaking in the dining room where he left me, the rage vibrates through my muscles. Once again, we are back to where we were two years ago, living as roommates with pure loathing for one another's existence.

A piece of the porcelain lies by my black boot, and I smash it to dust. Our unspoken rule, broken once more.

AYDEN PERRY 65

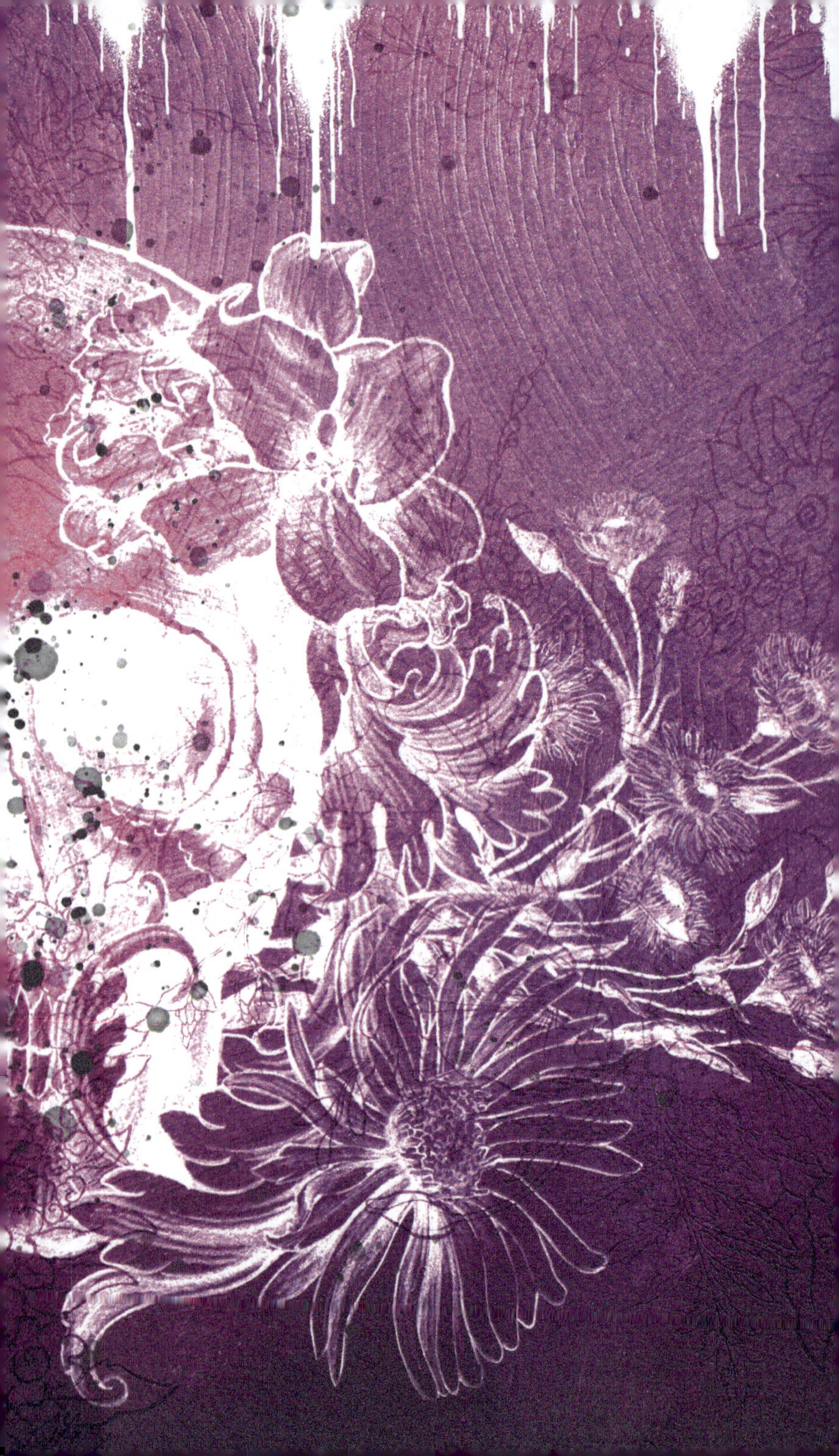

CHAPTER 5
VIOLET

He gave me one night. I convinced him to allow me one night to get my belongings together. Which I'm grateful for, considering I have to burn all my research books, and even my old driver's license that I'm attached to. I can't take it with me. The stakes are too high, so it must burn along with the rest of my belongings.

Staring into the dancing flames and popping embers, it feels surreal, like something from a movie. I'm dressed in all black with my hoodie up to hide my features as I take the papers and notes to the barrel between the brick buildings behind the apartment complex and light them on fire. I watch as the flames consume all my research and dance in unison as if the information is happy to be out of my care.

This morning, I called work and let them know about my car and that I wouldn't be in for the day to get it fixed. They were understanding and offered their condolences to my poor car. It was only slightly comical considering it fulfilled its purpose.

I'm waiting outside my apartment complex holding my bags. Everything I have fits into two duffels. The flimsy old furniture I bought will be left behind, since I won't need it at Wade's fancy residence.

While anxiously awaiting the major change in my life, I kick the gravel at my feet, and my eyes catch sight of a worm slithering between the cracks in the pavement. It's powering through the cluster of pebbles and debris until it finally reaches the open road. I equate myself to the little worm pushing through life, weaving through obstacles that get in its way. So strong, but *yet*, forgotten.

While I'm pondering the life of this cylindrical, squirming being, a sleek black town car pulls up, and out steps a driver in a suit. It's the same one who dropped me off the night of the auction. He is on par with expectations for a driver for the mayor. One who would have worked in the FBI in a past career. His clean-shaven jawline is set, and without saying a word, he opens the back door for me to get in.

"Violet." He greets me with a curt nod.

"Um, sorry, I didn't get your name the other night," I say before sliding into the back seat.

"Derek." He doesn't smile only answers my question, waiting for me to move.

I guess I won't be getting much out of this statue of a man. He grabs the bags from my hands as I slip onto the black leather seats. I sink in, leaning my head back against the headrest. *It's really happening. This is it.* I'll be living with the mayor. The only thing left is to get that ring on my finger. The car rocks slightly as Derek closes the trunk. He has to bend down as he gets in the driver's seat, and the car shifts again. This dude is a block of muscle with a mug that says *don't fucking talk to me*. He turns the wheel, and I can't help glancing back outside where the worm is still slithering along the pavement. Before we fully exit the parking lot, a bird swoops down and plucks the worm from the concrete. I gulp loudly.

"Everything okay?" Derek asks as I turn back around in my seat with my mouth hanging open slightly.

It's not like I didn't know that could happen. I mean of course, that's nature, but I connected to that worm. It was as if fate were trying to tell me something. Sometimes, I hate myself for getting attached so easily. After closing my gaping mouth, I shake my head at him as he peers at me through the rearview mirror.

"I'm fine," I say, pushing a stray hair behind my ear.

He doesn't say another word and continues driving, leaving my apartment complex behind. A strange sense of loss comes over me as I look out the window, and the brown bricks and multicolor graffiti blur in my vision. The apartments, the people, and the neighborhood I've grown familiar with go by in a flash. We ride in silence with only the sound of horns and the wind whooshing by as other cars pass us, until the terrain changes. The tires crunch on loose gravel, and the vehicle shakes on the uneven path.

"Wow, I didn't think the mayor would have a driveway like this." I can't keep the judgment from leaving my lips. I know I've seen pictures of his house on the internet, but this seems as if it was all a fake, and I'm slightly disappointed.

"The mayor is still in the process of renovating this area," Derek states, coolly. I watch his face through the rearview, and his eyes never leave the road or glance up at mine.

"What do you mean? Renovating?"

"Mr. Lynwood had this house built away from

town in the hopes of building more houses for residents." *Ah, that's right.* The Lynwood housing project in the suburbs.

"When did he have this place built?" I question Derek, already knowing the answer but wanting to keep him talking.

"A year ago."

"Oh, really. That's amazing," I say, a bit too forced for my liking, and that's when we come out of the cluster of trees we've been driving through. "Wow," leaves my lips involuntarily. A clearing in the trees reveals a glass house on a hill. It shines and sparkles in the morning sun. It's a bold choice to have a place such as this among trees.

"It's impressive," the driver states.

"It is," I admit, still in awe of the structure in front of us. Pictures don't do this place justice.

Derek pulls up the gravel drive until we reach the paved circle in front of the house. When he finally parks, I step out, not even waiting on him to open the door for me. I'm too eager to take in this uniquely built house. The only thing I can think is, *You know what they say about glass houses: don't throw stones*, but that's all I want to do as I stand here staring at it. The urge to tear everything down has this ball of energy in my chest wanting to burst. Self-destruction is what I do best, and I need to tamp down that strong compulsion because I'm about to get everything I deserve.

You deserve this, Violet.

All my life experiences, I've always told myself I deserve this. Whether the situation is good or bad, fate always has a plan for me. Whatever comes my way, I deserve it, so the saying keeps me in the right headspace. It keeps me strong in tough times and allows me to enjoy the good times when fate smiles down on me.

"Are you ready to go in?" Derek asks with my bags in hand.

His expression is stony, as if he is already annoyed with my presence. I lick my dry lips before giving him a nod and following him to the front door.

Derek presses a few numbers on the keypad to the dark oak front door, which gives the house an almost modern cabin appearance. He opens the door to a room framed in floor-to-ceiling windows. They are what creates the illusion that the house is completely made of glass. I'm taken aback by more of this house's beauty when we step into the foyer. The open floor plan of the living room is overlooked by the staircase that leads to a balcony of doors. It's so open I'm not sure anyone could hide in this house. One thing I'm thankful for is that the walls to the bedrooms aren't also glass. That would give me way more anxiety than I care to admit.

"Wade is at the office downtown. He sends his regards and is regretful that he couldn't be here to show you around," Derek states, setting my bags on the marble floor. "He also told me to let you know that your car should be delivered this evening." He stands ramrod straight, one hand holding the other wrist in front of his pelvis in a show of militant formality.

"Oh, okay. Thank you, Derek." I glance at him over my shoulder, dismissing him before I go back to ogling over the details of the house.

"If you need anything, I left the keypad code and my phone number on the counter for you." It's the last thing I hear from Derek before the front door closes behind him with a loud click.

A delayed automated voice announces, "Front door closed," causing me to jump out of my skin. *Fucking fancy shit around here.*

The farther I walk into the expansive space of the living room, the more I can see the view through the windows. It's breathtaking over the mountainside, and the way the sun illuminates and casts shadows over the horizon has me speechless. Maybe I should mention it to their PR team, because this could be a selling point on their housing project.

Now that Derek's daunting presence is gone, it seems I'm all alone at the moment, which gives me time to explore this big, beautiful house. I bite my lip, more excited than ever.

Starting with the kitchen, it looks like something out of one of those cooking shows where the two industrial stoves are stacked on top of each other. *Who needs all that?* It seems like a waste to me, unless he has a big family that comes over for holiday gatherings. Even the fridge is high tech with one of those touch screens that shows you what's inside without even having to open it. I'm not going to lie, it has me giddy.

The only thing I don't like so far is the robotic voice that announces every move someone makes in and out of the house. That's something I'll need to talk to Wade about changing, but then I find the box on the wall. *It's always better to ask for forgiveness, right?*

It requires a code to change the settings. Mm-hmm. I hold my finger to my chin, thinking. What if the code to the door works for this as well? I run over to the counter and snatch up the piece of paper Derek left for me and press in the numbers. A green light goes off, allowing me access, and I disarm that annoying voice. I guess I'll be telling Wade what I did, instead of asking. My curiosity can't control itself, and I begin opening doors on a whim. The first floor includes of course the kitchen, living room, a bathroom, and a door to the basement. All standard rooms you would find on the first level, but the one that shocks me the most is the indoor swimming pool. That's not something you'd find often in Southern California, that's for sure.

Moving on, I take the stairs to the second floor. This floor loops around as a balcony overlooking the living room and extends down a hallway of rooms. The first room is an office, which I assume is Wade's, lined with bookshelves behind a mahogany desk. *Classic and predictable.*

Continuing down the hall, I find two guest rooms, another room that looks somewhat decorated, which must be Wade's, with a large king-size bed and an attached bathroom, and a fourth room with black accents, a couch and a king-size bed. It looks as if it is normally occupied by a full-grown adult child. *Weird.* I thought when Wade said child, he meant *child*, not full-ass adult.

No one is here, and it's the only room that actually looks lived in, so I explore further.

The desk is covered in miniature tools and gadgets. I pick up one of the minitools, admiring how cute and tiny it is in my hands, when a noise from the doorway makes me jump. Quickly dropping the tool, I hold my hands up and back away from the desk. Only slightly regretting disarming the automated voice announcer now that there's a guy with wavy brown hair—long on top, shaved on the sides—and an arm covered in tattoos blocking my exit.

"I'm sorry, I didn't realize anyone was here," I apologize with my hands still up in the air as if I've been caught red-handed.

"That still doesn't give you the right to come into my space," he says with a sneer and one eye glaring at me under his mop of disheveled hair.

"You're absolutely right, and I am so sorry," I say, holding my hand out to him. "I'm Violet. *Eh,* new stepmom?" I'm not even sure why I threw in that last part. I guess so he didn't think I was some groupie for Wade who decided to break in to confess my undying love for him.

He moves past me into his room and holds on to the door handle. "And I don't give a shit," he says as I move past him out into the hallway, and then he closes the door right in my face.

I stand there awestruck by the way he is acting and still reeling from the fact that he's not a kid, but a grown-ass adult. A loud bang and a guttural roar comes from the other side of the door. Well, this is going to be fun. So much for new stepmom status. I might as well be the night hag that comes in to scare you while you sleep.

I head back downstairs and gather my belongings to pick one of the guest bedrooms as my own. I'd rather grab the one with the attached bathroom I think before I realize that every room has its own bathroom attached. So I just choose the one farthest away from everyone. Wade said I wasn't his sex slave or anything, so this should work out perfectly.

AYDEN PERRY 75

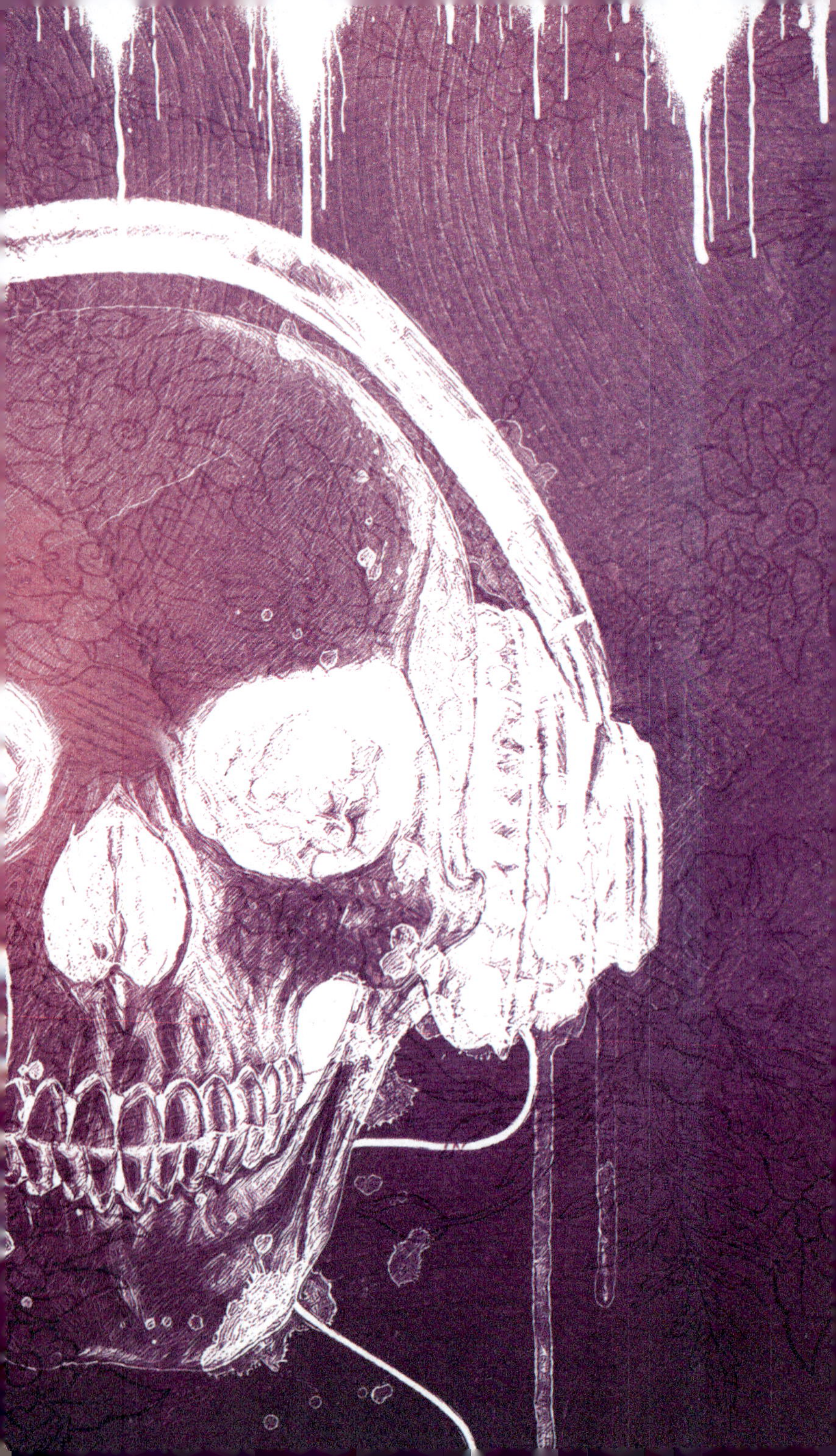

CHAPTER 6
MILES

  The door stands between us. Separating us. My new stepmom. I knew this was coming. She was in my safe haven. I take a few deep breaths and rest my hand against the cool wood to ground myself. Why the fuck would she come in here? My breaths come faster, and the fraying rope holding my anger together snaps. I scream, punching my door. I have to deal with this shit, *again*?

  Every new stepmom is worse than the last. One came into my room and threw all my books away. The next complained about how my robots got in her way, and the fact that my existence was enough to make her want to leave. *Fuck, leave.* The only way I got the last one to leave was fucking Christina right in front of her. I knew that would be the end of it, since Dad loves Christina. I thought after the last stepmom there would be no more. Even with Dad's political standing, the town loves him. He doesn't need the image. He's only doing this to piss me off.

I walk over to my desk where she was touching my belongings just like my first stepmom. I inspect the pieces, ensuring every item is there. Good, nothing is missing. *Yet*. I'll get her out of here just like the others. I turn on the stereo and blare my music to drown out my thoughts of the last stepmom.

A few hours pass while I sit in my chair tinkering with my last project. I'm more calm, and the anger that left my muscles has only made me tired. I'm considering lying in bed when my cell phone buzzes and lights up, a picture of Christina popping up on the screen. I hit answer and put it on speaker as I put my tools away.

"Yeah," I call out.

"Hey, do you wanna come to this party with me later?"

I don't say anything for a while, leaving her there on my phone to listen to the music. *What do I want to do?* I should probably get out of here with how angry I am. I'm not mad to the point of punching doors anymore, but I'm still angry. Plus, I can't fuck this up or Dad will have me doing more than what I already do for his cult shit. I have to play nice until my twenty-first birthday when I can access my trust fund. Only two more years which, thinking about it now, seems like a long time.

"Hellloooo. Millyyyy," she sings on the phone. She must already be there at the party, tipsy and wanting me to come take care of her.

"Yeah."

"What?" she girlishly screams on the other end.

"Yeah," I say a bit louder and turn down the music in order for her to hear me better. "Drop me a pin."

She squeals on the other end, and I hang up on her. *Fuck, me.*

After gathering my hoodie, keys, and phone, I

walk down the hall to leave. One of the guest bedroom's door is ajar. That must be the room my new stepmom picked. I'm not surprised by the fact that they aren't sleeping in the same bed. My father has never shared his bed with another woman since my mother. I'm not sure how he gets around that with them.

As I walk past the room, I pause, peering through the crack. My new stepmom is putting away her clothes in the dresser drawers. She doesn't seem to feel me watching her, and I can't look away. Her blonde hair is up off her neck, and she's wearing shorts now. When she bends over, the bottom of her ass cheeks shows, causing my body to heat. I should walk away. I urge myself to move, but I can't. She isn't like the last stepmomsters. She might actually be younger than I thought because there's no way the last ones would have worn an old beat-up T-shirt and shorts around the house. Father must be getting bold in his old age.

She straightens up, and I move away before she can turn around and see me being a creep. I smack myself in the head. *The party, fucker. Get to the party.* Then I can get this situation and *her* off my mind. I need to get my shit under control, because I only have a few more months before I'm out of this fucking town.

My hand's on the doorknob, and her small voice calls from behind me. "Hey, I was going to see if you wanted to order pizza."

Violet stands at the top of the stairs. Her short shorts show off her tanned legs, and her faded Def Leppard shirt hangs over them, making her almost look like she has nothing on underneath. She takes timid steps down the staircase, never dropping her gaze. I go to step back, to leave, but an imaginary pull anchors me in place. Her violet-blue eyes transfix me. She's nothing like the other stepmoms, but I can't be swayed. *Keep my distance.*

Get the fuck out of this town.

"Don't fucking bother," I snap with a scowl on my face as she gets to the bottom. Before she can say another word, I leave and slam the door in her face, once again.

When I pull up to Shawn's, there are too many vehicles in the driveway. Instead, I park in the grass. It will make it easier to leave when I want, anyway. Too many parties I've been blocked in and forced to stay the night with these fuckers. It was nice two years ago. A new woman in my bed every night, but that got old quick. Especially after a few pregnancy scares, and the clap. A shiver runs through me at the memory. That's enough to scar a man. Needless to say, I've learned my lesson to keep my dick in my pants, for the most part. I'll still make a few exceptions, but only for my two best friends.

Walking up to the door, there are already people passed out in the yard, and it's not even midnight yet. One girl sitting in another guy's lap grabs for me, and I pull my arm away from her before she can dig her claws into me.

She whines at the rejection. "Miles."

"Are you fucking my girl, dude?" the jock asks in his dude-bro voice.

I flex my jaw and keep walking, ignoring them. Always some fucking shit at these things. The first thing I do when I enter the front door is go to the kitchen. The kegs are lined up on the bar, and a cooler of punch is on the floor. I grab a red Solo cup and scoop up the jungle juice. All the alcohol in the house was thrown in with fruit punch. Chris even threw in some orange slices. She always goes to the extreme with aesthetics, like intoxicated young adults will care. I take a huge gulp of the sweet fire and relish the burn. I breathe out, feeling the sting in my mouth like a fire-breathing dragon, and finish off my cup before filling it back up again. The concoction of alcohol is already working on my muscles, effectively loosening up my anger.

After my second cup, I leave the kitchen to find Shawn and Christina. I can usually find Chris in the main living room with her girlfriends. I push through people to get there. The bodies pressing together radiate with heat. I'm already sweating from the alcohol. The beads of perspiration run along my hairline.

"Miles," someone screams in my ear over the music.

I turn to see Ashley, one of Christina's friends.

"Hey, Ash. You seen Chris?" I ask her.

Ashley wears a sheepish smile as if she has a secret to tell and grabs my arm, leaning in close. Her breasts are pushing against my arm she's holding, and I have to resist pulling away. "I think she went upstairs with Shawn."

I slip my arm out of her hold, backing away. "Thanks, Ash."

Her brows furrow, and her mouth turns down in a scowl. "Really, Miles? You're just going to run away from me like that?"

"Go find someone else to pray to tonight, Ashley," I yell over the bass. She pouts, folding her arms over her chest. I don't want clingy, and I don't need attachments. I'm almost done with this school and plan on leaving for my dream college soon. I don't want someone who's going to get attached and hold me back, making me choose between them or my future.

I make my way upstairs and go straight for the last room on the left, knowing that's where Shawn and Chris will be. I don't even wait to knock and just let myself in. Christina is lying on the bed with a joint between her fingers, and Shawn is at his computer, playing the latest shooter game. The lights surrounding his room cast everyone in an eerie blue light. I shut the door behind me.

"Milly!" Christina jumps off the bed squealing, wrapping her arms around me.

That's her nickname for me, as Chris is mine for her. No one else calls us that. I'd probably deck someone in the face if they called me Milly. That's only reserved for Chris.

Setting my red Solo cup down, I pluck the joint from between her fingers and drag in the herbal tang. I hold it in my lungs until a long, forceful cough takes over, expelling puffs of smoke from my mouth. I've always been told the longer you hold, the faster you get high. Better the cough, better the dope. I don't know if that's right, but it has never failed in my case.

"Hey, Chris," I say, collapsing onto the bed where she was lying before.

"I'm so happy you came. You never come out anymore," she whines as she plops down next to me on the bed.

"I know, family stuff at home. I needed to get out of my head," I admit.

"Is it your new stepmom?" Shawn asks from his computer.

"Word travels fast." I groan. Shawn's dad works for my dad. He knows everything, which makes being friends with him easy. I don't have to hide my true self from him or Chris.

"I figured you'd need to get out of your head, that's why I had Christina call you," he adds, never looking away from his computer.

"Thanks, man, I appreciate it."

Shawn sets his controller down before spinning his chair around to face us. "I hear your stepmom is hot. Want to give her my number for me?"

I grab a pillow off the bed and chuck it at his face, not wanting to talk about it. Shawn is quick to turn around, so it to hits the back of his chair instead of its intended target. I'm glad I have Shawn and Chris as best friends, because they grant me a safe space to drown out all the tension and anger I go through at home.

"Will you guys stop fucking around, so we can have some fun?" Chris asks, running her hand over my chest.

I take another puff of the joint before snuffing it out in the ashtray. The weed and alcohol are already taking effect on my body. Chris's hands leave tingling trails in their wake, causing a shiver to run through me. *This* is exactly what I need.

Chris gets off the bed, pulling me with her. She's playful when she's high. If she didn't love someone else, I would have enjoyed having her on my arm. She would have checked off my dad's box and made my life easier, but I won't keep her from the one she won't admit she desperately wants more than life itself. I'm a dick, but not that much of a dick.

I grab the back of my shirt, yank it off one-handed, and immediately a second set of hands wrap around my back. Shawn. I'm open with my sexuality. This started as practice, experimenting between friends, until one day we admitted that it was much more than that. We aren't together. We are very much friends that enjoy each other's company from time to time. No strings attached. We are there for each other to let off some steam.

Christina's lips capture mine, soft and pliable. I run my tongue along the seam of her lips to gain entry as strong hands caress my back and shoulders. My dick grows uncomfortable in my jeans, and Shawn begins working on the buttons to set me free.

Our kiss breaks for a second as I pull Chris's shirt over her head, and I move out from between them, allowing Shawn to take up my position. My pants grow even tighter as I watch them touching, feeling, and grabbing each other. The way they move together makes me want to jump them both. I want to be in the middle of that sandwich.

Removing my pants, my hardened length springs free, and I groan at the release. I grip my shaft and stroke it a few times. A bead of precum graces the head, and I rub it in with my palm. "*Fuck*," I groan.

"Quit fucking around and join us," Shawn says with a smirk.

"You don't have to tell me twice." I step in behind Shawn, running my hands over his back and shoulders, like he did mine. Once I get down to his pants, I grab hold of him through his jeans, and he thrusts into my hand. "You like that don't you?" I whisper in his ear before planting kisses along his shoulder. He shakes in my hold, which brings a smile to my lips. "Let's take this to bed."

"Yes, please," Chris pleads. She's already naked and glistening from Shawn's expert fingers.

I grab his hand that he used to get Chris ready. His fingers shine with her arousal and looking into her eyes, I suck them dry. Shawn moans as I run my tongue between his fingers. Chris licks her lips meeting my challenge. *Bring it on.*

Christina edges along the bed before spreading her hands over the comforter. She arches her back, sticking her ass out while Shawn and I watch. She's seductive in her movements, and she pushes back on her knees, putting her cunt on full display. Shawn and I crawl on the bed toward her, following her lead.

Once we are at the headboard, we are on either side of her. She looks at me, and I grab her by the hair before taking her mouth. The heat within me rises, and my length grows with the way her tongue massages mine. Chris's hand is so close to me that my dick jumps at her nearness. She smiles against my mouth and grabs hold of me with her dainty fingers. Shawn groans, letting me know that she's grabbed him, too. *Naughty girl*.

After a few strokes and spreading the precum around, she breaks our kiss to give Shawn some attention. I use this opportunity to play with her. Running my fingers along her seam, I collect her wetness on my fingertips and rub circles over her clit. She groans into Shawn's mouth, and I push two fingers inside of her. She grinds on my fingers before releasing Shawn's mouth. He lies down on the bed, and I remove my fingers to allow her to straddle him.

I get behind her and look over her shoulders down at Shawn, who is grinning from ear to ear. He knows what I'm about to do. Before Chris can even catch on to our playful banter, I grab on to her shoulders and push her down onto Shawn's cock. She lets out a screaming moan as Shawn fills her forcefully.

"You having fun yet, Chris?" I ask.

A low chuckle comes from Shawn, and Chris grunts out, "Fuck. You. Guys."

"You are, baby," Shawn says, and Chris smacks his chest while grinding on his dick.

I run my hand over Shawn's chest, slipping between him and Chris to find her clit. Once I find it, I pinch it between my fingers, which makes Chris shake and fold over onto Shawn. My hand is stuck, but my fingers are still able to rub her clit. She moans, and Shawn groans.

"Come on, Milly. I can't last much longer," she whines, sending a thrill of excitement down my spine.

"Is that you giving in?" I ask her, because I know if I don't, she will swear up and down she won this unspoken game.

"Yes, Milly, please fill me up. I need to feel you both inside me."

"Good." I lean over to the bedside table and open the drawer to grab the lube when the bedroom door opens. *Shit*, I thought I locked that fucker.

"Ayyy. Yo. Is this where the gangbang is?" A senior from our high school stumbles in.

I leap off the bed, grab him up by the collar of his shirt, and drag him out. "Get the fuck out and get people who are willing to fuck your shrimp-dick ass," I seethe before closing the door in his face and locking it.

After pushing all of Shawn's clothes onto the floor, I pop his spare chair under the door handle to make sure that doesn't happen again.

Once I get back to the bed, Shawn is pumping up into Christina from the bottom. She moans loudly, pushing her hands into her hair. I must've taken too long because Christina is looking at me with her brows pinched together, and her mouth is open in an O.

"That's one, Chris," I say, climbing onto the bed again. "Are you ready for another?"

"Come on, Miles. Please," she begs. "Fill me up."

I open the lube in my hand and coat my shaft. The cool sensation makes my dick twitch. Lining myself up behind Chris, the mattress dips with my weight. I take more of the lube on my fingers before running them along her crack and lingering on her puckered hole. I play with her ass until it opens up for me. She shivers and groans at my touch. I press my finger inside the tight ring of muscle, getting her relaxed and ready for me. She clenches around my digits, and I groan.

Shawn slows his pumping, giving me the chance to sink in, and Christina continues to grind on Shawn's dick trying not to lose that friction. I stretch her with my fingers a little more before lining up with her entrance.

"Come on, Milly," Chris whines, and I shove my dick inside her. Shawn's shaft presses against mine through the thin membrane, making me grow even harder. Christina lets out a loud groan, and I begin pumping into her faster. Her tight ass clenches around me, sucking me back in with each thrust. Christina's head falls back on my shoulder. I grab her breasts in my hands pulling on her nipples. She squeezes us. Her pussy flutters, and sparks of electricity race down my spine.

"Fuck," I groan, and Shawn grunts.

Christina is shaking in my arms, and we ride her through the second wave. Once she stops shivering, I release her, and she collapses on Shawn's chest. I pull out of her, and I look down at where she and Shawn are still connected. Cum leaks from each of her pretty holes. I trace my fingers through the mess we've made, causing Chris to groan.

"Please, Milly, I'm sensitive."

"Sorry, Chris. I couldn't help myself," I admit, grabbing a handful of her ass and giving it a squeeze. On wobbly legs, I find Shawn's boxers on the floor and wipe myself off with them. I'm a little fucked-up. Those fruit drinks were stout.

"Go to the bathroom, man," Shawn complains.

"I am. I thought you would want to keep a piece of me to jerk off to later," I say, chuckling.

"Fuck you, ass."

AYDEN PERRY

"You can have some too," I joke, walking into his connected bathroom.

I wash my hands and clean myself before grabbing a few towels for Chris and Shawn. When I'm done, Christina is snoring, sated from our quick fuck, and Shawn is trapped underneath her.

"Come on, man, help me out," Shawn whines, and I chuckle at him before helping him with Chris.

He cleans himself off while I take care of Chris and tuck her into his bed. We've all been friends since we were kids, and us fucking together is nothing new. I feel comfortable with them, but it's nothing serious. We have fun together. Help each other release some tension from time to time, but that's it. There's a mutual understanding between us.

"I'm going to go home," I tell Shawn. The exhaustion is hitting me about as hard as Chris.

"All right, man, let me know when you make it home."

I slap him on the back and dress, leaving my boxers for him. I wasn't joking. I love leaving stuff for him. He hates it, which means I love it. I mostly enjoy fucking with him. Once I make it back downstairs, I grab another Solo cup and fill it up, chugging two more cups of the sickly-sweet punch. My body sways without my full control, and I lean against the countertop, feeling slightly woozy. I shouldn't leave, but I need to get home. My robot competition is tomorrow, and I need to work on that first thing in the morning. Scratch that. There's no way I can sleep even after working out some of my tension. Anxiety claws up my spine, eager to raise its ugly head.

No sleep for the struggling, yet industrious engineer.

AYDEN PERRY 89

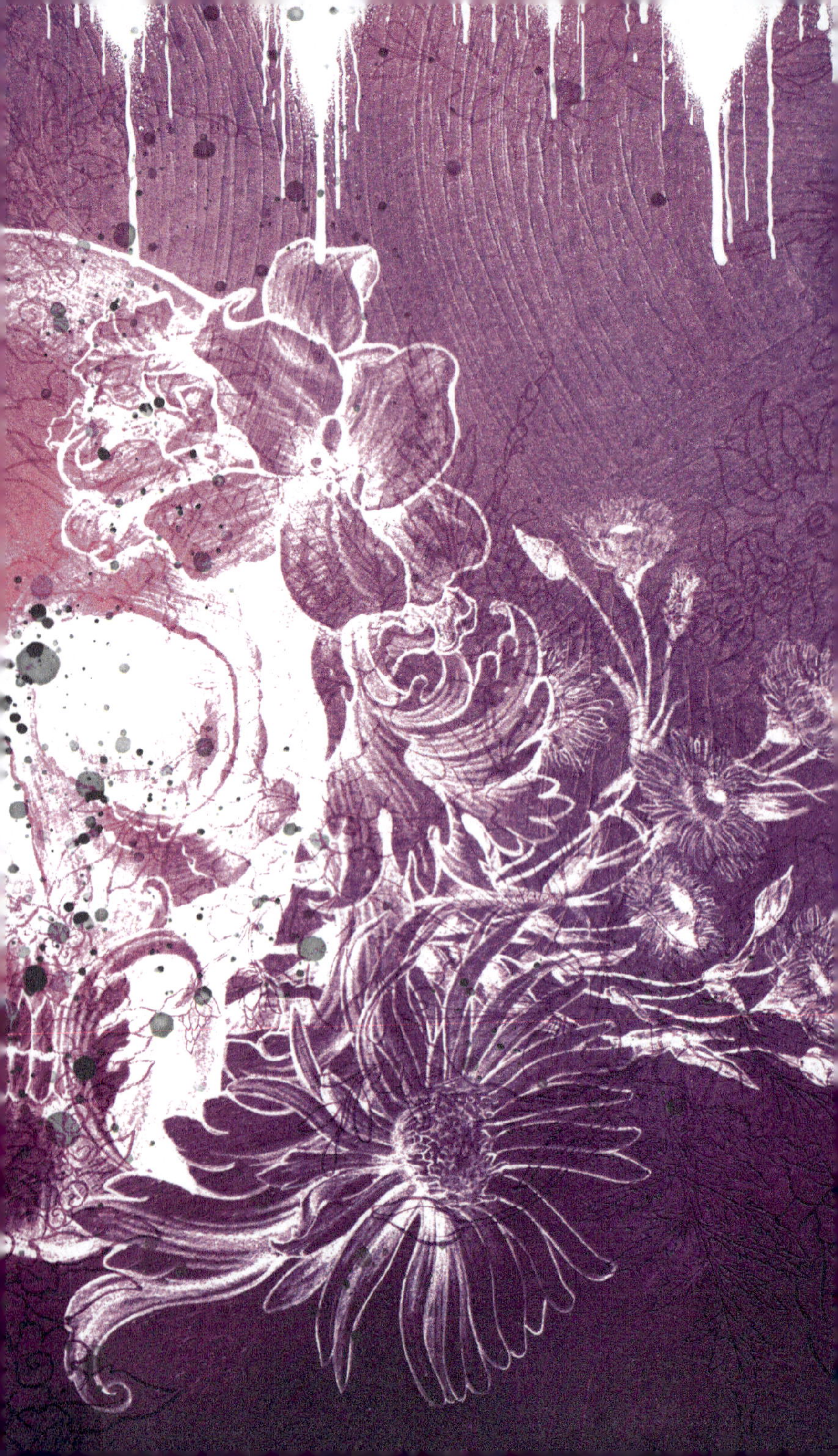

CHAPTER 7
VIOLET

    The first encounter with my stepson was a failure. I'm obviously not cut out for this, and I have no idea what the fuck I'm doing. I should just stop while I'm ahead.

    I nestle in on the couch with the Roku stick and put it on *Snapped*. I've already ordered the pizza. I guess it's a good thing that he didn't actually want any, because I kinda forgot to ask him before I ordered it. *Yep, I'm a bad stepmom*. Fuck it, he's a grown-ass adult. He can figure it out for himself.

    Pushing the nagging, obsessive part of my brain down into a locked box, I zone out for hours to episodes of *Snapped*. This one is about a wife who shot her husband and tried to convince the detectives that he was a bear. Another on an obsessed coworker who was persuaded to stab the spouse. The episodes continue for hours with women snapping, getting caught, and going to prison. My mind turns into peaceful mush until I hear the front door slam shut. I immediately hop off the couch. My heart racing as if I'd been caught red-handed. *You're not doing anything wrong*, I chide myself and go to see if it's Wade, which it is, so I can thank him for everything.

He's already halfway up the stairs when I call for him. "Wade."

He stops, and his shoulders are tense.

"Yes?" He turns to me, looking a little concerned with furrowed brows.

"I just wanted to thank you for helping me."

His shoulders seem to relax, as if that's not entirely what he expected.

He gives me a curt nod and says, "You have a spare key sitting on the entryway table, and a new Audi in the driveway."

"Oh," I say, sheepishly. I'm slightly taken aback. I didn't think burning up the car would do *that* much damage. Not so much that I would need a whole new car. Though I'm not upset about it, just surprised. My *oh* comes out as more of a question than a statement, and Wade takes it as such.

"Your car wasn't fixable," he grumbles, continuing on his path upstairs.

My heart is racing. *Does he know?*

"Thank you, again," I shout, but Wade is already out of sight.

The door to his office shuts, and I know I'll be alone again for the rest of the night. Well, that went as well as could be expected. Before I go back to watching crime shows, I check the entryway table, and on it sits two keys and a note.

The key is for if the keypad battery dies. -Wade

So much for the sweet notes, I guess. He's just like all the rest. Once rich men have what they want, they quit trying to sweep the damsels off their feet. I crumple up the note in my palm. The sharp edges serve as a reminder that this isn't permanent. Then I make a mental note to put the key somewhere easily accessible.

When I sit back on the couch, the TV is on an episode of a stepson killing his biological father, leaving his stepmom a widow. *If only*, I think before changing the show to a horror movie.

Almost three hours later, I'm stretching with my arms over my head and yawning. My box of pizza is almost gone. I should probably go to bed. Who knew sitting on the couch, binge watching shows and movies all day could be so draining. I gather all my trash and take it to the kitchen, cleaning up my mess before heading to bed. As I'm putting the last of my pizza in the fridge, my stepson walks in, staggering and stumbling. He knocks off a few of the canisters on the countertop, causing them to clatter loudly on the floor. He's *really* intoxicated. He must've gone to a party. It is Friday night, so that's plausible.

"Hey, I still have some pizza, if you want some," I say to him, offering the box of leftover pizza. "The bread and carbs will help soak up some of that alcohol."

Before I can even process what is happening, the pizza box is thrown from my hands, feet are shuffling along the floor, and my back is pressing into the counter. The edge jabs into my spine. An intoxicating mix of sex, alcohol, and weed overwhelms my senses, making my head swim. My eyes begin to water from the strong scent, and pain shoots up my back. My stepson has me cornered, caged in with his arms. I stare at his chest. His chain dangles in my face, and hanging from it is a small silver key. I'm having a hard time breathing, and the fire in my veins is blazing.

He's too close. I try to focus on his necklace to

ground myself, but my eyes betray me. They trail up his chest along his corded neck, continuing all the way up to his dark eyes glaring down at me. His hair looks wet hanging over his eyes. His lips are twisted in a snarl.

"You should leave," he says with a low, gravelly voice.

He moves a step closer to me, if that's even possible, causing my brain to spin. I back up farther, bending back over the counter as I attempt to put more distance between us. "Don't touch me," I whisper.

My thighs press together, and he looks down at me with a smirk. *Shame, Violet. Fucking shame.*

"No one is touching you, Violet."

His presence weighs heavily on me, and there is nowhere for me to go. My back bends at a weird angle. He leans over, and his lips barely brush against the shell of my ear. "You're fucking pathetic," he seethes.

A whimper escapes me. My palms press against his chest as I try to push him away, but he is a wall of hard muscle.

"Miles!" Wade exclaims from the kitchen doorway, making me flinch.

Miles slowly straightens his spine, allowing me to stretch my back out and ease some of the tension. He stands there as if nothing happened between us. I'm not even sure *what* happened between us, but something *did* and I'm not sure how I feel about it. He is obviously angry about me being here, and I hate that. Wade gives him a demeaning glare with his jaw set into a hard line. Miles smirks, as if this is a game to him, before sauntering off.

I'm still leaning against the counter, catching my breath, when Wade cups my cheek.

"Look, he's very troubled and has been since his mother passed. If he causes any more issues just let me know, and I'll take care of him," Wade says in a soothing tone while his thumb rubs over my cheekbone.

I shake my head, trying to clear the fog that has formed there. "Yeah, sure," I say meekly and allow Wade to guide me through the kitchen door. Once we get to the doorway, I remember the pizza box that fell on the floor. "Ahh. The pizza."

Wade continues to push me toward the stairs. "Don't worry about it. I'll take care of it. You just get some rest. It has been a day of transition for you. You must be tired."

"Yeah, you're right." I rest my hand on his hard chest and look up at him. His graying hair is mussed, like he had just come down from sleeping. "Thank you," I whisper. He holds my hand resting on his chest.

"No, thank you is necessary."

My chest warms at his sincerity. *This will all be fine*, I tell myself as I head upstairs to go to bed. *Everything will work out in the end.*

His body cages mine, and I look up into his hazel eyes. The pupils are blown, filled with lust. The faint cinch of wire wraps around my throat, restricting my breathing. "You shouldn't be here, Violet." His voice is gravelly in my ear.

His breath fans over my neck, causing a shiver to run down my spine. "I need to be here."

He steps closer to me, as if that's even possible. The space between us is no more than a foot, but it feels like we are wearing the same skin. He's so close.

"That's because you've been a bad girl." His lips

hover along my cheekbone. The only thing I can feel is his warm breath. My body is hot, and my breathing becomes ragged. "Do you like to hurt, Violet?"

"Don't touch me," I whisper.

"No one is touching you," he growls over my lips. "Yet." He grabs my neck.

His calloused palms replace the invisible wire that was once there, restricting my breathing again. My vision grows spotty as stars burst in white lights. I clench my thighs together, attempting to cool down the fire building inside me.

He tsks at me before using his knee, forcing my legs apart. "Such a filthy girl."

"Miles," Wade yells.

Miles looks at him, still holding my neck possessively with a smirk playing at the corner of his lips. "What's the matter, Dad? Don't want to share your playthings, or did you want to watch instead?"

I squeeze my thighs together, forgetting that his knee is there, and I begin to grind on him, trying to find that friction to cool my burning nerves.

My phone rings, waking me from a dream that I'll never speak of out loud. The scene in the kitchen last night, playing out differently and more erotic than it was. *Shame on me and my dirty mind.* I run my hand over my face, groaning before checking to see who is calling. Seeing that it's my boss, I check the time, thinking I'm late. Then I remember it's Saturday, and not only that, it's five o'clock in the morning. *What the hell?*

"You do realize it's five o'clock on a Saturday, right?" I ask, groaning into the phone as I roll over in bed.

"Yeah, I'm sorry about that. We have a case we need someone to come in and take care of. There's another missing parent, and a child who has no guardian.

We need you to come in and call around for any available next of kin."

Since Dani took care of the last late case, it's now my turn. I groan again, running my hand over my face. "Okay, give me an hour."

"Thank you, Violet."

He hangs up, and I throw my phone on my bed beside me. Here we go, another glorious morning, as my favorite witches would say. I quickly put on some semicasual but professional attire and toss my hair up in a bun before brushing my teeth. As soon as I'm done, I head downstairs to grab a granola bar.

When I enter the kitchen, Miles is standing in front of the fridge. His back is bare, and sweats hang low on his waist. My eyes linger on the two little exposed dimples above his ass. I bite my lip. *Fucking, hell.* This should be illegal to look at.

"You're up early," Wade announces, making me jump out of my skin.

"Yeah. Uh, work," I say, stumbling over my words. "Work called, they're needing someone to come in this morning, and I agreed to go." I rush out and walk over toward the cabinet where I saw a box of granola bars yesterday. Perfect for breakfast on the go.

"Well, that was noble of you," he says, adjusting his lapels.

"I could say the same about you. Does the mayor work every day?" I ask, stroking his ego.

He smiles and shrugs as he pours himself a cup of coffee. "It's a part of the job."

Miles slams the fridge door, and I notice Wade side-eye him with a glare that says *Keep it up and I'll take you out.* The tension between them is palpable, and I don't want to be in the middle of their explosion when it goes off.

No one says a word until Miles leaves the room. Wade pulls out a rolled-up piece of paper and sets it on the counter with a pen. "The marriage papers." *Wow, that was fast.* I look down at them, and he continues, "I know this isn't exactly how you imagined getting married, but I hope you will understand the need for a private ceremony."

The whole ceremony thing wasn't for me to begin with, so I shrug as if it's no big deal. I want to kick myself, because I have to at least show I care. Placing my hand over his, I say, "I've always wanted a big, beautiful wedding, but having you is all that matters to me now."

Please buy it. Please buy it. The mantra plays in my head as I lift the pen and scrawl my name on the dotted line.

"Thank you, Violet. I hope that this agreement will be mutually beneficial."

"Yes, me too."

My stomach sinks at how cold he seems. This is a business deal for him. Without another word, he leaves me there, standing at the kitchen counter all alone. We are officially married, and I question whether I'm doing the right thing.

After pouring myself some orange juice in one of Wade's to-go coffee cups, I head out, ignoring the disgusted glances Miles is giving me as he lingers in the hallway. His fists clench, like this deal is stripping something away from him. He's acting like I pissed in his Cheerios and forced him to eat it.

I click the matte black fob, and my jaw drops as a sleek black car flashes to life. *Oh, I'm going to have fun with this.*

As soon as I pull into my parking spot at work, the sun is just peeking over the horizon. This is my first time ever being here on a Saturday. The sensation of being out of my normal everyday routine throws me for a loop. I unlock the office door with a key Mark gave me for moments such as this. They don't happen often, but there are times when we have to stay late, and Mark wants us to lock up afterward. I sit at my desk, pulling up the file for Scarlet McIntire, and begin my round of calls.

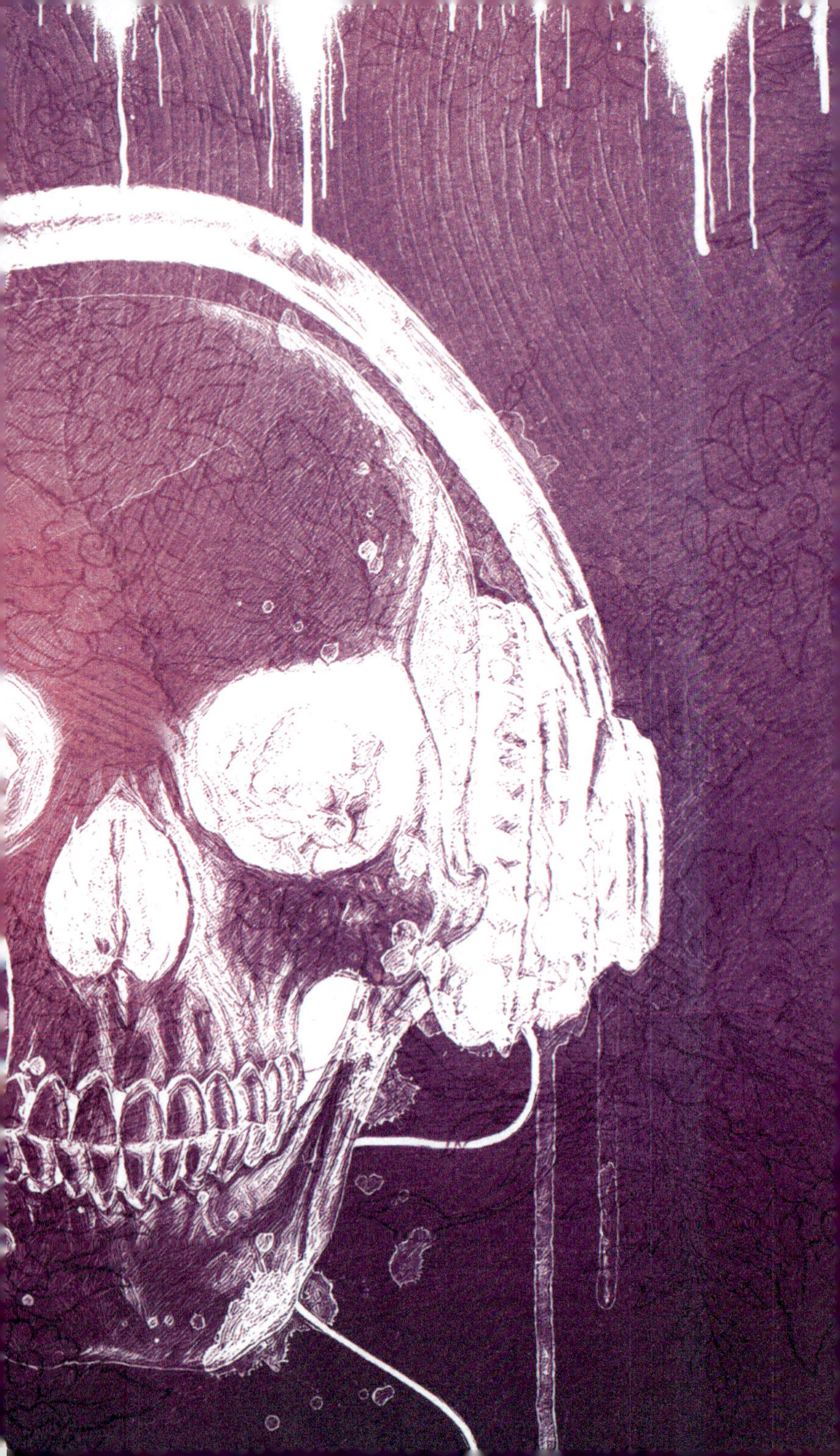

CHAPTER 8
MILES

All I can think about is her in the kitchen, leaning over the counter, and the way her eyes became saucers when she looked up at me. And those fucking pouty lips. *Fuckkkk*. I grab hold of my hardened length and squeeze to get it to go down. I can't think about her this morning, or ever. I have to focus on my own shit, like winning this scholarship. I can't rely solely on my father, who holds my dreams over my head in order to make me do his bidding.

My head pounds in sync with my heartbeat from the amount of alcohol I drank last night. That wasn't a very smart thing for me to do the night before a competition.

I gather my equipment for the battle of the bots, and by the time I make it out to my Jeep, Violet's and Dad's vehicles are both gone. Good, two fewer obstacles in my way. That fact alone makes the tension in my shoulders relax, and I can breathe a little easier.

After taking some of the headache medicine that was left in my console, I drive in silence. Hopefully, this skull-splitting pain is gone soon, because all I want to do is drown myself in music.

Once I make it to the parking lot, I park beside Shawn's ride. We don't come to these events with the same motives. While he does these competitions for fun, I do them out of necessity.

As I get out to walk around back and grab my fighting machine, a set of arms wrap around my middle. Christina's little arms squeeze me with excitement. "Are you ready for today?"

"I don't think I'll ever be ready for this," I say honestly. The low throbbing headache has completely subsided, and my stomach knots in nervous excitement.

"Aw, don't worry. You will do great," she encourages. Which is something she has always been great at. Always a supportive friend when I need it.

"Where's Shawn?" I ask as we walk up to the door.

"Oh, he's already inside. He saw you on the phone tracker, so I thought I'd meet you out here. We were getting worried you wouldn't show." She bites her lip, looking away from me. I know that part of it is guilt for getting me to come over last night when I shouldn't have before a competition.

"Thanks, Chris. I'm okay. Head hurts a bit, but it's getting better," I reassure her.

She gives me a smile before leading the way to where Shawn is set up. He's bent over, adjusting some of the knobs on his machine, and I clap him on the back. "You ready?"

He shrugs, nonchalantly. I'm glad he isn't serious about these competitions, because if anyone were to beat me, it would be him.

"It's time to get into position," the announcer calls over the loudspeaker.

My nerves have my muscles tensing as I get into position. Shawn and I are in the cages next to each other, and he gives me a nod of encouragement. The bells go off overhead, and the bots are on the floor.

Metal and electronics are crushed and tossed into the air. Alongside it are the dreams of each operator as the announcer calls out who is eliminated. Shawn, a new guy, and I are the only ones left, increasing the crowd's excitement.

"Destruction, Killer, and Corrupter are the only ones left on the floor," the announcer calls out.

I've never seen this guy, or his machine, Killer, around here before. My nerves start to build, and I set my controller down and crack my knuckles to regain focus and take off some of the edge. *You got this. You need this bad enough, and that's enough to get you through this.* I give myself a mental pep talk until I see this guy's bot. It's half a size larger than mine. I have to remind myself it's not about the size, it's about how you control it. *That's what she said.* I give the guy a smirk, radiating forced confidence. *I've got this.*

We get into position, and I grip my controller with a little more strength than I should. There's a pop in my hands as it cracks down the side. My chest tightens because there is no time for me to fix this. The announcer counts down, and I hold my controller together, hoping the connections aren't damaged.

No time to stress, but I can't help it. Copper fills my mouth with how hard I'm biting down on my lip. He moves his bot forward, and I worry that mine won't go. At the last minute when he brings the hammer down, my bot follows my control and moves out of the way.

Shawn passes by the guy to distract him, and I bring my miniature chainsaw out of its hidden compartment. I clip the new guy's machine, causing sparks to fly.

Yes. I pump my fist in the air at the move. While I'm rooting for my power move, the guy turns his bot and smashes mine with a hammer over the motor. Plumes of smoke begin to rise from it, and my shoulders slump. *Fuuuccckkkk.* I'm mentally kicking myself for celebrating early.

The announcer speaks overhead. "MilesBOT2004, Corrupter has been disqualified."

Before the next round begins, I go to the pit to collect my bot.

"It was a good match." The guy who beat me meets me in the ring. He grips my hand, giving it a firm shake. "I saw that you were having a hard time with your controller, and you still got a hit in."

"Yeah. That fucked me up," I admit, running my hand through my hair. "And I got too cocky there at the end."

"It happens to the best of us. Better luck next time, eh." He claps me on my shoulder.

After collecting my machine, I don't stop to see Shawn and Chris. Too caught up in my own disappointment, I drive home. Thankfully, the headache from earlier has died down, and I crank up Motionless in White and drive through the hills. I pass my house at least three times before I finally pull in. When I park, my chest doesn't feel as tight as it did, and I can breathe a lot easier.

The dash lights up with a call from Chris, and I hit answer before getting out. "Hey."

"You left without saying goodbye."

"Yeah, I was in a mood and hating myself," I admit.

"You know this isn't the last time. This is only the start. There's still all season."

"I know," I huff.

"You want me to come over?"

"Yeah, sure."

"Okay, I'll see you in a bit," she says eagerly, and I can only imagine that she has a huge-ass smile on her face. She's always had the secret touch when it came to cheering Shawn and me up as we grew older.

I go up to my room and play some music for a few hours while scrolling through the Snap pictures from the meet today. Shawn won the meet. There are pictures of him with the guy who beat me today as he holds the trophy. The fire in me burns again, and all that work I did to melt it away by driving around for hours is quickly undone. I have to fix my bot again and do better about controlling my emotions. I was much better at controlling them two years ago, but since I had a bit of reprieve, I'm having to discipline them all over again. While I'm festering in my emotions, there's a quick knock at the door.

"Hey," Chris whispers.

"Hey," I say without looking up from my phone.

"You saw the pictures, didn't you?" she asks, tiptoeing into my room to sit next to me on the couch.

I just give her a nod before closing out the apps and throwing my phone down next to me. "Does Shawn know you're here?" I ask her.

"Yeah, I told him you were probably upset with yourself. We both know how badly you wanted to win, but you know there are other meets coming up," she says, looking at me with round eyes. She feels for me. Her and Shawn both do, but they also know that I can't just be given a win. I need to do it for myself.

"I know."

"Do you wanna play a video game to take your mind off of it?" she asks, picking up my controller.

"Hell yeah." I jump off the couch and grab my other controller from the dock. Chris is not good with video games, but she deals with it because she knows it's one way I let out my aggression. After some time of us shooting down hordes of zombies, Chris's stomach growls. She doesn't bring any attention to it, but I get up to grab us some snacks anyway. "I'll be right back."

I race down the stairs and grab some cans of Coke and a bag of hot Cheetos. When I turn to leave the kitchen, a spark of fire lights in my brain. The little devil on my shoulder smiles something sinister and delightful. My belly warms with glee. I set the snacks down on the foyer table and open the front door. Violet's not back, yet. *Good.* I pop the cover off the keypad, remove the batteries, and click the cover back into place. The little devil on my shoulder rubs his hands together. I hope she gets annoyed and adds it to her reasons to leave. She needs to for her own good. I gather up the food off the foyer table but pause with my foot resting on the last step when gravel pops outside. *Oh, I can't leave. I have to see how she reacts.*

There's rustling outside the front door. She's grunting in frustration. What the fuck is she doing? The happy, bubbly cloud that was there in my chest dissipates with how long it's taking her to attempt to open the door. The smile that was on my face is gone, and curiosity wins out. I open the door to her settling back on her heels, her shirt still riding up on her stomach. My eyes linger on the smooth patch of flesh peeking out, and I yearn to feel her against my palm. She's fixing herself, and her cheeks are flushed a seductive shade of pink. When she looks up at me and our eyes lock, my instinct is to scowl. She can't know I was looking at her, and I slam the door in her face.

"What the fuck?" Violet cries from the other side of the door.

Taking the snacks upstairs, I can't stop hearing her adorable frustration playing in my head.

"What took you so long? I was beginning to think you started eating without me," Chris says when I walk through the bedroom door with my arms full of snacks.

"No way in hell," I joke. "I just fell down the stairs a few times from the mountain of food in my arms. I could've used a little help."

"Whatever." Chris blows me off, grabbing the bag of chips and a Coke then popping the top.

After a few more matches, I forget about Violet downstairs and the front door until someone clears their throat in the middle of a match reloading. My stepmom is at my bedroom entrance. I slouch with my elbows on my knees and grumble my indifference. Her being here makes me want to either slam her against the door or shut it in her face.

"Hey," Chris squeals, jumping up to hug my new stepmom and telling her all the mushy-gushy stuff she's probably always wanted to hear. *Ugh, makes me sick.*

I wish I'd shut the door, but I was so wrapped up in the joy of her frustrations. Then the snacks and video game distraction. *Yeah, fuck me.*

"Thank you. That's really sweet of you. I was wondering if the both of you would like to come down for dinner. I made spaghetti," my stepmom says, and Chris looks at me with a bright light in her eye.

"We're fine," I snap. "We don't want any of your fake-mom shit."

"Oh, okay. I just thought I would ask," she says with her shoulders dropping ever so slightly. Oh, she's good at this acting. She came in here just to fuck with me.

When she is out of earshot, Chris turns to me. "What the fuck dude?" I shrug. "Why do you have to be such a dick all the time?" She grabs her jacket and phone, and I give her another shrug. I can't let her know that we are in this silent battle, and this is just her form of payback.

I know she's not happy with my answer because she huffs loudly and storms out, leaving me there with the loading screen. The characters stand on the balls of their feet bouncing back and forth, waiting to be played with again.

I'm fucked.

AYDEN PERRY 109

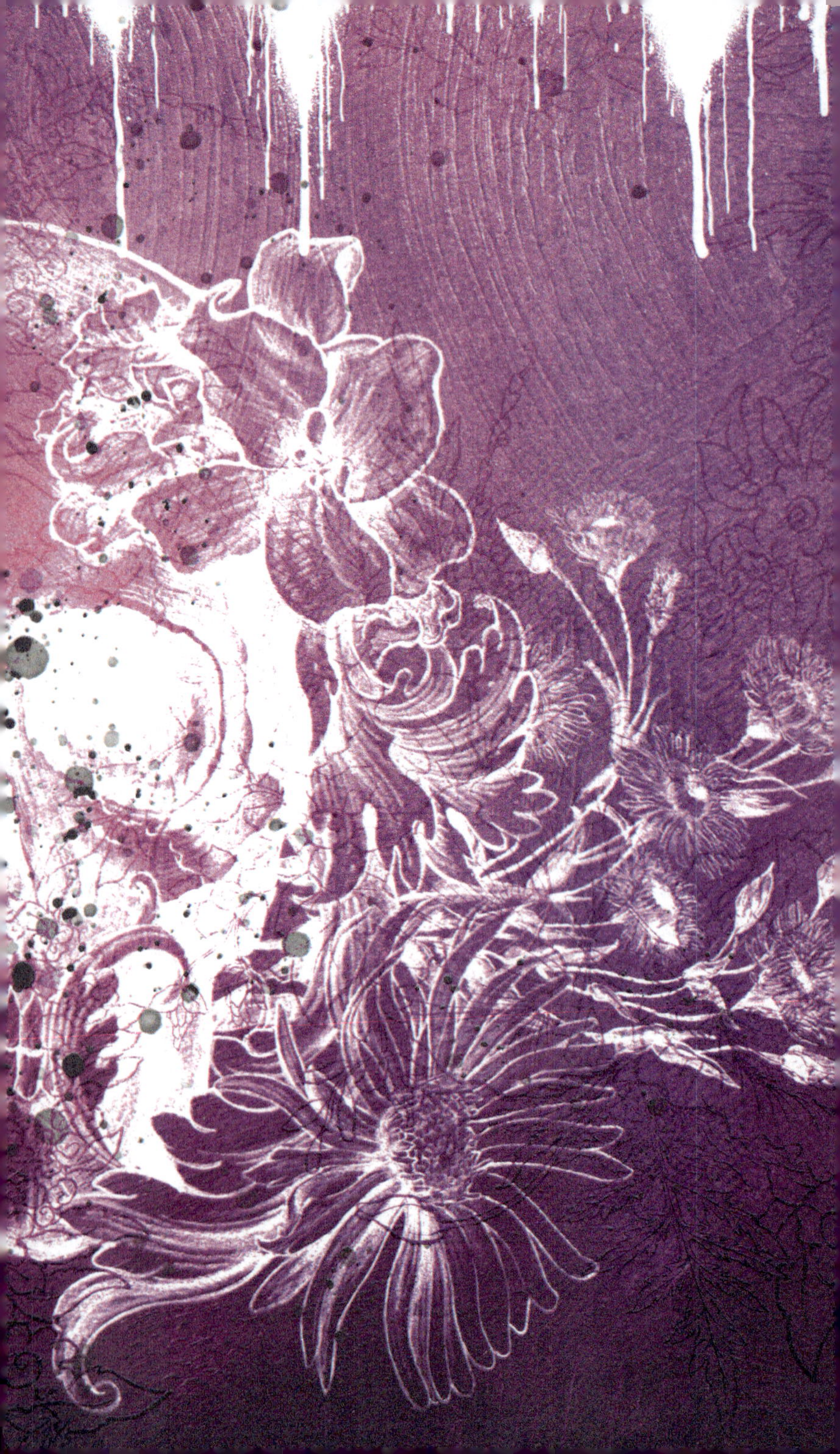

CHAPTER 9
VIOLET

After a long day of calls and a low throb starting at my temples, I close up the office, stop by the grocery store, and drive home. The traffic is at its normal level of absurdity with horns blaring and drivers leaning out of their windows with an angry fist. All things my head is at a low tolerance for, so I turn on my ASMR playlist and try to focus on it instead.

The tension in my head seems to ease a bit, and my scalp tingles from the rhythmic pops and clicks. I lose myself in the audio sounds until the pops move from inside my head to the outside. My car vibrates along the rumble strip on the shoulder, snapping me back to the present. My eyes bulge open, and I take in the roads around me. "Damn it," I say under my breath, hitting the heel of my hand on the steering wheel as I realize I passed the house.

Slowing down to a crawl, I find a beaten-down

path among the trees and pull in. My car idles as I look down the eerie road. Curiosity swirls in my belly, and everything in me tells me to see what is down here. My foot hovers over the gas, and I squint my eyes. *I wonder how far this trail goes?* Screw it. I check to make sure the doors are locked and step on the throttle. The path gets darker the farther in I go. My high beams light the base of the towering pines. Scraggly tree branches start to come closer to my car as the path gets narrower, and from what I can see, it only gets smaller. *Who uses this path? Does anyone come out here?* I shake my head. I have groceries in the car, and I need to get home. I pop it into reverse and back out the way I came. Thankfully, my mind didn't get too distracted, because it doesn't take long before I'm pulling into the driveway. A cute little minicoupe sits beside Miles's Jeep. He must have a girl over. *Perfect, maybe this is how I get on his good side.*

Before walking into the house, I pull the spare key to the door off my key fob and tap the end of it against my chin. The irrational fear of being locked out of this mansion and having nowhere to go makes me think hiding the key would be a good idea. *Hmmm. Where to place it?* Like a light bulb going off in a sea of bright lights, I think of the most obvious place—*above the door*. I stand on my tiptoes, stretching to reach the top of the doorframe. My side strains, and my shirt lifts with the motion. This might not be the best place to put the key. I don't think I'll be able to reach it, but finally my fingers are able to push the cool metal into place.

"Ugh. Finally," I huff. The door opens while I'm adjusting my shirt, pulling it back down. Miles glares at me before slamming the door back in my face. "What the fuck?" *What is wrong with this kid, and what is his obsession with slamming doors?*

I turn the knob, and it doesn't even budge. *He*

fucking locked it! Ugh! This is not the day. I push in the code for the keypad, and they don't even light up. I grind my teeth together in annoyance. That fucking dick with those hazel eyes that I dream about. *Fuck. Get it together, Violet.* I stand on my tiptoes again to grab the spare key, unlock the door, and place it back in its hiding spot.

Opening the front door, the sound of gunshots blares from upstairs. I'm guessing from Miles's room. He must be with his girlfriend and not wanting to be interrupted since he literally locked me out and closed the door in my face. I huff and groan with irritation as I carry the bags to the kitchen and put the spaghetti on. That piece of shit is trying to get on my last nerve, but he will have to try harder than that. I'll have to kill him with—I lift the box of garlic bread out of the plastic bag—garlic bread? *Eh, that's kindness enough.*

The sauce is hot, the bread is on the stove, and the noodles are drained. The aroma of the meal fills the air, and my chest, with warmth. It makes this cold house seem slightly more homey. Maybe that's all he really needs is for this place to feel more like a home.

I take my chance and go up to Miles's bedroom. The door is open slightly, and sounds of gunfire and girlish laughter filter out into the hallway. At least they are playing video games, so I feel a little better about interrupting them. Less like I'm invading his privacy.

At the doorway, I watch as Miles and a pretty, petite blonde girl play. They are sitting side by side, knocking elbows and laughing. I've never seen him in this space. He seems happy and almost carefree. I observe them like that for a while until they hit a stopping point. I hate to interrupt their happy bubble, but they still don't know I'm here, so I clear my throat to gain their attention. The girl shoots off the couch when she sees me and wraps her arms around me. She's perky. A stark contrast to

Miles's sour mood.

"Hey. You're Miles's new stepmom. You're so pretty," she squeals with the biggest smile on her face, making me feel more welcome than I've been since moving into this house.

Miles looks up with a pronounced frown on his face as if I've foiled all his happiness by being here. I've invaded his space, and I hate seeing that glow drain from his features. I've got to fix this.

"Thank you. That's really sweet of you. I was wondering if the both of you would like to come down for dinner. I made spaghetti," I quickly spit out, trying to justify why I came up here.

"We're fine," he snaps. "We don't want any of your fake-mom shit."

"Oh, okay. I just thought I would ask," I say sheepishly, but all my confidence coming up here has evaporated.

So much for kindness. I guess asshole is his only language. I've never had an adult figure to look up to, what with my life of moving into the foster system and bouncing from house to house. It took me a long time to decide to finally help other children who had been in my situation, but I definitely don't know what to do with kids for the long term.

As I make my way downstairs, I hear someone's footsteps behind me, but I don't look back.

"Hey, I'm sorry he was such an ass. He's not normally like that." The blonde-haired girl stops me in the foyer.

"It's okay," I say, placing a hand on her shoulder. "I understand. I'm new in his space."

She looks sympathetic and shakes her head. "It's not that. It's because you're a repl—"

"Chris," Miles yells from the top of the stairs.

We both look up at him. His chest is heaving, and I didn't even hear him run.

"I'm sorry," Chris whispers. "I have to go."

I give her a curt nod and watch her leave. By the time I look back at the top of the stairs, Miles is gone. *What was that all about?*

I gather my plate and grab a soda from the fridge before going to the living room to watch my comfort show, *Criminal Minds*. It's hours before I hear Miles slink downstairs. The microwave beeps and the smell of marinara fills the room, which brings a smile to my face. *Just one step closer to gaining his trust.*

This is the longest weekend ever in the Lynwood house. I've watched so many crime shows and *Cold Cases* on the couch that all my joints ache and pop when I move. I need to find another hobby, because I'm starting to feel my age. *Fuck that*. I can't even get any interactions with the guys. Miles stays in his room or out with friends because he fucking hates me for some unknown reason, and Wade . . . I mentally roll my eyes. He's working in his home office or working in his office in town. It's seriously so lonely. I think back to when I lived in my apartment just a few days ago, and the feeling of being alone didn't seem so daunting when my days were filled with spying and stalking to get my ass here. Now that I'm in this house with two other people who aren't talking to me, it seems intolerable.

When Monday rolls around, I'm more than happy

to leave for work. I crank up Def Leppard and roll down the windows. The wind blows through my hair, making me feel lighter. I pull into work, and Dani is by my car before I can even get a chance to turn it off.

"So, spill," she says, thrusting a Starbucks coffee into my hand.

"Spill what?" I ask, walking past her and taking a sip of the hot mocha goodness. "The coffee? No way."

"I'm about to knock that coffee right out of your hands." She makes a playful move toward my cup, and I guard it with my life.

"Well, I came in on Saturday and watched crime shows all weekend."

"Eww and eww," she says, wrinkling her nose.

"Hey! There's nothing wrong with crime shows," I whine.

"Okay, but you and the hot greyhound didn't get any pornographic, hot and steamy moments this weekend?" she asks.

"Greyhound? Really? And, um, no," I admit, pushing open the door to our building.

Before Dani can ask me anything else, Mark pops in with more cases for us to deal with and more phone calls to make. We split to our respective desks and get to work.

The day moves at its normal pace, and I actually forget about the whole stepson situation at home. During the last twenty minutes, Mark turns up the volume on the television, which is on the Seattle news.

"Up in the mountainy suburbs of Seattle, a young woman by the name of McIntire was found dead this past Saturday morning. After speaking with the local detective who was assigned the case, we've been informed that they found her throat slit as well as ligature marks around her wrist. Leading them to believe that a serial killer from twenty years ago has resurfaced. Stay tuned on Lion News as we bring you firsthand reporting on the task force's efforts to keep our streets safe. Back to you, Ron."

"Thank you, Veronica. Now, on to a little league softball team that saved a bear . . ."

My body freezes as if ice-cold water has been poured over my head. *That poor woman*. Mark sighs in exhaustion. The mood in the office grows heavy as our empathy over the situation with the mother and child weighs heavy on our shoulders. When the end of the day comes, we leave the office more solemn than when the day started.

On our way to our vehicles, I stop at my door, looking over the hood at Dani like we always do. "Dani."

"Yeah?" she asks, pulling on the handle.

"Does Mayor Lynwood have a kid?"

Her brows pinch as she ponders my question, then shakes her head. "Yeah, but I thought he went away to college or something. I haven't seen him since he was a child. Why do you ask?"

Interesting. "No reason. I was just wondering."

She shrugs, getting into her vehicle, and I do the same. I didn't find anything on him either before, when I was investigating Lynwood. He must be his best kept secret, and everyone is on his payroll to keep it that way.

As soon as I pull into the driveway, I sit there in my car, letting Metallica take the weight of the world off my shoulders. Miles and Wade are already home, surprisingly. When I walk in the house, I'm hit with the scent of spices. *Is that . . . tacos?*

After dropping my car key in the bowl by the door, I walk toward the kitchen. Curiosity gets the better of me. Maybe Wade decided to get us an in-house cook.

That would be marvelous. When I turn the corner to see who is cooking dinner, Miles is in an apron. If I could pick my jaw off the proverbial floor, I would. His wavy hair hangs over his brow, and the way the cords in his neck stand out as he bends over the stove has my attention. He turns toward me, and I bite my lip. *Shit. Fuck. Why am I staring?*

"What?" he asks with a deep frown.

"Nothing." I brush him off and grab a soda out of the fridge. I don't want to tell him how shocked I am or make a bigger deal out of it. Especially since I was just checking out my stepson. *Bad, Violet. Bad.*

I go to the living room to, *once again*, watch crime shows. When Miles is done with dinner and walking upstairs, I pounce on the tacos. As I fill my plate, my stomach growls loudly.

"Hungry, aren't we," Wade calls from behind me.

I jump, turning around with a plate full of food. "Does everyone sneak up on people in this house?"

"We aren't used to having a house guest. It's been a while," he admits.

I stand there awkwardly, blocking him from the food. I notice, which causes my cheeks to flush as I slide out of the way after the realization. "Sorry."

"It's no problem." He proceeds to fill his plate.

I turn to walk away when he grabs my attention again.

"Hey, Violet."

"Yes?"

"I do need you this week. There are functions I need you to attend during the day and at night. I just need you by my side for the image."

"Aren't elections months away?" I ask and bite my lip, hating that I questioned him. I shouldn't have, since this is a part of our deal.

"Yes, but we start prepping early. Is this going to be a problem?"

I look down at my plate of food. "My work. I—"

"If your job is going to interfere, then we will need to rethink this arrangement," he interjects.

"No. No, that's okay." *Threatening my job, that's where we are going now.* "I might have to put in my notice though, so that they can get someone else in to help fill my spot."

"Do what you need to do, but if this becomes a problem, then I won't hesitate to cancel our agreement." He grabs his food, leaving to go upstairs to his office. I guess that's the end of that conversation.

Before I go to bed, I shoot off an email with my two weeks' notice. It gnaws at my insides, but I know it has to be done. This isn't surrender but hope for the future. I lie in bed, staring at the popcorn ceiling, wondering when the best time would be to kill Wade. The only wrench in my plans is Miles. He is a variable I didn't anticipate.

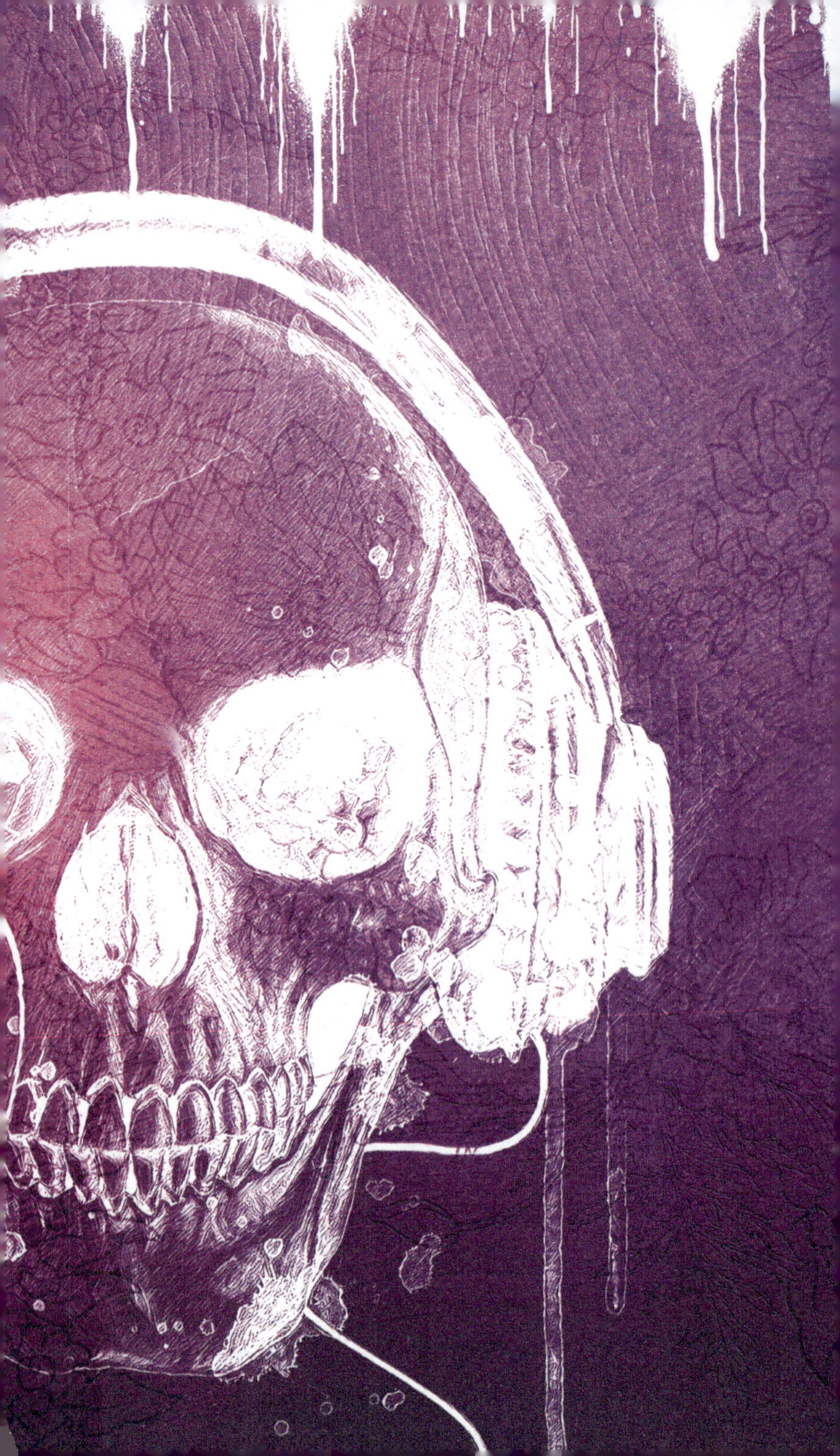

CHAPTER 10
MILES

It's been a couple of days now with no interactions with my stepmom. She must have gotten the hint from my last dismissal. Since my mom was killed, I'm only used to having home-cooked meals when my father calls the cook. It's something I don't like to think about because it breaks down the brick walls I've built to protect myself. Needless to say, I gave in and made tacos as a form of unspoken apology, and I haven't seen her since.

Part of me is happy about this newfound adjustment in our arrangement, but another part of me can't stop thinking of her at the top of the stairs. Or her with her lips parted and looking up at me. My dick swells at every thought of her. I grab it, applying pressure to get the fog in my mind to clear. I need to focus on fixing my bot. The next competition is coming up, and I need to go over to Shawn's this morning to grab some parts.

I walk downstairs, and a rustling in the kitchen stops me in my tracks. I stand in the doorway with Violet's legs and ass on display in her little short shorts. She's making coffee in a porcelain travel mug with her hair up in a messy ponytail. I just want to grab hold of the back of her neck and force her to look up at me again. The urge to coerce her into that position has all rational thought leaving my brain. *Fuck with her. Fuck with her. Fuck with her*, screams in my brain, and I grab the cup off the counter before she even realizes I'm there.

"Thanks," I say, and before I can fully turn to go, she grabs the cup from my hand and throws it down on the floor.

What the fuck? I thought maybe a snide comment or something, but not this volatile reaction. *Have I already pushed her too far?* I think, standing there with coffee spreading across the marble floor.

"What's going on in here?" my dad commands from the doorway as he takes in the scene before him, making Violet's eyes bulge. "Did you do this, Miles?" His face is already turning red with anger as he accuses me.

I open and close my mouth like a fish out of water, trying to find a way to explain what just happened. Before anything comes out, Violet is grabbing the gloves from under the kitchen sink and the cleaning supplies. She's scampering around spraying the mess on the floor.

"I'm—I'm so sorry, Wade," Violet stammers, looking up at us with innocent eyes, and I just know she's going to pin all this on me. I clench my fists in anticipation. "It's my fault. I wasn't expecting Miles behind me, and I ran right into him, spilling the coffee I made for you." She continues to clean the brown liquid off the floor, completely shocking the shit out of me.

"Violet." My father thrusts her up from under her

arms, and she collapses against his chest. He runs a hand over her hair to calm her. This moment seems off. She's acting, playing the part for him, and I can't seem to look away. "I can make my own. Don't worry yourself." He releases her and walks to the coffeemaker, then pours himself a cup.

When I glance at Violet, she is looking up at me, wiping away tears. It only serves to further my confusion. I was only trying to mess with her. She's the one who knocked the cup out of my hand. I turn, leaving this whole mess behind.

My father yells, "Where are you going?"

"Shawn's." I don't even give him the attention he so desires and continue down the hall toward the front door. I don't hear what else he says, and I don't really care.

On the drive over to Shawn's, I can't stop thinking about the strange encounter I had with Violet this morning. *What was that all about?* I thought maybe she wasn't like the other stepmoms I had who were always up Wade's ass, but maybe I was wrong after all. The peace offering I gave her didn't do what I was expecting. The last thought I have before I park my Jeep is, *She needs to go.*

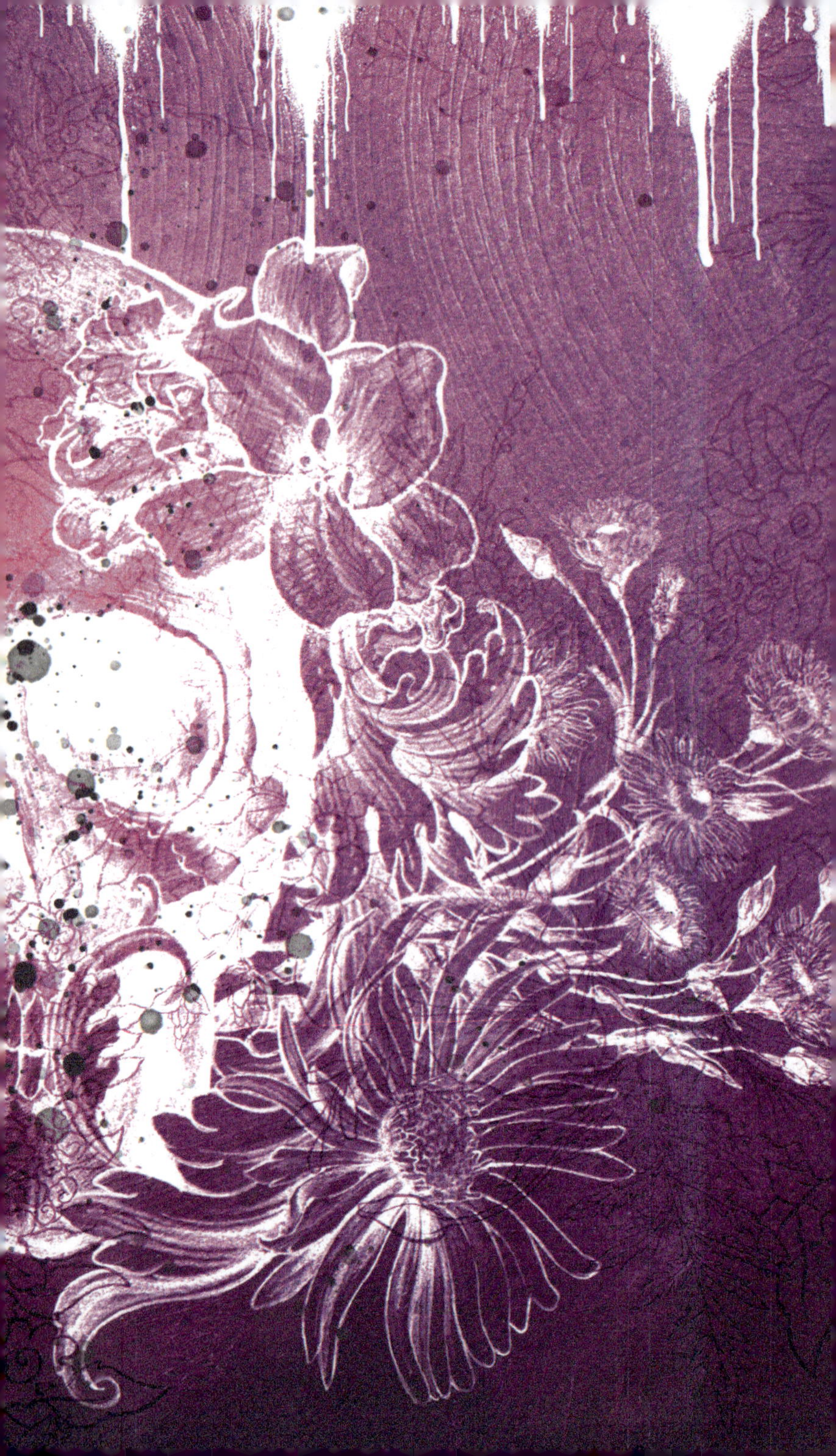

CHAPTER 11
VIOLET

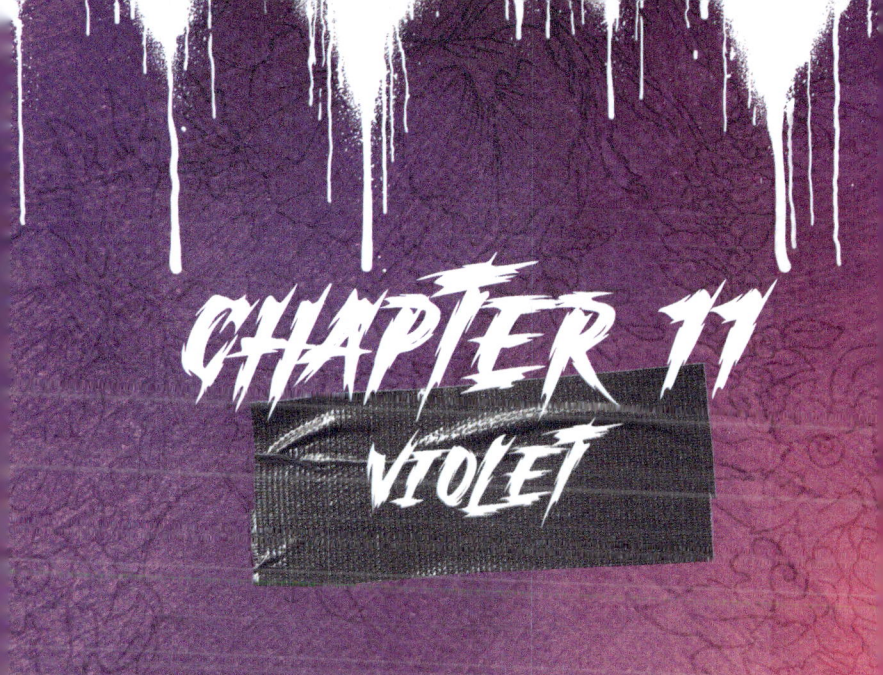

Miles almost ruined everything. I haven't seen him in days with Wade making me go with him to all these dinners, luncheons, and meetings. I thought this morning would be a good chance to try rat poison in Wade's coffee. Just a little bit to see what would happen, but I didn't think Miles would try to drink it. That wasn't part of the plan, so I had to create a diversion. I've noticed the tension between him and his father and knew he wouldn't say anything. I took the blame, so that solves everything. Well, almost everything. I'm sure I ruined the subtle compromise we built.

"We have a dinner to attend this afternoon," Wade announces when the front door slams shut.

Yep, I'm on his shit list again if we are back to the door slamming.

"Okay, I'll just call work and let them know," I say as I finish cleaning up the spill on the floor.

"I thought I told you," he starts, his palms resting on the countertop, "to quit that job."

I stand from my crouched position, confused by his demeanor. "I gave them my two weeks' notice last week. I can't just up and quit on them. They need a chance to find someone to fill my spot."

Wade invades my space, backing me against the kitchen counter. Like father, like son, I guess, but this feels different. This is more menacing. "And I thought we had a deal."

I stare at his chest, averting my eyes from the fire that is sure to be burning in his. "We do," I whisper.

"Good," he says, distancing himself again. When I glance up at him, he has a cool smile on his face and his to-go coffee in hand as if nothing happened. "I'll see you tonight."

"Yeah." I'm still holding on to the kitchen counter and just trying to breathe. I need to hurry this up and kill him soon. Then I'll be set for life.

When I get to work, I go straight to Mark's office. His head is bowed. He's working on something. I knock on the open door to get his attention. He's been the best boss I've ever had. I hate to leave him high and dry with no replacement for my position, but Wade's behavior this morning leaves me no choice. I can't hold off on this any longer.

"Hey, Violet. Anything I can help you with?" he asks, but he already knows. I had to call in and dodge work all last week. I give him my best puppy dog eyes and prepare what I'm about to tell him. "No. No," he cries, throwing down his pen. "He can't do this to me. He knows how much I need you. I have less than two weeks before you are gone for good."

"I'm sorry, Mark. He's saying he needs me for some function tonight." I lean against the doorframe, not wanting to tell him. Wade actually wants me to quit right this minute, but I'll drag it out as long as I can.

He throws his head in his hands, groaning in frustration. "Okay, fine. What does he need now."

"I have to leave work early today to go with him to some event," I say with some regret.

"Okay." Mark lets out another huff before begrudgingly saying, "Let Dani know, so that she can pick up the slack."

"Okay, thank you, Mark, and again I'm really sorry." I bite my lip before leaving his doorway at a slow pace.

He whispers under his breath when he thinks I'm far enough away, "Yeah, sure you are." That statement alone sends shards of glass straight to my heart.

I've worked with these two for months, and for Mark to think so low of me. My eyes water at the swell of emotions that seem to bubble up in my chest. *Fuck. Get it together, Violet. You have a job to do.*

The rest of the day drags until I collect my bag, and Dani waves me over to her desk. The bags under her eyes show how run-down she is from all the work I've been pushing off on her, but the curl to her lip is one of genuine curiosity.

"Are you going on a hot date tonight? I meant to ask you earlier, but you know." She gestures to the stack of papers on her desk.

"I know. I'm so sorry. Wade has a function tonight that he says he needs me for," I admit, but I bite my lip and push my hair behind my ear as if there could be more.

She shimmies her shoulders and shapes her lips into an O. She thinks we are going to have hot sex at the end, I'm sure, but little does she know that this is all a ruse. I'd never let that asshole touch me. I give her a smile and an eye roll, which makes her giggle.

"Well, don't do anything I wouldn't do." She winks.

"So, in other words, do anything and everything. Got it," I joke as I head out to my car. My insides flip-flop with nervous energy at what awaits me at home.

Miles's Jeep is here, but Wade's vehicle is nowhere in sight. I'm glad both of them aren't here. After this morning, Miles will have questions, so I run inside and upstairs to my room, avoiding him at all costs. When I open the door to my room, I'm greeted with a black dress draped over the end of my bed and a note folded on top.

For tonight is all the card says.

Oh, how sweet, very emotionally written and everything. I don't know why I'm bitter. The only reason I have for my sour mood is because of how he treated me this morning. I should be grateful, but I'm far from it.

Just get through tonight. I peptalk myself as I run my hand over the soft fabric, admiring the way it shimmers in the light. *There will always be another day to follow through with killing Wade.*

With that humbling thought in mind, I take off my work clothes and get ready. After some light pampering, shaving, hair curling, and finally makeup, I slip on the delicate dress. The cool air-conditioning kicks on, fanning over every exposed inch of me. My back prickles with goosebumps, and I turn to look at it in the full-length mirror. The dip in the back rests just above my hips, leaving my entire spine exposed. Well, this looks like it's a no bra and no underwear kind of night. The collar rests on my neck, the straps draping over my shoulders with effortless elegance. There's also a slit that runs all the way to my hip. Minimal movement will be key for tonight. I find a pair of black heels and pull my curled hair into a fashionable bun roll. *Perfect.*

As I take in the finished look, my bedroom door cracks open without even a knock. In the reflection, Wade is there in a black suit and white button-up shirt. He looks as sharp as ever.

"You are beautiful," he says with a practiced smile.

"Thank you." I glance at him over my shoulder in the reflection.

"I'll meet you downstairs. The limo will be here in fifteen." He doesn't even wait for my response before leaving.

My smile disappears as I stare at myself in the mirror, and I close my eyes, sucking in a deep breath. The door to my room opens again. I don't move or open them to see who it is in order to not disrupt the peace I'm attempting to gather within myself.

"You said fifteen," I say.

A warm hand touches my midback, and I suck in a sharp breath at the stark contrast against my skin. I refuse to open my eyes for fear of what I'll find staring back at me.

Lips touch the shell of my ear, and in a low husky drawl, Miles whispers, "I'm on to you. You gold-digging bitch."

A whimper escapes me, and I bite my lip to hold in any more that might try to escape.

"I'll uncover every last bone you're hiding in that crypt you call a heart. You can count on that."

He removes his hand and the sharp, cold air hits my back where his warmth used to be. I squeeze my eyes tighter to hold in the water threatening to leak out. When I finally open them, the only one left standing there in the mirror is me with red-rimmed lower lids.

You deserve this, Violet. Fuck these assholes.

The ride in the limo is a lot longer than I expected. Apparently, the event we were going to is a whole town over. When we get to the place, there are string lights to guide the cars where to go, and we are dropped off at the front door. It's familiar in a sense, only this time I'm not being dropped off in a cab.

My door is opened for me by the valet, and I have to hold my dress in the opposite hand to make sure I don't trip when I get out. The people here are all dressed to a T, so I'm grateful for the dress that Wade picked out for me. Even though with every move I worry I'll end up flashing someone by accident. *At least I shaved, right?*

Wade offers his arm to me, and I place my hand in the crook, allowing him to guide us through the event. I'm just meant to smile and nod. The arm candy for the night. He introduces me to everyone we meet, even though I've met them a few times and can never remember any of their names, nor do I care too.

At some point I'm passed over to a group of the wives where I hold a champagne glass and just stand there with a permanent smile. They are all gossiping about the other guests here, and then they finally get to Wade and how handsome he looks tonight. Just a good old bystander while these women gawk at my husband.

One of them even mentions my name as if I'm not standing a mere foot away from them. Then I hear that word again, *gold digger*. My mind pulls me back to that moment in the bathroom. I'm not sure why it hurt so much more coming from him than it does from these prudes.

When it's time for the charity auction to begin, the announcer calls us to our seats. I see Wade off in the crowd with a man in a dark corner. I notice it's one of the men from the luncheon, the same one who pulled over when my car broke down and grabbed me. Wade called him Richard. I hesitate as I walk toward them and stop dead in my tracks when I hear the name McIntire. *Like Scarlet McIntire? The foster kid?*

"You should have done a better job," Wade seethes.

The other man doesn't look pleased to be berated at an event like this. Before he can say anything else, the man turns to me with a smirk on his lips as if he knew I was here the whole time. Wade turns his head, meeting my eyes, but the scowl never leaves his face.

"We will continue this conversation later," he whispers under his breath to Richard before coming to my side. "We are over here." He points to a table, and I follow him to our seat. The rest of the night is filled with numbers being yelled out but no pressure for me to get on stage this time, since I'm married now. No one wants a woman who is already taken, and by the mayor of Seattle of all people. It would only look bad for him.

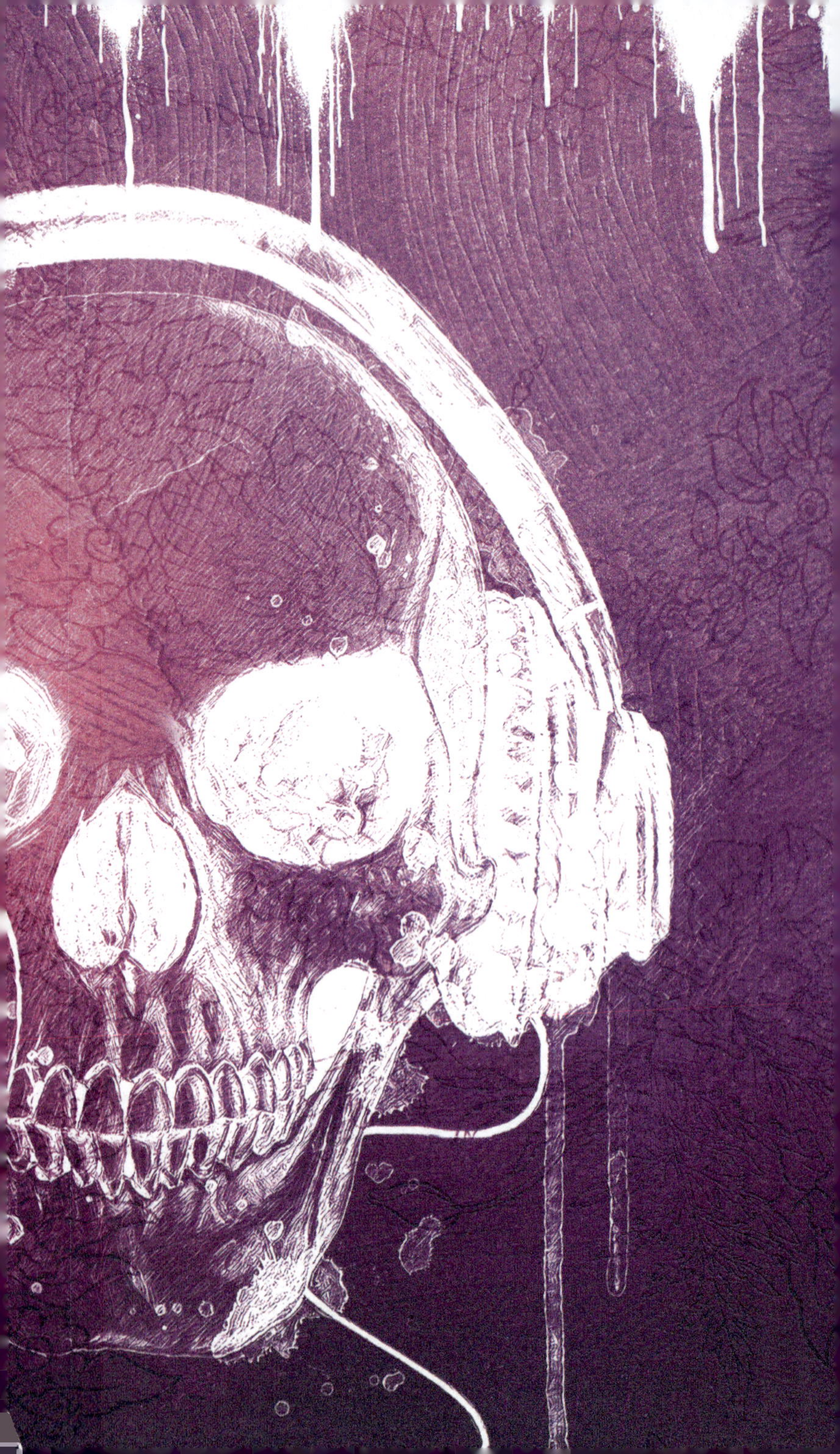

CHAPTER 12
MILES

Another event is coming up, and my bot is not ready. The pieces aren't coming together as they did before that fucker melted some of the panels and wiring to bits. I can't fail another meet, or I won't be in the running for the grand prize at the end. I need it if I plan on getting out of this house on my own terms. It's late in the afternoon, and I don't feel like calling up Chris or Shawn for a distraction. Instead, I throw on basketball shorts and a pair of old, worn-out tennis shoes. A run will help take the edge off.

The trail in the back of the house is one I would escape to growing up for different reasons, but the most common was always to get away from my father. When I was younger, before my father rebuilt our small home and made it into this obscene glass house, I got lost in these woods, and my father was furious that he had to call a search party for me. Once the cops found me, they could've used my ass as their emergency lights for a month. Needless to say, I only ever *purposefully* got lost after that.

I start by running behind the house, into the trees, and along the beaten path. My calves begin to burn with each step, that sweet, searing sting of relearning how to let loose on the trail. The power pumps through my legs, and the adrenaline in my veins alleviates the tension that has coiled itself in every fiber of my being. It unfurls like a bear coming out of hibernation. Its long, sharp claws extend, scratching against packed earth. I run until my lungs are on fire, and my sides are screaming for a break. I forgot how exhilarating and alive this makes me feel.

My home life dissipates like the dust behind me. It's been more tolerable around here since the last stepmom kicked rocks, but that seems to be changing daily. I can sense my newest one in every room, almost as if she's a beacon luring me in. A growl rocks through me, and I dig in harder to forget about her. She's a siren, and I know that nothing good will come of her. If she has her way, she will drag me to depths of the sea and leave me to rot.

Around the last bend leading back to the house, I cut a corner and almost trip over a fallen branch. It's a close call that has me fumbling before I gain traction again and right myself. I can see the house's porch light in the distance as the sun starts to set. The sky is a purple and pink hue, not fully dark yet.

My strides slow to a light jog when I get a good ten feet from the house. The perspiration drips from my forehead. I push the sweaty strands of hair out of my face as I plod up to the front door. My steps weigh heavily from exhaustion, and my eyes burn. I almost miss the hood of my father's vehicle being open from wiping all the sweat from my face. That's odd. I slow down to a walking pace and see Violet staring down at the engine.

"What are you doing?" I ask her.

She jumps, hitting her head on the hood and releasing it to slam shut. Her hands fly to her chest. "Oh, ah, I heard something. Rattling around in there." She points to the hood, and I continue to stare at her. She really thinks I'm going to buy that crock of shit. The keys to my father's ride jingle as she passes them from hand to hand. "When I was coming out here to take out the trash. It was like something was in there," she continues.

She's nervous. She should be, because I call bullshit. I don't believe her, and everything inside me screams not to.

"It must've been a squirrel that took off." She shrugs before going inside, leaving me standing there dumbfounded. Come on, she can't be that simpleminded to think I would believe that. She's up to something, and she's not good at it, whatever it is she's planning. All I know is, she's fucked with the wrong one.

"Shawn," I call out, waving my hand in the air to gain his attention.

He was already out of his car and across the school parking lot when I pulled up. I have to jog to catch up with him, but thankfully he stops and waits for me. My muscles are sore from pushing them yesterday. It's been a while since I've run, and it shows.

When I finally catch up to him, he holds his hand out for me to grab, and we give each other a half hug with our shoulders. "What's up, man? Why are you walking all funny?"

"I ran on the trail yesterday," I say, pushing my hand through my naturally messy hair.

Shawn quirks a brow at me. "You ran in the woods? Dude that's serious. You haven't done that since your last stepmom. Is Stacy's mom really that bad?" He jokes with that last question, and I shove his arm.

"Really, dude?"

"What? She's fucking fine. Even if she is a little overbearing, my disco stick is still available. It doesn't shy away from a challenge." Shawn laughs at his own lame joke before he finally fixes his face. "Okay, okay. Seriously. What's the matter?"

Attempting to put all my worries into one coherent thought, I start with, "I'm stressed about the competition, for one. Then, Violet is acting super sus, dude. She's hiding something, and I think she only married my father for one reason. His money."

He shrugs. "So, wasn't that every one of your father's ex-wives' goals? Bag the bachelor, stash the cash? That seems like it would just come with the territory."

Okay, he has a point. Shawn pushes open the school's large oak double doors, and we walk into the sea of students. I lower my voice so no one around us hears. "No, she's different."

"You think she's different, because you have the hots for her, man," Shawn says, and we stop in front of his locker. He turns the dial, entering the code until the lock clicks. The metal door swings open to reveal a mostly bare space, aside from a lone backpack, which he pulls out and hoists over his shoulder. "Maybe you should give in and fuck her."

His comment makes me think of Violet looking up at me with those perfect pouty lips. The way I want her on her knees in front of me with them wrapped around my dick. I close my eyes in an attempt to force that image out of my head. *Fucking hell, I'm screwed.*

"Besties!" Chris squeals from behind us, wrapping her arms around both Shawn's and my waist.

"Hey, sweet cheeks," Shawn says before kissing Chris on the temple, and her cheeks flush bright pink.

Shawn and I both rest our arms on Chris's shoulders as we walk down the hall like the three musketeers.

"What's up?" Chris asks, and Shawn is more than happy to catch her up on my latest home fiasco. "You're probably just overthinking it, Milly. She seemed really sweet that day I came over, and you were a complete ass to her."

"You're probably right," I admit to get them off my back. I know what my gut is telling me, and it's telling me she's a fucking snake. She's hiding something. I'm sure of it. "Where were you this morning, Chris? You're never this late," I ask to change the subject, but it seems I've thrown a dart and hit something unexpected.

Chris's face falls, and she unravels herself from our arms. "I have to go," she whispers.

"What's the matter?" I ask her.

Her eyes begin to water, but the bell rings. The students in the hall begin to clear, going to their homerooms.

"Maybe later," she whispers before running off.

I turn toward Shawn confused. "What was that about?"

He claps me on the shoulder, shaking his head. "You've missed a lot with your head stuck up your ass. Her and her stepsister are fighting. Something with her parents wanting to send her to a private boarding school for kids with problems or some shit."

"Fuck, man. I had no idea." I feel like a shit friend. I've been so worried about my own insignificant problems that I haven't even thought to check in with Shawn and Chris. I figured if they hadn't called me then everything must be fine.

Well, fuck me running. Ah, my legs.

AYDEN PERRY 139

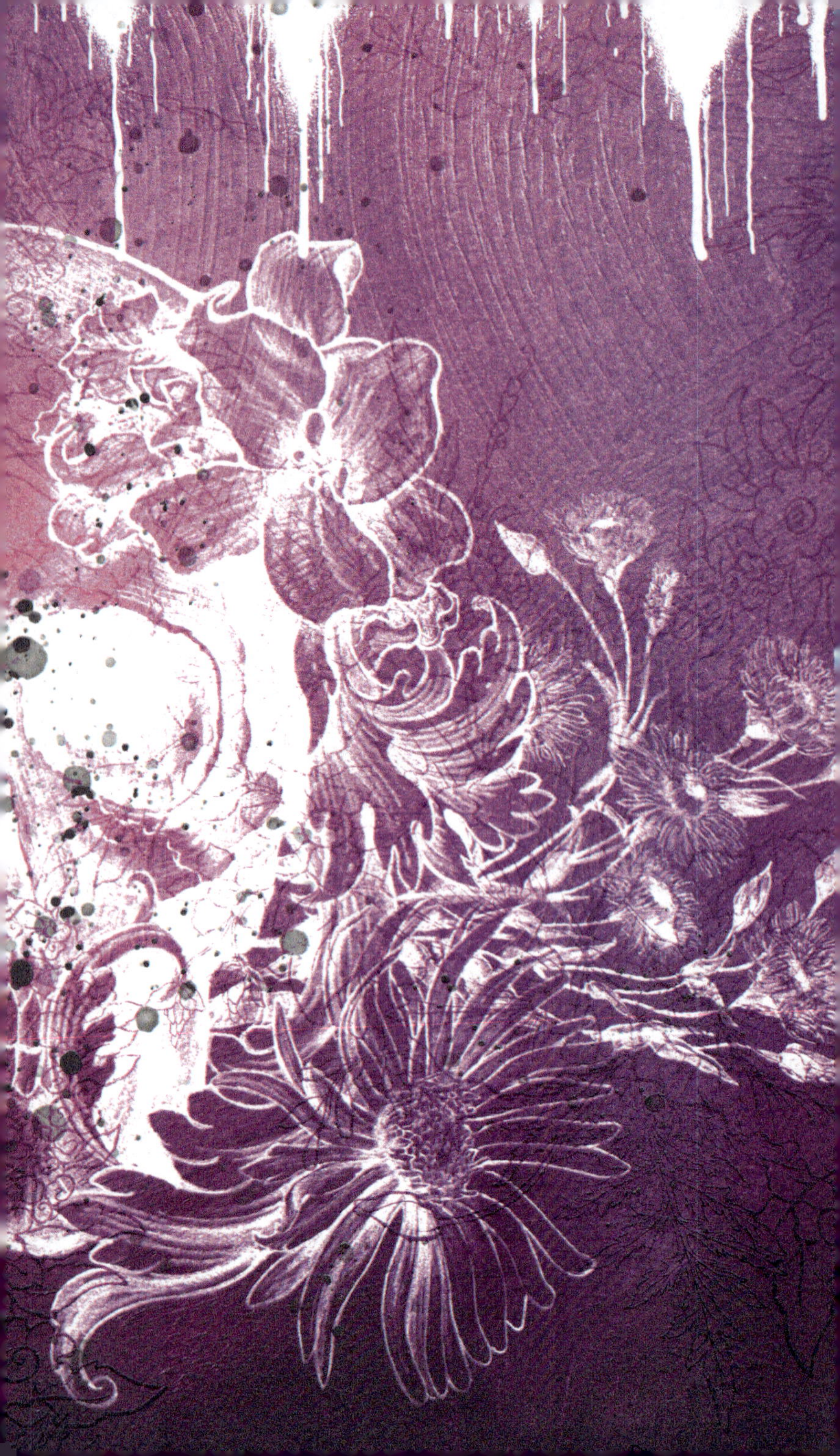

CHAPTER 13
VIOLET

Another crime episode plays on the flat screen TV. The photos they show of a happy couple are old, amber, and vintage. People sit in a nondescript room in front of a camera and discuss their interactions with the couple. Those close to them give their accounts leading up to the moment the happy, adoring wife snapped. They explain how she wasn't as happy as she seemed to be. That they suspected something was off about her before the final event of bloodshed. My skin prickles as I think of Miles recounting my actions in front of a camera.

"What was she like?"

"She knocked coffee out of my hand, and she was looking under the hood of my father's car when she clearly had no experience with vehicles. She was also obsessed with crime shows. All these strange events led up to the moment my father was murdered."

I chew on my lip as all this plays out in my mind.

Miles was never supposed to be here, and I don't know what to do. I don't know shit about cars. I'm obviously not good at being sneaky with poison. I've been out of work for a week, and all I've done is watch crime documentaries and go to fancy parties with Wade. The only thing those people think of me is that I'm a gold-digging whore. *What should I do?* I'm failing miserably with every attempt, and I'm becoming one with this couch. My muscles twitch with the urge to move, go, do something.

Miles was on a trail in the woods last week when I was trying to find the brake line in Wade's Audi. I was not prepared for how high tech it would be. Old cars, sure. I did pretty good with cutting my coolant line to make my car overheat, but these new cars? They are one solid mass of engine with a cover hiding everything in sight. The tension in my body coils tight within my core, and I let out a groan of frustration.

Maybe I should find that trail Miles was on and see if it gives me any ideas, or at the very least clear my mind. I run upstairs with a newfound surge to be productive. Sifting through my clothes, I find a sports bra and a pair of compression pants. *This will work.* One last thing: shoes. I find an old pair in the back of my closet and throw them on before racing downstairs.

Behind the glass house, a well-beaten path is carved out from the trees. I walk through the opening, leaving the sun behind. Squirrels hop along the path and scamper away when I get close. Their cute little bushy tails flick back and forth. The shade and absence of wind makes it seem as if I'm the only person left in this world. Calm settles over me, and I begin to jog. My muscles warm, and the stiffness in my joints begins to loosen. I've never run on open terrain like this, but the shade is cooling against the perspiration that's starting to collect along my hairline.

The movements flow through me. I run, legs pumping, and I fly, hopping over fallen branches as if I'm a natural. Birds flap their wings, rustling the leaves in the trees when I pass. Some of them sing as if cheering me on to keep going. I've never run a day in my life. The only activities I've ever done as far as working out have been spin classes and yoga in California. This is all new to me, but the dopamine coursing through me is all the same.

There's a dull pang in my ribs, and I keep going till it's nearly undetectable. I push my legs harder. The fog in my mind is clearing, and I think this could be my newfound hobby. *Or* maybe gardening, since there aren't any flowers around the house. I could plant violets. The thought makes me happy, and I lose track of the curves and bends of the path.

On my next leap, my toe catches the edge of a large branch, and I'm tumbling down a small decline. A sharp pain lances through my knees and my temple when I make contact with the hard-packed earth. Dirt coats my lips, and I inhale particles, which cause a coughing fit. *I just had to go running, didn't I?* A pounding erupts in my head. I attempt to move, but pain ignites in one of my knees, causing black specks to fill my vision.

"Violet! You no-good, gold-digging *whore*!" James spits at me. "You fucked me."

"I only took what I deserve," I say, grinding my teeth together.

He's in my face with his fists, but he doesn't touch me. I have to force myself to stand straighter, willing him to hit me. He unfurls his hands and runs them through his hair, ruffling it up more than it already was. I push him, egging him on. Antagonizing him. I know I shouldn't, but the way my chest has been cracking open lately, I'd almost rather wear the pain on the outside for a bit.

He spins around on his heel and grabs my throat. His teeth are bared. This is all I've ever wanted from him. A reaction. Something other than just passing each other like ghosts. I can't live in this tomb any longer. My insides are screaming to be held, to be touched.

"The people I work for will be coming for you soon," he says in a hoarse whisper so close to my lips that I almost yearn for him to close the gap.

He releases me, walking away. All the muscles in my body give out. All the fight I had in me dies as I go limp. I'm in a crumpled heap on our unblemished hardwood floors. Just like everything in his life—pretty, perfect, and *untouched*.

"*Fucking talk to me*," I scream with tears running down my cheeks.

He continues walking away from me, unfazed and unbothered, because I'm just another thing he can replace. A pressure within me builds, and I clench my teeth. My limbs are shaking with rage. Before he opens the door, I jump off the floor and run at him. He doesn't even realize I'm there until I spin him around to face me.

"I'll make sure they don't even believe *you*," I hiss.

His mouth is turned down in disgust, and he shrugs my hands off him as if I'm a germ or grotesque parasite he's trying to get rid of. Once he's fully removed me from himself, he leaves, shutting the door behind him. I'm old, used up. He doesn't have a need for me anymore.

My heart breaks into pieces, and the rage within me overflows until I'm screaming. My throat burns, but I can't stop. I even grab hold of my hair, pulling it as if that will be the switch that turns me off, but I can't stop. My insides are ripping to shreds. *You deserve this, Violet. You can't make someone love you*, that pestering voice in my head nags. Which only makes my muscles tense, coiling tight like a snake preparing to strike, and I do.

Our pictures fly off the tables, the mantel, and the walls. The cell phone with the messages from his secretary he was fucking behind my back is held tight in my palm. The tips of my fingers are turning white, and I smash it face first on the marble countertop over and over. The glass shards of the screen fly off into tiny pieces. Some of the shards embed in my skin. The crimson veins branch and spread down my arm, but I can't feel it. My anger, still not satisfied. It's a monster within, growling and snarling, begging to be fixed.

The rage vibrates through every muscle in my body, and I need to snuff it out. I go to the bathroom and run a hot bath. The water rises with the stream until it's overflowing, and I sink in, sloshing it over the sides. I'll make them believe me. They will believe me. The pain I'm feeling will be seen on the outside for all the world to see. Thrusting forward, my eye blossoms with pain. The faucet shines red with my blood, and the noise in my body subsides. That monster inside curls up, eyes closing. The still-running water like white noise is relaxing. Soothing. Sleep. I close my eyes.

Thump. Thump. Thump. Shhhhhh.
There's a pounding on the outside of my body and my head before a shower of small particles rains down on

AYDEN PERRY 145

me.

"Violet? Violet!" a voice calls to me. "Violet, wake up." A sharp sting lands across my face, and I blink a few times against the harsh, bright light. I straighten my legs, and lightning shoots up my right leg. I let out a low groan. The greens and browns blur in my vision, and I continue to blink, clearing the film over my eyes. Before I can even gather my bearings, a set of strong arms wraps around me. My cheek rests upon warm, hard muscle, and my head is cradled. I fit perfectly here. The scent of pine mixed with fresh linen and a slight hint of musk fills my nose, causing my heart to nearly burst with butterflies at the sense of safety I feel in this moment. I'm gently rocking in a nice bouncing rhythm. Only a few times do the bumps become intense enough that a low throb pulses up my leg and pounding erupts in my temple. A small groan leaves my lips, and a soft whisper follows. "I got you, almost there."

Cool air fans over me, and the soft cushion caresses my back. I want to drift off to sleep again, but another sharp sting lands on my cheek.

"What the fuuuuckkk," I groan.

"You can't sleep. I think you have a concussion."

I peek through my lashes at the glistening bare chest of my stepson. My heart ricochets in my chest. Pushing my hands beneath me, I launch to a sitting position with my back pressing against the arm of the couch. My whole body screams with the movement, and I whimper at the pain. Miles scowls down at me before wiping the expression off his face as if I had imagined it.

"You have a skinned-up knee and a deep cut on your forehead. You shouldn't move," he says, placing his warm palm on my good knee. The urge to pull away from him is intense, but I hold still. He isn't doing anything wrong. He's only trying to help me. I scold my devious body for going against my brain and making this out to be more than what it is.

"I'm sorry," I whisper.

His eyes light up. "The first aid kit," he announces, running upstairs, and before I'm left to ponder my own thoughts, he's back at my side opening up the blue bag with the medical symbol on the front.

He pulls out the antiseptic ointment with a few cotton balls and sets them down on the coffee table. After soaking the cotton balls, he brings one to the cut on my head. Our eyes catch, and it's as if time stops. I've never paid that much attention to his eyes, and the only time we were this close was that night in the kitchen. I'm captured by his hazel irises, and the colors interlock and blend together, making the green look like stars bursting. An electrical charge passes between us, and he glances up at my wound, breaking the connection.

My cheeks heat, and I avert my gaze. *I shouldn't have these thoughts or react this way. It's wrong.*

The antiseptic is cold with a slight sting to my open wound. I suck in a sharp breath between my teeth and wince before I can catch myself. "Sorry," I whisper.

He doesn't say anything, just continues to work on cleaning the cut. Once he is done with my forehead, he moves to my knee. His brows pull together as if trying to decide what to do.

"You have to take your pants off," he says with a straight face.

"What?" My voice comes out high-pitched.

"I can't see all the damage. Only a small amount through the tear in the knee." He's so clinical about it. I hesitate, thinking back to what I have underneath, and I freeze. My muscles tense up. He must notice, because he asks, "What?"

"I, um, I—" I hesitate. *Why am I being so*

nervous? "I need a towel to wrap around myself," I spit out, hating myself for being so timid.

He finally catches on and smirks. "You think I want to look at you?"

His words slice through me like a surgical knife. Of course he doesn't. This is all in my *fucking* head. "Okay. Fine," I huff, building my defenses. I even give him an eye roll for good measure, as if I'm as unaffected as he is.

Hooking my thumbs under the waistband, I push the compression pants down as far as I can before the pain in my knee becomes too much. I flop back on the couch, taking in deep breaths. *Why did I have to wear these tight things?* Before I can gather up the momentum to try again, Miles places his hands on my thighs, and I freeze. Miles freezes. Even time itself freezes. And my breath is frozen like a block of ice at the bottom of my lungs.

His hands hook beneath the band and slide my skintight pants off the rest of the way. "Breathe, Violet. It's just pants."

Yep, it's all in my head. Just knock it off already. He's your stepson. If my head didn't hurt so much already, I would bang it against the wall for my dirty thoughts.

Miles drags the antiseptic wipes over the cut on my knee, which doesn't look as bad as it actually feels. That may be a different story tomorrow. Good thing I don't have to go to work anymore, so I can just lie around, ice it, and elevate it. As soon as he's done disinfecting it, he dresses it in a compression wrap.

"I'll get you a bag of ice to put on it," he says before leaving the room.

Miles didn't stare at me during that whole exchange while I sat in my sports bra and underwear.

Super professional about everything, but I still feel weirdly exposed. Thankfully, I like to keep throw blankets on the back of the couch for bundling up to watch TV. There's a knit throw at the end of the couch. It's a bit of a stretch, but I go for it. The pain in my knee throbs with the movement, but I push through it. I grip the edge of the soft yarn between my fingers and pull. It unravels from its neatly folded spot, and I wrap it around me. *Ah, much better.*

Miles comes back with a glass of ice cubes, which has me pinching my brows together. "What, couldn't stand to be around me in your panties and bra?" he asks with a smirk.

"That's inappropriate. You're my stepson." My heart is racing at his comment, and I just want to smash it to make it stop.

"I guess we should never go swimming together then," he retorts.

"That's different," I say with a bit more snark than I intended. "You know you are supposed to put them in a bag, right?" I point to the cup in his hand, attempting to change the subject.

"Are you trying to mother me right now?" He stands over me with the ice, perspiration already collecting on the outside of the glass like dew.

"I mean." I give him an awkward one-shoulder shrug with a weird one-eye squint.

He chuckles, sitting back down on the spot he was before. "Well I don't need another mother."

The glass is in his hand between us. He grabs a piece and places it on my sore knee. It sweats, leaking on the dressing. I knew this was a bad idea, and I press my lips together, trying to keep from being a whiny bitch about it. When it melts completely, he adds another. The bandage soaks up the liquid, and it begins to drip down my inner thigh. Miles follows the trail with a heated gaze. I go to squeeze my thighs together, but his hand stops my bad knee from moving.

"You shouldn't use this knee for a while." His voice comes out husky, and he grabs another piece of ice out of the cup to place on my knee.

Putting up a hand to stop him, I say, "I think we're good on the ice."

"Okay." He throws the piece of ice he was holding back into the cup and picks up the Roku stick. "Want to watch something?"

"Yeah, sure." The racing in my heart slows down.

Miles flips through a few channels until he finds a scary movie playing. "You like scary movies, right?" he asks, his voice deep and breathy.

When I look back up, his dark eyes are on mine. My core throbs with the need to be touched, and it's as if he reads my mind, because he begins to follow the trail of water running down my thigh with his eyes.

"Miles," I whisper, trying to break the trance.

"My name sounds good coming from your lips," he rasps, and with the Roku remote he smears the trail of water.

"You can't touch me. This is wrong." The last part comes out so soft I'm not even sure if he heard it.

He continues, and it's as if a line of fire and ice is shooting straight to my clit. We break eye contact and both look down to where he is still holding the remote.

"But I'm not touching you." He smirks as he follows the water line farther up my thigh. When he reaches my panty line, he says, "The remote is." He presses the rounded plastic on my clit, and my breath hitches in my throat.

That sinister pull of his lip only intensifies with my reaction. He rubs the remote around in a circle, sending pulses straight to my core. You would think the ice water running down my leg would help with the heat boiling inside me, but it does the opposite. I bite my lip to suppress the needy whimper that begs to be released, and I squeeze my eyes shut so that I can pretend he is someone else. The only problem is, his face follows me there too. His chest. His arms. The cords in his neck, and the way his hair hangs down over his eyes. My breathing becomes erratic when he pushes my panties to the side and glides the remote lower, collecting my arousal on the hard plastic.

"Do you want me to stop?" His low husky whisper washes over to me. Every nerve ending in my body is at war, because my brain is screaming yes while my body is saying quite the opposite. Then he says, "What are you hiding, Violet?"

That has my eyes springing open and everything in me dies. I grit my teeth. "Get off me," I say in a low, cruel tone.

Miles lets go of the remote, letting it fall to the couch between my legs. His brows are furrowed and his jaw is set. Then the muscles along his jawline begin to flex. My thought is that he is going to just get up and leave, pissed that his plan to seduce information out of me didn't work. But instead, I'm met with a completely new surprise. He pushes my hurt knee down and out. The stabbing pain makes a groan leave my lips, but it's quickly cut off by his hand wrapped around my throat. Miles glares down at me. That soft, wavy brown hair dangling over his eyes. "You say anything about this to my dad, and I'll expose you."

"You wouldn't." I mouth the words, sucking in air around his tight grip on my airway.

"Try me." Then he releases me, stalking up to his room.

I'm left with a half-melted cup of ice, a wet bandage, a remote I won't be able to look at the same, and even more self-loathing than I started with.

AYDEN PERRY 153

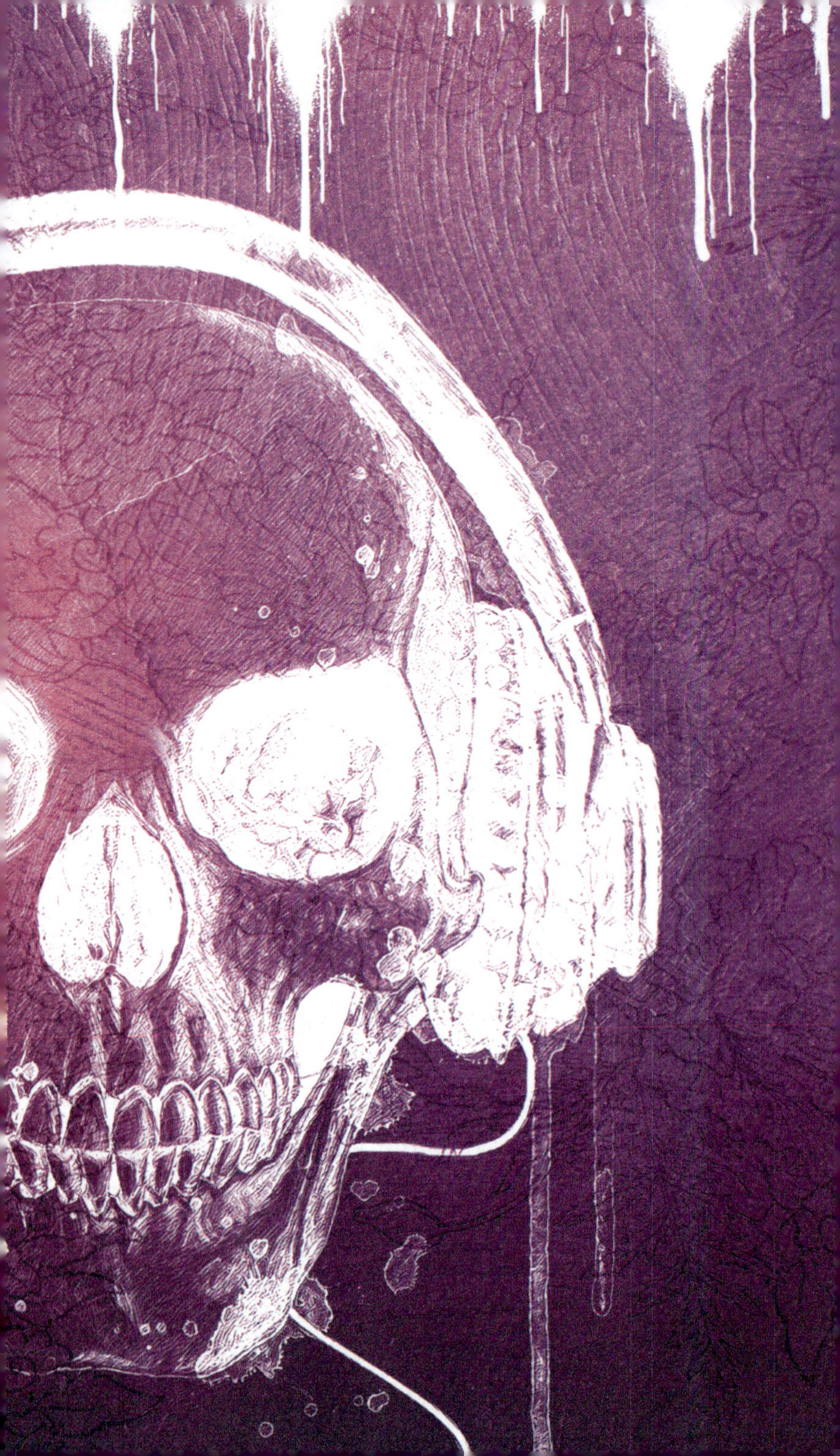

CHAPTER 14
MILES

Ever since that day with the remote and the ice cubes, Violet has constantly been on my mind. I've tried to rebuild my bot, but I'm distracted. The way she looked lying on the couch with her bottom lip pulled between her teeth... She was suppressing her baser desires. *For what? A moral code?* One thing I do know is she's not like the girls my age. Those who throw themselves at me or fake it as if they've watched too much porn. Or like Christina, who has no real chemistry with me. We just fuck to clear the black swirling chaos in our minds. *No*, Violet is a woman unlike any other. The fire. That light within her. When she told me to stop, and the way her eyes shone with excitement when I held her throat in my hand, that's what I want. That burn of the rope as we play tug-of-war.

I may get burned, but it's the craving for a fight I don't want to back down from.

Again. The energy in my muscles shakes with tension at the thought of her. I have to work this out, and the only way to do that is to go for a run.

The trails, as always, are a reassuring space for me. If I can't fuck the stress out, then I'll run it out. Set the dopamine off in my brain.

Violet's been hobbling around the house, or lying on the couch with her leg propped up, since I found her that day in these woods. Most people don't realize how unforgiving nature can be until they experience it. I hope she learned a lesson she'll never forget, especially when my hand was wrapped around her throat. I threatened her for fucking with my future. Whatever she's planning, I'll get to the bottom of it.

I continue running, letting out my pent-up energy. I jump over fallen logs and rocks. The one Violet fell over is still there, and I search the rocks for her blood. The thought of her face pinching in ecstasy and her biting her lip to suppress a moan fills my head again, causing my steps to falter. I stumble to a light jog, furiously groaning at no one but myself. The birds fly out of the trees around me. Their calls in the sky raise the alert of a predator in the territory, and still the only thing I can think about is her.

Fuck me.

I walk the rest of the way to the house, still frustrated with myself when I see a truck backed up in the driveway. It gives me pause. *What is a landscaping truck doing here?* A man unloads sacks of dirt with Violet standing over him. Her hip is cocked to the side. *What is she doing?* When she bends over to sign the paperwork, the guy checks out her backside. She's wearing those tiny shorts that allow the bottom of her ass cheeks to show again, and the fire within me blazes.

"Go in the house," I command when I get to them.

"Wha— No," she stutters before the realization sparks in her eyes, and she crosses her arms over her chest. "Are you serious?"

I fume in frustration, and a deep rumble reverberates low in my chest. I'm furious with her. I don't have time for this. Grabbing the man by his collar, I pull him toward his truck and open his door for him. "It's time for you to leave."

He resists me, pulling out of my grasp. "This is uncalled for," the man screams.

I shove him into his truck, and he falls into his seat with a shocked expression on his face. "If you ever come back and fucking look at her again, it will be the last time your eyes look at anything, I promise you that," I whisper through gritted teeth before slamming his door shut.

The man gives me a hard look, starting his truck up. He knows exactly what he was doing. I turn. The sound of gravel pops behind me, letting me know the man took my advice. Violet is standing in the same spot, hip still cocked to keep the weight off her hurt knee. Her expression is one of confusion. I continue to walk past her and into the house, but she follows me.

"What the hell was that for?" she asks.

My foot is on the bottom step. I don't even turn to look at her. "Drop it."

But she doesn't and follows me upstairs. "No, I'm not. Tell me what the fuck is your problem."

Once we are at the top of the stairs, I turn to her and look down at her bare thighs in those short shorts that she decided to wear outside for everyone to see. I trail my gaze along her body till I reach her face. My mouth forms a practiced grimace before I reluctantly tear her down a peg. "If you're going to act like my fucking mom, maybe you should try dressing like one."

Her eyes turn glassy. I walk away before I can even hear her response and overthink what I just did. I need to call Shawn.

When I close my bedroom door, I grab my phone and dial his number. He answers on the first ring like I knew he would.

"Hey, Shawn. Do you mind if I bring my bot over? I can't figure out what wire is misfiring. The electrics aren't responding like they should." I know what's wrong with it, but I need to leave. I can't stay in this house and work on this with her around.

"Yeah sure, dude," he says. "The door will be unlocked when you get here. Just take it to the garage."

"Thanks, man." I hang up, then gather all the things I may need.

When I get to Shawn's, the door is unlocked like he said it would be, and I walk through to the garage. I hit the button to open the door and bring my bot in. Shawn stands in the doorway that connects the garage to the house with his hands stuffed in his hoodie pocket.

"What's up, man?" He knows I'm a fucking liar.

"Nothing, just need help troubleshooting."

"Uh, huh." He goes through the motions same as I would, and the issue is glaringly obvious. I know it. He knows it. There's no hiding that it's just a fried wire. He replaces it, and when he turns it on again the lights flash, letting us know it's ready to go. With his arms crossed over his chest, he says, "Now, tell me the real reason you came over." He looks at me with one brow arched, and I let out a groan. "I'll go grab us a few beers from the fridge."

I give him a curt nod, and while he is gone, I load Corrupter into the Jeep. After closing the door to the garage, I find Shawn waiting in the hallway for me with a beer in hand. We walk up to his room, and he sits back at his computer, where I'm assuming he was before I came over because his computer is open on an underground news article. On it is a picture of an old hospital and across the top in bold letters it says, *The Mourning Cloak Devils Have Escaped.* That's as much as I get before he minimizes the page. He looks up the strangest stuff being a horror fanatic. I think he's on those deep dark net pages and helps with investigations in Reddit forums or some shit in his free time. If he only knew what was so close to home. I sit down on his bed and take a swig of the cold beer.

"So, spill." He swivels in his desk chair and leans over, resting his elbows on his knees.

"It's my fucking stepmom, man." I take another sip of my beer.

"Have you fucked her yet?" he asks.

"No." I cut my eyes to him, and Shawn gives me a smirk before chugging his beer.

"So the SMILF isn't giving in, and you're sexually frustrated, but you don't want to admit it, so you came here instead?"

"Ugh, man, really?" I grimace at his use of the acronym. I don't think of her as a stepmom.

He shrugs, leaning back in his chair. "What? Everyone has their kink. No need to be ashamed of it." I grab a pillow off his bed and throw it at his head. He ducks at the last minute, causing it to miss him. It hits his computer screen instead, making it rock slightly. "Come on, man. Don't throw shit," he says, letting out a huff at his prized possession being put in jeopardy.

"Sorry." I run my fingers through my hair and cradle the beer in my hands. "She's getting under my skin."

"So fuck her?"

"It's not that easy, man. She's hiding something.

I know it." I feel it in my bones. The only thing I need is for her to confirm it. That way I can put my suspicions at ease and get my plan B out of the frying pan. If not, my father will go up in smoke, along with the money for college.

He looks at me with furrowed brows. "What do you mean? How do you know she's hiding something?"

"I don't know. It's just a feeling I have. Nothing solid yet, but I feel like my ticket out of here is at stake."

"So you just need to get rid of her like you did with the last one?" he asks with a glimmer of mischief in his eyes. This dude is evil. I'm just glad I've never been on the wrong side of him.

"I've tried everything, ignoring her, giving her the cold shoulder when she's nice. I've been rude, demeaning, and I've even tried to fuck her. I'm all out of options at this point," I say, exasperated.

"Not *everything*."

"I'm not sure that will really help."

He only smirks at me before swiveling around in his chair. Then, I hear him say under his breath. "It's because you don't want to hurt her."

"Not so fucking subtle."

He turns back around in his chair, and that smirk is now a full fucking devilish grin. "Oh, but it's so much fucking fun. Plus, we need another sex tape." He rubs his palms together.

No one ever said being a troublemaker was easy. While Shawn is the quiet, destructive type, I'm more of the glorified Satan when it comes to bad shit. The only reason is because people see it, and I don't give a fuck. Shawn is much more evil with his silent work.

"Fine. We will do it your way."

If Shawn's grin got any wider, I think his face would break in half.

AYDEN PERRY 161

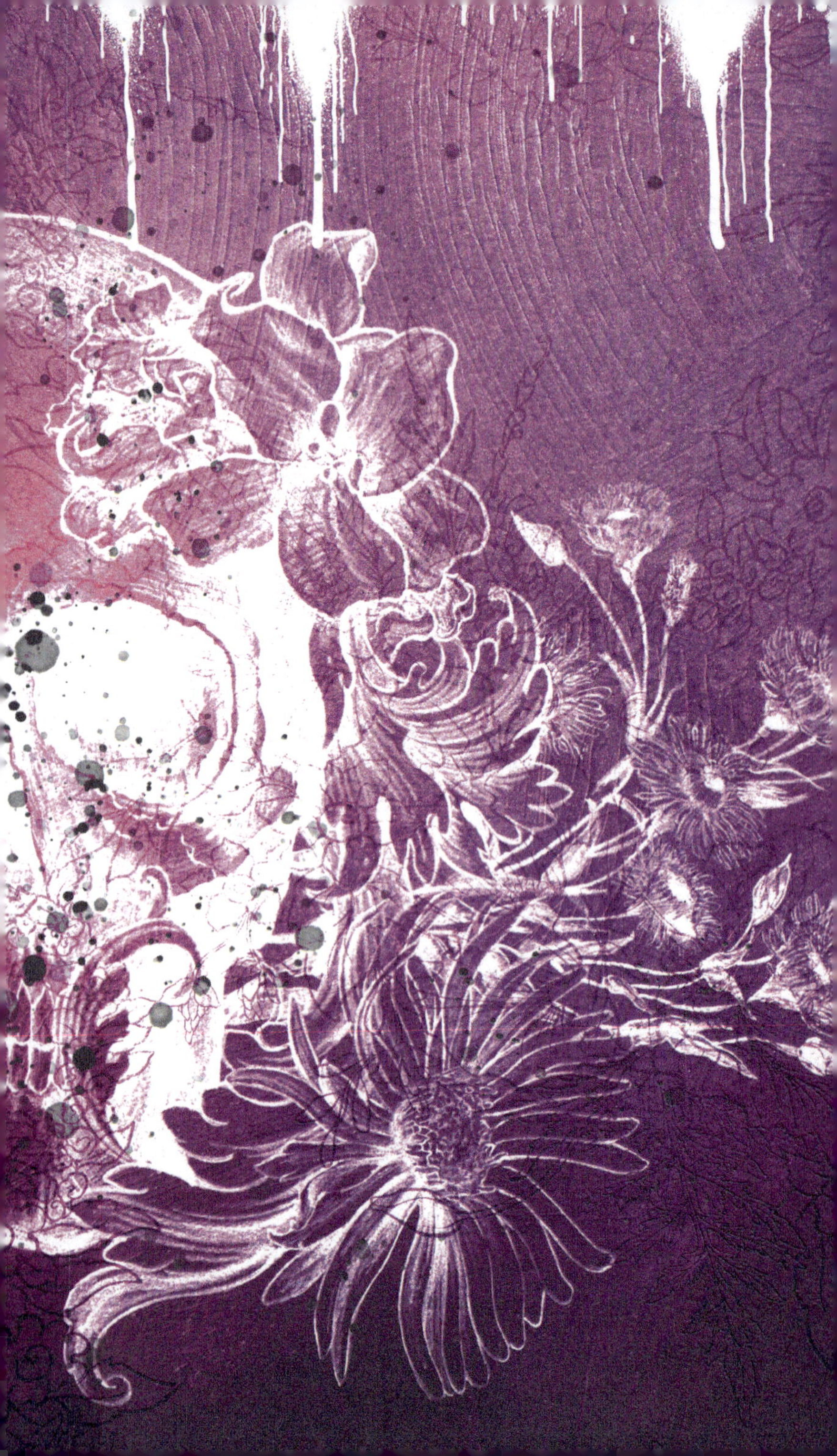

CHAPTER 15
VIOLET

Miles's words hit a little too close to home. My mind took me back to my ex-husband, James and the things he used to say to me. *Why are you wearing that? You should dress more classy. You're too old to be wearing stuff like that.* I was never going to be as good as his young hot secretary, so I have no idea why I even fucking tried. This though, was a whole new low, because I am actually being myself, dressing like myself. Then Miles had to go and cut deep with his words, deep enough to scrape the bone.

Standing in front of the bathroom mirror, I throw water on my face to cool the heat that is burning me up from the inside. The redness that surrounds my eyes doesn't lessen in the least, and I take a few deep breaths before going back outside.

Miles's Jeep is gone. He must be really upset with me, because I turned down his advances, or because he wasn't getting the information out of me he was looking for. His motives bounce around in my head. Is he genuinely attracted to me or just a really good actor? Was he only looking for information? *Why should it matter*, I scold myself.

I walk around the house and begin digging up the spot I marked in the backyard. I'm not sure how Wade would feel about me placing a flower bed in the front of the house, so I decided to make a spot for myself in the back where no one would see but me. I dig and shape the bed into a square. I figure if I hollow it out, I can border off the edges and fill the inside with gravel and a wrought iron bench, giving myself a nice sitting area when I'm done with it. A place to clear my head. And it will give me something to do in the meantime, since running isn't an option. I work until the sun begins to set and my bad knee starts to ache.

I gather all my tools, then place them in a pile for me to work with again tomorrow. When I walk—hobble—back to the front of the house, Miles's Jeep is back in its usual spot. The little voice in my head gets on its perch and demands I make things right with him. Food is the first thought. Hell, who am I kidding. Food is a constant thought. *What makes people happier than food?* It worked last time, so why not this time?

When I walk into the house, Miles's music is blaring as always, and I set to cooking homemade pizzas. I make one with regular pepperoni and one with jalapeños and pineapples, because that's my favorite. I don't know what Miles's favorite pizza is since he never talks to me, but who doesn't love pepperoni, right? That seems like a safe, generalized option anyway. Maybe I can have a talk with him, set some boundaries, and break bread over melted cheese and pizza sauce. I get everything ready before walking up to his room and to let him know there's food if he wants any.

Once upstairs, the music in the hallway is overbearing, and the bass vibrates the pictures on the wall. *Did I really upset him that much?* I continue edging down the hall, one step at a time. I'm holding my breath as if he could actually hear me over the music. I think it's more for myself than anything. He might blow up at me again, and that's what I'm most worried about. His bedroom door is wide open. The music is at ear-splitting level.

Once I'm at the doorway, I'm frozen in place by what I see. Miles's chest shines with perspiration, and he is balls deep in the blonde-haired girl he called Chris from a few weeks ago. He's looking down at her, and she's looking up at him, brows creased in ecstasy. They haven't seen me yet, and my brain tells me to run, but my feet are cemented in place, and I can't look away.

His hair over his brow swings, and his abs flex with each thrust of his cock. My core tightens, and I squeeze my thighs together. My body is betraying me at every turn. I'm about to turn around and run when the music stops. The moment hangs by a frayed thread. I can't breathe. Then he glances up at me. His eyes hold mine, and his lips perk up at the side in a half smirk. My chest and cheeks heat at being caught watching them. *I shouldn't be here. This is wrong.*

He never stops pumping into her, and he never breaks eye contact with me. He only pushes her knees to her ears, leaning over to pick up a black remote. The music is back but at a lower volume.

He leans down as if he's whispering in her ear but loud enough for me to hear. "What if my stepmom comes in and sees us like this?" The blonde girl only groans in response, and he continues, "Should we ask her to join us?"

AYDEN PERRY 165

"Yes, oh god, yes," she moans.

"I think she would be too much of a prude," he says gruffly as he pounds into her, flexing his hips. He moves in a rhythm like the waves of the ocean, and with the way her legs are bent, I know she is feeling his cock hit her cervix.

She screams out, and I'm sure her cunt is milking him for everything he's worth. "She doesn't. Know. What. She's missing." Her words come out breathy as she tries to catch air between the thrusts he is giving her.

"Oh yeah? And what is she missing? Scream it so she can hear," he growls.

His eyes never leave mine, and my thighs are slick with my own arousal. My clit is pulsating in time with my racing heart to the point that it hurts, aching to be touched.

The girl screams, and her legs shake in his hold. He rides her through the waves, and I can't stand it any longer. I run down the hall to my room, forgetting about everything downstairs. The pizza. The making up with Miles. There's no making up with him. He's started an all-out war.

AYDEN PERRY 167

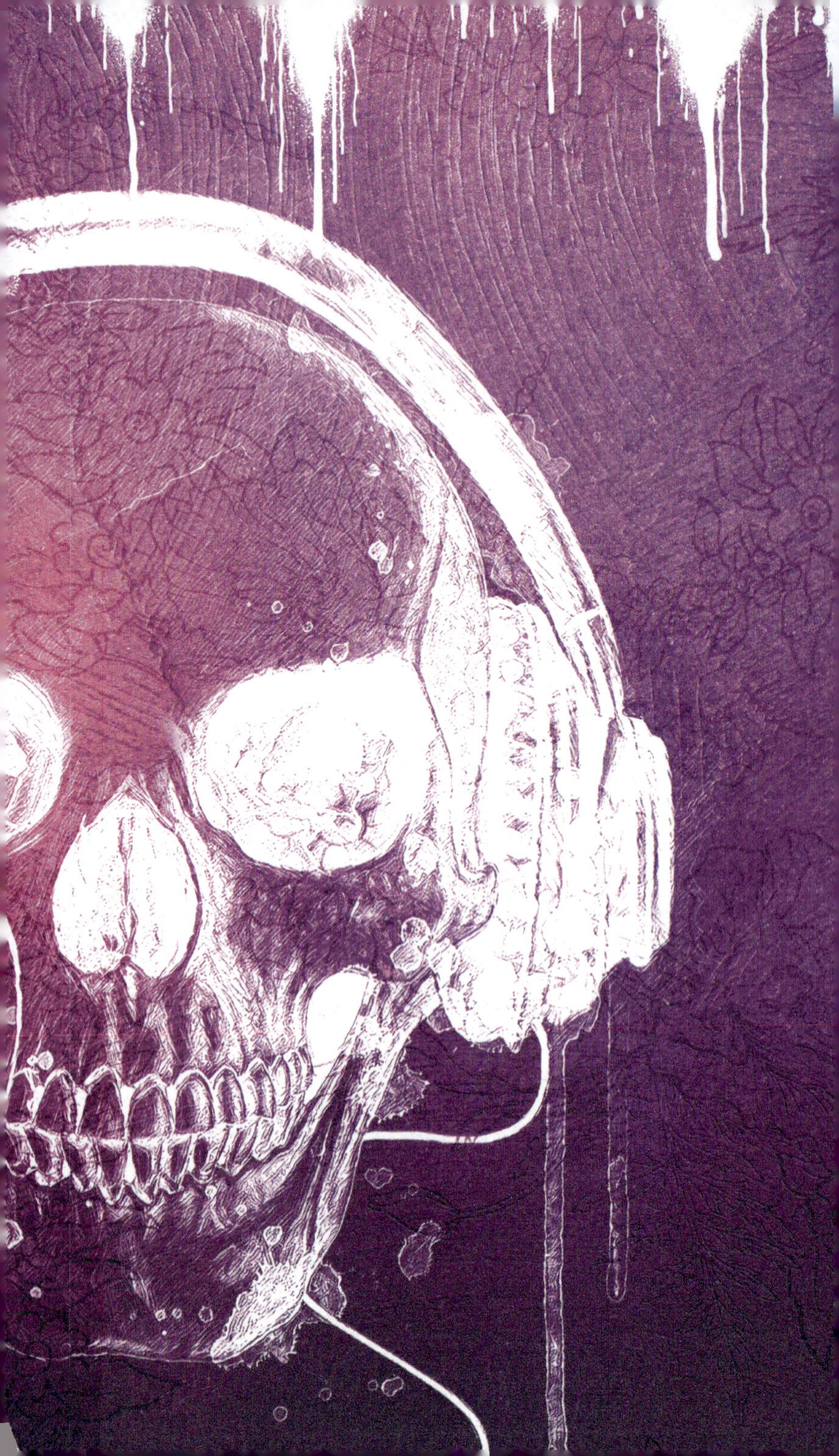

CHAPTER 16
MILES

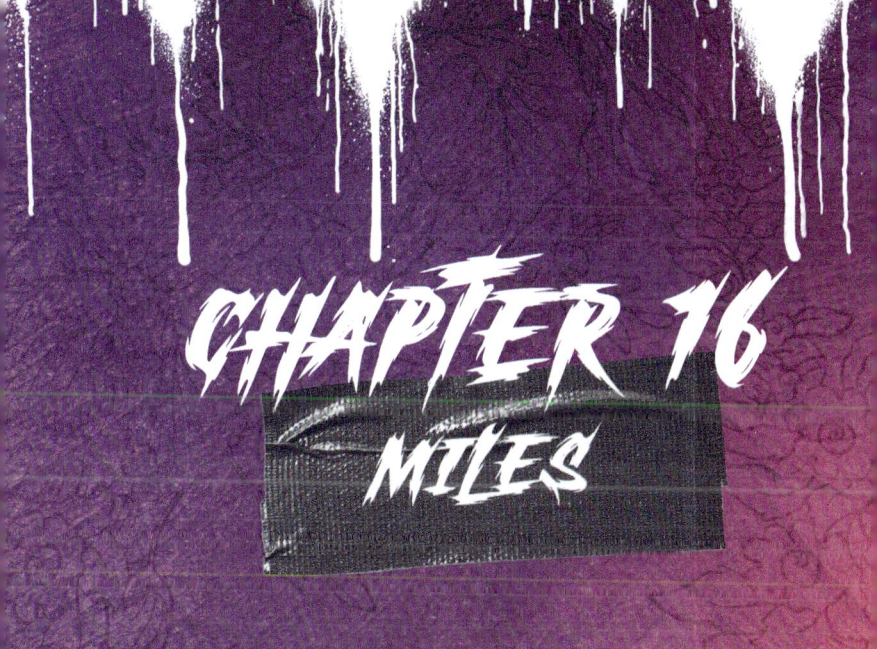

    The music is loud enough to kill my eardrums, but I need it if I'm going to be able to go through with this. Chris's noises just aren't cutting it for me and are actually turning me off, so I need the music to drown her out.

    I'm pumping slowly, making it look good. Swirling my hips, holding her legs back to give a good visual. It's when I feel a burning sensation that weighs heavily on me that I look up to see her standing in the doorway. I smirk, because she's not running. Or yelling. Nothing like the other stepmom. Just as I suspected, she's not like the rest. This was never going to work. Her eyelids grow heavy and her thighs clench together. That's the moment I start imagining it's her I'm fucking instead.

    My dick is rock-hard, throbbing with the need to come watching Violet's face. She's spurring me on and doesn't even realize it. The music stops, and I hear Chris. I push her legs back to rest on either side of her head in order to grab the remote and turn on something a bit lighter, so Violet can hear me.

"What if my stepmom comes in and sees us like this?" I whisper into Chris's ear. She groans in response, and I continue staring right at Violet's thighs rubbing together. "Should we ask her to join us?"

The way I wish she would break down those walls and join makes me want to break Chris in half. My balls tighten with a low pressure settling in my lower back. *Fuuuck, I'm getting turned on just by her watching.*

"Yes, oh god, yes," Chris moans. She's always down for a fun time.

"I think she would be too much of a prude," I reply. My eyes bore into Violet's, challenging her. Pushing her to come play with us.

I pound into Chris, rolling my hips as I do. She screams out every time I bottom out inside her, which makes Violet clench her thighs together even more. *Come on. Let go, Violet*, I scream in my head.

"She doesn't. Know. What. She's missing," Chris huffs out with each thrust of my hips as if she is catching her breath after each word.

Violet continues to hold my gaze, and I can't help pushing her more. I want that fire behind those bright eyes of hers. "Oh yeah? And what is she missing? Scream it so she can hear," I growl.

I quicken my pace, holding her stare. Her thighs rub together, trying to find that friction she's missing. *Come on, baby. Come play with me.* I'm urging her, wanting her beneath me instead of Chris.

Chris's legs shake in my hold, breaking my concentration on Violet, and I'm reminded again of the fact that it's not *her* I'm balls deep in. My dick grows soft at the thought, and I'm starting to realize I may need more of a connection, because just sex isn't doing it for me anymore. I have to pick up the pace to get through this. *Speed this up, get Chris to completion.* Then I can play with my little flower, but when I look at the doorway, she's gone. A sharp pang resonates in my chest. I grunt out a faked release as Chris spasms in my hold. When she's done, I pull out, releasing her legs. She lies there, panting, leaking onto my sheets. *I'll need to clean that up later.* Walking over to my desk, I remove the empty condom and jerk at the cool air that deflates my manhood even more. I'm disgusted with myself. This isn't how I planned for this to go. *Where is Violet? What if Shawn was right? What if I hurt her?* She's the only thing I can think of right now.

I pull on my sweatpants as Chris gets dressed. The camera continues to record. I grab it off my desk, cutting it off.

"Thanks for your help," I say, handing over her equipment.

"I'm guessing she saw, since you switched the music." She takes the black hunk of plastic out of my hands and shoves it into her bag. When she looks back at me, her lips are puckered. "You didn't get what you wanted from her, did you?"

"Why do you say that?" I ask, looking back at the empty doorway.

Chris shrugs her shoulders. "You've never given it to me like that before. You've also never asked someone else to join us." She walks to the door, but stops, unfinished with her assessment of me. "You need to figure out your shit, Miles. Before she's gone. You need to figure out what's more important to you. Her? Or getting out of here? Because she could be both, but if you choose to be selfish, you may just lose both."

She has a point, and one I need to think long and hard about. Looking out of my bedroom window,

I wait for Chris to pull out of the driveway before I go downstairs, looking for Violet. I need to talk to her.

I walk down the hall, stopping at the sound of running water. Violet's door is cracked, and curiosity takes over. I peek inside, but she's not in her room. I push the door open farther. Her reflection in the mirror that hangs over the bathroom door catches my attention. She's fully nude, dipping her toes in the bathtub with the water still running. Her hair is pulled up, exposing her neck, which is begging for me to sink my teeth into it. She submerges herself in the water, and I have a full view of her luscious ass. I just want to take a handful of it and squeeze, marking her as mine with red prints for anyone else to see.

My dick thickens in my sweats, coming back to life at the sight of her. Palming myself, I have the thought of leaving to take care of myself, until her hand disappears under the water. *Is she . . . pleasuring herself? From watching me?* Why didn't she join? I would have thrown Chris out so fucking fast to have Violet beneath me.

My muscles tense, and rage courses through my veins. She makes me so angry. The longer I stand there watching her, the more my thoughts grow sinister and spiteful. Before I can second-guess what I'm doing, I barge into the bathroom. Violet jumps, sloshing water over the edge of the tub.

"What are you doing in here?" she asks with shock and anger written all over her face.

"You watched me."

Her eyes narrow, and she definitely knows I'm up to no good.

"Please, don't stop on my account."

Her beautiful lips are set in a hard line, and she pushes her shoulders back. With closed eyes, her hand goes back to working on her clit. She's accepted the challenge. *Good girl.* My dick is hard as a rock, throbbing in my sweats. I pull myself out and fist my cock.

"Look at me, Violet. Look at me while you touch yourself." Her lids flutter open, then grow wide at the sight of me out on display for her.

She lets out a needy moan, working her hand faster. I want to touch her and pull more of those beautiful sounds from her, but I don't. We are at war here, and I'm determined to make her regret it.

We both work ourselves faster, chasing that high. Her mouth falls open in another moan as her other hand slips under the water to help herself.

"*Fuck me,*" she begs, eyes hooded with wanting.

"No touching, remember?" I say with a smirk, and her eyes flare. She's understanding it now, and it only serves to make the pride in my chest rise.

Her groans fill the air. Electricity sparks down my spine, and I work faster on my cock.

In between her panting, she breathes, "You're. An asshole."

"Good, because you're my little bitch." She comes all over her hands in the water at my words. I follow right after, making sure it lands on her neck in a string of pearls. She looks at me with her mouth wide open in shock. "You look good with a set of pearls around your neck."

"You're. A. Fucking. Asshole," she screams, drawing out the words.

Water sloshes around her as she stands. Her fists are clenched at her sides, and her chest heaves with anger. My release drips down between her breasts. *God, she's gorgeous when she's angry.*

"I never said I wasn't." I smirk, leaving her to clean herself, more satisfied than I was earlier.

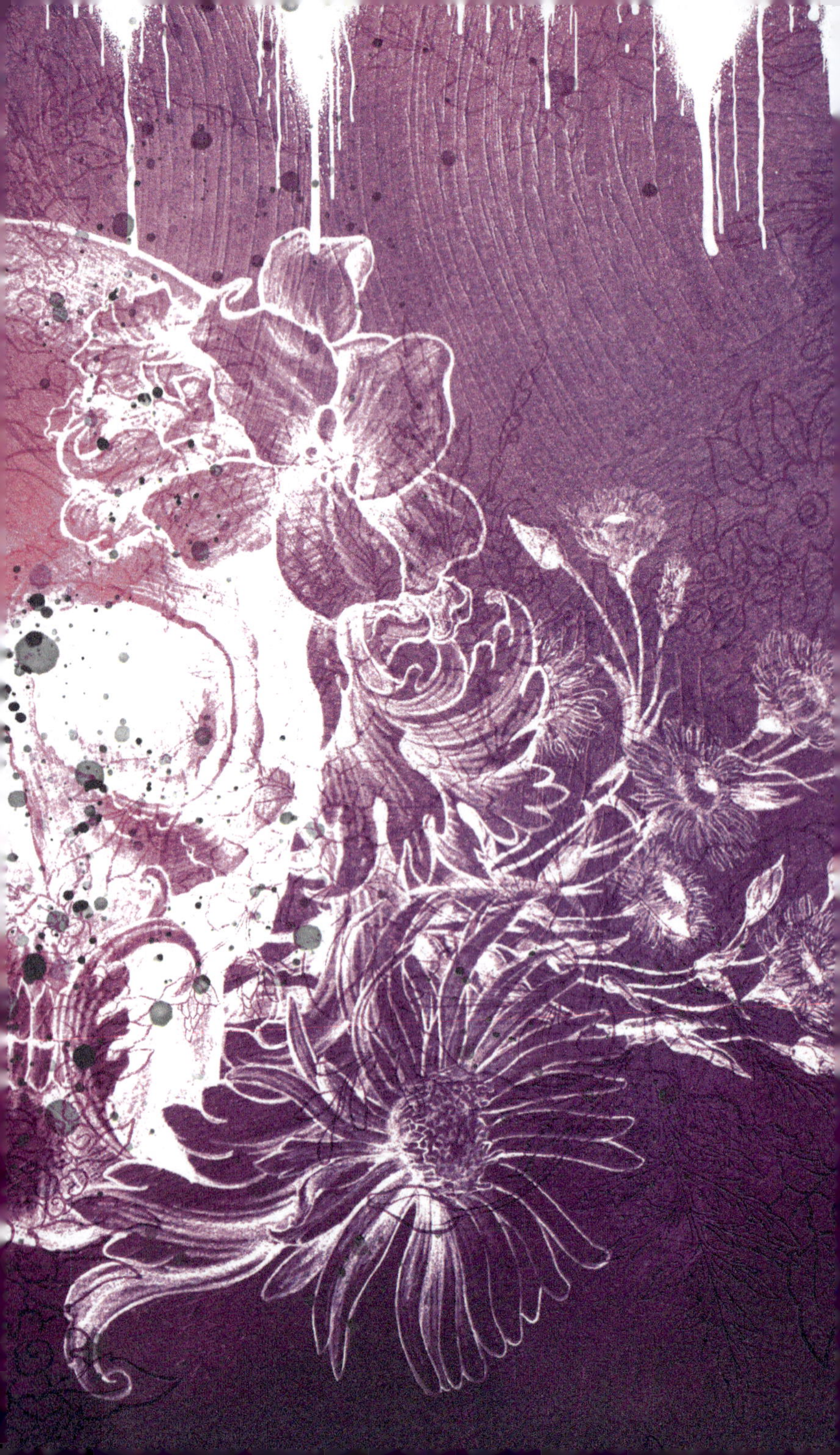

CHAPTER 17

VIOLET

Fucking Miles. He is getting under my skin, so much so that I've lost focus on what I even came here for, which is killing Wade. I haven't thought of another way to accomplish it, but I have to try harder and get more creative.

While I'm pouring my orange juice, Wade comes in ready for the day in a sharp navy-blue suit.

"How's your knee feeling, Violet?" he asks, making his to-go coffee.

Small talk, great. "It's doing a lot better, actually."

"Good. I have an event to go to tonight, and I want you to come," he says, turning toward me with his back to the counter.

"Okay, I'll take a trip to the city to find a nice dress to wear." I put the juice in the fridge, cleaning up my mess. If only all my messes were that easy.

"Make sure it's something that will make me look

good for the governor of California."

Before he fully exits the kitchen, I ask, "Do you mean revealing?"

He stops in the doorway, and without turning around, he says, "That's right."

Guess, that's the end of our conversation. If he is meeting with the governor of California, he must be trying to get in good standing with him to further his election. Will he make it to the next election? *Honestly, I hope not.* I hope he's dead before then, but I have to keep up the image until I can figure out what to do next.

I finish eating breakfast. A small granola bar, like always, with a glass of orange juice. On the way out the door after getting dressed, I see Miles walking down the hall, shirtless and ruffling his messy hair. I can't help the anger that flares inside me. *Do I hate him? I might just hate him.* Especially for the position he is putting me in, or for the sheer fact that he's enjoying torturing me.

He smirks as he passes, and I throw him a glare. He doesn't let that slide though. He corners me, caging me in with his arms on either side of my head.

"Change your fucking attitude," he commands.

This fucker. "Stay out of my way."

He leans down by the side of my face and in his warm gravelly voice says, "Not a chance, little flower." His warm breath brushes over the shell of my ear, causing a shiver to run down my spine.

Then he pushes off the wall and saunters toward me. I clench my fist. My nails dig into my palms, grounding me. *Ugh!* Why the fuck does killing someone have to be so hard? The universe is laughing at me right now. I just know it.

I drive into town and find a dress shop on the main strip. My mission is to find the nicest, most seductive dress I can find. The one I wore last time was good, but I need this one to make even Miles lose his mind. I didn't want to cross that line with him, but if that's what it takes to get him off my back, then that's what I'll do.

"Can I help you, ma'am?" The sales lady stops me at the door.

Like with most places like this, they have to size you up at the door to make sure you can afford their prices. Her name badge gleams in the light, and engraved in the metal is *Margo*.

"Marge," I say, purposely mispronouncing her name with my best Valley girl voice, and push my blonde hair over my shoulder. "I need something hot, but classy, to wear for tonight."

She has her resting bitch face on until I hold up Wade's black card. Her eyes sparkle, and her smile grows so wide I think she might break her Botox. "You got it."

She's excited to make a massive sale and will probably hand me the most expensive items in the store to try on. I don't really care as long one of them works for what I'm looking for. I'm sure Wade will be on the same page. I'm escorted to a changing room, and it doesn't take Margo long before she's handing me a stack of silky, soft dresses in varying colors. Most shades are flattering on my skin tone, but I don't feel comfortable in them. I prefer the darker hues. Thankfully, people find that classy.

I try on all the dresses, regardless of the color. All different types, shapes, styles, textures, you name it, Margo is throwing it at me over the stall door. By the time I'm finished trying all the ones she's given me, she throws one more over the door.

Out of breath she says, "This is the last one."

My chest is tight in anticipation, desperate for this to be *the one*. I slip it on over my head waiting for that aha moment, but nope. Nothing. It doesn't set the tone I'm looking for. I throw the dress back over the door with a huff of annoyance.

"Did this not work?" Margo whines from the other side of the dressing room door.

"No, Marge. It didn't," I snap, some of that California high society that I've tried so hard to get rid of slipping out. I hate that I'm feeling edgy with anxiety. That always tends to bring it out.

When I open the door to leave, Margo is fawning and schmoozing to get me to reconsider one of the other dresses she thought looked good on me. I only ignore her and keep walking. Maybe I can find another shop on this street, because I don't have time to go to another town for a dress. My hand rests on the cool metal of the shop's door when something flashes in the corner of my eye. I turn my head slowly, trying not to lose that glint that caught my attention. If the angels could pull apart the clouds above my head and have sunrays shine down on the dress on the mannequin in the window, this would be the moment they write songs about.

"Margo," I exclaim, catching her attention when I actually use her name. I never take my gaze off the dress for fear it will disappear and be a figment of my imagination.

"Yes, Mrs. Lynwood?" Margo comes up behind me, eager to please.

Let's hope she's eager enough to give me the dress off the display. Pointing to it, I say, "Margo, why didn't you give me that dress to try on?"

"I-I-I—" Margo stammers.

"I want that one in the dressing room in five minutes." I swish my hips as I make my way to the dressing room again. Once I'm inside, I shut the door and collapse on the bench, happy to give up the act. I'm crossing all my fingers and toes, hoping this will be the one I've been looking for. I need this, more than anything. She drapes it over the door, the edges shining. I strip down and pull the dress on over my head. It hugs all my curves, accentuating my hips in a tight bodycon style, but it's the top part of the dress that caught my eye. It cuts down in a V that ends right above my navel with a shimmery lace along the trim and sleeves. Last but not least, it's black, checking all my boxes. Elegant, classy, sexy, and pretty all in one to make the perfect dress.

"This is the one," I say, almost breathless as I admire the sleeves glistening in the dim lighting.

"Oh, thank god," Margo whispers under her breath, and I have to suppress a laugh. She definitely got her work in with me today.

Margo packs my dress up, wrapping it in sheer tissue paper. It rings up to almost four thousand dollars, so she got herself a pretty commission off that sale for all the hard work she did. I tried on every dress in this store, and it took me nearly walking out to find the perfect one. It's even my favorite color, *and* my size, so it was meant to be.

Once I'm back home, I go straight to my room, missing Miles altogether this time. Then I begin primping, teasing, curling, tweezing, shaving, and polishing. The bathroom fills with steam. When I walk into my room, the stream follows me out in rolling waves. My skin vibrates with anticipation, and the chill from the air makes goosebumps spring up on my arms. I slip my dress on, tease my curls, and complete my seductive ensemble with ruby-red lips. All done and ready to suck the life out of any man who challenges me.

Miles leans against my doorframe, blocking my way out. I try to push past him to go downstairs, but his stance is unwavering.

"Are you wearing that for me?" He bends over, invading my space. His warm breath fans over my collarbone. "Because if not, then you should change into your soccer mom attire, or people will begin to get the wrong idea about you."

He straightens with a smirk playing on his lips. My mouth hangs open slightly at the implication that I would dress for him. *Am I? No.* The fire burns under my skin, boiling over my neck and cheeks.

"If I were dressing for you"—I stand on my tiptoes, getting in his face—"then you would be on your knees worshiping me."

He shifts on the balls of his feet so he is looming over me. His finger trails down my cleavage, sending electricity straight to my core. "Should I call you Mommy while I praise that perfect pussy of yours?"

My jaw drops. *No, he didn't just say that to me.*

He smirks, that must have been the exact reaction he wanted out of me.

"Miles," Wade growls from behind him. Miles's spine visibly straightens, and his jaw tightens. "What are you doing?"

Miles angles himself to look between Wade and me. His face shifts from holding his smirk to an expression that is calm and collected. "Oh, I was just telling mommy dearest here how much of a slut bag she looks like in that dress."

It's not long before Miles is pushed against the wall with Wade's hand around his throat. "You remember what I told you?" Wade's teeth grit as he hisses the words. "I'll force you to . . ."

I don't hear Wade finish before Miles is pushing him off. "I know," he grumbles.

And that's the end of it. Miles walks back down the hall toward his room, then slams the door. This man communicates in slamming doors, and I know he's pissed.

"Come on, Mrs. Lynwood, our carriage awaits." Wade crooks his arm in a gentlemanly gesture for me to grab. That's not really needed here in the hallway before we go downstairs, and I suspect he doesn't want me to ask what that was all about, or about what he told Miles. "Don't worry about Miles. He's a troubled boy."

He brushes the whole thing off, and it makes my stomach twist into knots. What could he have over Miles that would make him back down like that? And so fast, without a fight?

The ride to the dinner isn't long, only an hour drive to the governor's summer home. Thankfully it's in silence, because I can't stand small talk. We arrive at a set of wrought iron gates, and they open up for the driver to pull through onto the circular paved driveway. It looks like a miniature of the White House. *I'm sure there could be some ego-stroking joke found in there.*

Wade gets out of the car, walks over to my door, and lets me out before giving me his arm again. We walk in behind another group of couples. The ones directly in front of us, I recognize them from somewhere. I just can't put my finger on it. The woman's blonde hair is pinned back in an updo, and the man's dark black hair is slicked back with gel. That's all I catch of them before we are ushered in with the other guests.

The dinner table is set with white card stock name tags etched with gold foil writing. Once I find our assigned seating, I go to pull out my chair when Wade places his hand over mine, stopping me. *Does he really have to do everything for me?* I think, but I'm taken aback when I look around and see that everyone else is standing behind their chairs as well. *This is strange.* Everyone is just standing around as if this is normal. The hairs on the back of my neck stand on end as a strange sense of foreboding washes over me. I link my forefinger and thumb around my wrist and hold it against my pelvis to ground myself discreetly. *What the fuck are we doing? Does the governor of California have his head so far up his ass that he needs to have an audience when he walks in?*

It's silent in the dining room. A pin could drop and pierce the dead air with a light ringing. The woman and man I noticed earlier stand across from us. That sensation of familiarity washes over me again, but before I can place its meaning, a burly man comes in. Everyone's head turns toward his jovial laughter. His reddened cheeks and curly white mustache jiggle along with his belly.

"Everyone sit. Sit." He acts as if no one is trained for this. Like he doesn't have them conditioned to stay standing until he tells them to sit. *Definitely an ego with this guy.*

The waitstaff are all females with short, pleated skirts and push-up corsets that make their breasts look as if they will spill over the top at any moment. My face must be showing some of my inner thoughts because Wade places his hand on my knee and gives it a little squeeze.

"Compose yourself," he whispers.

The waitresses set the plates of filet and glasses of merlot down in front of everyone. We all look toward the jolly clown sitting at the head of the table, anticipating his permission to dig in. *I guess I learn fast.* The smell of the butter and garlic mixture coming off the slabs of meat is enough to make my mouth water. My stomach growls loudly, and the king himself laughs in a boisterous manner.

"Dig in," he bellows with his arms in the air.

After everyone has eaten at least half of their meals in silence, too busy salivating over their plates, the governor bangs a gavel on the table. *I swear this guy thinks way too highly of himself.*

"Attention," he yells. There is no fuss. Everyone immediately stops talking, looking his way, but he bangs the gavel once more with a happy cheer. "Perfect! I am happy to have you all here tonight. In the matters of state, I have concerns to bring to your attention."

Murmurs around the table permeate the air as the guests try to figure out what the latest tea is and if it could possibly be about them.

The waitresses come out, pushing a man in a chair. There's a black cloth bag over his head. He's strapped down and there is no hope for him, but he thrashes in his seat regardless. I suck in a deep breath. The tightness in my chest grows even tighter with every minute that passes. Wade's hand is on my thigh again, squeezing. I look over at him, and his eyes are sharp, his brows furrowed, as if in warning to keep fucking quiet. *Why the fuck am I even here?*

My insides are flipping upside down, rolling on waves at what Governor Bryson has in store for us.

"In light of recent press releases, I'm sure everyone knows of Mrs. McIntire's untimely death." The mayor speaks with his chest out as he stands from his chair.

The murmurs around the tables grow softer as he starts talking. Everyone is on the edge of their seats, eager to know where he is going with this. The McIntire case has been all over the news at this point. He strides toward the man in the chair and pulls the sack from his head. Sharp intakes of breath draw in around the table, and a few gasps ring out. *Richard.* Copper explodes in my mouth as I bite down hard enough on my cheek to draw blood. A line of crimson drips from his forehead, and his mouth is wide in a silent scream as blood coats his lips and drips down his chin. *What the fuck did they do to him?*

"With the . . ." The governor clears his throat. "Business side of operations, it seems someone has been acting upon their own agenda. Shh, shh. I know I know," Governor Bryson coos as if soothing a crying baby. "You will only be made an example." He smiles down at Richard who begins to silently weep. "Sit him straight and grab me a mirror," he orders the waitresses, who are dressed and ready to serve him in any way that he pleases.

The man is pushed back into the chair, straightening his back.

"Now look at yourself and show everyone what they should be doing instead of betraying me." He holds the mirror up to him. "Look real hard at yourself," he orders before grabbing a fistful of Richard's hair and pulling back.

The whole top of Richard's head comes off like a hinge, exposing his brain. One of the waitresses holds the mirror up for him to see, and screams reverberate around the table. I'm glued to my chair. I haven't screamed, but the taste of copper continues to fill my mouth. Wade quits holding my thigh to intertwine his fingers and press his hands against his turned-down mouth. He seems to be handling this as well as I am. *Which is barely.*

We are all in a state of shock. My chest is still tight, and spots begin to rain down on my vision. The man vomits, and the governor laughs. My stomach twists, wanting to expel my own dinner.

"You see people?" he addresses the dinner party. "Even the brain is disgusted with itself." He turns away from the man, letting go of his hair. The top half of his head still hangs on, leaving his brain exposed.

Why did he even give us a meal if this was his goal the whole time? To what, prove a point? Then the lady next to me throws up on her half-eaten meal. I glance back up at Governor Bryson, who is grinning from ear to ear. It dawns on me then. This is what he wanted to feed us for. He's thriving on our reactions, and I wasn't going to give him that. *No, I refuse.* My insides toss and turn, but I hold the bile in my throat down.

He waves at the waitresses, and they take poor Richard away. The governor uses the gavel as if he is enacting justice in this space. "Use your fucking brains, people. If there is another fuckup like this again, I'll have all of your heads." He makes eye contact with everyone in the room. "You may now leave."

Chairs begin to scratch on the floor around me as everyone gets up to leave. I don't move from where I'm sitting because I'm still swimming in my own head over what I just saw.

"Come on, Violet," Wade commands.

I blink up at him. The blurry film over my eyes makes the world around me hazy. He offers his hand, and I grab it, leaning on him to stand. The crowd exits fast, eager to leave this mayhem behind. As soon as we step outside, the cool night air hits my face. I drag air into my lungs, relishing the feeling of breathing again.

"You wait here. I'll grab the car," Wade says before taking off.

I'm more than happy to have a moment to myself after everything I just witnessed. I have so many questions to ask Wade, but I'm also hesitant. *What do I even ask him? What do I start with? Why did you bring me here, for starters.* While I'm lost in my head, my feet guide me toward a bench near the front door.

"Hey. Mind if I sit with you while I wait for my ride?" asks a lady with a sweet, slightly southern accent.

"Yeah. Go ahead," I say absentmindedly. I glance at the woman who sits down next to me, and my heart stills in my chest. It's the women from earlier who felt so familiar. Now that she's closer and looking directly into my eyes, I know exactly who she is. "Codi."

"I was wondering when you would notice us," she says just as the man she came here with walks up beside her.

"Violet," Azrael grumbles. "We need to talk."

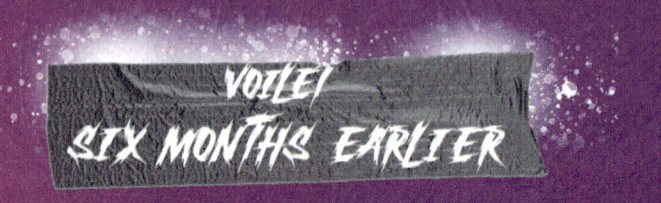

VOILET
SIX MONTHS EARLIER

If anyone can help me out of this situation, it's my sister, Anna. That's why I'm riding in a taxi down the Vegas strip. Otherwise, I wouldn't be caught dead here in this part of town. The undertone of darkness sends a shiver down my spine, and the hairs on my arms stand on end after every dark alleyway we pass.

"We're here. That will be twenty-five dollars," the driver announces.

"Are you serious?" I scoff as I pull out two crinkled-up twenties from my pocket. The last ones I have in my possession.

The driver takes them from me and says, "Get out."

I groan loudly before stepping into the downpour. I slam the door when I get out, and the driver revs the engine. This is why I hate coming to these places, because they see what I'm wearing and think I have all this money when I have none. I have to jump back before he rolls over my Jimmy Choos. The only pair of heels I was able to escape with. At least they are my favorite.

The rain beats down on me, and I pull my tan peacoat over my head to block some of the onslaught. It's two in the morning, and tourists continue to walk the streets, hooting and hollering. Not a care in the world. I wish that was me. My heels clack on the pavement as I approach the metal double doors and the neon sign that flashes above. *Darling Girls*. This has to be the place. Grabbing the handle, I pull to open the door, but it's locked.

Groaning, I yell up at the sky, "Fuck you, world." I stomp my foot, and it lands in a puddle, soaking my toes. A shiver runs down my spine, and the cold water drenches my shoe, only serving to make me more annoyed and angry.

With the heel of my palm, I beat on the metal door. I only stop when my hand begins to hurt and I've lost all hope. I don't have any money to get a hotel. I have nothing left. I walk to the curb and sit. Who cares about the rain now? The storm inside my chest is showing itself on the outside, just as I've always wanted. I fold my arms over my knees and rest my head in the crook of my elbow. I have to think of something. I can't go back to James. I can't.

It seems like hours pass before a cough makes me jerk. *Did I fall asleep? What woke me?* I glance up to find a girl with pink hair. Her head is cocked to the side, and her brows are furrowed.

"What are you looking at, freak?" I snap.

"You, obviously," she retorts.

I'm lashing out at everyone for my misfortunes, and I need to stop. She's wearing a string bikini top and a miniskirt, unfazed by the cold, damp air. I'm assuming she's one of the dancers from the club. Maybe she could help me.

"Did you just come from there?" I ask her,

pointing at the club's metal doors.

"Maybe. What's it to you?" she sneers at me.

Yeah. I've fucked up, yet again. "I need to talk to my sister."

The pink-haired girl pulls out a cig and brings the butt up to her neon-pink painted lips. Her chest rises with an inhale as she lights it. On the exhale, she blows out before asking, "Why should I help you?"

My eyes burn from the cloud of smoke that lingers, and I wrinkle my nose. At least the rain has calmed down to a light mist. I try to find the bright side as I get up from the curb and try to reason with her. A booming male voice comes from behind me, causing my spine to stiffen.

"Is this person bothering you, Codi?" he asks, and I glance back at him. His face has a row of stitches tattooed over a scar, and one of his eyes is entirely blacked out.

"I can handle myself," she scoffs at him, and he gives her a nonchalant shrug.

I'm between them, and my heart is racing in my chest. I knew my sister had gone down a different path than I had, but this wasn't what I expected. Then again, I didn't really know what to expect. The last time I saw her, she was begging on my doorstep, and I had turned her away. My chest tightens at the memory. I should have been a better sister, but I was too stuck up James's ass to care about anyone else.

"I'm just looking for my sister," I whisper to make myself smaller.

"Violet?" the scary man asks, saying my name as if he knows me.

"Yeah?" I cock my head to the side to look at him more closely, but I can't place if I've ever seen him before. "Do I know you?"

"From another life." He grins as if telling himself an inside joke and gestures for me to follow him into the club. "Come on, I'll take you to Anna."

Without another question, I obey. I follow him to the club's entrance, and he pulls out a key to unlock doors. He glances back at me before opening them with a loud screech from the rusted hinges. My eyes widen to take everything in. The floors are concrete, the walls are red brick, and the only lights are from purple and blue neon signs. Smoke still clouds the club from the patrons earlier this evening, and a man in a navy jumpsuit is mopping up a mess on the floor. I can't tell what he is cleaning up due to how dim it is in here, but it looks dark. My hands grasp each other in an attempt to suppress the shivers building in my muscles. I continue to follow the man toward the back of the club, then through a room with a ring in the center, and even farther toward the back where a set of stairs descends into a basement.

When he starts walking down into the dark, I pause. "Are you going to kill me now?"

That gets a chuckle out of him. "No, I'm done working for the night." He glances over his shoulder with an arched brow and adds, "Unless you want me to kill you."

"No. I'm good for tonight. Thanks, though, maybe next time," I answer him and fold my arms across my chest.

He chuckles again and proceeds to walk down, farther into the dark, and I follow behind him. Once at the bottom we are met with another door, which he raps on with his knuckles in a rhythm.

Knock, pause, knock, knock, pause, knock.

The door opens, and the light that streams out is bright, nearly obscuring my vision. The silhouette is tall with a lean figure, and as my eyes begin to adjust, I can see the outline of a face and long brown hair. *Anna.*

"Awe, look what the cat dragged in," Anna coos. "Thanks, Azrael. I'll take her from here."

He gives her a curt nod before heading back the way we came.

Anna places her hand on her hip and leans her forearm on the door, holding it cracked. "And what do you want?"

"Look, I know I don't deserve it, but I need your help," I beg her. I don't deserve it, and I know it, but I'm hoping she is a different person than I am.

"Come in." She steps out of the way, holding the door farther open, just enough room for me to pass through.

The strong aroma of bleach fills my lungs, and coughs begin to rack my body. I'm hunched over in a fit as Anna walks past me and sits in a chair that looks as if it were stolen from a dentist's office.

When I finish, Anna asks, "What did you do, Violet?"

My eye is still throbbing, and I'm sure it's still swollen and bruised enough for her to see. "I need your help. I've stolen from James. I needed to get out, but before I could, he caught me." I lie to her through my teeth, not wanting her to know how pathetic I am. That I gave myself a black eye.

"So you, what, stole some money from his wallet, and he gave you that shiner?"

"Worse," I admit and release a huff of air before continuing. "I forged his name and stole from his company. Now the men he works for will be after me."

Anna shakes her head. "Mm-hmm, mm-hmm, mm-hmm. Greedy."

"I know. Please help me, Anna." I get on my knees and grovel. "I know I don't deserve it from you of all people, but—"

"You're right, you don't deserve it," she interrupts, sneering down at me. "But lucky for you, I am nothing like you."

My body heats with warmth, and my eyes burn with unshed tears. I knew my sister was better than me. She will help me get out of this mess.

"But there's one condition."

"Anything, Anna. I'll do anything," I say, still on my knees for her.

"I need you to kill the man who tore us apart."

My heart seizes in my chest, and the blood in my veins runs cold.

VOILEI
PRESENT DAY

"Your sister sent us to check on you," Codi states.

"Well, you've checked on me. Are you both done?" I ask, worrying that Wade will be back with the car any minute. Anna must be worried that I'll betray her and fall in love with Wade because he has money. She doesn't know me. No one does.

"Not quite," Azrael says, picking at his face. I can see now that he's wearing a prosthetic over his scar because the makeup is starting to peel. With the contact in, he looks like he did when we were kids. "You're closer, now. You've seen what the governor of California is doing. Don't worry about him. Codi and I will take care of him, in time. Wade is still your main goal."

"But I've never killed anyone. Can't the both of you take care of him for me?" I'm nearly begging, on the verge of whining, after what I just witnessed. I may be able to bag a rich man, but killing people has never been a side hobby for me.

"You know we can't. Your sister wants you to prove your loyalty to her," Codi explains.

I know all this already. *I fucked up, but damn, killing someone?* "I keep trying and failing. Can one of you at least give me a pointer or two?"

"You have to figure that out on your own. Prove yourself. We'll be around." Codi gets up, dusting off the back of her dress.

They both hop in a car right before Wade pulls up. This time, he doesn't bother to open my door for me, and I let myself into the passenger seat. He drives us home, and we don't speak a word to each other. The silence is almost unbearable. After the hour of riding in the car with him, we finally pull into the driveway.

"Wade," I whisper as he turns off the car.

"Yes?" he asks, looking at me with a quirked brow.

"Why did you bring me tonight?" I ask the question that's been pinging around in my head the whole way home.

"Because Governor Bryson would have thought it suspicious if my wife were not there," he explains as if it's the simplest answer in the world and not like we just saw Richard with his head cut open.

"Why, so we can be a *family unit*? Then why didn't Miles come too?" I continue questioning his logic because I know there's more to it. *There has to be.*

"He's not ready for this life," Wade hisses, losing some of his straightlaced composure.

"Then why didn't you warn me first?" I ask because I can't stop pushing. My palms lie open in my lap as if I'm waiting for all the answers I need to fall into my hands so I can grasp onto them.

"I wanted to see how well you handled yourself."

I glance up at Wade as he speaks and turns in his seat toward me. His eyes take me in for the first time all night. Their path burns a trail up my thighs and my cleavage.

"You held your own tonight. I expected you to be weak, but you proved me wrong," he admits, and his hand cups my face. "I'm very proud of you."

I should be happy that I made him proud, but unease washes over me instead. His thumb brushes my cheekbone before tracing my jawline. His fingers continue along their path down my cleavage, sending an unwanted shiver through my body. "I don't think I've told you how beautiful you look in this dress." He leans in close, eyes boring into mine. "I want to rip it off your body," he growls before his lips take hold of mine. An instant sense of revulsion comes over me, and I place my hands on his shoulders. I push, but he doesn't let up. He continues kissing me, forcing his tongue down my throat. I push him again, finally breaking our lips apart.

"Stop," I say. My breaths are coming fast from the intrusion. *I can't do this. Not with him.*

"What was that?" Wade asks, and there's venom in his tone.

"I'm sorry, I can't do this." I wipe my mouth with the back of my hand, smearing my lipstick.

Wade's eyes flash with hatred, and he rubs his jaw in disbelief. "Are you denying me?"

I'm not sure how to respond in a way that won't upset him, but I try anyway. "I'm not ready for this yet. You said this was for show, and if more came along then—"

He's on top of me with his hand wrapped around my throat, cutting off my words. My hands grip his shoulders again, but this time pushing him doesn't work. He still has his hands on me, groping my breast, and before I know it, his forefinger and thumb press down over my pulse. I can hear my heartbeat in my head. The pounding is loud in my ears, and I can barely hear him when he says, "No one denies me."

I grab hold of his hand, attempting to pry his fingers off me. I need the blood flow back before I pass out. "Please, stop," I beg.

His teeth are bared, and his eyes are menacing as he glares down at me. He cups my pussy underneath my dress, igniting an unwanted need in my clit. "This is mine. I own you, Violet, and you need to learn your place."

My vision swims with spots, and my arms grow weak, falling by my sides. *Fuck you*, I think before the world around me goes completely black.

AYDEN PERRY 195

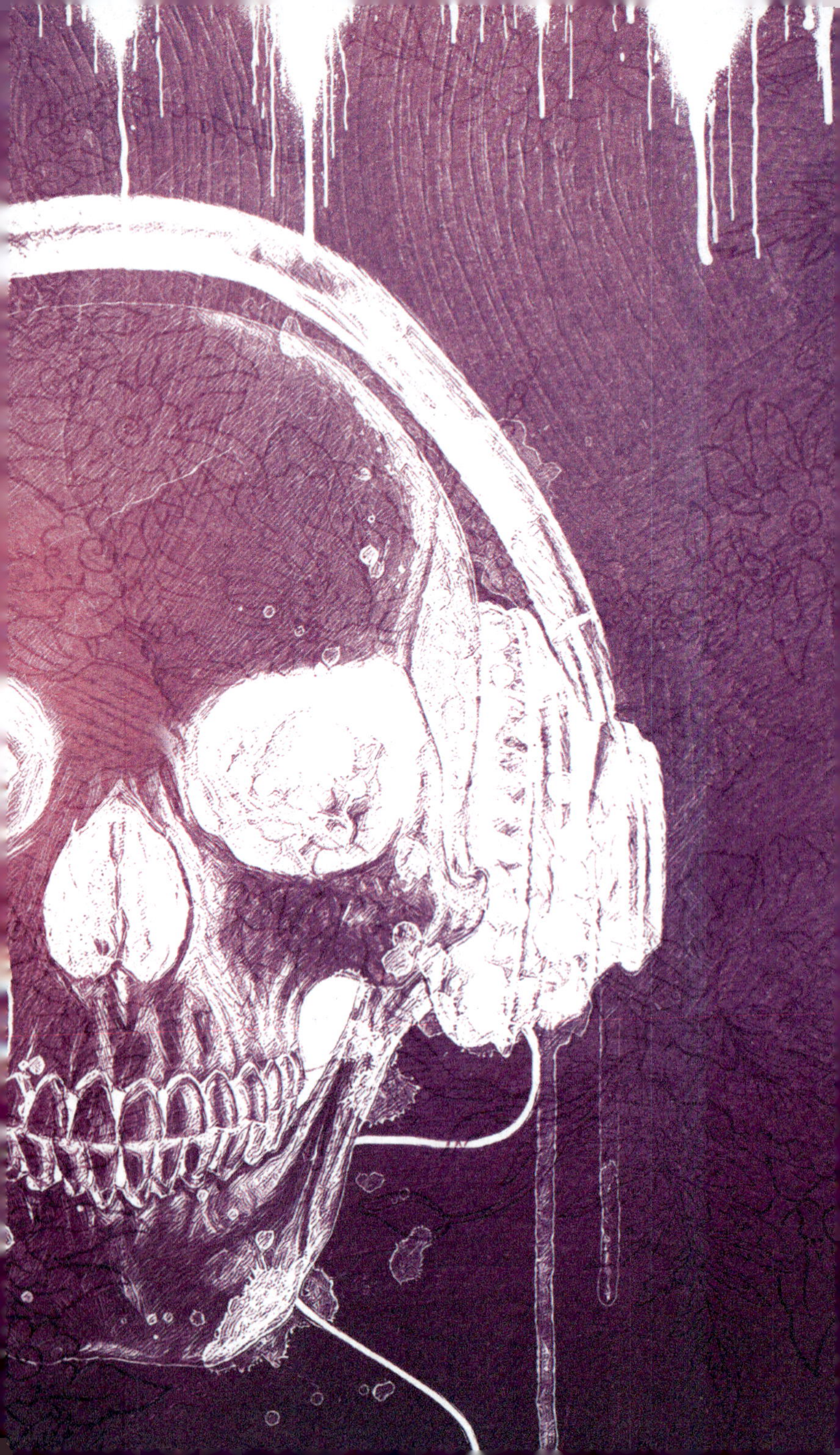

CHAPTER 18
MILES

I'm lying in bed, looking up at the ceiling, when there is a loud bang from downstairs.

"Miles," my dad screams. "Come here."

My heart rate kicks up, but I'm more angry than scared of him. *What has he fucked up this time that he needs my help?* I clench my hands at my sides as I clomp down the steps on heavy leaden feet. I'm fuming until I see Violet is in his arms. She's passed out, looking like an elegant sleeping beauty. I take the steps two at a time, racing toward them.

"What happened? What did you do to her?" The questions spill out of me, showing that I'm concerned for her more than I care to admit.

"Just take her upstairs," he says, blowing me off.

"It was the governor, wasn't it? What did he do *this* time?" I scream at him.

He only glares back at me, because he knows it's

fucked. What he is doing in his spare time will kill us all.

"Just take her upstairs," he barks out, and I grab her from him before he can drop her on the floor out of annoyance.

He doesn't care about Violet, never has. He will use her till he's done with her. And whatever she witnessed tonight, she'll never get away alive like my last stepmom did. That thought settles heavy in the pit of my stomach. Dad doesn't even spare us a second glance as he makes his way toward the kitchen and pours himself a drink.

Before I turn to leave, I ask a question I already know the answer to. "Why did you even take her tonight?"

He slams his glass down on the counter, irritated with me. "You know Governor Bryson would have his suspicions about me if I didn't."

With that, I finally give up this pointless argument and take Violet upstairs to her room. He will never change, no matter who he hurts on his path of destruction. *Selfish bastard.*

I cradle Violet in my arms. Her cheek nuzzles into my chest, but her eyes remain closed. My chest warms at the little unconscious gesture she does when she's near me. I think back to the day I found her on the trail. When I was carrying her, I could hear the inhale of her breath, and the way she clung to me. There's something about this woman I'm afraid to admit to myself. I think I may be falling for her.

Once I'm standing in front of her bedroom door, I'm regretting letting her go before I ever put her down. My stomach is in knots thinking about what she might've seen tonight. I need to try harder to convince her to leave. I nudge the door open with my foot, and I'm hit with her scent of lilacs and honey. A smell that's all her. One I'll never be able to forget.

She nuzzles into my chest again, mumbling something inaudible in her sleep. *What are you saying, Violet?* I want to know what she talks about in her sleep. Her lids are still closed, and the light shimmer on them is just as perfect as it was before she left this evening. The only thing out of place is her lipstick, which makes my blood boil. This wasn't the work of Governor Bryson, this was my father. *That fucker.* What Chris said plays in my mind as I lay her down on the bed. *You need to figure out what's more important to you.* I grab the light cover at the end of her bed and drape it over her legs. When I turn to leave, I hear her whisper again. I freeze, straining my ears to catch her words, but nothing comes. My chest tightens with disappointment. I let out an exasperated breath and turn to leave, giving up on hearing what she's saying.

"Miles," she murmurs in her sleep.

My heart lodges in my throat and a husky, "Yeah?" comes out. *She wants me?*

She doesn't say anything else, and I can't wait any longer before I'm climbing into bed behind her. Hooking my arm around her waist, I pull her to my chest. Her hair presses against my nose, and I draw in a deep breath, inhaling the sweet scent of her. She hums and presses herself closer to me. I'm unsure of how long we've lain like this with her breaths slow and even. My eyes might have closed for a moment. I'm not really sure, but my brain is suddenly awake.

"Violet?" I call her name to see if she's awake.

She hums at me in response. My senses are heightened with her body pressed so close to mine. I run my fingertips down her arm, the material of her dress as soft as I remember her skin being. She's still in the dress she was wearing to the dinner last night. I never got the chance to take it off her.

"Violet," I say her name again, and this time she doesn't respond. I take this opportunity to tell her everything I want to say, because I know she won't remember. "You have to leave. Don't stay here. I don't know what it is you're looking for, but the money, the status, none of it's worth it. It's not worth risking your life over." I run my hand over her hair, tucking a stand behind her ear. She huffs and rolls over, snuggling into my chest. "You're beautiful, Violet. You can have any man you want, and I think I'm falling for you." *Fuck, emotions. What the fuck am I doing? What the fuck is this woman doing to me?*

I ease out of the bed, unraveling her from my arms. She still doesn't wake. Her breathing is an easy rhythmic cadence. *Good.* I pull her throw blanket up higher to cover her arms, and I push her hair away from her face again. Without much resistance left against this woman, I lean over to plant a kiss on her temple. "Night, little flower."

I toss and turn in bed the rest of the night. My body aches from the lack of sleep. *Can I not sleep without her now?* I groan at myself and this whole situation. Giving up on sleep, I get ready for school. Now that spring break is over, I can't fuck around anymore. I have to put all my focus on getting out of here and getting into my dream college. Violet is only serving to distract me.

Pulling up to the old catholic private school, I'm reminded of why I hate being here. The cliques are grouped together in packs, ready to pounce on anyone that they see is below them to tear them down further. It only serves to make them feel better about how awful their own lives are. I thought we left that kinda shit in junior high, but nope. Their shitty behavior followed us here to high school. The only newer development is that they hang over me, begging to suck my dick because I bulked up. Ever since sixth grade when I met Shawn, we've been on the outskirts. The mysterious loners who could fuck you up. We could fit in, but we choose not to with our fuck-off demeanor. No more was I the mayor's hidden-away, strange kid. No. Now I'm the bad boy women drool over.

"Hey, Miles," Christina calls, waving her hand in the air.

Christina, being the most grounded out of all of us, is dressed in her Hilltower cheerleading outfit. Gold and black. Wildcats. "Whoa, go team," I say with sarcasm dripping from my lips.

She slaps my arm. "Shut up. You're here early."

I rub the back of my neck. "Yeah, I couldn't sleep. Though I didn't expect the both of you here this early either. What's up?"

Chris lifts one of her shoulders in a half shrug. "Same. Couldn't sleep, so I called Shawn."

"Home life still a fate worse than death?" I ask, because I feel bad I've been all about myself lately and haven't asked about her life. She nods but doesn't say anything further, effectively dropping the subject.

"So how did it work out for you?" Shawn raises a brow at me.

"If you're talking about my stepmom, not well. She's still around." I look down at my combat boots and kick the dirt on the ground.

"Ha! I knew it." Shawn laughs. *Mischievous little fuck.*

"What do you even know?" I ask, trying to

throw him off.

"I know how you looked on that tape, and dude, you have it *bad*."

"Just shut up," I say, hoping he will drop it. I know I have it bad. Violet infiltrates every part my mind and causes me to lose focus. Thankfully, he leaves it alone and goes back to what he was doing before I walked up.

We sit on the concrete bench in the middle of the courtyard. Christina scrolls through her socials, Shawn is on his laptop, and I sit on top of the table, watching everyone. I find them interesting. How they act when certain people come around them. Especially when they plaster on their fake masks to appease the social crowds they have chosen in order to avoid being a pariah.

A girl with long black hair and fishnets hides in the shade, reading a book. That's Christina's stepsister, Evalyn. She's more of a loner than we are. We are too much for her apparently. Doing things like partying while also being an outcast is an anomaly. Christina's sister is innocent, extremely goth, and introverted to the point of talking to the spiders in the trees. When people try to pick on her, Christina jumps in right away, ready to take the world down.

"Your sister is looking cute today, Christina," Shawn says, and I can't tell if he means it or if he just playing with Christina. *Probably both.*

She takes it literally because she smacks him over the head pretty hard. "Don't even think about it."

He rubs his hand through his hair, paying special attention to where Christina just knocked some sense into him. "What? I was just joking."

She folds her arms over her chest. "Uh, huh. Sure you were."

The bell for class sounds, and we separate to walk

only serves to make them feel better about how awful their own lives are. I thought we left that kinda shit in junior high, but nope. Their shitty behavior followed us here to high school. The only newer development is that they hang over me, begging to suck my dick because I bulked up. Ever since sixth grade when I met Shawn, we've been on the outskirts. The mysterious loners who could fuck you up. We could fit in, but we choose not to with our fuck-off demeanor. No more was I the mayor's hidden-away, strange kid. No. Now I'm the bad boy women drool over.

"Hey, Miles," Christina calls, waving her hand in the air.

Christina, being the most grounded out of all of us, is dressed in her Hilltower cheerleading outfit. Gold and black. Wildcats. "Whoa, go team," I say with sarcasm dripping from my lips.

She slaps my arm. "Shut up. You're here early."

I rub the back of my neck. "Yeah, I couldn't sleep. Though I didn't expect the both of you here this early either. What's up?"

Chris lifts one of her shoulders in a half shrug. "Same. Couldn't sleep, so I called Shawn."

"Home life still a fate worse than death?" I ask, because I feel bad I've been all about myself lately and haven't asked about her life. She nods but doesn't say anything further, effectively dropping the subject.

"So how did it work out for you?" Shawn raises a brow at me.

"If you're talking about my stepmom, not well. She's still around." I look down at my combat boots and kick the dirt on the ground.

"Ha! I knew it." Shawn laughs. *Mischievous little fuck*.

"What do you even know?" I ask, trying to

throw him off.

"I know how you looked on that tape, and dude, you have it *bad*."

"Just shut up," I say, hoping he will drop it. I know I have it bad. Violet infiltrates every part my mind and causes me to lose focus. Thankfully, he leaves it alone and goes back to what he was doing before I walked up.

We sit on the concrete bench in the middle of the courtyard. Christina scrolls through her socials, Shawn is on his laptop, and I sit on top of the table, watching everyone. I find them interesting. How they act when certain people come around them. Especially when they plaster on their fake masks to appease the social crowds they have chosen in order to avoid being a pariah.

A girl with long black hair and fishnets hides in the shade, reading a book. That's Christina's stepsister, Evalyn. She's more of a loner than we are. We are too much for her apparently. Doing things like partying while also being an outcast is an anomaly. Christina's sister is innocent, extremely goth, and introverted to the point of talking to the spiders in the trees. When people try to pick on her, Christina jumps in right away, ready to take the world down.

"Your sister is looking cute today, Christina," Shawn says, and I can't tell if he means it or if he just playing with Christina. *Probably both.*

She takes it literally because she smacks him over the head pretty hard. "Don't even think about it."

He rubs his hand through his hair, paying special attention to where Christina just knocked some sense into him. "What? I was just joking."

She folds her arms over her chest. "Uh, huh. Sure you were."

The bell for class sounds, and we separate to walk

to our classes.

I sit through Spanish, Algebra, and English in a daze. Violet is constantly on my mind, and I can't stop. *Do I need to try and fuck her out of my system?* I've tried that already, twice, and it did nothing. It only made me want her more.

When the bell rings for lunch, I'm thankful to finally get out of these desks that trap me in daydreams of her. Ones I'd rather not have while in the middle of classes.

Collecting my tray of square pizza with a side of corn, I plop down beside Shawn. Over half of the lunch period goes by before I ask him where Christina is. I need her to talk some sense into me again. What she said about choosing what I want before it's too late plays over and over in my mind. Violet is my stepmom for crying out loud. *Can I really get what I want? Socially, it's unacceptable, but do I really care?*

"You didn't hear, man?" Shawn asks, bewilderment clear on his face.

"No?"

"Where have you been? It's been all anyone has talked about," Shawn says, pulling his phone out of his pocket. He faces the phone toward me, and I have to stare for a while before understanding what I'm seeing.

Someone took a photo of Christina and her sister from over the top of a bathroom stall. Evalyn's face is clearly etched with pleasure, and Christina is on her knees, pushing Evalyn's skirt up.

"They were expelled," he says before taking the phone away and slipping it back into his pocket. "Yeah, man. That's exactly how I looked too."

"The fuck! When was it taken? What happened to the person that had this photo?" As many times as I have been caught with a women's mouths on my dick in the school bathrooms, no one ever expelled me.

"The girl was only given detention since they are of legal age, and apparently, she's been keeping this photo since the beginning of the year, waiting for Chris to come at her again. The girl's been bullying Evalyn. Remember when I told you Chris was having problems at home?"

"Yeah?" I ask, waiting for him to tell me more.

"It was about her and her stepsister getting caught," Shawn explains.

"No shit?" I say with an inflection as if I didn't already know. It just wasn't my place to say anything. Chris would have told us when she was ready.

"Yeah, seems we have some pearl clutchers around here." Shawn's voice rises. "Fucking prudes. This is a hate crime."

"Hey," one of the teachers in the lunchroom calls out, glaring right at Shawn. "Watch your mouth, Mr. Cromwell."

What am I going to do? Who am I going to ask for advice now that Christina is gone? I hate myself for only thinking of my messed-up situation. I can't imagine what Christina must be going through right now. I've known for a while that Chris loves her sister. She's her stepsister, so I never saw the problem. She never actually said it, but I could read between words she never spoke aloud. Her parents are pretentious assholes and think their image is everything. With that thought, Chris might be helping me out more than she intended to today.

The rest of the school day goes by in a blur, and by the end, I have a hard time keeping my eyelids open. When the final bell rings, I head out to the parking lot to find Shawn leaning against my Jeep.

"Hey, what's up?" I greet Shawn.

"I just wanted to make sure you knew about the

bot meet this weekend."

I knew, and I also know that I need to be on my A game. The last meet of the season is coming up in three weeks, and I can't fail. The grand prize is what I need to get out of this place and follow my dreams. Where I can run away from my father's funds. Where I won't be held over the fire and be pushed and manipulated to do his bidding anymore.

"Miles? You going?"

"Yeah, of course. You know I wouldn't miss that for the world."

"Okay." Shawn gives me a nod. "Let me know if you need any more help with your robot."

"I will, man. Thanks," I say before getting into my Jeep and heading home.

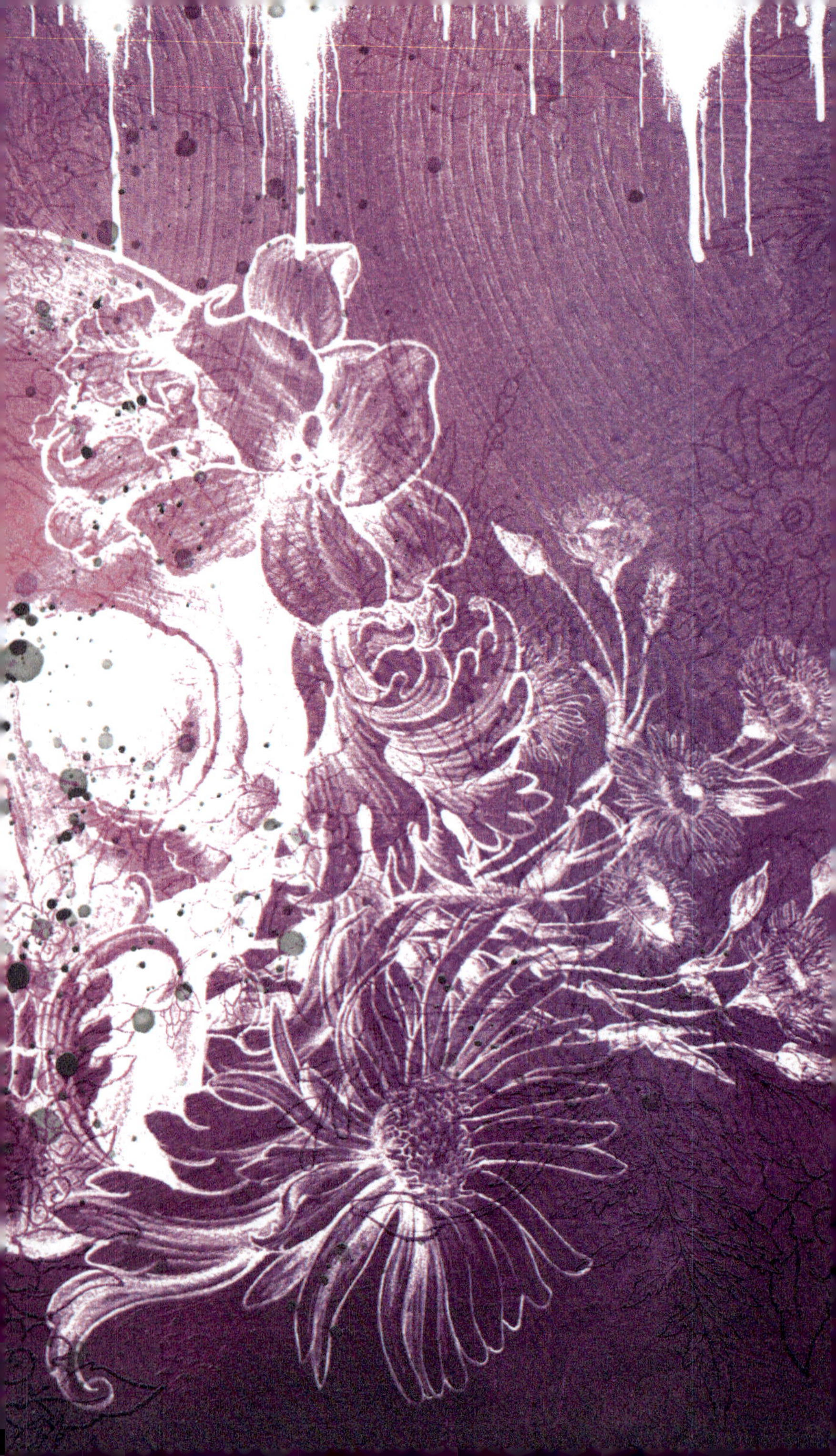

CHAPTER 19
VIOLET

After last night, I need to speed up the plan of killing off Wade. The plan to leave is imperative, and I can't keep letting my stepson get under my skin. I grab a bag of dirt, and I carry it to the back of the house. My in-progress flower bed is dug up and ready to be filled. I don't care if they think I'm a gold digger, because I'll be long gone before they find out. I'll leave Miles with violets as the only thing to remember me by.

I pack in the filler and place the seeds. Once I'm done with my work, I head back toward the house to shower. Miles hasn't come home from school yet, but at least Wade is home. He's probably in his office. I can go talk to him about the girls' getaway weekend with Dani. I should really call her. It's been a while since we've talked.

I walk upstairs, and Wade is right where I expected him to be. He's hunched over his desk full of papers, probably reading a new bill that's trying to be passed. I knock on the doorframe to get his attention.

Wade looks up from his papers for a moment before waving me in. "Violet. Is there something you wanted to talk about?"

He's back to his hard demeanor I see. *Come on, Violet, you can do this.* I take a seat in front of his desk. I can't look him in the eye for fear of seeing that menacing person I saw in his car when he grabbed me and told me he owned me. *Stop, Violet. Stop thinking about it.* This is the only thing I have left. *Pull yourself together.* "I was hoping you didn't have any plans for me this weekend."

He purses his lips before responding, "Nothing that I know of."

"Well," I start off shyly. "I was wondering if it would be okay to go on a girls' trip with Dani for the weekend."

"Where will the both of you be going?" he asks. I thankfully have this already thought out.

"Just the next town over. Some light girl hangout time and pampering. Nothing the media will have a field day over or anything. I wouldn't want to ruin your image." *Pull it back in, Violet.* The sarcasm is leaking from the corner of my mouth. "I just haven't seen Dani in a while and I thought . . ." I trail off. *Shut up, Violet.* My eyes are still cast down as if I'm a child ready to be scorned, but he surprises me.

"I don't see why not. You've done an amazing job so far," he says, without giving me any more attention. When I glance up, he's already back to his work.

"Really?"

"You have been hospitable with everything I've asked of you." He looks at me with one dark brow arched. "You haven't asked me anything else about the dinner with the governor of California. Which I hope remains under lock and key," he says, then that menacing flash in his eyes comes back. "I'd hate it if anything happened to you."

I stare at him with my mouth slightly unhinged. "Is that a threat?" That didn't take long. I was wondering when he would show his true colors again.

"Not unless you want it to be," he says, steepling his fingers with his elbows resting on the desk.

My heart is lodged in my throat, and I swallow, trying to resolve my feelings of uncertainty. "I understand."

I stand to leave and when I get to the doorframe Wade calls out, "Enjoy your girls' trip, Violet."

I don't look back as I continue down the hall toward my room.

With my bag lightly packed for the girls' weekend, I walk down to my car. Wade is in his office, pouring over papers, and Miles is still not home. It makes leaving a lot easier for me. What if I just leave and never come back? The men I stole from will come after me, then there's Miles. The thought of Miles hanging out with his girlfriend, blaring music, invades my mind. His toned abs glistening with sweat as his hips rock against her. That prominent Adonis belt that I just want to sink my teeth into. My stomach is alight with butterflies, but my mind lingers in a dark place. *I shouldn't be this way. I shouldn't even think this way.* Jealousy is never a good look, *especially* not over my stepson.

I hold my key over the handle, and the doors to

my black Audi unlock. The one Wade bought me as a gift after my other car finally died out. I'd bought it cheap with cash only, so I hadn't expected much from it. It had served its purpose. It got me here.

I throw my travel bag into the back seat harder than I anticipated because it falls off the seat and onto the floorboard.

"Fuck," I whisper under my breath. *Focus, Violet. Don't let emotions get in the way.*

I slide onto the cushioned leather seats and start the car up with the press of a button. The lavish life of luxury. Rubbing my palms over the silky, smooth steering wheel, I'm reminded of what I must do and back out of the drive.

The smooth pavement under the wheels lasts a good five minutes before I hit the gravel-paved one-way road. I turn down the side path I found when I'd lost track of time and stumbled upon it on my way home. It's wide enough for a car to go about a mile deep before the trees close in and begin to scratch up the paint. I drive onto the well-beaten path, just far enough before I start damaging the car. After turning off the engine, I climb into the back seat.

My travel bag on the floorboard looks how I feel. Defeated and thrown around. My emotions and my head are all over the place. *Snap out of it.* I smack my head, trying to get my priorities straight. After a deep breath to calm my nerves, I pull out my hiking jeans and thick jacket. I pull on the suffocating layers. The lack of air circulating in the car has beads of sweat collecting along my hairline. The muggy heat outside only intensifies the feeling of being smothered. I take slow deep breaths to trick my mind into thinking I'm cooling myself off before pulling on my thick black combat boots.

There's a small loop of fabric on the top of the

back seat. Once I locate it, I pull it down and climb into the trunk. The lack of light makes it difficult to find the quick release. I should have prepared better rather than done this on a whim. My hands touch every surface until I've located the bar, and I pull. The trunk fills with a cool breeze.

My boots crunch on the dead, dry grass, and I shake my hair out. The cool air runs over the sweat along my neck, bringing down my temperature a fraction. *All this to prevent the scratch marks on the paint*, I think to myself before letting out a frustrated huff.

The long strands stick together at the nape of my neck, making me even more hot. I run my hands through the clumped strands before pulling them up into a high pony. *Almost ready.* The last thing I need is in the spare tire hatch. A tube of Vaseline. Gotta protect my face. I read online that wrestlers use it to control the cuts and bleeding. Let's hope they are right. The foliage and trees are thick and will take me a while to get through. I know I won't come out scratchless, but I need it to be the bare minimum to cover up later.

Before locking up the trunk, I grab the tarp and spread it over as much of the back of the car as I can. The material is hard plastic, making it difficult to open up with one person, so I do my best. I doubt anyone will come this far into the woods, but one can never be too cautious when they are on a mission to kill their husband.

The trek back to the house is a long one. The twigs and dead leaves crunch under my feet as I maneuver under branches. One smacks me right over my cheek, and a fresh sting blooms in its wake. With one hand, I push the stubborn branch out of my way, and with the other, I swipe at the pain on my cheek. A warm liquid coats my fingertips, and I peer down at them to see blood. *Great. That shit Vaseline trick didn't work.*

My steps are loud, but thankfully my goal isn't to be silent, only to not be seen. The sun has set after two hours of walking. It takes another fifteen before I finally make it to the tree line surrounding the house. I let out a deep breath from exhaustion. I only drove five minutes down the road, but it takes way longer than I thought walking through the woods. My face didn't make it unscathed, but at least I didn't fall in a hole or trip and sprain an ankle. I need to be ready to run if this doesn't go as planned.

I quickly sprint to the back of the house and edge my way around to the front. Wade's black Audi and Miles's two-door Jeep are in the driveway. I glance up at the windows, and the lights are out, except for the ones coming from Miles's room. *Good, he is right where I need him to be.* At least that part is going as planned. Now I only need Wade to be asleep and not still working in his office. That would make everything so much easier. The only thing that will grace me with more luck is if Miles is distracted enough for me to slip out again. Then my chest tightens at the thought of him with the blonde girl again. *Fucking focus.*

Once this is all done, I'll be on a real girl's trip of one. Me, myself, and I in a hotel with a hot tub and a tall glass of wine.

I press in the code to the keypad, and the numbers don't light up. *Fuck you, Miles. I have a backup plan.* I run my hand over the top of the door seal, but I come up empty. *I left a spare here for this reason. Where the fuck is it?* My only thought is that maybe Miles saw it and decided to mess with me by moving it. I lift up the door mat, and again, nothing. I grind my teeth together to contain the frustration that is slowly building, but not even that helps. In my moment of anger, I kick around a few rocks, trying to come up with another plan. *What do I do?* I need to stop before someone comes to find out where all the noise is coming from.

Then my foot hits a rock with a hollow thunk. I stop in my tracks. *What the hell?*

I lift the fake rock and underneath is the spare key Wade made for me. *That fucker! I knew it.* I groan low, releasing some of that pent-up tension still coursing through my veins. *Focus.* I need to focus.

Get in, kill Wade. That's the goal. Then I can spend my night relaxing in the hot tub and ease all this stress I've been carrying around.

Picking up the silver key, the weight of the cool metal is like a boulder in my palm. The heaviness matches the way my insides feel right now. *This is it. I can do this.* I push it into the lock and twist until there is an audible click. The door doesn't creak when I open it. This expensive-ass house, I would hope it wouldn't. But as in every scary movie it would be just my luck that the door would creak before the final moment. *Is this my final moment? I sure hope not.*

There's a slight bass throb coming from upstairs. *Perfect.* Mentally, I'm rubbing my palms together and shoving down any excessive thoughts that try to spring up. When I walk toward the stairs, I step softly—heel toe, heel toe—until I make it to the carpeted staircase. My palms are sweating and my heart races. *I can do this.*

As soon as I place my foot on the bottom step, a soft shuffle from the carpet fibers on the second floor catches my attention. If I can hear it over the bass coming from Miles's room, then whoever it is must be close. I quickly race underneath the staircase and into the first-floor hall. My pulse pounds heavy in my ears, but I'm able to hear the thumps coming from the stairs. *Thumps!* my mind screams. Which means multiple pairs of feet. I can't stay underneath this staircase for long without getting caught. I race on the toes of my boots, trying not to make a sound as I run to the basement. The knife in my utility pocket slaps against my thigh. Once I open the door and close it behind myself, I rest my forehead on the cool wood. *I can't do this.*

My eyes sting as I bare my weakness. *Fuck, fuck, fuck.* I want to cry because I'm nothing but a fucking failure. I'm withering in my own self-loathing, so I don't notice the footsteps on the concrete stairs behind me, or when the husky voice near my ear breathes my name, until it's too late. His hand covers my mouth pulling me down farther into the abyss.

"I knew you were up to no good." His lips press against the hollow spot behind my ear.

A rush of warmth fills my core, and my head naturally tilts to the side, giving him better access. *What the fuck is wrong with me?*

His lips graze over my pulse, and I know he feels it racing, because the pressure of his mouth against my skin curves into a smile. He whispers, "Are you scared, little flower?" My thighs automatically clench together, and I groan into his hand. *Fuck.* My insides are screaming to be filled.

The light in the basement cuts on, and brightness sears my pupils, making me squint as I wait for them to adjust.

"Where's Miles at?" a man at the top of the stairs asks.

Miles's arm wraps around me, gripping me tighter as he pulls us into a utility closet. He closes the accordion door, hiding us, and the hand covering my mouth grips my cheeks. I think he's scared too. My suspicions are confirmed when he fiercely whispers in my ear, "Stay, fucking quiet."

I nod, but his hand doesn't move. I'm grateful for

it when I look through the slats in the door. During our exchange in the dark, I missed who was in the room with us. In the middle of the basement, a naked woman hangs with chains wrapped around her wrists. She's one of the women from the first charity event, something Davis. My mind races trying to piece this together, but I can't fathom it. *Why?*

"He probably went back up to his room when he finished doing what I asked of him," Wade says, talking to a group of men trailing behind him. All of them in matching black robes, but their hoods cover their faces. "He doesn't necessarily enjoy this part."

"Won't he be taking over for you, though? Will he be able to accomplish what you have done for us?" one of the men asks him.

"He will come to terms with it," Wade says, but his jaw flexes in annoyance, and Miles's arm tightens around me.

He doesn't want this. My chest tightens for him at that newfound information. I grip his forearm and rub it to give some solace, some reassurance. Transferring my understanding and sympathy for him into my touch. His grip on me loosens a fraction as he relaxes.

A sharp slap against flesh rings out, breaking us from our moment.

"Emily, you have been chosen," Wade says. He lands another slap over Emily's cheek, and a groan leaves her lips.

She blinks a few times before her eyes go wide with understanding. The chains rattle as she thrashes, drowning out her words. Her feet dangle over a bucket of water. I know, because the concrete floor is turning a darker shade with each kick she makes. Liquid sloshing over the sides.

"It's okay, Emily, we'll make this quick for you,"

Wade says with a calm demeanor.

It's only when the chains stop rattling, and Emily's face remains contorted in a scream, that I realize no words are actually coming from her. A hoarse, cracked sound, but no actual words. My breath catches in my throat as I remember Richard's silent screams. Miles grips me tighter. Wade's smile is one of wicked delight. He's enjoying this. My insides twist in disgust for this man. "You know why they blindfold prisoners in the executioner's chair?"

The woman shakes her head, tears falling down her cheeks.

"Because their eyes pop out."

She thrashes harder against the chains, and the men who surround her laugh hysterically. *Fucking assholes.* I move forward, clenching my fists, wanting to take every single one of these men out, but Miles holds me in place. He's the only one tethering me to reason. If it weren't for him, I'd be strung up alongside Emily.

Wade's finger hovers over a button on a black remote in his hand, holding it up to Emily's face, antagonizing her. "The electricity will course through you at a low voltage as we take our pleasures from you," he drawls, but Emily's not hearing it. She shakes her head, and Wade grips her cheeks to hold her steady. "If you don't cooperate this will take longer than it needs to." She lets out a whimper before Wade announces, "All right, line up." The men hoot and holler.

My stomach twists into knots, because this is exactly what Anna wanted me to witness. Heaves rack my body, and Miles continues to hold me.

"Close your eyes, now," Miles breathes against the shell of my ear. He doesn't have to tell me twice. I close my eyes immediately. I wish he could cover my ears as well. His fingers trace the seam of my jeans, a calming sensation that causes the muscles in my abdomen to relax.

The sounds of electricity, voltage, chains rattling, and water sloshing fills the room. My muscles tense and Miles says, "We are the only ones here. Just focus on my hand and my voice, Violet."

He runs his lips over my pulse, pressing a soft kiss there. My chest and face heat at his words. This seems wrong, but I can't deny the olive branch he's offering in this moment. His fingers slide down farther, distracting me from everything that's happening outside this closet. I beg to forget everything as I lean back against his chest and feel his hard length press into the curve of my ass. My hands rest against his muscular thighs, and I squeeze them, wanting more. He dips his fingers down lower, finding my sensitive nub and circling it. I'm drenched, soaking my panties. I can't move or open my eyes for fear of what my brain will do when this all doesn't seem like a dream any longer and my morals come crashing down around me. The rational part of my brain is screaming for him to stop while my body aches for more. *None of this is real. It's all in my head.*

I lift my hips, begging him to fill my needy cunt, but our bubble of escapism bursts. I'm broken from our warm, safe space, and Miles pulls his hand from my pants. My lips turn down in a pout behind his hand. I'm going to mentally torture myself for that later.

"That should be good, boss. Her flesh is starting to burn," says one of the mayor's henchmen.

"We're done here." I open my eyes as Wade turns to leave, and his little cult follows him. "I'll see you all out and have Miles take care of this mess."

The door to the basement closes before Miles is pulling me out, removing his hand from my mouth. I know this is not a good time to ask him questions. Emily hangs in the middle of the room as blood runs from her neck down the front of her body.

I scrunch my nose at the smell of burned flesh, but I'm barely given enough time to take it in before Miles is pushing me up the stairs, and fast. Not that I want to spend any more time down here anyway. I don't want to inspect Emily any further and find out why they were saying she was starting to burn. He's looking around the corners and leading me toward the back door. When we get there, he pushes me out.

"Run, Violet." The look in his eyes is one of pity. I have a moment of hesitation, but Miles's jaw flexes. He doesn't yell but instead hisses at me in a sharp whisper, "*Fucking* run."

My heart speeds up again, and adrenaline courses through my veins. Doing what I do best, without wasting another moment, I run.

The pounding of my footsteps echoes in my head all the way back to my car. Those words will haunt me, forever. Knowing I can't this time. The fact I can't fully run away weighs heavy on my shoulders.

AYDEN PERRY 219

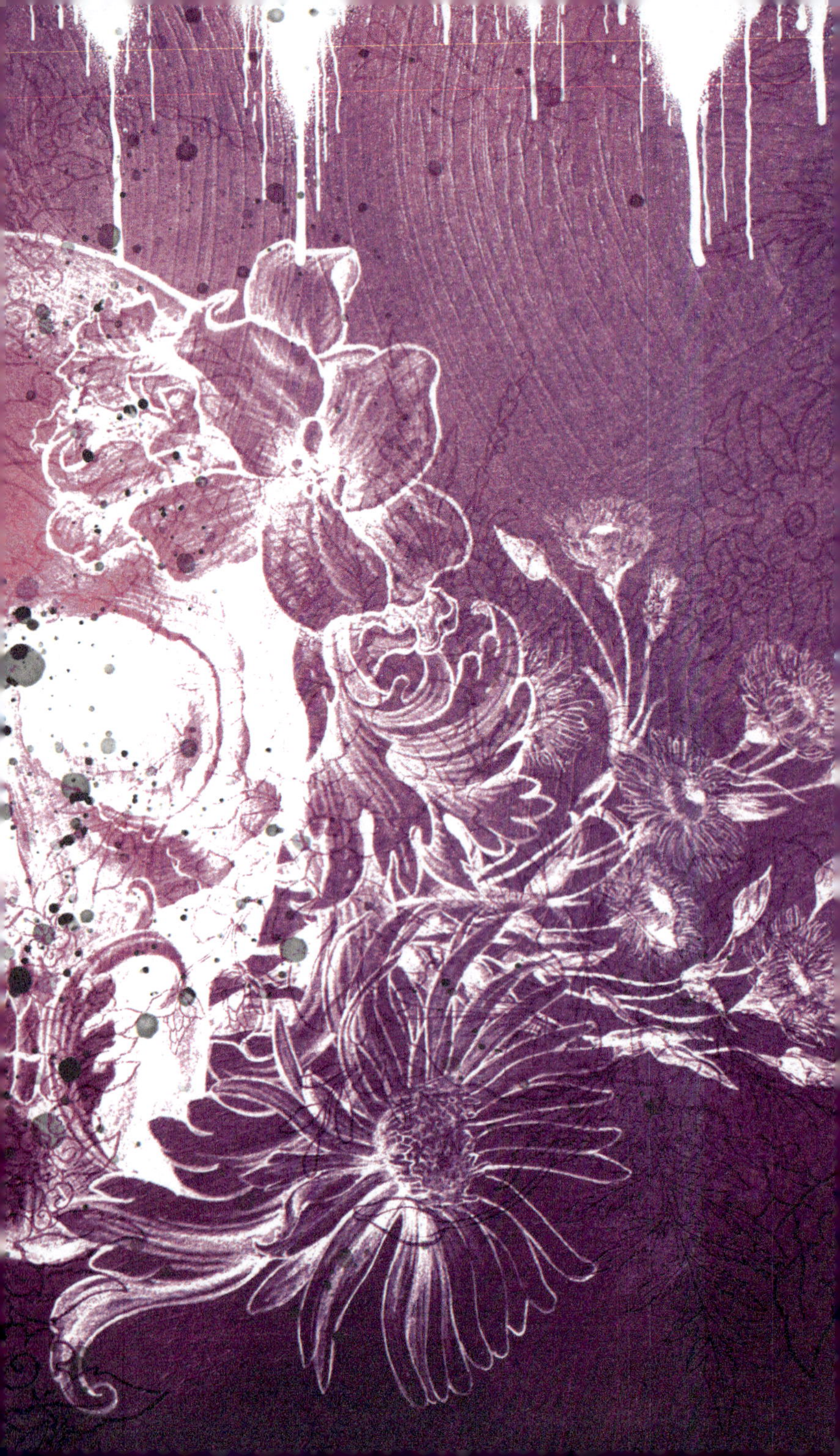

CHAPTER 20
VIOLET

The luxury hotel room Jacuzzi tub is filled with steaming hot water and bubbles. I dip my toes in to test the temperature, which is hotter than the devil's ass crack, but it's the shock to my system that I need to clear my head. I slip in, drowning myself beneath the layer of foam coating the top of the bath. Once I'm fully submerged, I open my eyes. The bubbles from my nose burst into rippling waves, and the world is muted around me. It's the sensation of letting go that's soothing, until my chest tightens, screaming for air.

Breaking through the surface, I inhale oxygen, re-expanding my chest walls. It's cleansing. Rejuvenating in a way. *What am I going to do now?*

I'm lost in my mind. The rivulets of water still drip down my face when a knock on the door sounds. I snap to the sound, my heart racing. *It's only room service. You're fine, Violet. Calm the fuck down. Miles wouldn't rat me out. Would he?*

I pull myself out of the safety of the bath, and I wrap the hotel's fuzzy robe around myself. After padding over toward the locked door, I peek through the peephole on my tiptoes. The fish-eye view of the hallway is empty. *Strange. I know I heard a knock at the door.* To clear my head of the worry, I unlatch the chain and turn the lock with an audible click. Easing the heavy door open, I peer through the crack, and still see no one.

My anxiety-riddled brain is playing tricks on me. I'm so scared of getting caught by Wade and his cult that I'm starting to make up things that aren't really there.

I push the door closed. My breathing eases.

But before the door fully closes, it's ripped out of my grasp. The handle's edge scrapes my palm, and the breath is knocked out of me.

Miles's fingers hold my chin, forcing me to look up at him. "What the fuck are you doing, risking your life like that?"

His eyes are dark and glaring down at me while his curly hair hangs over his forehead. "I have my reasons," I whisper through gritted teeth. "How did you find me?"

He holds up his cell showing a map with a blinking red light. "Tracked your phone. You're going to get yourself fucking killed." His eyes soften a fraction as if he is pitying me. *Fuck his pity.*

I roll my eyes. "What the fuck do you care?" I ask, because as much as he pushed and pulled at me, I don't understand why he even bothers. It's not like he even wants me around.

"I've tried so many times to help you get the fuck out," he pleads, letting go of me. The absence of his touch makes my insides go cold. He paces the room, running his hands through his hair, frustrated with me. "What the fuck are you in this for, huh? The money? It honestly can't be good enough to risk your life over."

"It's what I deserve." I scream, *"You will never understand."* Tears prick my eyes, threatening to fall, but I grit my teeth and clench my fists to hold it together. I can't break, not now.

He invades my space again, forcing me to look up into his eyes before he grabs my throat, holding me in place. "Then make me understand," he says, and his lips are on mine.

My insides are on fire. His lips are soft, and his tongue invades my mouth, consuming me. I run my hands under his shirt, forcing it over his head, our kiss only breaking for a moment before his lips are back on me. This moment has been building within me. I've denied myself due to social norms, which I'm not even sure matter in the long run, and my own debt to Anna.

His hands grip my waist, lifting me so that my legs wrap around him. My hands are in his hair, running through his curls. The soft strands intertwine between my fingers. I grab hold, pulling his head back, breaking our kiss. His lips are swollen and red. I lick his bottom lip, and a groan leaves his throat. My legs clench around him tighter, and my cunt weeps at his noises.

"Tell me, so I can help you," he says, his voice husky as he strides toward the open bathroom door and sets my ass on the cold counter. His eyes are hooded as he takes in the view of my partially open robe. The way he looks at me says that he is the luckiest man in the world right now, and that alone has me grabbing his face in my hands, pulling him back in.

His forehead pressed against mine and his lips a breath away, he groans out, "Gah, you're so damn beautiful. I want to fuck you every way possible, but I need to know."

I look up into his eyes with him so close to me. His eyes are fully consumed with lust and wanting. "I'll tell you everything, but first. Take me. Fuck me like you hate me." My words come out more breathy than I anticipate, giving away how much I want him.

"Noted," he says before consuming my lips again, sucking my tongue into his mouth.

Then he pulls my bottom lip with his teeth, biting, lacing this fog of lust with a bit of pain. He kisses me again, and our kiss tastes like copper. I grab hold of his pants, roughly unbutton them, and push them down around his ass, all while never breaking our kiss. He grips my neck to hold me steady and lines himself up with my entrance. I hold my breath, waiting for his intrusion. The sweet stretch of pain and pleasure. He pulls back, looking into my eyes.

"I want to see your face as you take me," he growls.

I barely have time to nod before he grabs hold of my hips, slamming me down on his cock. My pussy clenches at his girth, and my brows furrow at the burn. A sharp moan leaves my mouth. Gripping the back of his neck, I pull him in and run my teeth over the cords in his neck. As he thrusts into me, I clamp down, sinking my fangs into his flesh. If I were a vampire, I'd drink him in, just to have him living in my veins, putting me on this high of ecstasy and pleasure every day of my life. He grunts at the pain, pounding into me harder.

My palms rest on his chest before I push him away. He looks angry. Fuck, my pussy is weeping, and I crave the assault he's giving me. He grabs me off the counter, flips me over, and smacks my ass. I push out, arching my back, wanting more.

"Needy for the pain, little flower?" he asks, landing another rough slap to my ass. He rubs in the sting, gripping my ass cheeks in his palms. "I'll give you all the torture you think you deserve."

"Please," I beg, tears brimming my eyes. *If only he knew.*

He grips my hair, turning my head so that my cheek presses against the cold counter. His other hand grips his shaft as he runs his dick over my slit, paying extra attention to my clit, teasing me.

"Fuck. You," I groan as he continues to tease me.

He chuckles. "What's the matter, baby? Not enough for you?"

I groan again, but it's cut off quickly when a sharp sting lands on my clit. I inhale sharply at the pain that makes my bundle of nerves pulse, begging for more. Before I can even ask for more, he gives me another smack over my clit before slamming back into my drenched, needy cunt. His hips connect with my ass with each thrust of his cock, causing me to press into the cold, hard counter. My insides tighten, holding on to him. Every time he pulls out, my pussy clenches on the empty space he leaves behind, begging him to come back. My breaths quicken, and the heaviness in my swollen clit throbs, wanting to be touched. I begin to reach down to touch myself. He spins me, lifting me up to wrap my legs around his waist again.

"I'll take care of you," he breathes, before capturing my lips.

My chest tightens, because I want to say I deserve this, but I don't feel like I should. I still want to wallow in self-loathing.

When he walks us into the bedroom, I break our kiss. "I don't deserve you," I whisper.

"Let me show you how much you deserve this," he says before throwing me back on the bed.

I bounce a bit when I land on the soft cushion

mattress top. It doesn't take Miles long before he's looming over me. His chain dangles over my mouth, and I lean up, latching on to it with my teeth playfully. Miles grips my cheeks, making my lips pucker, and his eyes are piercing and serious.

"Don't touch that," he sneers. *That's his limit.* I make a mental note of it.

"Got it," I respond. He runs his teeth over my neck, sending electricity straight to my core. His lips trace over my collarbone, down to my chest. My nipples are straining for attention, and I arch my back for him to move down further. "Fucking, bite me," I growl.

His teeth latch on to my hardened nipple, and the pain is a craving I can't get enough of. My moans fill the room. I'm panting for more. His length glides between my lips, and I lift my hips for him. He slips in easily, and my greedy, wet pussy grips every inch of him.

"Fuuuck," I moan as I throw my head back.

"I love your moans, Violet. Especially when you finally let go and give in to what you want." He pounds into me faster, and my hips meet him at every thrust. My core clenches, the build becoming unbearable. I close my eyes, focusing on the sensation of waves crashing against a shore, wiping away every mark that's ever existed against my soul.

He grunts his release just as the tension inside me bursts. We come down together with his chest resting against mine. Our breaths mingling, I attempt to catch up with reality. When he pulls out of me, I feel empty. I miss the way he fills that spot inside me that's deeper than anyone else has ever reached. Lifting up on my elbows, I wait, watching him. I am expecting him to get up and head straight to the bathroom to clean up, but instead, his head dips low.

"What the fuck are you doing?" I ask him,

confused.

He smirks up at me slyly. "Cleaning you up," he says before his tongue runs up my slit, lapping up his cum. If I could get any wetter for this man, then I would. He crawls back up to me, taking my mouth. Our releases meld together as our tongues intertwine. The sweet and salty, a perfect combination.

When he sits back on his haunches, he smiles before coming back to plant another soft kiss on my lips. My head is swimming, and I don't think I'll ever want to make it back to shore. This man is *perfection*. And something I definitely don't deserve.

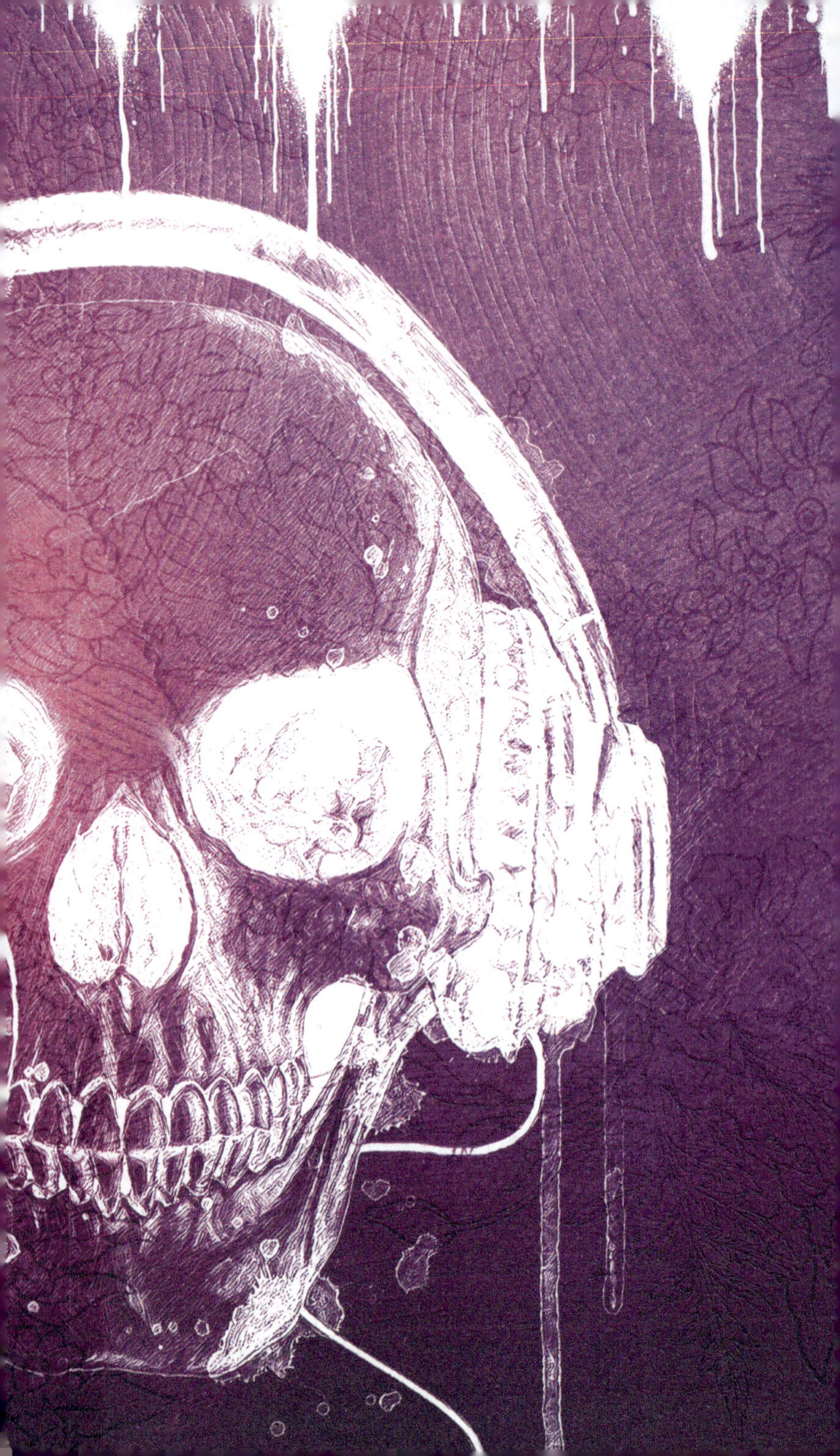

CHAPTER 21
MILES

    Her soft snores make my chest warm with affection. I pull her closer to me, fitting her curves into the crook of my body. I've refrained from feeling this way for anyone. I couldn't be happy living under the same roof as a monster. My thoughts go back to finding her in the basement with her back to me. She was dressed for a mission, but one she wasn't ready for. I couldn't let her get caught, then this would be all over.

    She moves her head, readjusting her pillow. The scent of her—floral and honey with an added hint of berries—engulfs my senses. Her hair is fanned out on the pillow next to me. I press my nose into her soft strands, taking it all in. Committing her to my memory. There's a pang of longing in my chest, as if she is already packing her bags and walking out of the door. As if this is one of those loves you only experience once in a lifetime, that burns bright and dies fast. I can't think about that right now. I need to take in as much of her as I can. While I'm reveling in my thoughts, her ass presses into my already straining length. I let out a groan and press against her, just wanting to ease the building pressure in my cock, but she grinds against me in return.

"Fuck, me. I can't get enough of you," I whisper in her ear.

"Please, never do." She arches her back into me, and I take the hint.

I run my hand over the curve of her ass and up the side of her breast. She shivers under my touch, and my dick jumps in response. I pull back slightly allowing my cock to drop between her thighs. The heat of her core has my abs tightening in anticipation. *Fuuuckkk*. She could be my weakness and possibly even my downfall. Moving my hips back and forth, I run my cock through her arousal. She releases a low moan which brings warmth to my chest in delight at her reaction. I never want us to leave this bed.

"Stop fucking teasing me," she moans.

I chuckle at her begging me to fill her. She doesn't even know how much I'm holding back and wanting this to last forever. Or the fact that I want to slam into her as much as she wants me to. I need to take advantage of this moment.

"Are you going to tell me why you're trying to get yourself killed?" I ask her, still stroking my dick through her wetness, making it slick with her arousal. She tenses in my arms, letting me know this is a no-go for her. I need to keep pressing, make her comfortable. "If you don't tell me, then how can I help you?" I whisper in her ear, causing another shiver to run over her. My dick jerks at the reaction. I'm not sure I can hold out teasing her much longer, but I need her to trust me.

"You would want to help me?" she asks, a little

breathy.

"You said you'd tell me, and I didn't turn you in," I say and lift her leg over mine.

"That's true," she admits, "but you still could."

"I guess you'll have to trust me." I align with her entrance and push into her tight, soaked cunt. Electricity shoots down my lower spine at the way her pussy grips my cock.

She moans out and grinds against my dick, swirling her hips. Her cunt clenches me in rapid succession, and I have to pull out slightly because she feels too good.

"Fuck. You're milking my cock with your needy pussy," I growl.

She groans, grinding down harder, faster, pressing her ass into me, and I meet her with each thrust. Flesh slapping, chasing that high of release. While she is still lying on her side, I lift her leg over my shoulder and straddle her knee.

As I hit her at the right angle, she cries out, "Oh, fuck."

"You like that, little flower?" My dick is hitting her deep, and she quivers in my hold.

"Yes. Please, make me come," she begs.

"Will you trust me?" I ask her, slowing my speed, keeping her on the edge of release.

"Yes," she cries. "Yes." That last yes comes out as an angry *don't fuck around*, and I take the hint.

My hips pivot, pumping into her. The pressure builds. Sweat drips from my temples as I work her over. Her legs shake, and I grip on to her calf, thrusting fast. That race to the end. The lights in my eyes are bursting. Violet screams out my name, and I grunt out my release.

After readjusting her leg, I lie down beside her. We are both panting, catching our breaths. I rest on my hand, leaning over her. One of my brows arches up, letting her know I'm waiting. She huffs and rolls over.

"I'm a fuckup," she starts, and I wait for her to continue. "I stole from my ex-husband. Not because I'm a gold digger." She looks over her shoulder at me, side-eye, before rolling over to finally meet my gaze head on. "I turned my sister away when she needed me most. Now, she's making me pay for it, in order for her to help me get away from the men I stole money from. The men my ex-husband works for."

"What does she want you to do?" I ask, trying to piece the puzzle together.

She looks up at me with glassy eyes and says, "She wants me to kill your dad."

AYDEN PERRY 233

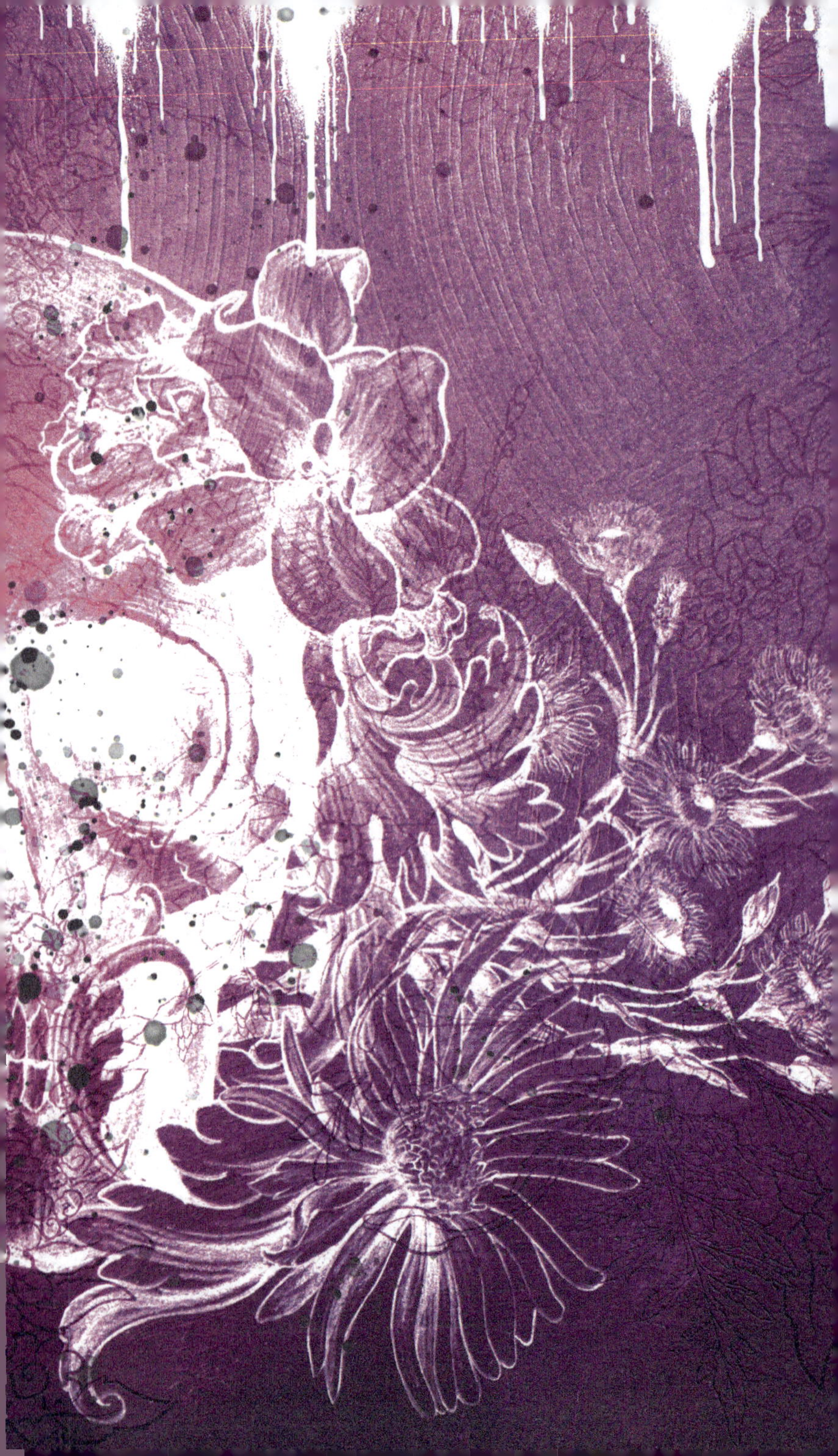

CHAPTER 22
VIOLET

Sitting on the bed, I zip up my boots that Miles got out of the car for me. I'm wearing the clothes I left the house in yesterday, but I don't think Wade will care or even notice.

"Where will you be?" I ask Miles. He can't leave and show up at the house the same time I do.

"I have somewhere to go," he says, and my traitorous body tenses up.

I avoid his eyes and pull my hair out of my shirt. He catches me by the arm when I walk past him, pulling me into his embrace. His thumb runs over my cheek. "It's not her."

Looking up at him, my chest tightens. I shouldn't care, and I hate that he even noticed my reaction. Shrugging, I say, "It's none of my business."

The corner of his lip quirks up, calling me on my bullshit. "Yeah, okay." Then he pushes a stray hair behind my ear. "I'll figure this out. Trust me."

"I'll try," I admit, because that's all I can do. Trust doesn't come easy for me, and allowing my fate to rest in another person's hands isn't something I want to do. I did that with my last husband, and it's definitely not something I want to do with Miles.

"You're working really hard behind those violet eyes of yours. What are you thinking?"

"It's just. . ." I chew on my lip, not wanting him to know everything about me just yet. "Trust is hard for me. And you helping me, I don't deserve it."

He grips my shoulders, giving them a little squeeze. "Don't say that. There's nothing you've done that's bad enough to get yourself killed over."

"I've told you everything. I've stolen, accused my ex-husband of beating me to get out of it, and when my sister needed me years ago, I turned her away," I urge.

"You've made wrong decisions. You learn from them, but that doesn't mean you deserve to die for it. Plus, I've seen you. You could never kill someone," he says, and the air around us weighs heavy with unspoken words, but he doesn't push. "Come on, I'll walk you to your car."

We don't speak. I'm not sure either of us know what to say right now. One thing we do know is that I'm a problem that he's not obligated to solve. Once we make it to the driver's side of my car, Miles places his hand over the handle. "Now, don't do anything stupid." I purse my lips and fold my arms over my chest. "Don't look at me like that, little flower. I've caught you every time." He pushes me up against the car, looming over. "You're only potentially dangerous, not deadly."

"Maybe I just want you to think that," I sass back.

His lips softly press against mine, lifting my soul out of my body. Our kiss breaks, and I'm let back down to this awful world. "Well, if that's the case, you're doing a great job."

That causes a laugh to bubble up from my throat. I am awful. I've never killed anyone. It's not in me. I'd rather help people, and sometimes, I can't even help myself. I'm a perfectionist to the point of self-destruction.

Miles holds my chin up between his fingers. "Will you be good for me, little flower?"

My insides melt at his pet name for me. It makes me feel special.

Letting out a huff, I give in. "Yes, for now." I can't keep the smile from my lips. *Why do I have to keep poking?*

He gives me a stern look before opening my door for me. I slide onto the leather seat, gripping the wheel as he shuts the door and walks away.

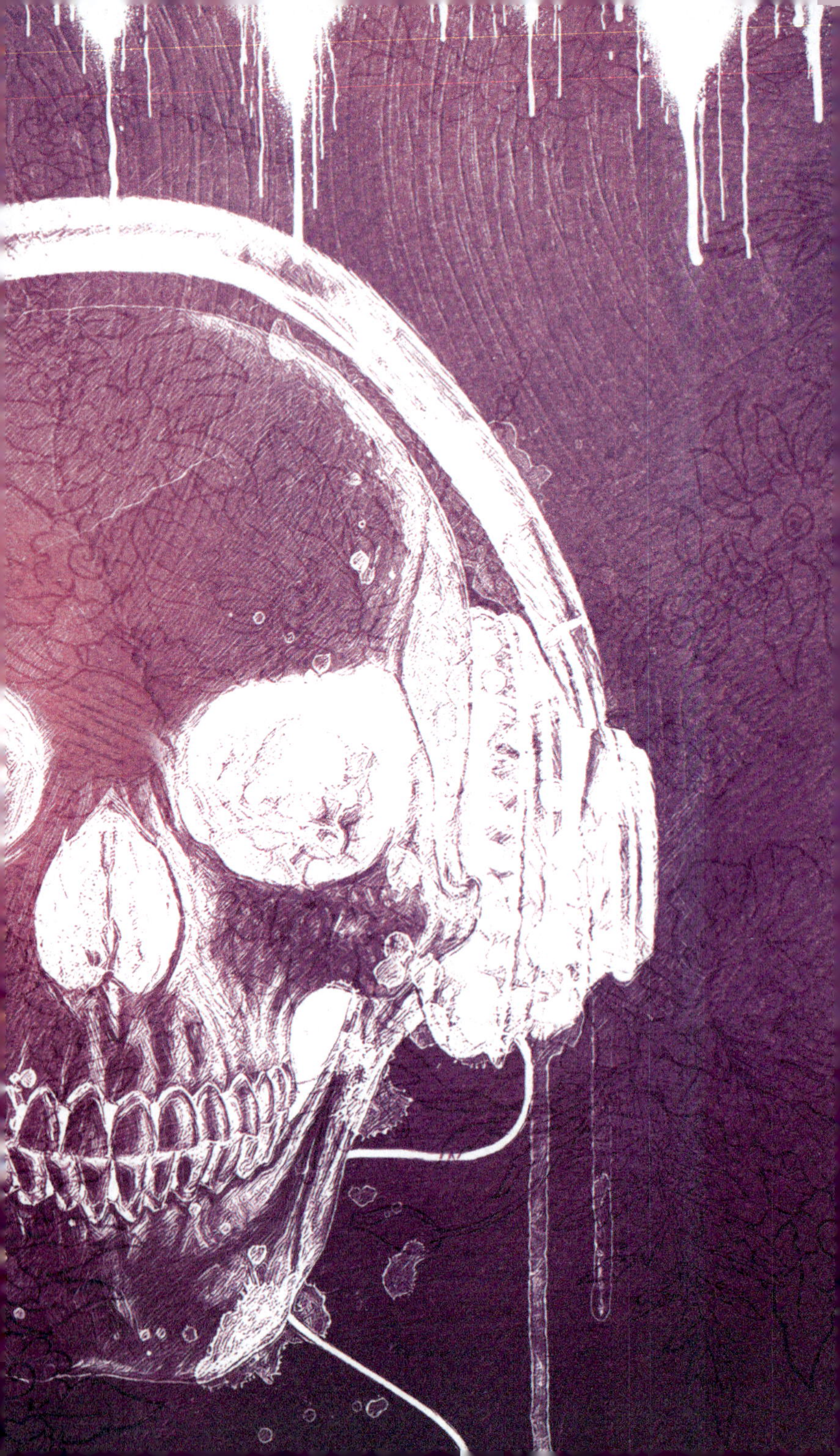

CHAPTER 23

MILES

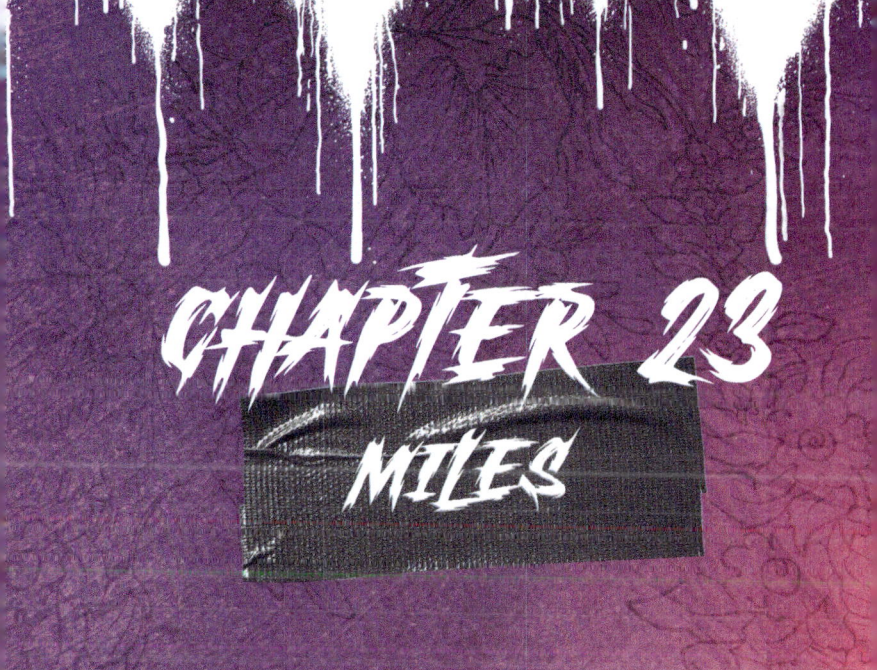

My Jeep is parked on the other side of the parking lot. When Violet drives by me, I'm still walking toward my Jeep. I have a meeting, then I need to go see Shawn about our battle bots competition. I unlock the door with the key and turn on the stereo. "Crazy" by Kid Bookie blares through the speakers. It's connected to my phone, playing the last thing I listened to. It sets the mood perfectly with how much my head is spinning at the moment.

There was always something more to Violet. I just never wanted to see it, because it was easier to see her as just some gold-digging bitch. Nope, that would be too easy for me. Then, all this has to happen while I'm trying to get the fuck out. My forehead rests on my steering wheel as I sit and ponder my options.

My cell phone rings and I answer it. "Yeah."

"He's ready for you."

"What are you doing here, Miles?" Shawn asks.

"I need your help." We walk up to his room, and I can't stop my heart from racing. Once we are in his room, he takes his usual seat at his computer chair.

He spins around, rests his elbows on his knees, and his hands are together in a prayer over his lips. If only that could be enough to help me right now, I'd lie down and sacrifice myself.

"This sounds serious," Shawn says.

"It is." I sit on the edge of his bed. This is our friendship. A mutual understanding of being there for someone when they need it. "I need to win the battle this coming weekend."

Shawn straightens his spine in his chair, rolling his eyes. "Man, that is nothing new."

"The stakes are higher now," I say, which makes him lift a brow.

"Continue." He gives me his full attention, but I can tell he's still skeptical. Maybe it's because I always dramatize the need to get out from under my father's thumb, but things *have* changed.

Now, Violet is in the mix and running from her own demons. I'm in deep with her, and I know I'm in trouble.

I tell Shawn everything from the beginning with catching her, the suspicions, the threats and bullying I've used to get her to leave. All the way to tracking her phone to the hotel where she was supposed to be having a girls' trip. After catching her in the basement dressed to the nines in gear, ready to kill my father. Not leaving out the part where she is doing this to get back in her sister's good graces.

Shawn's eyes are bugging out of his head. The whole time I'm telling him all of this newfound information and catching him up, he's sitting on the edge of his seat. When I finish, his smile is gleaming with mischief.

"So? Will you help me?" I ask him.

"Are you fucking with me?" Shawn leans back in his chair, still taking in everything I've laid in his lap.

"No?" My brow arches at him.

"Of course, I will help you. Under one condition," Shawn says with a wicked smile, rubbing his hands together.

I run my hand over my face. "Name it."

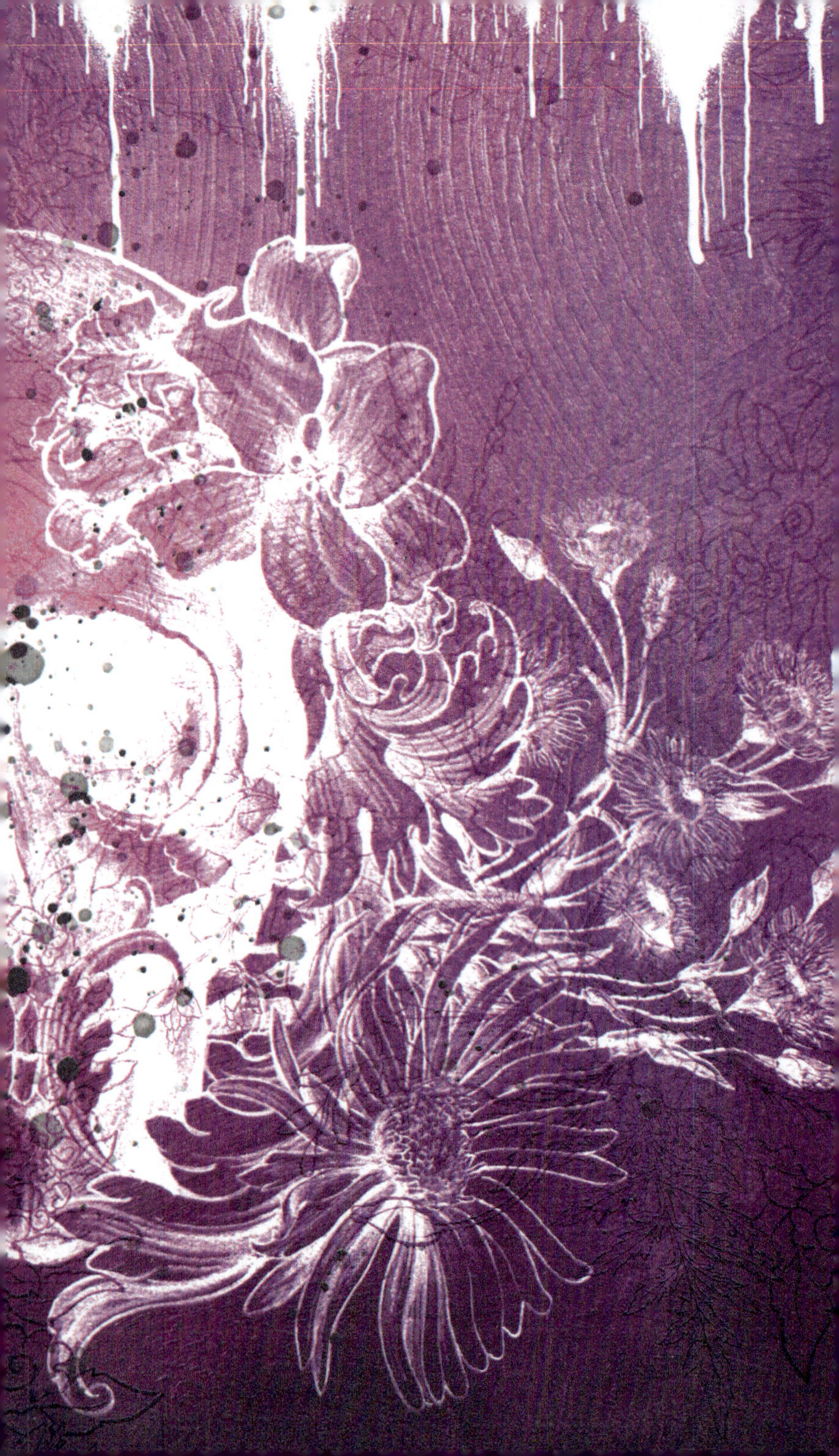

CHAPTER 24
VIOLET

My drive back to the house is filled with tension as I drum my fingers on the steering wheel. The local radio station plays oldies, but when "Smooth" by Santana with Rob Thomas comes on, I turn it up loud. The guitar solo consumes me, and my body rocks to the beat. The anxiety that has wrested itself into a frustrated knot of overwhelming thoughts begins to loosen.

The trees are a green and brown blur, and the road in front of me becomes one black blob. I wipe my face and wetness comes off it. *I'm crying?*

My phone rings on the dashboard, showing a picture of Dani. I know I need to talk to her, but now is not the time. A loud horn catches my attention, and when I look up a truck is coming at me head on. At the last minute, I jerk the wheel back over into my lane. Shock hits me first. Then, the freefall of my hair, and the sound of glass and metal twisting. Last, comes the pain.

"Violet. Violet." The sound of my name repeats over and over. It's a serenade to my ears. He's calling for me.

"How can you be so *fucking* stupid," the voice seethes. Pain burns through my chest, and my breath hitches. *I've fucked up again.* I crack my eyes open to the bright white lights. "Oh good, you're awake," my husband says, annoyed.

Not my husband. My ex-husband.

There's a pool in my head. No wait. A bathtub.

He rushes at me. Angry. He's angry with me.

My brow furrows, and my head throbs. I want to curl into a ball. I don't want him like this. Make it all go away.

"You deserve this." He points a finger at me. "You're fucked in the head." His pointer finger presses into the spot that's throbbing on my head. I cry out in pain, and his words come out as a hiss. "Shut the fuck up. You brought this on yourself. I never loved you. You were just a means to an end."

There it is.

The final stab to my heart.

Venom creeps in, settling deep within my soul.

He walks away. His back is silhouetted in the doorframe. The hospital monitors beep in time with my racing heart. All I wanted was real love. Love that could be smooth, but that was something I was undeserving of.

"And Violet, don't come back. Ever. Or I'll have them kill you." His words shatter the rest of me into pieces, leaving me to paste my heart back together.

Rubber melted, sealing the cracks, and the black seeps like sludge from the wounds.

Rubber. Rubber. Burning Rubber.

"Violet," he calls. "Violet." His strong hands grip my forearms, but I pull back.

"Don't touch me," I cry. "Please."

"Violet the car is smoking. You have to get out. I have to get you out," he urges. The desperation in his voice calls to my aching heart.

Something drips from my lashes, and I brush it away.

"No, I deserve this," I whisper.

His eyes are soft, but that dies fast and is replaced with a hard edge. "Fuck you, Violet. You *are* getting out of this car."

He grabs hold of my forearms again, and I writhe and kick in his grip. Sharp, shooting pain lances up my side, but I keep fighting until he throws me to the hard earth. Dirt clouds around me, and I suck some of it up into my lungs. The tickle in the back of my throat has me coughing. They rack my body trying to expel the dust, which has me bent over with eyes watering.

"Why, not let me *just fucking die*?" I scream.

My head throbs from the pressure. Miles's pants are dirty, and his arms are covered in blood. My blood. I take it all in. The whisper of the memory lingers on my chest. It's heavy.

Miles's jaw ticks before he lunges at me. He pulls me up by my arms and shakes me like a rag doll.

This.

This is what I deserve.

But then, he holds me. "Why do you think you deserve to die?" he whispers. He says it so softly. Not in a way that he's asking me or expecting me to hear it. He holds me at arm's length, and the hardness is back in his expression. "I'm not leaving you to fucking die, Violet." We hang in the balance of time, and my breathing slows.

"Why do you even care?" I ask, not counting on an answer from him. I hate that I sound like a whiny bitch right now, but all my life it's been one let down after another.

It seems as if a movie is playing behind his eyes, contemplating our options before he pulls my arm toward the road where his Jeep is parked. My pulse kicks up, and I dig my heels into the compact dirt. "Wait. Shouldn't we help the others?" I ask.

He stops attempting to pull me and turns on me. "What others, Violet? Please, tell me. Because it seems like two steps forward and three steps back with you." His brows are furrowed, but his eyes shine with a certain sadness.

I swallow the lump that has formed in my throat. "From the wreck," I squeak.

He points behind me, and I turn to see what it is he's trying to show me. It's the first time since exiting the vehicle that I actually look at the damage. I didn't kill anyone. I didn't hit another car. Not even a dead animal carcass splayed out in the wake of my disaster. No. Just me and my own self-destruction is before me, if you don't count the earth I tore up.

My car is a hunk of twisted metal wrapped around a tree in a patch of dried grass and dirt. The hood smokes as if a fire is already going. *I survived that?*

I look back at Miles with a renewed perspective. His eyes are soft again. "Yeah, we need to get you to a hospital." He pulls on my arm once more, but I hold firm, standing my ground. "What the fuck is your problem, Violet?" He holds my face in his hands, forcing me to look into his eyes.

"I don't know," I admit. I place a hand over his. "Just no hospital, okay?"

He seems to wage a war behind his gaze, but gives up, clearly knowing he won't win. A groan leaves his lips. "Fine. You better not die on me though, or I'll scour every corner of hell, every deep, dark cave in the mountains, and every evil fucking place just to bring you back to kill you all over again myself."

"Wow, you really do care," I say and allow him to drag me the rest of the way to the Jeep.

"Shut up." A smile touches his lips, but he hides it, turning away from me when he closes my passenger side door.

We ride back to the house in silence since my head is pounding. I don't want to tell him it's splitting me in two even in the quiet because he may turn the Jeep around and take me to the hospital instead. I can't stand another visit like the last one I had. The trauma and anticipation of that happening again haunts me.

He pulls into the drive, parking the Jeep closest to the front door. I know he did that for me. It's the small things. My chest warms with the gesture. He walks around to the passenger side and helps ease me out. Splintering pain stabs me in the chest when I move so he takes it slow for me.

The numbers on the keypad beep as he presses in the code. I guess he fixed that last night before coming to find me. When he opens the door, though, we are met with a face I did not want to see at this moment.

"What happened?" Wade asks in a no-nonsense tone.

"I found her car wrecked on the side of the road," Miles explains while I stand there looking like I should have been sent off in a body bag. I should've been taken out of this world. That would have solved all my problems. "She didn't want to go to the hospital, so I brought her here."

"And the car?" Wade asks as if this is a business deal. *That is what I am*, I remind myself.

"I already called Tommy." Miles is tense, and I hate he has to deal with this line of questioning for me.

"Good," Wade says before turning to me. "Go get cleaned up. You're not leaving this house until you look 100 percent again."

Miles, still holding onto my arm, guides me toward the bathroom. What Wade said about not leaving the house chews at my already fragile brain. I know why. I know, because it's why I didn't want to go to the hospital. Not only because of my own experience, but because my chance for redemption would be over. Image is everything to Wade.

Miles runs a bath for me while I attempt to remove my bloody clothes. Every inch of skin is covered in tiny cuts from the shattered glass, and the pain shooting up my side has me moving at sloth speed. I try to pull my shirt off, but it gets stuck with my arms halfway up in the air. A stabbing in my ribs makes me pause, and a groan leaves my lips, involuntarily. Warm hands glide up my sides until they reach where my top is stuck. A shiver runs through me, reminding me of every strained muscle in my body.

Once my shirt is off, our eyes lock on each other. Warmth spreads over my face and neck, thinking of last night and this morning. "So, I guess I won't be leaving this prison anytime soon," I whisper.

His look is one of pity. "It's an image thing."

"I know." I reassure him that I know the deal. I've been through it before. The image of perfection is one of those toxic traits I tried so hard to maintain. It's the reason I turned Anna away when she needed me. She was frail, dirty, and covered in track marks. I was too vain to help her, and I'm kicking myself every day for thinking I was better than her.

"It's easy for him to play off bruises on his kid, but his wife is a different story. The media will eat that shit up," Miles states, guiding me into the tub.

"I'm sorry." I apologize because it's the only thing I know to say.

"Don't be." It's the only thing he says while sponging the dried blood off my arms.

The rest of our time in the bathroom is spent with Miles cleaning me up in silence. The lack of noise weighs heavy, because I know I'm in trouble if I don't end Wade soon. I can only imagine what Miles thinks of me now. He helps get me dressed and in bed before speaking.

"Don't do anything stupid. I've got a plan," he whispers.

"Okay," I reassure him, knowing damn well I won't stop searching for an easy way out.

"I'll bring you some pain medicine. Until then just relax, watch TV, or *read a book*," he says with a smirk.

"What? I read." I put my hand over my chest, offended by his implication.

"Oh, I know you read." He chuckles.

My cheeks heat. The phone. The tracking app. *My Kindle app*.

"You fucker," I say, grabbing the pillow beside me.

He races toward the door, and I attempt to throw the fluffy puffball at him. I immediately regret it when my side lights up with pain again. *Fuck*. The sad sack of fluff doesn't even make it off the bed. Miles laughs under his breath, shutting the door.

AYDEN PERRY 251

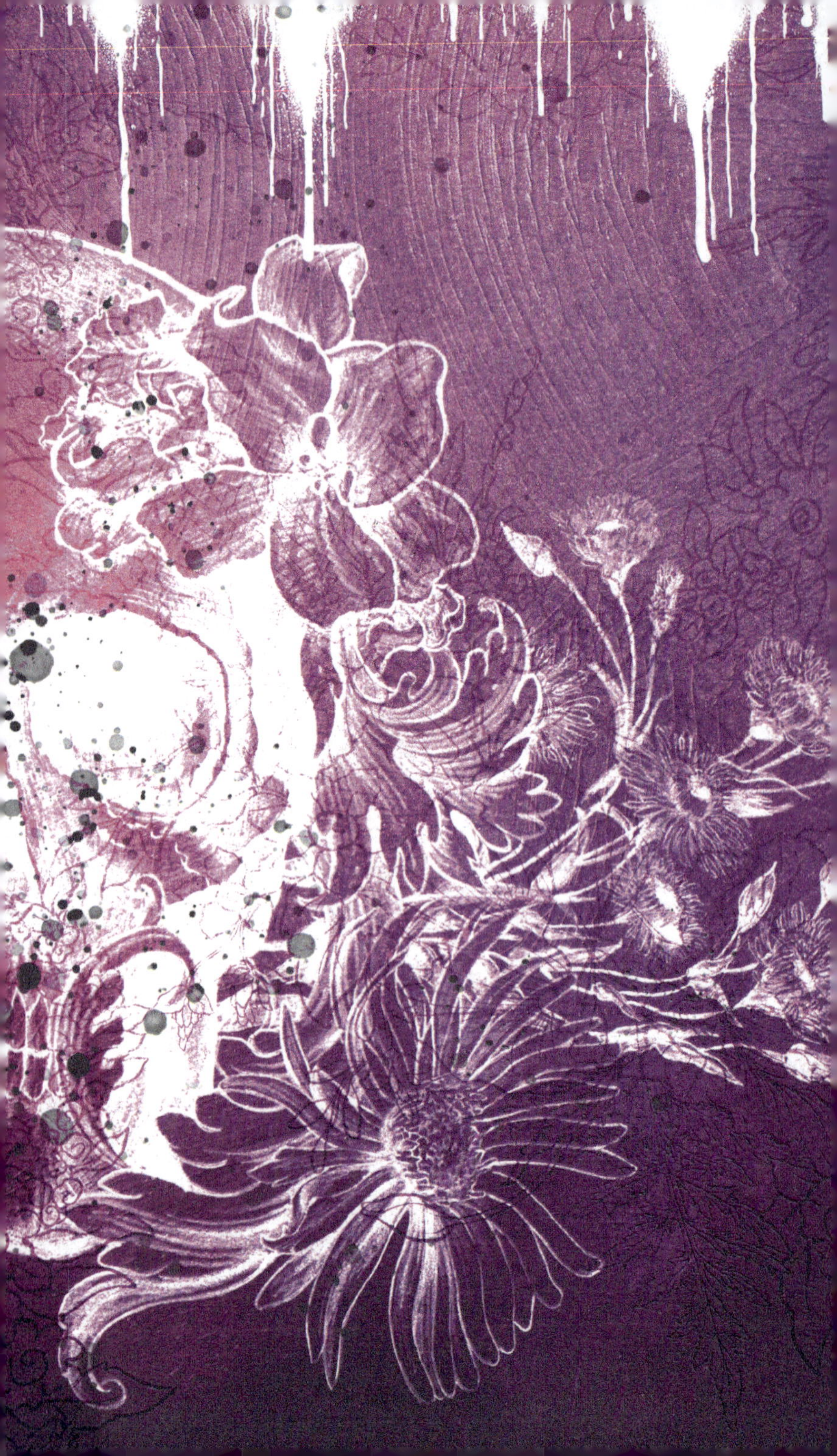

CHAPTER 25
VIOLET

"You keep an eye on her and don't let her out of your sight," Wade commands.

He's outside my bedroom door. It's still dark. The sun hasn't even come up yet. I blink a few times and glance at my alarm clock. It's five a.m. and the alarm symbols aren't showing up, letting me know someone has turned them off. My brain is floating on clouds, sleep still blanketing my rational mind. I don't ponder for long who Wade could be talking to at this hour. It's probably Miles. Has to be. The thought of questioning it flies high above warm pink fog, and before I know it, my eyes drift back closed.

When I wake again, the TV is on *Criminal Minds*, and on my bedside table sits a glass of water along with more pain pills. A heaviness presses in my lower abdomen, letting me know I need to pee. I can't stay in bed forever. I begin to ease back the blanket, and my muscles scream with every inch I move. *Ugh, this sucks.* It's like walking through quicksand while being pelted by rocks on the way to the bathroom, but I finally make it. I plop down on the cold seat and sigh in relief.

"Good to see you're awake," the familiar voice states from the doorway, and I nearly jump out of my skin, teetering on the toilet. "Whoa whoa, calm down." Miles grabs my shoulders, steading me. I groan at the tightness in my neck and the soreness in my chest and muscles. "Not feeling too hot, huh?"

I shake my head at him, but it's as if I'm wearing a neck brace with what little movement I make. "No," I whisper, so he gets an answer.

"Need me to help you?" he asks, still holding my shoulders. He's looking at me like he doesn't want to leave me, but I need to try and do this by myself.

"No, Miles. I've got it. I might be as slow as a turtle, but I'll make it." My voice comes out groggy. I'm assuming from the pain medicine still lingering in my system.

"Okay well, I'll stay close by just in case," he says before going back to my room. I finish up in the bathroom and wash my hands. Once I finally exit, Miles is sitting on the edge of my bed with a smirk playing on his lips. "Took you long enough."

I glare at him before taking the medicine on the bedside table. He pulls the covers back for me to get in, and I slowly lie down. The aches and pains from muscle stiffness and the bruising on my chest is the worst.

"You relax. I'll come back to check on you." Miles tucks me back in. He pushes my baby hairs behind my ear and kisses my forehead. The small gesture causes my chest and cheeks to warm. "Sleep tight, little flower."

I get the strange sense of déjà vu before I close my eyes to sleep.

We continue this routine for a week. My muscles are slowly getting back to normal, the cuts on my arms and face scabbing over, and the bruises getting darker before they get better. Miles even helps me bathe and get dressed. I've never felt more helpless in my life, besides my one time in the hospital.

After another week, Miles makes me move around the house more. Slowly easing me back into everyday life in between going to school and working on what he calls his bots with Shawn. I'm impressed by the patience he maintains with me as I bitch and moan, because all I wanna do is sleep, watch TV, and read on my phone, but Miles isn't having it.

The screech of the blinds rips through the room, and the bright light assaults my eyes. I throw my arm over my face and groan. "Really? You fucking asshole."

"Ah, come on." He throws something on the bed that weighs heavy on my legs. "I have plans for us today. Get dressed."

I whine, bitching and moaning as I pull back the warm blankets. "I just wanna lie in bed."

"Too fucking bad. You have to keep moving to get better."

I know he's right, but the pain meds just make me so tired. I pull on the clothes Miles threw on the bed, and when I'm ready, he drags me downstairs. His pace is faster than he normally has been with me in the last two weeks, showing his excitement. When he opens up the front door, my heart beats fast against my bruised ribs. Wade's *You're not leaving this house* rings out like an alarm in my head.

"Where are you taking me? You know I can't leave the house," I say as a reminder, but I'm just as excited as he is. The need to break the rules has my adrenaline pumping.

"You'll see." He doesn't give me any hints but continues toward the trails.

I follow him as the aches in my muscles begin to ease, but still the undertone of soreness sings through. The breeze blows through the trees, and the birds chirp as we walk. My pace slows as I take in the soothing fresh air. So much better than being cramped in that house, and I relish the sensation of being free. Then Miles veers off the beaten path, walking among the trees. I stand on the outside, watching him maneuver among limbs.

He stops to look back at me. "Come on."

"Are you serious?" I arch a brow at him. I was all for this little walk, but getting lost in the woods is not on my agenda for today.

"Yes, Violet. We are almost there."

"Ugh, okay," I huff, pushing back the limbs and following him.

We walk for at least five minutes before I ask him again, "Where are we going?"

"Violet," he warns, shooting me a glare.

"Okay, okay, just trust you, I guess," I say with a hint of sarcasm.

"Yes, you should." He chuckles, and we keep moving.

The trees are extra thick in this area, and I have a hard time maneuvering. *Gah, where is he taking me? Maybe, this is where I die. He didn't want me to kill myself. He wants to do the job for me. How nice.* I think, and my foot catches a hole. "Ahh."

Miles catches me before I hit the ground. He's holding me in his arms, looking down at me grinning. "See, trust me." I roll my eyes at him, and he sets me back on my feet. "We're almost there."

"You said that like ten minutes ago," I whine, following him.

He pauses, grabbing one of the tree limbs, and looks back at me. He pulls it back, exposing a clearing with a tall metal tower. My words are taken from me as I walk out into the open area, looking up at how high the thing goes.

"Wow, how did you find this?" I ask.

"I used to come out here to get away from my dad. I found it and would hide at the top until the sun started to set." He stands beside me admiring it. "One of my safe spaces, before I found my friends."

He grabs the railing and begins climbing.

"We're going up there?" I ask, chewing on my lip.

"What? Are you afraid of heights?" He smirks down at me.

"No. Maybe." I hesitate, because I totally fucking am, but I don't want him to know that. He laughs and continues climbing. "Fuck you."

I follow him up the ladder. The tower sways and creaks as the wind blows against it. My palms begin to sweat. This doesn't seem safe, but I push through it mentally, reminding myself not to look down. I know if I do, I'll be stuck there, clinging to the ladder.

Once Miles gets to the top, he looks down at me, grinning. I reach for the last rung, and he grabs my hand, pulling me the rest of the way up. My heart ricochets against my ribs painfully. *This is how I die. This is it.* Miles holds me tight in his arms, and I grip his shirt, burying my face in his chest. I'm panting until my breaths slow down.

When I'm finally composed, Miles's chest rumbles with laughter. I pull away, glaring up at him and smack him hard on the chest. "You asshole."

"Never said I wasn't." He smirks, letting me go before walking to the railing. "This is what I wanted you to see." I shake my head. *I can't do it. I can't look over the edge*. He holds his hand out for me to grab, but I don't take it. "Come on, Violet."

"I can't. I can't do it." My knees are weak at just the thought of looking over the edge. We are about two hundred feet in the air, and all I can imagine is one of the railings breaking, causing me to fall to my demise.

"You can. Just close your eyes." He shakes his hand that's still extended toward me. "I've got you."

I let out a deep breath and close my eyes before grabbing his hand. I shriek as he pulls me to where he is. My knees are shaking. He holds me in his arms, grounding me. Then his mouth is against my ear. "Open your eyes."

I don't obey, immediately. I try to relax my rapidly beating heart and screaming brain that's telling me how insane this is. When I finally feel calm enough, I open them, and my breath is taken away. "This is beautiful."

"I know, the view is what got me too," he admits as I take it in.

The mountains and trees are even better than the views from the house. It makes me feel so small, as if the world is so much bigger than my little worries. The birds fly in a group over the trees before disappearing off into the horizon. Miles's hand grazes my breast before he grips my throat.

"Do you trust me?" His warm breath brushes the shell of my ear, and I close my eyes leaning into his chest.

His lips move to my extended neck, brushing over my pulse and behind my ear. "Yes," I breathe.

"Good," he says.

His voice is gravelly, causing my clit to pulse with need. He nips my lobe, shocking my system with a bit of pain. I groan, wanting more. His fingers graze the skin of my abdomen, which causes my muscles to clench. He chuckles in my ear before doing it again. I groan, wanting him to know I want more. His fingers go lower, sliding beneath the waistband of my pants. He dips down even lower with each gentle pass of his fingers. The sensation has my clit throbbing.

"Stop teasing me," I whisper.

"Mmm," he hums in my ear. "As you wish."

He immediately lets go of me and pulls my pants all the way down. Before I even have time to think, he lays his palm between my shoulders, pushing me over. "Miles!" I scream, gripping the railing. I'm looking down at the ground, and my palms begin to sweat. His foot moves one of my feet, which are cemented to the metal tower floor, spreading me wider. Before I know it, the cool air breezes over my exposed pussy. I'm dripping. "Oh god."

His tongue licks up my inner thigh, catching my release. He bites the sensitive area of skin, and I groan again. *Fuck, me. This is thrilling.* Adrenaline courses through my veins from my fear of heights, but I can't move. *This feels too good.* His warm mouth captures my sex as his tongue swirls around my clit. I press back into him, needing more. His fingers replace his mouth as his tongue rims around my ass. The cool air whips my hair around, and the force of it shakes the tower, but I'm so lost in his touch I couldn't care less if I died right now.

He leaves me completely, and the fear comes back. "Miles," I say with urgency, but I can't move. My knees go weak remembering how far up we are.

"Relax, Violet. I'm just admiring this pretty pussy of yours."

"Well, hurry u—" The whine that leaves my lips is cut off by a moan.

The soft skin of his dick separates my lips. He

moves back and forth slowly, collecting my arousal on his shaft. The sensation makes my eyes cross and my knees go weak. Miles is there gripping my hips as he plunges his dick in. A gasp leaves me as he stretches me, filling me to the brim.

"Fuuuckkk," he groans. "You grip me so well."

A fire lights in my core at his words. I grind back into him, and he lets me. Our breathing increases the closer we get to falling over the edge of his tower. The pleasure within soaring as high as the birds over the trees. I grip the railing, trying to hold on as he pounds into me. His balls slap against my clit with each thrust, causing the bar to screech, and before I know it, I'm falling forward. The metal rod clattering against the tower on its descent. Miles fingers dig into my hips, and he follows me down to my knees. I'm leaning over the edge. My pulse pounds in my ears, but Miles doesn't stop. I whimper at his assault as he presses the pads of his fingers to my clit, circling it. Building that pressure in my lower abdomen until I finally erupt all over his cock.

He pulls me back against his chest as I sit in his lap, breathing hard. Then he breaks out into laughter. I pull him out of me, turning on him.

"Jerk," I say, slapping his chest.

"I told you to trust me. I wasn't going to let you fall and let that pussy go to waste." I give him a piercing look, and his crooked smile lingers. "Come on, let's go back and clean you up."

After getting our clothes back in order, he guides me back to the ladder. I freeze. I didn't think about going back down. My palms start sweating again. The fear resurfacing.

"I'll go down first," he reassures me. Miles begins climbing down, and I hesitate to follow him. "You got this, come on."

260 CORRUPTING VIOLET

I breathe in and out a few times, trying to get out of my head. When I calm down again, I grab hold of the ladder and ease my way down. When we make it to the ground, I have a strong urge to kiss it.

"I did it. I did it," I scream, jumping up and down.

"Okay, my little thrill seeker," he says, grabbing my hand.

We make the trek back through the woods. My steps are lighter than they have been in weeks. I'm glad Miles decided to get me out of the house, because I was starting to grow roots. I'm sore as we walk the path to the back of the house, but at least I'm not as stiff as I was. When we walk around to the front, we both freeze. Wade's vehicle is in the drive. *It's too early for him to be home, right?* The sun hasn't even started to set.

We walk in the front door, and it's quiet. Hairs stand up on my arms. Now I'm not so sure going out for a walk was the best idea. Miles goes up the stairs first, and I follow behind him. We walk as quietly as possible. Wade has to be in his office.

"What are you two doing?" Wade asks from behind us. *Where the fuck did he come from?*

"I . . . Um," I begin, but Miles comes down the stairs fast, blocking me.

"I took her out for a walk," Miles explains, holding his palms up.

"And I told *her* not to leave." Wade points a finger at me. His face is turning red with every word that leaves his mouth. "What makes you think you can change the rules around here," he demands, pushing that same finger he was using to point at me into Miles's chest.

Miles squares his shoulders. His jaw flexes before he says, "She needs to get out and walk around, or she won't get better."

He seems reasonable, but Wade doesn't seem

to think so. He grabs hold of the collar on Miles's shirt before thrusting him into the wall, getting nose to nose with him. "It's not your place to decide what she needs." Wade's fist clenches at his side.

"Well, I don't think—"

"Stop," I cut Miles off when I see Wade pulling his elbow back, getting ready to lay into him. Wade looks at me, glaring.

"Don't get in the way of me disciplining my son," Wade seethes.

I hold up my hands. "I'm sorry, but I asked to go outside. It wasn't his fault," I lie. I lie straight through my teeth to protect him.

Wade huffs, letting go of his shirt. "Both of you, to your rooms," he commands, scolding us like children. Like his property.

Miles stands in place with his shoulders back till Wade leaves, going back to the kitchen. He stomps upstairs, and when we get to the top, he doesn't stop. Miles keeps walking to his room, slamming the door. *What the fuck.* I couldn't not say anything and just stand by and let him get beaten. I couldn't do it. I go to my room and take a hot bath, some pain medicine, and then lie in bed with my phone. I'm not sure what I did wrong, and it's all I can think about as my eyes grow heavy.

AYDEN PERRY 263

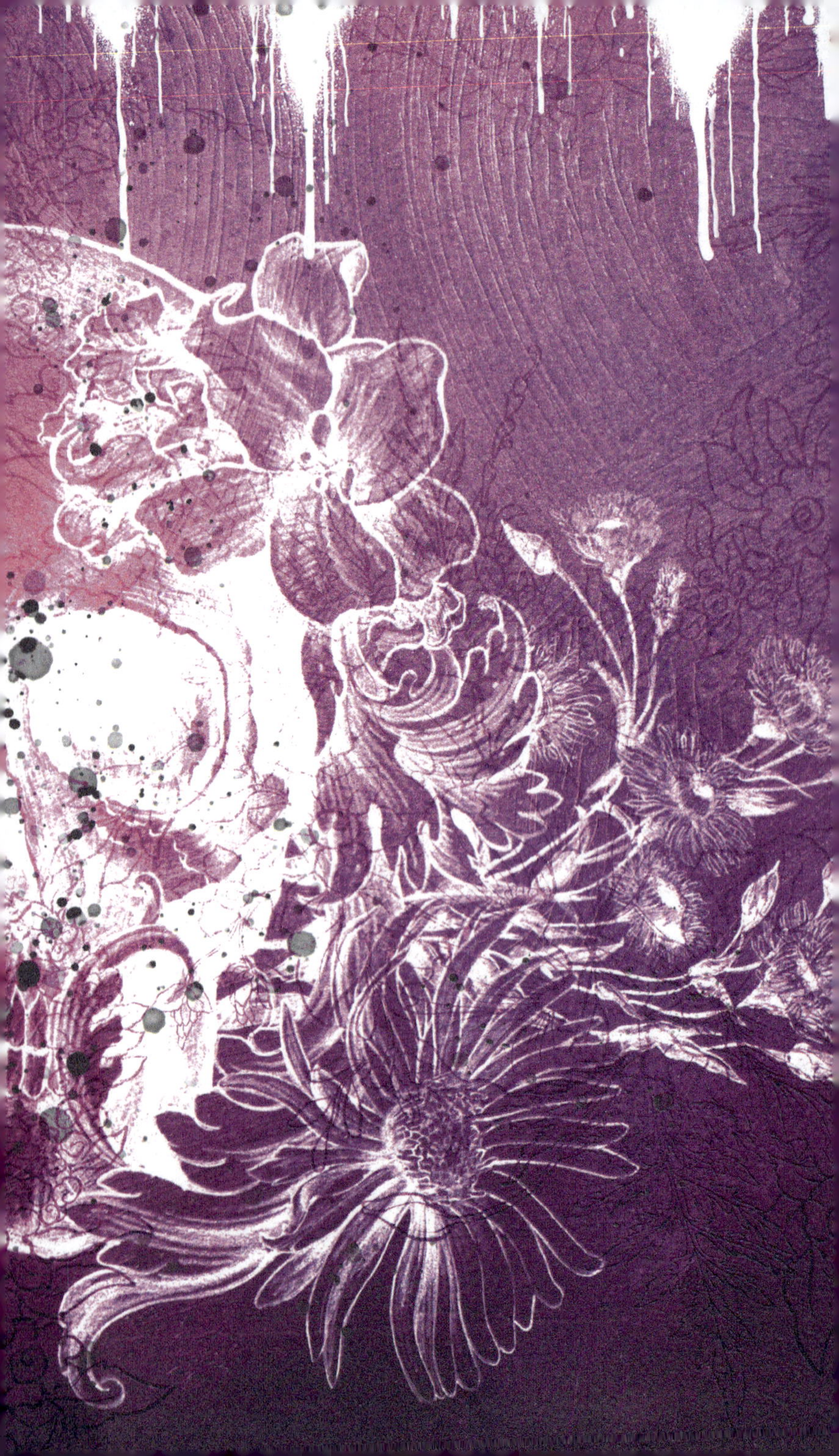

CHAPTER 26
VIOLET

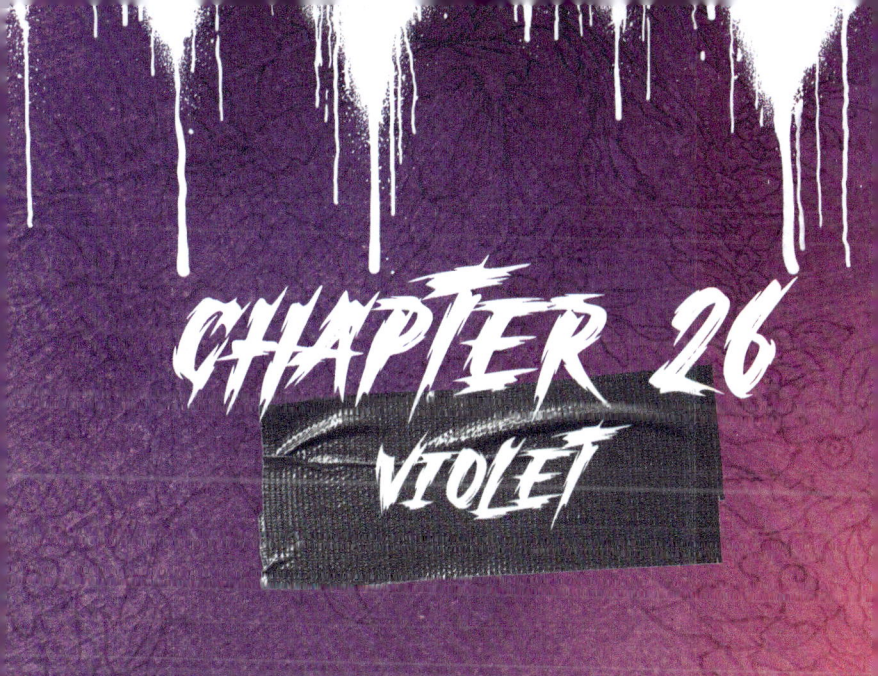

I wake to cool air kissing my skin. The pressure of my covers rests on my knees, as if I'd been fighting them off, but now I'm covered in goosebumps. I'm about to open my eyes and pull the blankets back up around my shoulders, when I feel the warmth against my back. A hard rod pressing into the curve of my ass.

Fingers trail lightly over my arm, and his hot breath fans over my hair. I know it's him. His pine, clean linen, and musk scent, unique to him, envelopes me in a warm cocoon. My sex clenches with anticipation, ever the betraying bitch that it is. I continue to keep my eyes closed, not wanting him to know that I'm actually awake.

His hand lightly grazes my naked thigh, and on reflex, a shiver takes over my body. I pull away from his touch. The tingling he left behind lingers on my skin. A low moan escapes my lips, but my eyes remain shut. I hope he believes I'm still asleep. I want to be taken, and having someone take me while I'm unaware is a kink I've never told anyone about. I'm aroused by the thought of being taken while helpless.

The rough pads of his fingers trail paths over every exposed area before finally swiping gently underneath the hem of my silk nightgown. He grips my hip, and my sex heats. I clench my thighs together, attempting to suppress the longing need throbbing in my clit.

"You like it when I do this?" Miles whispers in my ear as he repeats the motion, tracing his fingers down my spine, causing another shiver to race through my body. "I know you can hear me. You can continue to keep your eyes closed and pretend, but I know better," he says before running a palm over my bare ass, the tips of his fingers grazing my exposed sex from behind. The only thing stopping him from shoving his long digits into my cunt, which is already soaking, begging for attention, is willpower. I'm sure he can feel it too.

He repeats the motion again, this time pressing harder and lightly slipping between my lips from behind. My back arches into him, and his hard length presses into the curve of my ass. A whimper escapes me before I can lock it inside a box to never be heard. I feel so wrong for wanting more of this, more of him. He's an asshole, and my stepson.

"Is that your body begging for me?" he asks, adding pressure just over my entrance that is clenching on empty space, wanting to be filled. I'm mentally screaming from the way he is edging me, right now. He runs the tips of his fingers through my arousal and sinks one of his fingers into me. He is slow. Filling me one knuckle at a time until I feel the knuckles of his other fingers brush my clit. He slowly pulls out of me. My hungry sex grips him, not wanting to lose that fullness.

"You're so needy for me." His voice is low and gravelly. The darkness behind my eyelids makes me feel like I'm lost in a dream state. *Fucking take me already.*

He pushes his finger into me again with more force this time. Curling it inside me as he drags his other finger against the front of my sex, he rubs that rough spot before he pushes back in. He repeats the act until my sex is dripping. Weeping for more. He pulls out all the way to slip and spread my arousal over my throbbing clit. I moan at the contact and my ass perks up, spreading my legs farther apart.

"Look at me, Violet," Miles commands, but my eyes refuse to open as I fist my pillow, not wanting this to end.

"You shouldn't be here," I whisper. "If your father finds you here . . ."

He plunges back in with two fingers this time, scissoring his fingers and causing that nice stretch. My pussy clenches tighter, building a low pressure in my abdomen as my whimpers beg for more. He picks up the pace of his fingers, pumping into me faster as my clit throbs with the need to be touched. The moans leaving my lips are absorbed in the pillow.

"I don't care about my father. I just want you to look at me," he pleads before pumping into me harder, faster.

I finally look at him. There is need and wanting residing in those hazel eyes. My abdomen tightens as the rising tide in me crashes into a sweet release. I relax back onto the bed. My body weak and sated.

Miles pulls me close, molding into my body and curving around my ass as he presses his enormous length against me. I hear him suck and smack his lips before his warm breath is by my lips again. The sound is aggressive, filled with a touch of malice.

"Your whimpers sound pathetic, but I've never tasted anything sweeter than forbidden fruit." His words are grit, grounded in fury. No matter how angry he may be, his words still have an effect on me.

"I'm only trying to protect you," I admit.

"I wish you wouldn't," he says. "Just let me take care of it."

His weight on the bed lifts, but before he leaves his footsteps come to my side of the bed. My heart pounds in my chest at what he may do. Will he leave? Or will he put us both at risk sneaking around this? But he only pulls the cover up over my shoulders and plants a kiss on my forehead. The sound of his steps recedes, and the click of the knob lets me know that he has opened the door.

My ears strain for the second click announcing that he's left, when I hear him whisper under his breath, "You deserve everything, Violet."

I fist my pillowcase hard, trying to contain my rage. Fury burns inside me at my situation. All the confusion I feel, hatred, and desire are wrapped in a bow over my heart.

AYDEN PERRY 269

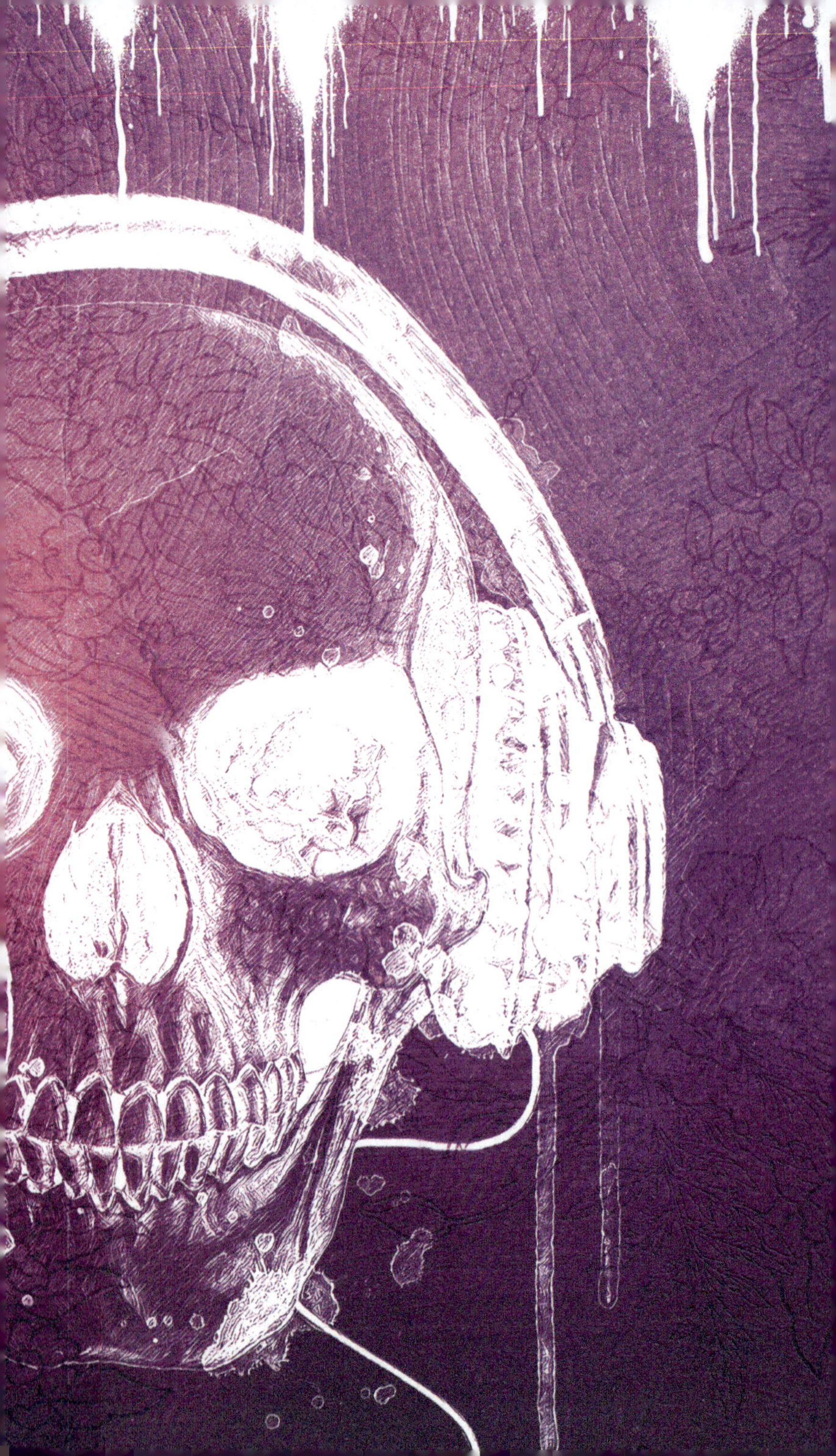

CHAPTER 27
MILES

It's been three weeks since Violet got into her accident. I've taken care of her every chance I had in between school and working on the bot with Shawn. I've even received my acceptance letter from the engineering school I want to go to in California. I just need to win the final battle bot tournament.

I walk downstairs to find Violet curled up on the couch, watching another episode of *Criminal Minds*. She said she grew to love the suspense of these shows when she was looking for ways to kill my father. I'm sure she knows by now, she's not cut out for murdering someone.

"Hey, how are you feeling today?" I ask her.

She looks at me with a smile. "Better. A little sore in the ribs when I move certain ways still, but better every day." I move her legs and place them on my lap. "Is today the day?"

I knead my thumbs into the soles of her feet,

causing a moan to leave her lips. "It is."

"Mmm," she hums. "Can I go with you?"

That causes me to pause. She was scolding me for sneaking into her room last night, and now she wants to disregard my father's rules, again. This woman is giving me whiplash. If my dad were to find out she left the house with cuts and dark, yellowing bruises still visible on her face, he would kill me. Then her because she can't help herself from butting in. There'd be no need to win this event to get us out of here because we'd both be dead. Yesterday was only minor for him. She hasn't seen what he is capable of, and I hope she never does.

"You could, but then you can't help saving me," I say.

Her eyes are downcast. "You're right."

"I'll be back as soon as it's over. I just need you to trust me," I say, going back to rubbing her feet.

She sinks back down into her bundle of throw blankets. *I know she's sad, but it's for her own good.*

Lifting her legs off me, I get up. "Wish me luck?"

"You don't need luck. You got this." She gives me a smile before going back to watching her show.

If only there were something I could do.

I pull up beside Shawn's truck. The battle bot in the back is covered in a tarp. We worked so hard on it the past three weeks. I'm absolutely positive we will win.

He gets out of his ride with a shit-eating grin. He forfeited the independent battle to help me, but what he asked for paymentwise makes me wonder about his mind.

I told him everything to expect down to the last detail. The information only intrigued and excited him more. He pulls the tarp back, exposing the beautiful metal trap. The shocking purples and gleaming silver are stunning.

"You like it?" Shawn asks.

"Holy shit, man." I touch the smooth paint of the electric-violet hues. "This is amazing."

"I figured you'd appreciate that." He's still grinning, feeding off my reaction. "Let's go fuck their shit up."

"Hell yeah," I say.

We get the battle bot inside still covered by the tarp. The crowd tonight is massive, all because it's the final battle. This is when all the work we've put into perfecting our robots comes into play. All the events leading up to this moment were ways to analyze our components. Like many of the rest, we've paired up. The cash prize is large enough to split, but with the school I've applied for, I'll need all of it. That's where Shawn and my agreement comes into play.

"Everyone to your places. The battle royal will start in five minutes," the overhead speaker announces.

"It's going to be good, man." Shawn claps me on the shoulder, reassuring me.

My hands are sweating, and I wipe my palms on my jeans. We get into our respective corners of the pit that's been gated off in an octagon. The other opponents are doing the same. Some of them look as nervous as I am, while others are grinning ear to ear with excitement. The ones who have the same anxious energy as I do must be just as desperate for the prize money as I am.

"The battle will begin in *three*." The speakers vibrate with the announcer's voice. "*Two*." The voice grows louder, and the wait between the countdown grows.

Shawn and I hold separate controls that operate different parts of the bot. Even the crowd is growing restless with their screams and chatter. I put one of my earbuds in to help keep me calm and keep me focused.

"*One*. Time to rumble," the announcer finally calls.

Shawn gives me a nod. Our play is in action as we move in time like dancers. The floors move with spikes coming up in sections, ready to take out the tires and undercarriages. There are even rows of fire along the edges of the pit for those trying to take the exterior of the octagon.

One of the players comes near our bot. I swivel the claw and hammer while Shawn moves the bottom of the bot closer to them. They make a simple mistake of backing into the fire line. Their paint singes, and before it causes any real damage, they are forced to come to us instead. I use the claw to hold them and the hammer to beat into the top of their chassis until the wires begin to show.

"Corrupting Violet just took out Mass Destruction, EmCarBot1998," the announcer screams in excitement.

"That was quick, Charlie. I wasn't expecting one to go out that fast," the partner announcer says as they chat back and forth, describing the scene before them for the audience members who are too far back to see.

"Right. Then that hammer action." Charlie whistles.

The battle continues, other bots getting taken out left and right. Metal pieces scatter the floor, and the smell of burned electrical wiring fills the room. The event coordinators open the doors to let out the smoke. I bounce in time with the music in my one earbud, getting comfortable with my movements.

"The Green Monster is on fire. Did you see that,

Marty?" Charlie calls overhead.

"Yeah, I saw that. It was pushed into the spike strip by Machine Killer. He's made quite a few upgrades, but I think Corrupting Violet might be the one to beat with the way it's smashing everyone to pieces," calls Marty.

"Don't get too cocky, Miles," Shawn hisses from my side.

I give him a curt nod, furrowing my brow. I can't let my guard down.

Metal clanks together as more bots are destroyed. I'm beginning to feel good about our odds until Machine Killer is in our way. The same guy who took me out the first time squares up. His bot has been modified and stands taller than ours. My heart races at the comparison.

The crowd calls out both our bots' names in a chant and stomps their feet.

"These are the last two opponents, Charlie. Who do you think will be the last one standing?" Marty asks.

"I don't know. The crowd is pretty split on this one," Marty says.

Shawn moves us slowly before he cuts me a side-eye. I get ready, holding my controller in position for the grab and smash method. Then we get a glimpse of what Machine Killer has been hiding. He flares a line of flames from one of the tubes. I've been so focused on taking out the bots in front of me and completely forgot to keep an eye on him. I have no idea what his moves are, or what he has been doing to take out the other bots.

I'm guessing Shawn can see the panic in me, because he whispers, "Just trust me, Miles. Keep doing what you've been doing. When I give the signal, be ready."

We sit there, inching forward. Slowly. The anticipation is killing me, but I have to stay calm and trust Shawn. Even the crowd must be feeling the weight of this moment with how quiet they are. They are leaning on the edges of their seats, waiting.

Shawn clicks his tongue, and I hold the controller tighter. He presses a button causing Corrupting Violet to rev, speeding toward Machine Killer. The crowd gasps in unison. We've been holding on to this trick for the whole match, waiting for this moment.

***

"That is going to be remembered as the fight of the century," Marty says.

"One we will never forget." Charlie whistles.

My hands are still clenched around the controller, and the overhead announcer calls out the winner.

We gather our parts and head for the exit. The crowd is still pushing through the doors when a black hood falls off a blonde-haired woman in front me. *Violet?*

I weave through the sea of people, trying to reach her.

"Miles. Miles!" Shawn screams, but I'm trapped in the sea of bodies crushing each other to get out of the door.

I'm so close to the person who looks like Violet until she gets past a bulky, tall guy, and I lose her. Continuing to push past people, I finally make it outside. With my head on a swivel, I look around, but I still don't see her. Maybe she was a figment of my imagination. She would listen to me and stay at home. Right?

"Hey, what did you take off for?" Shawn asks from behind me.

He's still pushing the cart with our broken bot inside. "I thought I saw blonde hair. I thought it was her."

"Maybe it was all the stress from the match." He claps me on the shoulder. "Or maybe it was just someone who looked like her."

"Maybe," I say, letting out a breath.

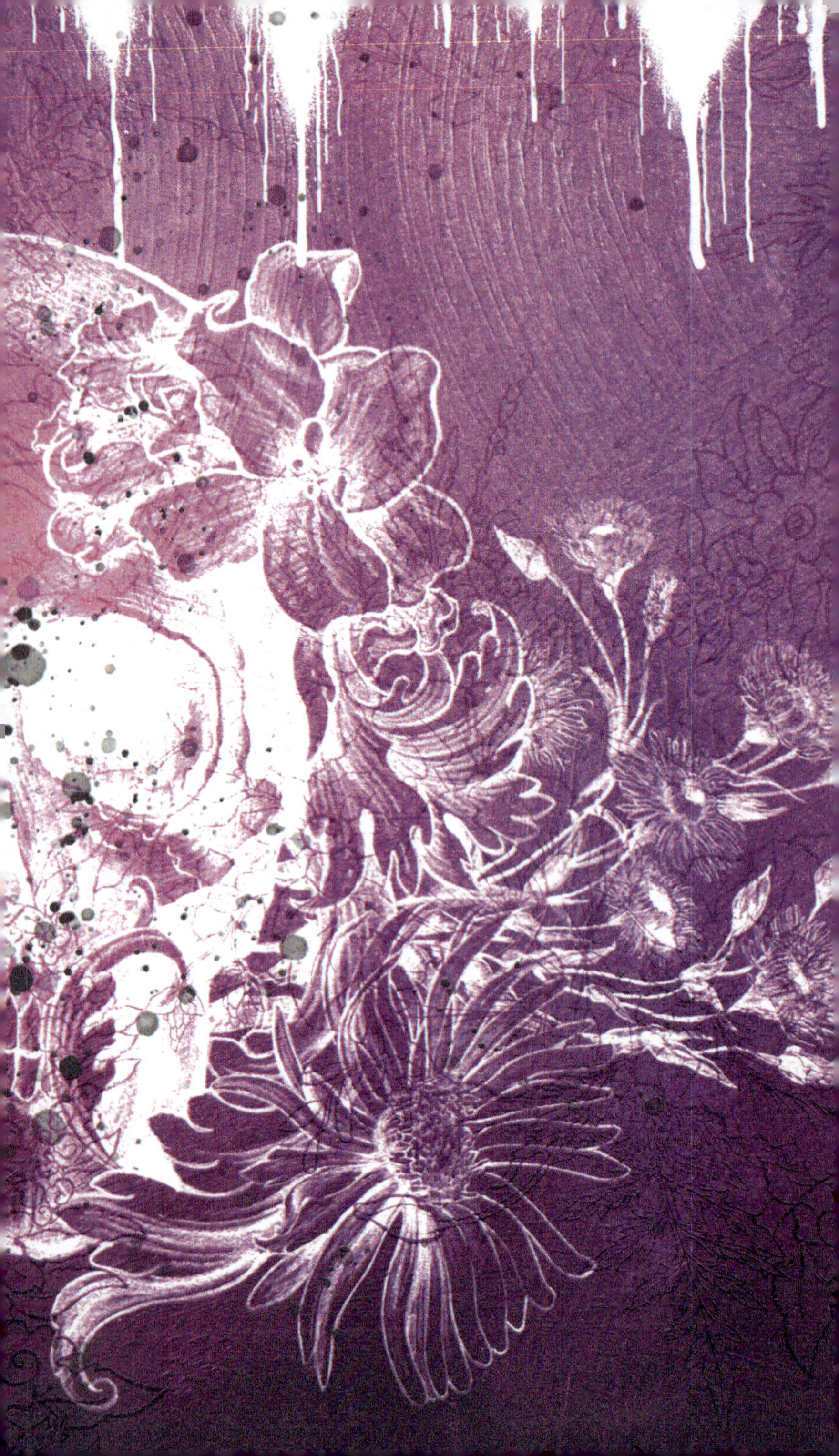

CHAPTER 28
VIOLET

I couldn't stay at home. It's not that I don't trust Miles. The only thing I can blame it on is trauma, and my inability to trust people in general.

I'm squished between fans in the bleachers with my hood over my head. Miles is in a box with another guy as they control this robot that's going around fighting other robots. This is way more intense than I thought it would be. When he told me about it, I thought it was cool, but I definitely didn't think it would be like this.

The robots are down to the final two. The others were taken out by moving each other into the spikes or the flames that lined the cage. But the whole time, I couldn't keep my eyes off the electric violet that dominated my field of vision. When the announcer called Corrupting Violet for the first time, tears sprang to my eyes. He named his robot after me. *Me.*

I've never felt so cared about in my entire life,

and he didn't want me to come see this. I knew it wasn't him. It was his father's image. If someone saw the marks on my face and the faint bruises that are still too dark to cover up without looking odd, they would make up some wild media story about how the mayor is abusive or something. Or if they had found my car wrapped around a tree, they would think I wasn't in good enough mental health to be at the mayor's side. People would flip the vote just to save me in some way saying, "Oh she is struggling, he needs to get down off the throne, so he can spend more time with her. Blah, Blah, Blah."

    I watch Miles as he focuses on the battle. His hands are gripping the controller with intensity, and his body is leaned forward to get closer to the fight.

    The last robot on the field is just as ruthless as his, and the announcers overhead say as much. "This is a fight to remember," they say. When the Machine Killer shoots out flames with its flame thrower, my heart rate kicks up a notch. I cross my fingers, an old superstition, I'm not even sure where I got it from, but I'm pushing all the luck in my body toward Miles. He needs this just as much as I do. I'm not sure what his plan is, but he seems to think this is the key.

    I'm on the edge of my seat as they inch closer to one another. One inch at a time. The people sitting next to me are whispering about what they might be doing, but I can't focus on them. I'm in my own bubble, and the world around me is void of color and sound, except for that piercing violet.

    Corrupting Violet speeds forward right into the Machine Killer. I thought they had it until Machine Killer lets out this spring mechanism that has it going back a few inches. Only a few, not enough to push it into line of fire, which I've seen Miles doing, cornering his prey. Violet springs forward again, grabbing the robot by one of its parts to hold it in place while a chainsaw comes out of a hidden compartment. The crowd gasps in unison. Both opponents are tearing each other apart. Pieces are falling off. Sparks are flying. Flames are consuming Violet, but it's so close to the Machine Killer that the flames consume it too. The ring fills with smoke and the battling robots grow quiet. The employees opened the doors, but the fumes aren't clearing fast enough for us to see.

Everyone is holding their breaths, sitting on the edge of their seats, waiting for the smoke in the ring to clear. When it does though, the whole crowd riots. Bodies around me stand, yelling, and people are arguing over the money they bet.

"I'm not sure we can call this one," Charlie states. "Both bots lie in pieces."

"Right. This is going to be a hard one to judge since the smoke made it hard to tell who gave in first," Marty says. "We will have to reconvene everyone. Check the website next week to see what we decide."

The people in the stands move in an agitated way. It's almost like a beehive as we move in unison toward the double doors. I pull my hood tighter around my hair, so that I don't get caught by Miles. Even though I know he will be distracted with the turn of events, it's always better to be safe than sorry.

"That is going to be remembered as the fight of the century," Marty says.

"One we will never forget." Charlie whistles.

They got that right. I'll never be able to forget this moment with the violet machine fighting for me. It warms my chest just thinking about it.

I push through the crowd as we all get through the small doors. An elbow flies toward my face, and I duck, barely missing it. I don't need another bruise to add to the catastrophe that is currently my face. Though it missed, the appendage did skim the top of my head, pushing the hood away. I'm almost outside at this point, so I don't bother fixing it. *There's really no point now.* Once I'm outside, I suck in a large breath of clean air. It was extremely smoky inside. And with the pressing bodies, I'm surprised we all didn't pass out.

In my new car, I turn on the radio playing the alternative rock station and soak into the feels. It's the only thing I can do considering Miles's efforts were all put into this one event that failed us. I'm almost certain he didn't think of another plan. My stomach churns, because like every other man in my life, I'm let down once more. It's not Miles's fault. I know that. But my life is over, and that's a hard pill to swallow.

When I pull into the driveway, Wade's car is there. A cold sweat breaks out over my skin. I'm stuck between going inside and facing the music or sitting in my car and never going inside, ever again. But Miles's face passes through my mind, and for some reason, I can't just walk away. Instead, I inhale a deep calming breath and turn off the car.

I ease the front door open, hoping Wade will be in his office. It's a dumb thing to wish for, considering my car was missing. Wade leans against the foyer table, rubbing his hand over the stubble on his jaw.

"I had someone call me," he states, still not looking at me.

"What?" I'm not sure where he is going with this.

He looks up at me with hard eyes. "I said, someone called me. They saw you leave the house."

"You had someone watching the house?" My voice squeaks. I wish I hadn't gone. I'm fucking shaking.

"Where were you, Violet?" he asks, stalking toward me.

My feet backtrack. "I wasn't anywhere. I just went for a drive."

"I'm not sure I believe you," he growls. "You could ruin my career, you know."

The adrenaline in my blood is pounding in my ears. I can't give Miles away. He never told his dad about his battle bots because it was his only way out. My legs act before I can register what I'm doing. Flight takes over, and I run into the kitchen, looping around to the living room. I do this all in the hopes of throwing Wade off. I just need to get back out the front door. *Leave, I just need to leave.* The front door is within my reach. *I'm so close.*

"No. The fuck. You don't," Wade hisses, and pain spikes through my scalp. He grabs a fistful of my hair and pulls me back to his chest. "You'll answer when spoken to, you little bitch."

Tears prick my eyes at the pain. *I can't tell him. I can't betray Miles like that.* I'm clenching my fists, ready to rear back and connect my elbow with his ribs or side, whatever I can reach, when the front door opens.

Miles is standing in the doorway. His eyes are wide for a second before they narrow. "What's going on here?"

"*Our* little bitch here, decided to leave the house." He pulls on my hair, causing me to hiss in pain. "And she won't tell me where she's been."

"Is that right?" Miles asks. There's only a slight change in his demeanor before he stalks toward us in a calculated manner. It takes me by surprise how quickly he can take on his father's persona.

"Where have you been, little slut?" Wade's words are harsh in my ear. This is unlike anything sweet or sexy. Nothing like the degrading way I like so much from Miles. No, this is pure cruelty.

"I told you where I was," I hiss. My teeth clench together in an attempt to hold back tears.

"She was with me," Miles says with a twisted smile on his face. *What the fuck is he doing?* I'm sure he can see the shock in my eyes, because his smile grows.

"And why the fuck was she with you?" Wade asks, not letting up on his grip.

"Because we've been fucking for the last month," Miles states in a nonchalant way.

The grip on my hair loosens as I'm thrown to the floor. Wade lunges at his son, throwing him against the closed door. "You little shit," Wade roars.

"What? You weren't fucking her, Father." Miles is still smiling while Wade is only a hairbreadth away from his face. "I figured, why waste a good piece of ass?"

What is he doing? Wade balls his fists up at his side. My palms are sweating, and my heart is racing. *No. No, no, no, no.* Wade begins punching Miles in the face. He just stands there taking every blow. Wade isn't letting up. With the rate he's going, he may kill him.

"Stop, please. Stop," I cry, running toward them. I grab hold of Wade's forearm, slowing his blows. "Stop. He's lying. Please."

Wade turns on me, and I fall to the floor on my ass. "I won't let a cheap piece of ass turn my son against me." Then his shiny black shoe connects with my side, my back, and last, my head. The last thing I see is bright red blood coating the shine of his shoe.

I blink my eyes multiple times, clearing the film

that covers them. A pounding in my head thunders loudly as sharp threads of pain pierce my jaw. I groan and try to move my arms with no luck. Biting my lip, I try again. My shoulder blades grind together with every attempt, causing me to cry out. Tears stream down my cheeks.

The moisture clears from my vision. I rest my head against my arm as I look up at the chains holding my wrists in place. I'm in the basement, held in place just as my mother was. In this very spot. The pain in my body throbs, and the fire in my belly grows. Grinding my teeth together, I suck in air and bellow out a scream that reverberates in the semi-empty room around me.

Can you hear me? Whoever in the fuck is up there that has some control over my fate, fucking hear me.

As soon as I think this, the door upstairs opens with a whoosh, and multiple pairs of feet walk downstairs. Everybody who surrounds me is covered in black robes and hoods that shadow their faces. I can't make out who anyone is. One of them stands in front of me and removes their hood. My heart clenches in my chest at the sight of his chiseled, defined face and curly, soft brown hair. There's a lump in my throat, and a whimper escapes me, revealing my agony at the sight of him before me. He's with *them* of all people. *He betrayed me?*

"Why?" My words come out as a sob, and the tears stream down my cheeks more fluidly. I can't hold them back any longer.

The cloaked figure next to Miles removes his hood with his cruel smirk. *Wade.*

"Did you really think my son would fall for a gold-digging whore like you?" He ponders with his forefinger on his chin. "No, wait. You're not a gold-digging whore. Well, you once were. Weren't you, Violet Viceroy?" He grabs hold of my side, and a sharp throb spikes up my arms as I sway over the bucket. My toes only skim the bottom where an inch of water lies.

"I bet you didn't tell him how your mother begged me to help you and your sister. I found you a good home, did I not?"

I grit my teeth at him. That wasn't the point. I might have gone to a good home, but my sister didn't. He separated us.

"My mother paid your price"—I seethe—"with her life."

He clicks his tongue at me. "Then why are you here?"

The pain I feel all over is well deserved. "My sister needed me to end you."

"Why didn't she come to kill me herself?" Wade asks.

"Because it's a part of my redemption. It's something I needed to do to earn my forgiveness."

Wade chuckles. "You are one of the worst assassins I've ever met, and," he says, pulling my hair back so that I'm looking him in the eyes, "trying to have sex with you wasn't worth the trouble. I'm not even sure what my son sees in you."

His words don't hurt me. "I've never cared for you, nor your opinion." I spit in his face, then grit my teeth from the low throb in my scalp.

"Well, maybe Miles can show you how much he cares about my opinion." He pushes my head, letting go of my hair. My body swings, and I grab hold of the chain to make it more steady and decrease the pinch on my wrists.

Miles steps forward, grabbing the remote from Wade that must control the wiring connected to the chains holding me. "Do you know why they blindfold prisoners before execution?" He repeats the line that I heard his father say when we were hiding in the closet. That moment he caught me, held me, kissed me, and followed me to the hotel.

My chest aches at the look in his eyes. They are full of sorrow.

"So they can't see their eyes bulge out of their head," I say, repeating the punch line.

He shakes his head at me, glances down at his feet before looking back up at me. "No," he whispers. "It's so they don't see the pain in their eyes at their last dying moment."

I bite the inside of my cheeks so as not to cry. This can't be him. *What did Wade say to change his mind?*

Well, this isn't how I end. I refuse to let him take me down without feeling some regret for it. I'll leave a mark on his soul and haunt his ass forever. I push my shoulders back the best I can and hold my head high. "Well as a prisoner, I have one dying wish."

Miles's brows furrow in confusion before he glances back at his dad.

"Oh, this is glorious," Wade says. "What would be your dying wish? Humor me."

I lick my dry lips and make it a point to stare at Wade. I'm not going to look at Miles as I say this, because I don't want to see his reaction. I'm afraid of what I'll find there. I want to go down fighting. "I want your son to fuck me like he hates me as my eyes bulge out of their fucking sockets."

A piercing whistle rings out from Wade's lips. "You're a feisty little cunt. No wonder my son loved that lying pussy so much." He shakes his head. "Well, guys. This is going to be more eventful than I anticipated."

Miles's jaw flexes, but other than that slight movement, I can't decipher what he's thinking.

"What's the matter? Can't handle the challenge?"

I ask with acid lacing my tone.

Fuck this fucking family. The fire burning in my veins fuels my hatred. I'm not going to lie down and die. I refuse. If he wants to kill me, then he will have to look me in the eyes while I fucking die on his cock.

"I guess I've fully corrupted Violet," he says before glancing at his dad. "I'll accept her challenge." The name of his bot. My eyes sting at the realization.

Wade laughs and claps his son on the shoulder. "That's my boy." He turns toward his followers all smug. "I told you he would step up to the plate when it came time."

Miles undresses, removing his black cloak and jeans. He's still as beautiful as I remember. With every move he makes, his muscles flex in the light shining overhead. When he comes up to me, still holding the black remote, he grabs hold of my legs, wrapping them around his waist.

"Why are you doing this, Violet?" he whispers.

"Because I deserve better, and I refuse to let you get away with this with a simple push of a button. If you're going to kill me, then I'll make you remember every fucking minute of it," I seethe. The hatred boiling inside me. I grit my teeth at the pain that stabs me in the side with every move. I refuse to let these assholes see me cry.

He pushes into me slowly. "Get it over with, Miles. We want to hear her scream," Wade says from within the shadows.

He and his posse of brainless followers are hiding within the shadows, so I can't see their expressions.

"Fuck you," I scream, earning a round of chuckles from the void.

Miles begins moving inside me. The pain is there, but it's not something I can focus on while he fucks me. I grind my hips into him, moaning in ecstasy. I'll give them a show they will never forget. He presses the button on the controller as a shock of electricity courses through my wrists. I grit my teeth and groan.

"That's it. Break her," Wade commands.

I can't speak. The waves of energy course through my arms, shoulders, all the way down to my clit. The pulses that land there are ones I don't expect. The mix of pain and pleasure at its finest. If this is how I die, then at least this is a good way to go, coming on the cock of my executioner.

Miles is feeling it as well because his movements slow. His lips brush along my neck. Everywhere we are connected the electricity is more intense.

"You should have trusted me, little flower," he whispers. I shiver in his hold when his warm breath fans over the shell of my ear. The lights around us flash, but Miles never stops fucking me. "Look at me and only me," he commands.

Flashes and bangs go off around us, and a whirring sound is the last thing I hear before the lights flashing in my eyes go completely dark.

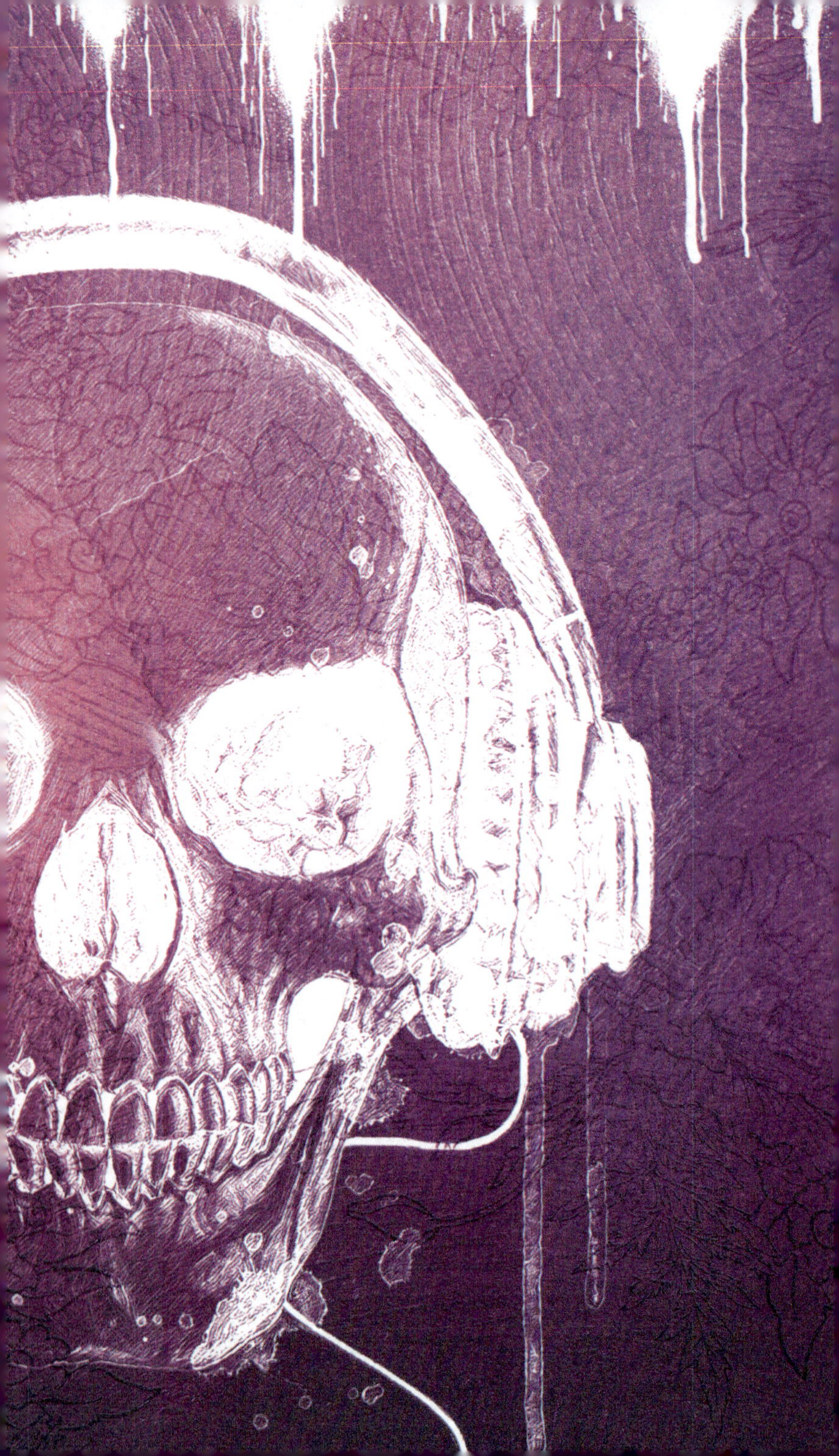

CHAPTER 29

MILES

It takes everything within me to push the button on the remote to stop the low shocks of electricity, since I lost all feeling in my fingers. I corrupted the remote with Shawn's help to decrease its settings. Dad would have never known with Violet's injuries that it was lower than normal.

We've been planning this for weeks. It just seemed like the perfect time to play into my father's wrath, so I sent off a quick text to Shawn to let him know it was time. I slide out of her sopping wet cunt and gently uncurl her legs from around me. My limbs are slow, like I'm running in water, but they will slowly come back to life soon. The pins and needles are already starting to creep down my arms and fingertips as the feeling comes back to them.

The bodies of my father's followers lie around me, blood and brain matter oozing down the cement walls. I grab my black robe and jeans off the floor and pull them back on. Shawn comes out of the closet, grinning ear to ear.

"Fuck, man. That was hot," Shawn says as he hands me the controller of our backup bot.

"I'm going to kill you. You're no son of mine. You'll regret the day you ever came into this world. The governor of California will have your head on a spike." My father spits and sputters. The bot's claws are wrapped around his neck, holding him in place on his knees, and the hammer hangs over his head.

Violet is still dangling from the chain wrapped around her wrists, and her head is flopped over. *I can't leave her like that.* My limbs, still feeling the pins and needles, move as if they are foreign objects. I grab the key from my father's pocket, ignoring his berating words. He tries to grab me, and I dodge him until he finally latches onto my robe.

I glare at him with gritted teeth. The need to get to Violet is fueling all my moves at this moment. "If you don't let go of me, I'll drop that hammer on your head."

He lets go of me, quicker than I thought he would. "You will regret this."

"I don't think you even know how deep in shit you are. The governor of Washington knows everything. He won't let your precious governor of California touch me," I spit. Shawn stands off to the side, waiting for an order to follow. "Your plan to move up, take over Washington, and partner with Governor Bryson is over."

"You really think he will let you go, just like that?" my father asks.

"No, but anything is better than living under your rules," I snap.

"That's what you think now."

I grip the keys tight. The grooves cut into my

palm as I run over to Violet. I place my fingers against her neck, checking her pulse, and it thuds weakly under my fingertips. *Fuck.* I need to get her down. I quickly unlock the chain and grab her around the waist. She falls limply against my shoulder.

I lay her down on the floor, gently, my hands cradling her head. "Violet. Wake up." She doesn't move and the pulse in her neck is gone. My heart is pounding rapidly in my chest as it echoes in my ears. "Violet, don't you dare fucking die on me."

With my hands over her chest, I pump. "Violet," I cry. "Please. I promise to treat you right and give you everything you truly deserve. You deserve the best of everything in this world, and if you come back to me, I'll prove that to you until my very last breath," I pant out between each thrust on her chest. Pleading with everything in me for her to come back.

Her chest rises as she sucks in a sharp breath. I grab her up into my arms, cradling her against me and wrapping her up in my cloak.

"You can't do that ever again," I whisper, tears streaming down my face. I never cry, but the thought of losing her is enough to break me.

"If I were to die, dying on your dick is the best way to go out," she says hoarsely, making me chuckle.

"You fucking bitch."

"Only for you." She wraps her arms around my neck, crawling into my lap.

"Umm, I know the two of you are having a moment and all, but we have business to attend to," Shawn says, waving a hand toward my father, who is grabbing the bot's claw that's clamped around his neck. He's attempting to pull it off but failing miserably.

"I think we got it from here, Shawn. You're good to go."

"I just wanted to make sure Violet is cool with our agreement."

"I'll talk to her about it. Don't worry. I'll explain everything when she is more with it," I say.

"Okay, man. Call me if you need anything else." He waves before ascending the basement stairs.

I sit there holding Violet, appreciating this moment with her. I'm not sure how much time passes before I hear my father screaming. He apparently fucked up one of the claw's springs because it's now tighter on his neck. His eyes are round as saucers as he scratches at the bot in panic. *He shouldn't have fucked with it.*

"Can you stop that screaming? My head hurts," Violet says with her eyes still closed.

"Yeah." I stand to carry her upstairs.

"You're just going to leave me here?" my father screams, his voice shrill and strained.

"Yeah, we'll be back to get you. Better stop fucking with my bot, or it will blow up with you in its clutches." I chuckle before turning off the basement light and closing the door. His screams grow faint the farther we get away.

I continue up the next flight of stairs, and Violet nuzzles her face in the crook of my neck. The movement sends a shiver down my spine.

Fuck, she is perfect.

AYDEN PERRY 295

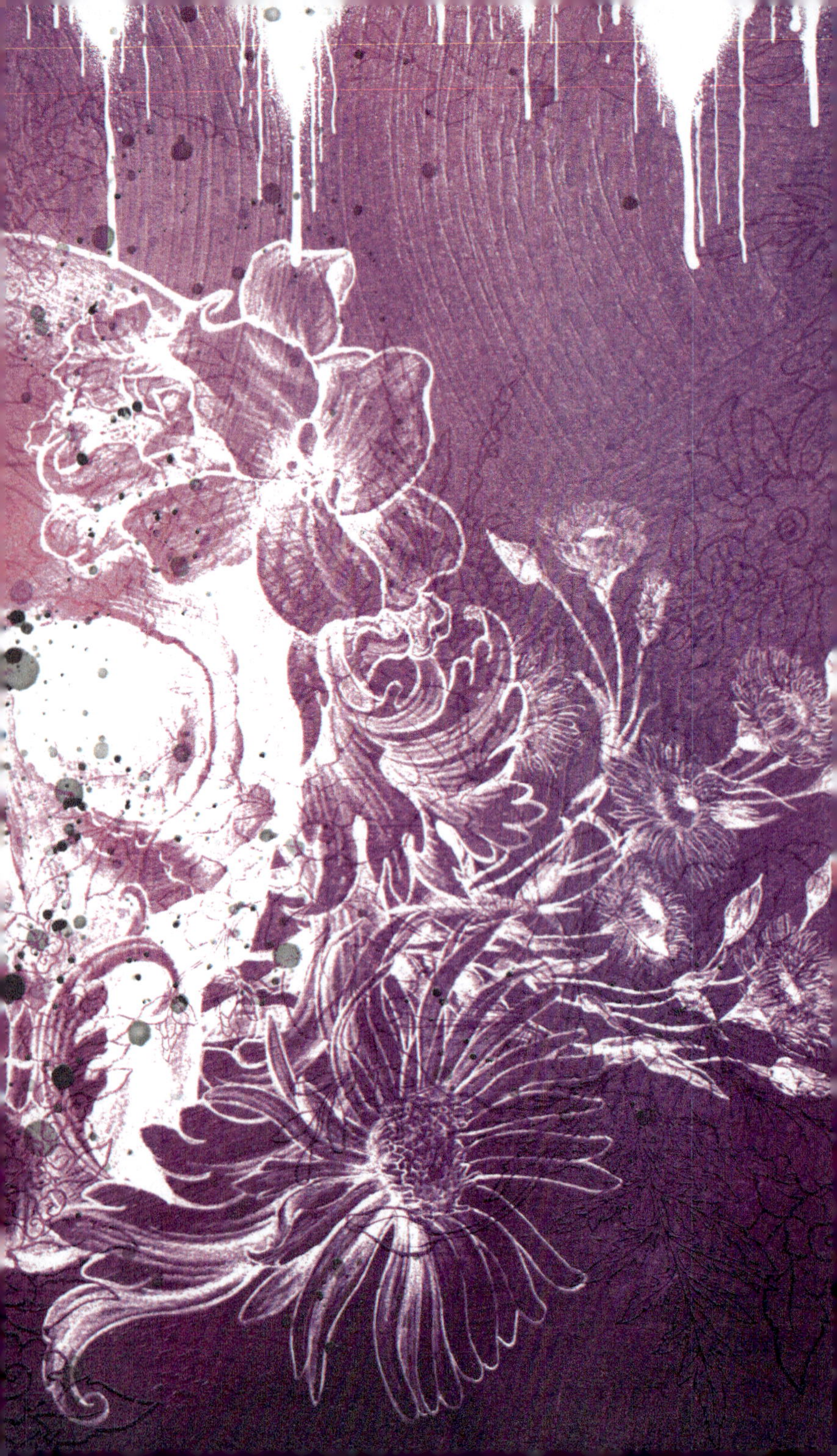

CHAPTER 30
VIOLET

The last thing I remember is the look in his eyes, wet and shiny from crying. His words ring in my ears. *You deserve the best of everything in this world.* My chest aches. Not the kind of ache from the obvious cuts, bruises, and—I'm almost positive—broken rib. No, that you're loved so thoroughly that your heart can't expand any further or it might combust, kind of pain. I've never had that before.

A heavy weight holds me down. I stretch, causing sharp aches to spring up all over. A groan leaves my lips, followed by his warmth leaving me.

"Are you okay?" He's leaning over, checking every inch of my naked and bruised body.

"I think I'm fine, just a little banged up." His eyes are softer as he looks down at me. "Don't pity me, asshole."

That brilliant smile of his flashes across his face,

stretching out his split lip and causing some of his bruises to pinch together. "I would never."

"Huh, yeah, sure," I chide him. Sitting up in bed is harder than I expect. Miles is there helping my every move like a mother hen. This should be the time I ask him. "What deal did you make?"

He freezes, which isn't a good sign. "I was going to ask you, but everything happened so fast. I—"

I hold up my hand, cutting him off. "Just tell me."

"I had a plan the whole time, you know. The battle royal wasn't the only card up my sleeve," he explains, crouching down in front of me and grabbing my hands. I know he's trying to soften the blow from the bomb he's about to drop.

"I'm sorry I didn't trust you. I went to see your match because I was nervous. You know my trust issues. It was never you," I say, letting go of his hands to hold his bruised cheeks. "It was just trauma, and I need to have more faith in you. I'll work on that."

"I know, and I'm sorry I had to involve you," he admits. "My father has been abusive with me, but never like that. Nothing like that."

"It must be in combination with finding out who I am," I say, placing the puzzle pieces together in my mind. "What did you promise Shawn?" I ask him, needing to know everything.

"He got a sex tape out of it." His lips draw into a hard line.

I laugh, doubling over, holding in the pain lancing through my abdomen. "That was all?"

His brow arches at my reaction. "You're not upset?"

"No, I'm alive. What does he want with the sex tape anyway? It's not like he can post it online anywhere. It would be evidence with everyone dead."

"The dark web," he states with complete seriousness.

"Holy shit. I guess that's not far off considering your dad, and that dinner I had with the governor." I shudder, remembering that night. My sister is involved in some dark dealings, but I honestly don't ask. Maybe I should have asked before getting myself involved.

"Yeah." He strokes my cheek. "You might have come in with dark plans, but you hold innocence and pain in your eyes, little flower." That causes tears to spring to my eyes. "I never wanted you to be tainted or corrupted with this life, as you already know. I tried to get you to leave."

"I know. You just weren't good at it." I smile sheepishly at him.

"I underestimated you and downplayed my feelings." He stands, extending his hand to me. "Let's get you dressed, and I'll make you some coffee."

"What about your dad?" I ask, taking his hand and using it as leverage to stand.

"I don't think he will be going anywhere anytime soon." He hands me a shirt and helps me pull it over my head.

We both get dressed and head downstairs. Miles helps me every step of the way, and my insides come alive with butterflies with the way he handles me. He's so caring. Something I deserve. I have to start appreciating the good in my life. I can't dwell on the bad any longer. My new mantra in life will be *I deserve better*, because I do. I might have done many things in my life that I regret, but torturing myself shouldn't be what takes over my life. If I want to make things right, I have to start by forgiving myself.

Miles puts on the coffee as I ease myself into the kitchen chair. My muscles ache slightly with the move. It will take a while before *all* the pain is fully gone. I shiver as a chill runs over my body. *Fuck. Why is it so cold?*

"Miles?"

"Yeah?" He grabs coffee cups from the top shelf and places them on the counter.

"Do you mind grabbing my throw blanket? I'm fucking freezing," I say, grabbing my arms and rubbing them for warmth.

"Yeah, sure."

He runs to the living room, leaving me trying to curl into myself at the table. I hope I'm not getting sick or something. This house is always cold, but right now it feels like a walk-in freezer. Maybe it's finally coming down from weeks of an ongoing adrenaline rush. As I'm leaning over the table, attempting to rub a fire into my arms, I'm yanked out of my seat by my hair.

"*Ahhh*," I scream, but that's all I get out before hands cut off my breathing.

Wade is in my face, leaning me over the table. The blood vessels in his eyes are broken, and blood is smeared across his cheeks. I glance down at his neck, and it's bruising with scattered cuts, though they all missed both his arteries and airway. *Lucky fucker.*

"If I'm going down, you're going with me," he hisses through bared teeth.

The only thing that comes from me are squeaks as I try to breathe. I scratch at his forearms, attempting to dislodge him, but nothing. My chest is on fire with the lack of oxygen. There's a loud crack as wood shards rain down around me. Miles must've hit his father with a chair. I can't see him. My vision is blurry. I run my hands over the table until my fingers brush a splintered piece of wood. Footsteps are pounding in my ears, and I'm jerked up with Wade. Miles can't dislodge him. The only thing left to do is kill him. I muster all the strength I have left in my body and ram the piece of wood still in my grasp into his neck.

His hands loosen their hold around my neck as a shower of warm blood pours down on me. The look of shock in his eyes brings me satisfaction. My lungs scream as I gasp for air.

"Violet, are you okay?" Miles is by my side, crouched on the floor.

"Yeah."

The gravity of what I've done hasn't hit me yet. My head is swimming as if I'm mentally doing laps in a river of quicksand, and the room seems even colder now. I shiver and hold myself again. Miles wraps my blanket around me before he guides me to my feet.

"Come on, let's sit outside." He continues to guide me. My head is in a daze. He sits me down on one of the metal porch seats that looks over the horizon. He squats down to look me in the eyes and squeezes my thighs. "You did what you had to do, Violet. Do you hear me?" I nod at him, but I can't seem to make words come to my mouth. "You sit here. I'll bring you a cup of coffee, and I'll dispose of the bodies."

He stands to go inside, but I grab a hold of his forearm. "Can I ask you one thing?"

Then he's back at my eye level, holding my hands. "Anything."

"Can we bury your father in my garden?"

The longer I sit here thinking about what I did, the less I care.

The only thing I regret is not killing him sooner.

Warm summer air blows my hair, whipping it in my face. The trees extend over the hill with the sun coming up over the horizon. My hands shake as they grip the coffee mug. I'm attempting to collect its warmth because the black cloud swirling inside me is sucking all of mine out. The breeze isn't as cool as it is high up in the tower, which I'm thankful for.

I flex my fingers to stop the itching. The blood caked on them has started to crack and peel, leaving them dry. Hazelnut aroma fills my nose, and I breathe in deep.

Where do I go from here?

The question repeats in my mind until a strong set of hands squeezes my shoulders.

"Hey, cuz," Azrael says.

"How did you find us?" I ask, but my heart isn't in it.

"Shawn posted the sex tape on the dark web. We had a talk with him, gave him money for the tape. Which you can have if you want." He pauses to gauge my reaction, but when I don't give him one, he continues, "We signed a few autographs and wiped everything from the web. We found it before the buyers got to it."

"Autographs?" That makes me laugh, but I don't even turn to look at him. "Why can't we call you Alex anymore?"

He takes a seat beside me. "Because one, I'm on the run, and two, I wanted a fresh start."

I nod, looking down at my mug and the blood on my hands. "What do I do now? Do I need to change my name?"

"No," he says calmly. "Find what sets your soul on fire and speaks to you on a level that no one else can reach."

I laugh. "Really? That's all? Anna's not going to

use this to twist me into one of her henchmen?"

"Anna never expected you to go through with this. She only wanted you to get as far as you could to show your loyalty," he explains.

I scoff and glance at him. "Was that all it was?"

"No." His brows furrow. "It was so much more than that. You needed to let go and forgive yourself. And to discover and come to the understanding that the both of you were only the by-products of an evil man who changed both of you irrevocably."

That takes me aback. I thought my sister was only trying to get back at me, but she was actually trying to show me where she was coming from. That day she stood on my doorstep, begging for my help, I turned her away because I was so focused on my image. The perfect wife to the perfect man, living in a perfect home, but life is so much more than material things. It's about so much more than that. To fight through life and realize that every day is a gift. That's what she wanted me to see.

"I'll leave you to your thoughts. It seems your friend may need our help disposing of the bodies." Azrael claps me on the shoulder, and I place my hand over his.

Then he's gone, leaving me to do just that. I wonder what life will be like after I've killed a person, how it will change me, even as they dig up the middle of my flower bed and dump all the body parts inside. I sit and watch Codi and Azrael come with the gravel as Miles packs down the dirt. The thought of losing him ignites a deep, visceral pain in my chest. That's it. My life from here on out will be about what I want, and what I deserve, living every moment as if it will be my last. Fuck what anyone else thinks.

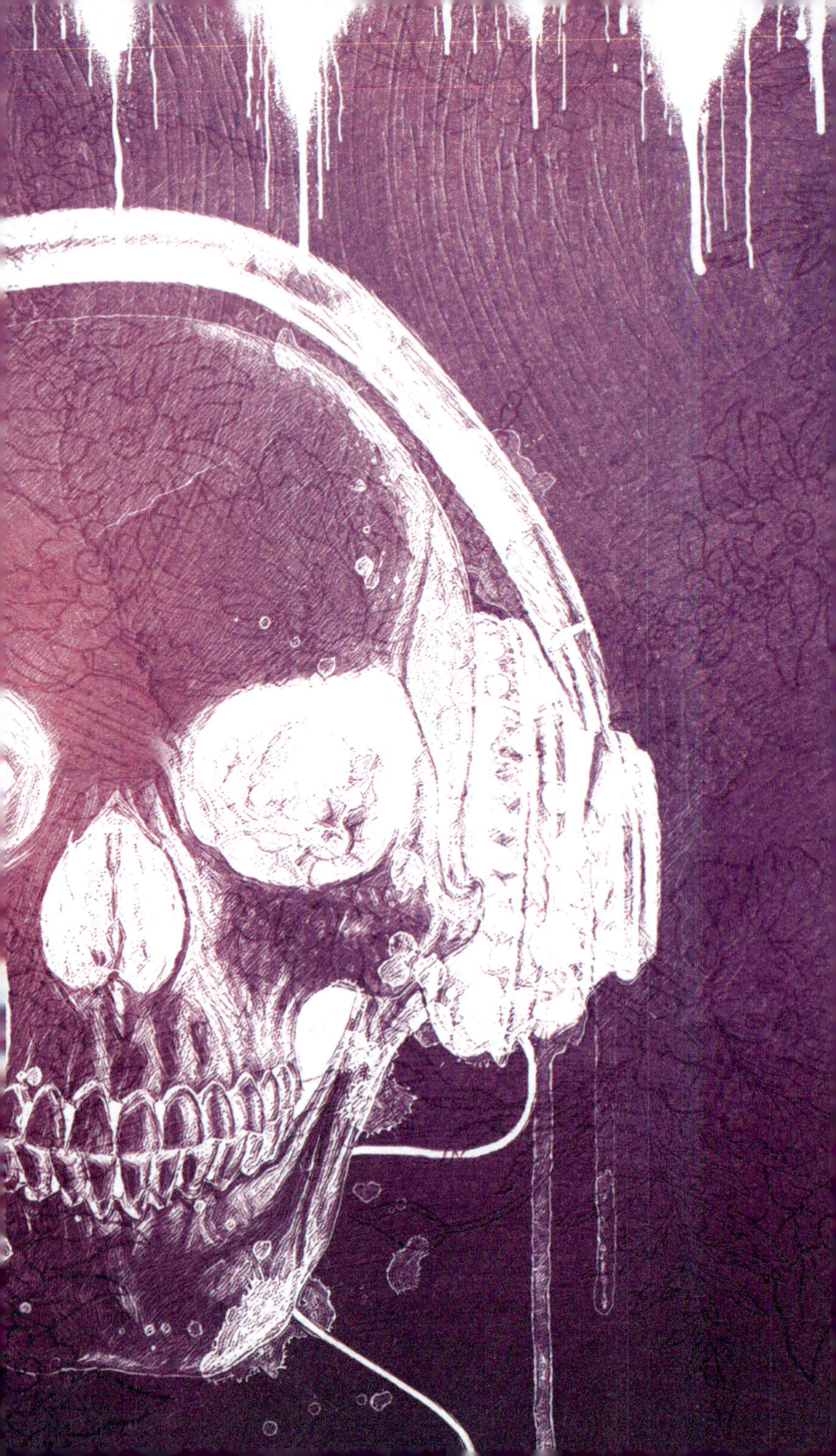

EPILOGUE
MILES

The audience erupts as Anna delivers a forceful uppercut, causing her opponent to land with a resounding thud in the middle of the boxing ring.

"Who's next?" Her question can barely be heard over the cheers of the thunderous crowd.

Several hands raise immediately, eager to take on the queen of The Death Moths. Her dark brown eyes are triumphant as she scans the crowd. Her grin spreads across her face when she finds the opponent she's looking for, and I can see the resemblance between her and Violet. It's in the way they smile, the way their noses crinkle when they are displeased. Their mannerisms are alike but different in so many ways.

The new fighter slinks between the ropes, and it's no time before the bell rings signaling the start of the next match. Violet cringes and jumps at the impact of each punch. I wrap my arms around her chest and pull her into me. She does so willingly and tension seeps from her body as she snuggles into me. Her blonde hair tickles my nose and I greedily inhale her floral essence with its hints of vanilla and raspberries.

"Come on." I grab her hand, and we get up from the stands in the middle of the match while everyone is distracted.

"Where are we going?" she asks. I cut her a look, and she laughs. "Trust you. Got it."

The turbulent crowd makes for an interesting obstacle course but I don't let that slow me down. I pull her through the neon lights of the bar, past the tables and the stage, never letting go of her hand. That is, until we get to the bathroom. It's quieter here as most of the patrons are still watching the fight.

"Miles?" Violet's brows are bunched in question at my sudden trip to the other side of the club.

"Shut up," I growl as I turn her to face me, wrapping one hand around her neck and guiding her through the metal door of the men's bathroom. The smell of her hair and the way her body fitted so perfectly into mine. I couldn't wait any longer. I claim her mouth with mine, telling her without words how I intend to claim the rest of her body.

She opens for me, willingly. I know she's ready for what I'm about to give her. I'm rough as I push her against the wall. When our kiss breaks, she's looking up at me with those pouty lips I love so much. "Now, let me praise that perfect pussy of yours, Mommy."

Her mouth opens in a gasp, but I don't give her the chance to scold me for calling her that. I'm already down on my knees, grabbing her leg, and placing it over my shoulder. Her dress rises up, giving me full access to her perfect cunt. Her hands are in my hair. She's running her nails over my scalp.

Fuuccckk.

With my knife, I cut the seam of her black lace underwear. She gasps and her nails dig in hard, egging me on in my pursuit. I drag my index finger through her lips, collecting her arousal before bringing her sweet taste to my lips.

"Mmm," I hum. "Tastes even better when you're married to me."

She's the only one to ever bring me to my knees, and I'll let her do it over and over again till the day I die.

"Stop playing around, Miles, or I swear to god," she snaps.

"No, you'll swear to me and always me," I say before my mouth is on her sweet pussy. Licking, sucking, and nibbling on her clit until she cries out my name. I release her from my mouth, but my fingers continue to work her toward the edge as I look up at her face twisted in ecstasy. She's beautiful, and she is mine. "I love pulling my name from your lips."

She groans at my teasing. "Stand up, asshole. It's my turn."

I do as she says, standing up and getting out of the doorway. I walk farther into the bathroom, and she pulls my arm, twisting me around. She's just as rough as I am when it comes to sex. *I fucking love it.*

She gets down on her knees in front of me, undoing my pants. Her eyes look up at me seductively through her lashes. I'm already straining in my pants. When she rips them down roughly, my cock springs free. Her hands grip my thighs as a wicked grin takes over her sweet, innocent face. Then she rakes her nails down, sending an electric buzz to my already throbbing dick. I'm so fucking glad she chose me. She could've had anyone, but she chose me. She continues to tease me, payback for everything I've done to her. We love to play these games with each other.

Her warm, wet tongue licks the bead of precum from the tip of my dick. The sensation electrocutes my core, causing me to jerk back.

"Oh, no you don't, baby boy," she chides while she grips my ass cheeks and pulls me in close.

"Fuck you," I growl.

Her lips wrap around the head of my cock as I run my hands through her blonde strands before grabbing a handful of it at the base of her neck. She wraps her delicate fingers around my shaft while her head begins bobbing up and down. I help her with the motion, building that euphoria to its brink.

The door to the bathroom opens, and a man walks in. I give him a devilish smile, continuing to work Violet on my cock. He smirks, but his smile falls when my eyes flash with fire. I mouth, "Mine." He gives me a curt nod, then turns to walk out. The pressure in my lower spine builds. I want everyone to know she's mine.

She grabs my balls, giving them a gentle pull. Knocking on the door to the devil's gate to play with my demons. I pull her off, throwing her to the bathroom countertop. Her hands splay out on the mirror. I grip her hair, pulling it back, forcing her to look at herself. She laughs, smiling at me, because she knows what she did to me.

I brush my lips against the shell of her ear. "You can push me all you want, but I'll always be the asshole who tamed the bitch. You're my queen, little flower, and I want everyone to know it."

With my teeth, I graze her neck, causing a forceful shiver to run down her spine. "I wouldn't have it any other way," she breathes.

I bite into her shoulder and ram my dick into her tight, wet cunt. She screams out at the intrusion, but it doesn't stop me. I want everyone in the bar to hear her scream for me. I watch her face in the mirror as I pound into her pussy. She grips me, milking me for all I'm worth.

"Is that all you've got, baby boy," she teases.

"Fuck no," I grunt.

I lift her thigh up on the counter while one foot remains on the floor. My dick hits her cervix, squeezing the head of my cock with each thrust.

"Fuckkk, yes, just like that," she moans.

Her brows bunch, and her jaw drops when my thumb rubs over her puckered hole, then plunges in. The moans that come from her are guttural. The lust, passion, longing, and love coming together in a sweet release. I keep pumping until her legs are shaking, and her pussy stops quivering.

I run water, grab some paper towels, and clean us both up while she lies on the bathroom countertop, passed out in lustful bliss. She stands on shaky legs, adjusting her dress back into place.

"You ready to go back?" I ask her, grabbing her hand, but I quickly let go because I completely forgot why I pulled her away from the match in the first place. "Ah, hold on." I pull out the wedding present that I've been hiding from her from my back pocket. When she sees it, her hands come up, covering her shocked expression. I hold up the leather strap choker with a heart lock. It fits the key my mom left me. If anyone could unlock my emotions, it would always be Violet. "Will you be the lock to my key forever?"

"Are you kidding me?" she asks before turning around and lifting her hair off her neck. "I already married your ass."

She makes my chest warm with her no-bullshit attitude. Once I clasp it, she turns back around, fingering the lock. She's beaming at the significance of this, how important it is.

"Do you like it?" I ask her.

She cradles my face. "I fucking love you. Now, kiss me, you asshole." Then her lips capture mine.

As much as we've both been through, we both deserve this little piece of heaven.

"You're so fucking perfect," I whisper against her lips.

She shakes her head and grins up at me. "Fuck perfect, it never existed."

"Well, if that's true, then you are imperfectly perfect enough for me."

AYDEN PERRY 311

312 CORRUPTING VIOLET

ACKNOWLEDGMENTS

First and foremost, I have to thank my husband for allowing me the time to write this book, taking care of our little one, and always making sure I'm fed when I'm up writing and working at all hours of the night—You can thank him for all the pizza references in this book, since it was my main source of food, lol. On another note, this character holds a lot of your characteristics. It's the small gestures. I love you, asshole.

Next, I have to thank all the people—Allie, Brookey, Sam—who have encouraged me to keep writing and keep the negative thoughts at bay. That impostor syndrome is a real bitch. I can't forget about my biggest hype man, Dr. J. The student has finally become the master. Congrats on your first book. I can't wait to read more from you.

Lastly, the readers. Ya'll encourage me to keep going the most with your kind messages, posts, and sharing my books with the world. Ya'll are amazing!

Now if you made it this far (looks around nervously) get ready because Chris and Anna will get books, and so will Gertrude and Shawn at special requests. When, is the question, and that all depends on when time permits it.

Printed by Amazon Italia Logistica S.r.l.
Torrazza Piemonte (TO), Italy

VIOLET

I only have one person in mind, Wade Lynwood, the mayor of Seattle. He's looking for a trophy wife to carry on his arm, and I'm up for the task. If I can use my knowledge about rich men, then maybe I can lure him into my trap.
The only problem is he comes with extra baggage. A son.
I don't want to be a mother, and Miles isn't looking for one. Far from it. This should be a piece of cake, right?
Wrong.
There's something way more SINISTER going on in this family than I can anticipate, and my SILENCE is imperative.

MILES

I have a skill for getting rid of stepmoms, but now that I'm getting older, my future hangs in the balance. This one might be a bit more difficult than the last and better TAKEN DOWN while on my knees.

The only thing better than beating the ENEMY is sleeping with them.

Ayden Perry
There is Beauty in Death.

ISBN 9798867818821